Summer
in the City
of Roses

Also by the author

All of Us with Wings

Summer
in the City
of Roses

Michelle Ruiz Keil

Published in the United States by Soho Teen
an imprint of Soho Press, Inc.
227 W 17th Street
New York, NY 10011

Library of Congress Cataloging-in-Publication Data
Names: Keil, Michelle Ruiz, author.
Title: Summer in the city of roses / Michelle Ruiz Keil.
Identifiers: LCCN 2020052760

ISBN 978-1-64129-171-2
eISBN 978-1-64129-172-9

Subjects: CYAC: 1. Brothers and sisters—Fiction. 2. Supernatural—
Fiction. 3. Social action—Fiction. 4. Musicians—Fiction. 5. Punk rock
music—Fiction. | Portland (Or.)—Fiction.
Classification: LCC PZ7.1.K41513 Sum 2021 | DDC [Fic]—dc23
LC record available at https://lccn.loc.gov/2020052760

Interior design by Janine Agro, Soho Press, Inc.
Rose illustration: © elenavlas/Shutterstock
Printed in the United States of America

10 9 8 7 6 5 4 3 2 1

For Luciana & Angelika

Summer
in the City
of Roses

ACT I

Whoever drinks from me will become a tiger

1

THE FIRST ACQUAINTANCE WITH A PART

I t's the middle of summer, but of course there's rain. Clouds race past, covering and uncovering the moon. Iph's high heels squish with water, insult to the blistered injuries that are her feet. Her mother's cashmere sweater, already two sizes too small, is now a second skin. She stops at a wide, busy street that might be familiar if she'd remembered her glasses. But those, along with her purse, are far away, sitting innocent and hopeful on the white tablecloth in the hotel banquet room.

A guy across the street beams a glance her way and walks backward a few steps so he can keep on looking. She concedes a point to Dad. Earlier tonight, when she swanned into the living room in her white movie-star dress, he nodded approval at the first impression—glamorous but appropriate—followed by a jaw-drop of horror when his eyes reached her chest. Iph turned without a word and got the sweater out of her mother's closet— oversized and beachy on gamine Mom, not-quite-button-uppable on Iph. Although Mom has trained Dad against the sexism of policing his daughter's clothes, Dad insists on a basic truth: *Men are malákes.* Disgusting. A wolf whistle follows her around the corner, bringing the point home.

Iph turns away from the busy street—Burnside, she thinks, squinting at the blurry sign—and walks back the way she came. A car drives by a little too slow. More men, more eyes. This never happens in Forest Lake. She isn't scared . . . but maybe she should be? "The trick to bad neighborhoods," Dad once told her, "is to act like you belong." She was twelve or thirteen then, brought along to pick up a load of salvaged building materials from a part of the city people called Felony Flats. Staring out the rain-spattered window of his truck at the small houses with their peeling front porches and dandelion gardens, Iph wondered what exactly made a neighborhood bad.

An older woman wearing a blanket instead of a raincoat shuffles past on the other side of the street. A car whizzes by, blasting the Beatles. "Yellow Submarine" to go with the weather—a childhood road-trip favorite. Iph would give anything to be in that silver Volvo now, sharing a pillow with Orr in the back.

She stops. She can't think about her brother. Can't stand here crying in the rain with no coat.

She takes a deep breath and starts walking again. Each step cuts like her gold heels are the cursed shoes of a punished girl in a fairy tale. She passes an alley. The same creepy car that slowed down before is turning in. A group of kids, some who look younger than her, are leaning against the wall, smoking. Iph hurries by. The scent of wet asphalt and urine wafts toward her on the wind. Iph wills her nose to stop working. So yeah, this neighborhood is probably what her father would call bad. She should go back and face him. Find some way to make him change his mind. But there's no making Dad do anything, not when he thinks he's right.

It's humiliating how useless she is out in the real world. Like a jewelry-box ballerina waiting to be sprung, she's dreamed her life away in her pink suburban bedroom, sleeping as much as possible, rewatching her favorite movies, and rereading her favorite books. She always thought she'd be one of those kids who got their driver's license the day of their sixteenth birthday so she could drive into Portland whenever she wanted. Like

Mom, she loved the city. But sixteen came and went without even a learner's permit.

Once, years ago, Iph heard Mom talking on the phone to her best friend. "If I'd have known how white it was in Oregon," she said, "I would've made Theo transfer to NYU and raised the kids in Brooklyn."

City-girl Mom made the best of it. Portland was still mostly white, but more liberal and diverse than Forest Lake. She'd taken Iph and Orr into Portland weekly since they were little—for Orr's cello lessons and Iph's theater camps, trips to museums and plays and record stores and summertime Shakespeare in the Park. Most often, they go to Powell's, the enormous bookstore downtown that covers an entire city block. The streets around Iph look a little like those.

But really, all the streets in downtown Portland look like this—art deco apartment buildings crowded next to the sooty turn-of-the-century low-rises Dad calls brickies; parking lots next to Gothic churches; nondescript midcentury offices and newish high-rises, shiny with rain-washed glass. In Portland—or everywhere, really—Iph has been content to let Mom do the driving, the thinking, the deciding. They all have. And now, after two weeks without her, their family is broken, and Iph can't imagine a fix.

She stops at an intersection and squints at the sign. The streetlight is out, so it's only a blur. Something hot is oozing from her heel. Her fingertips come back bloody. Blood has always made Iph feel faint. Sometimes, she actually does faint. She looks for somewhere to wipe her hand.

On the corner is a box with the free weekly paper. She rips the cover page in half and does her best with the blood. Doesn't see a trash can and settles for folding the sullied paper and sending it down the storm drain—a lesser form of littering, she hopes. She breathes through the pain in her feet. She needs a break. A plan. She leans against the nearest wall. The stucco snags Mom's sweater. What a waste. And for nothing. The whole outfit, the whole evening, was a con.

Iph cringes at her three-hours-ago self, proudly walking into that hotel on Dad's arm. When the band began "Fly Me to the Moon," he even asked her to dance. They waltzed easily, him singing the words so only she could hear them. When she was little, they'd bonded over Ol' Blue Eyes, which is what Dad calls Frank Sinatra. He twirled her and dropped her into a dip, a routine from their father-daughter dance in middle school. His coworkers smiled, and Iph remembered what it was like when she and Dad were close.

"Sweetie," he said as the song ended, "I need to talk to you about something."

2

SENSING
THE HUNTER'S
FOOTSTEP

Orr sees stars. Thinks about the phrase, *He saw stars*. Words for a cartoon head injury, a cast-iron pan to the head. He gags—a sudden rancidness. The scent of an unwashed pan. The way the kitchen smells when Dad's away and Mom leaves the dishes in the sink all week. But this isn't kitchen grease. Or a dream. It's the smell of the men pulling him from his bed.

A sack covers his head. His arms ache where hands grip him, lift him. The upstairs hall tilts by in the shadow world outside the thin black fabric. Orr remembers to scream. He flails, knocking into a chair, the countertop. He reaches out to the bumpy plaster wall of the entryway and claws at the worn spot next to the phone, but the men yank him away.

The alarm beeps its familiar goodbye as the front door slams shut. Orr quiets. Listens. The night is cool and smells like rain. He is strapped into a vehicle. Like Agent Scully on *The X-Files*, he is being abducted.

His sockless feet are clammy in his shoes, tied too tight by his kidnappers. His breathing is shallow. A meltdown builds. He reaches inside for the ghost in him, the thing Mom calls *tu alma*—his soul—but the ghost is gone, hiding or fled.

With his index finger he traces the map line of the West Coast on his leg, from British Columbia to Baja California. Questions form: *Where am I? Where are they taking me? And why?*

He breathes a little deeper. Wiggles his toes, tells them it's okay. Waits for the world to settle.

He is in a large car, possibly a van. The cracked vinyl seat is a fanged menace under the worn flannel of his too-short pajama pants. Summer rain hisses under the tires. The radio switches on, a sports station blaring. Orr reaches for music—his battered *Klengel, Volume 1* with its old-world yellow cover and pages of punishing drills he's grown to love. He recalls every detail of the slick round stickers his teacher placed on the fingerboard when he was a beginner. He remembers the deep cramping of new muscle in his wrist and hand. His right elbow crooks around an invisible bow. His legs shape the cello's curves until he can almost feel its purr.

The radio drones on and on. *Baseball.* Orr knows more than he cares to about the game. For Dad's sake, he's tried to love it. The announcer's voice is deep and comforting. The rhythm of *thwack, cheer, talk* surprisingly helps Orr think. Details coalesce. The silent house, the men. The way he never heard them enter. The alarm's familiar sequence of beeps, because . . . because . . .

They knew the code.

They *knew.*

Orr narrows his eyes in the solitude of the hood. Fucking Dad. That's what Iph would say. This whole ordeal is because of Dad and that awful brochure.

The van stops. Orr is unsure how much time has passed.

"Okay, kid," a voice says, and the sack is pulled from Orr's head.

The waxing moon is bright as a bare light bulb in the star-exploded sky. Crickets chirp. Frogs harmonize in the deep forest hush. The gravel parking lot is a stark landing pad in a tree-circled compound. Orr nods. This has been a long time coming.

Finally, here he is: a prisoner at the Fascist Reeducation Facility

for Inadequate Specimens, also known as the Meadowbrook Reha-
bilitation Center for Boys.

Boot camp.

He's heard of it, of course. A place for kids who do drugs or
kids who fight—kids with something they need to change. What
is Orr supposed to change? He doesn't get into fights. Has no
interest in drugs. He's quiet, but silence is part of him, heads to
the tails of his music.

The driver closes the van. Another man guides Orr toward a
building that looks like some sort of lodge. A third walks ahead.
This one is taller than the others, with a back like a bull's. One
second, Orr is fine. Then he's not. He sees now that his calm in
the van was only his mind's clever ruse to protect himself and
fool the men. Sound boils in the tar pit of his stomach, but Orr
won't let it out. It's an experiment, an untested suggestion from
his therapist: *Contain the meltdown without dissociating. Talk to it.
Make it your friend.*

The lodge looms closer. The mountain silently watches. Orr
morphs the meltdown into a tactical step. Sound transmutes
to animal knowing. He feigns a slip, a twisted ankle. The man
releases his arm and bends down.

After that, Orr doesn't think. He just runs.

3

FUNDAMENTALS
OF ART MATERIAL

A pay phone beckons at the corner. Iph keeps thinking about last winter—her and Dad finding Mom crying at the kitchen table, the acceptance letter from the residency in one hand, a pack of contraband cigarettes in the other.

"Theo," Mom said, handing him the letter, "it's three full months."

"He'll be fine," Dad said, pulling Mom up and wrapping her in a hug.

"It's just the summer," Iph said.

And she believed it then. She would take care of Orr. Dad would take care of her. But she hasn't. And Dad certainly hasn't. And now what? Call Mom and tell her that Orr, who's never lasted the night at a sleepover, is in a militaristic boot camp for wayward boys? Iph is at the phone, hand on the receiver. She picks it up. The streetlight goes dark overhead. A sign?

Something warm touches her ankle. A soft breath. A dry little tongue.

"Scout!"

The small, stocky dog pulls away and sits at attention, looking up. Iph follows the yellow gaze to a mohawked boy on a beat-up ten-speed. No, not a boy. Or . . . maybe not?

"I'm George." A boy's name, but not a boy's voice. "This is Scout." The miniature brindle pit wags its stubby tail. "Are you okay? Do you need help?"

As if in league with the pair, the sky clears and the moon appears. Iph shakes her head. Is that . . . a bow and arrow slung over George's shoulder?

George pulls an index card from a back pocket and reads. "Are you in need of medical attention?"

Iph looks down and shakes her head. Her feet are bad, but Band-Aids will fix them.

"Are you being pursued?"

She shakes her head again. Dad didn't follow her when she stormed out. *Why* didn't he follow her?

"Are you a victim of trafficking or domestic violence?"

Does lying count as violence? How about betrayal? If so, maybe she's as guilty as Dad. Iph shakes her head. "No, I'm fine."

Scout whines and quivers for attention. Iph bends down in a weird sideways twist, constrained by her dress, to stroke the dog's brindle fur. "So soft!" she says. "She's adorable!"

Scout vibrates with happiness.

"And knows it," George says.

Close enough now to defeat her nearsighted astigmatism, Iph takes George in: bear-brown mohawk, bright black eyes. Well-shaped ears with five earrings in the right lobe and three in the left. A silver septum ring in a small, slender nose. Crisp white shirt, ankle-cuffed jeans, and oxblood Oxfords. A sort of dandy archer with an adorable mini pit-bull sidekick. They look like they belong in a story that starts with, *Once upon a time . . .*

"Thank you," Iph says to Scout, who's licking her ankle above the worst of the blisters. "I'm feeling much better now."

The dog offers her paw. Iph takes it and laughs.

"Are you sure there isn't something we can do?" George's skin is pale olive with hints of gold. Iph wonders but would never ask. She hates the question herself—the inevitable *What are you?* Maybe George is like her—a little of this, a little of that.

Iph stands, wobbly in her demon shoes. "I was at a work thing with my dad. We had a fight and I ran out. I left my glasses there. I'm lost without them."

It's an oversimplification of the ugly truth. In reality, Iph had a tantrum and ran away instead of staying to fight for her brother.

"Do you feel . . . safe going home?" George is being careful, like maybe it's common to find girls in sensitive situations alone in the city at night. Is that what the bow and arrows are for? Iph flashes back to the alley, the smoking kids. The men in the car.

"It's not like that," she says. "My dad—he did something awful, and I found out about it."

George's eyes widen. Even Scout is at attention.

"No, I mean, he's not . . ." Iph can't find the words for what Dad is or isn't. Not after tonight. "Look, if anyone needs to worry about their safety at my house right now, it's probably my dad."

"I see," George says, nodding like of course Iph is a powerful angry goddess whose father should fear her. "Can I help you get home, then?"

"It's far," she says. "Way out in Forest Lake." The second she says it, she wants to take it back. To most people, Forest Lake means money and white people and Republicans.

George just nods. "No bus out there this time of night."

"My dad's probably still somewhere around the hotel, looking for me. Could you give me directions back?"

"Of course," George says with a formal bow. "I'm at your service."

Iph can't help smiling. "Thank you kindly," she says. "I'm Iph."

"If?" George grins, then furrows, then drops to one knee and begins to recite.

> O, if a virgin,
> And your affection not gone forth, I'll make you
> The Queen of Naples.

Iph laughs. It's familiar, but not *R and J*. Not *Two Gentlemen of Verona* or *Twelfth Night*, either. "Ha!" she says, tapping her forehead. "*The Tempest!*" She should've known right away—she stage-managed the play last year. "Ferdinand to Miranda."

"Wow!" George grins. "No one ever knows what I'm blathering on about. But seriously, your name is If?"

"*I-P-H*. Short for Iphigenia. We're named after our dad's side—he's Greek."

"We?"

"Me and my brother."

"Why not your mom's side?"

"Good question." Mom's side of the family is a no-fly zone—even nosy Orr has learned to back off about Mom and her past.

"What hotel is it?" George adjusts the bow and arrow so naturally, it's clearly habitual.

"The one with the fancy doormen? With the breeches and big hats?"

"The Heathman," George says. "It's not too far."

Iph takes a step forward and hisses in pain—standing still for so long had been a mistake. Scout runs to her and whines.

"Blisters?" George asks.

Iph nods. There's no getting around it. She has to take off her shoes. She reaches down, but George stops her.

"If you take them off now, you'll never get them back on. They won't let you into the hotel without them. I have alcohol wipes and ointment, but only two Band-Aids—I need to restock my first-aid stuff."

Iph looks around for a place to sit where her dress won't be completely ruined. White seemed like such a great idea at the mall.

"Let me," George says. "We can at least do the heels."

"It's so gross," Iph says. "There's blood."

"I have gloves." George produces a pair of latex gloves and a first-aid kit from a well-worn messenger bag.

"So you just . . . ride around at night, helping lost maidens and shooting ne'er-do-wells and dressing strangers' wounds?"

"Yep," George says. "Lift your foot up, but not all the way out." The cleanup and bandaging is gentle and precise. "There we go." George takes off the gloves and stows them in a Ziploc bag.

"Thank you," Iph says. "That's way better."

George smiles. "It's nothing." In a fluid motion, the messenger bag and bow and arrows are back in place.

"Have you ever shot anyone with that thing?"

"Once." There's a beat, a shift. Iph notes it and files it away. She's always on the lookout for these in-between moments where everything breathes. "Find them onstage," Mom's director friend from New York once said, "and you can make magic."

Iph waits. George breaks the silence with a gesture at the ten-speed leaning against the wall. "Why don't I take you? If you sit sidesaddle on the rack and hold on, I think we'll make it. It's not far."

"Are you sure?"

George grins, one hand holding up the bike, the other holding open the flap of the messenger bag. Like a tiny gazelle, Scout leaps in. Even though it's the worst night of her life, Iph laughs.

"Milady," George says, gesturing to the bike like it's a chariot. Iph hobbles over and wriggles on. The relief of getting her weight off her feet is sweet enough that she doesn't even care about her butt, which is far from comfortable on the narrow metal shelf. George stands to pedal, calf muscles impressive as they work.

Iph grips the sides of the rack, careful to hold her feet away from the gears. Her shoes twinkle in the streetlights, cruel but pretty with their shiny gold leather straps and chunky four-inch forties heels. She found them in a box of Mom's old stuff and brought them with her when Dad handed over his credit card and told her to get something nice for the party.

The white cocktail dress saw Iph coming with its retro vibe and thick damask satin with the perfect amount of stretch—a necessity for serious boobs and hips. The wide straps hid her bra, and the sweetheart neckline did something amazing for her waist. When she put the shoes on and stepped out to look in the big three-way dressing room mirror, the saleslady whistled.

"Just like a Spanish Marilyn Monroe!"

Spanish. Mom has always hated being called that. The Spanish were, in Mom's words, "*pendejo* colonizers." She also hates *Hispanic*, which she considers basically same thing.

Still, Iph knew what the saleslady meant and took it as a compliment.

She held on to that good feeling all week. Which made it so much worse when Dad told her the real reason for the evening out. He didn't invite her because he wanted her company. She was there so strangers could come into the house and kidnap her brother without her braining them with a cast-iron skillet.

Take care of him, mija.

That was the last thing Mom said when she left. Orr was too upset to come to the airport, so Dad and Iph were the ones to see her off. There had been a scene the night before. Mom almost didn't go. Iph found her after Orr was asleep and Dad had retreated to his den, frozen in front of her closet, still not packed.

"You have to," Iph told her. "It will be me next year. Show me how to be brave."

Mom's eyes cleared. She nodded. They held each other tight. They had been a team for so long, taking care of Orr. Making sure the world didn't break him. "I've got this," Iph told her. "He's going to be fine."

Iph's spine straightens. She opens her eyes to the now-clear night. She will find Dad. She'll convince him. They'll drive straight to that boot camp and get Orr back. Mom can stay at her residency, and Dad can deal with her fire-spitting fury when she gets home at the end of the summer and finds out what he did.

George sits to coast down a small hill. The clean wind cools Iph's face. She holds out her arms for a second, perfectly balanced. Scout peeks out of the messenger bag and grins. Even if everything else about tonight is abysmal, being rescued by these two is undeniably great.

Orr lies on a thin mattress that feels slightly better than nothing. Rocks press cold into his bones, but the pressure is oddly painless. Is this what it feels like to be dead?

He rubs the thick paste stuck in his lashes but doesn't open his eyes. He imagines he is Uncle Marcos on the Greek side of the family, who would open one eye to light his first cigarette of the day and only open the second when it was smoked down to the filter. Marcos sat propped against his pillows and drank coffee for cigarette number two.

One eye is all Orr needs to see that it's very dark. He hears the woods around him, fur against fir, frog song, the rustling of dreaming birds. The second eye is easier.

He's in a tent. A dirty-sock-smelling sleeping bag is draped over him.

He sits up. Something is wrong. It's a static in his ears, something missing. A sting on his earlobe where the clippers have cut.

Orr remembers now: the barbed-wire fence that stopped him, being dragged back to the lodge with its wood-fire common room and silent, watching boys. The adults were the ones from the van.

The Minotaur man kept him still, his muddy boot resting on the chair an inch from Orr's crotch.

There was a string of words meant to unnerve him. Things he heard in middle school, names people called him. Words Mom said no one should ever use. Orr pans out on the memory, adjusts the angle. It's one of his tactics, maybe his best. He can turn the sound of any memory on or off. He can pause, rewind, fast-forward.

He zooms in on the scene in the lodge. The men holding him look less like men and more like older teenagers. College age at most. They're in charge, though. Of him and all the other boys.

One of them, maybe the one who drove him here, is saying the worst things. He's angry Orr ran, angry he won't stay still. Maybe Orr hurt him with his flailing. He keeps the sound on at first. The driver is holding his shoulders, calling him *dirt surfer*. This is a new one—probably a slur for hippie, referring to Orr's long hair. It's a dumb insult and easy to reject. Orr and his hair are always clean.

The sound goes off. He knows what's coming next—a bad word for someone who is Chinese, also inaccurate when it comes to his ethnicity. But Orr is used to being misclassified. The whole Santos Velos family has a look Dad's New York family jokingly calls "mystery ethnic." Mom and Dad both dislike the term but let them say it anyway. "It's not the worst thing I've been called," Mom always says.

"We're American," Dad counters, raising his thick eyebrows at Mom like he's daring her to disagree. "As American as anyone."

"Ha!" she says. Then she sighs. "I don't know, my love. The kids are *mestizo*, right? Mixed."

But Orr doesn't like that one, either. It makes their family sound like cake batter.

Orr knows the Meadowbrook guys don't care what he is, not really. They want to find his weak spots. The worst one wants to punish him.

Orr fast-forwards to a slur for a gay man or boy, something Orr has heard countless times since elementary school. It's a throwaway in terms of insults. Mom's dancer friends visit a few times a year from New York and use that word with affection or neutrality. But Mom never uses it, so neither does Orr. He's still not sure if it applies to him. Mom says he can decide when he's ready.

The final insult is kind of ironic. Another elementary school taunt with roots in one of the best things about being half-Mexican—Mom's creamy, perfect refried beans, the ones she says are like her *abuela*'s. Not that he would know. He's never met a single person on Mom's side of the family, and she refuses to talk about it. Ever. "I took the food and left the rest," she always says. "It was the one thing worth taking." Orr wonders now, like he always does, why that's true. Why nothing and no one from Mom's past is worthy.

By the time Orr thinks that one through to its logical end, he's not angry, only hungry. Or he would be, except he's not in his body anymore. Just floating around like a big naked brain in a giant pickle jar. This is Orr's way. He can spend full days in his head uncoupling sense from sensibility. It takes time and precision, like disarming a bomb. But now, in this cold, lonely moment, Orr needs to do something real.

He tries a formerly rejected calming exercise of Mom's to make it safer. He lies back down. The ground is there, holding him. He sends a cleansing breath in through his nose, past his heart, solar plexus, belly, and root chakras, down into the molten core of the earth.

In. Out. In. Out.

Images emerge, abstract at first. Ordinary moments at home. Dad. Iph. Mom.

Mom. The night before she left. Her suitcase. Clothes piled on the bed.

NO.

Orr shakes his head like it's an Etch A Sketch he's erasing.

He goes back to the van, his attempted escape, the lodge.

The chair, the men, the silent, watching boys. The memory stops.

He rewinds a little. Presses play.

Metal bites his neck. The Minotaur-man moves him like he's a puppet.

That's Orr's crime, the reason he's here. His father wants a real boy.

"*Bad Pinocchio,*" Dad says, "*believing that fox was your friend.*"

"*Bad people,*" Mom says, "*villainizing the fox. It's men who lie, not animals.*"

"*Corvids can.*" Dad grins. "*Crows, ravens, and jays. They're smart enough to lie.*"

When Orr was little, he was afraid of everything: the vastness of the sky, the weight of a roof over his head, the grating sounds of machinery, the feel of certain substances on his skin. But Mom had been there. Mom and Iph.

From the start, he understood that they were a team. When Dad was home, he always pushed. He wanted his son to throw and catch, to ski, to snowboard, to golf.

Dad called it love, but it wasn't love.

Dad pushed so hard, it was almost like he wanted to prove Orr's unworthiness. In the end, Orr's high-pitched keen always exposed Dad for the fake he was. He would yell and slam doors. Things the kids were never allowed to do.

To be fair, when Orr was three, four, even five, the wailing upset Mom, too. It probably upset the entire county—it was that loud. Sometimes, back then, Mom covered her ears and rushed to her room and closed the door. A few times in the car, she even cried. Orr hated upsetting her but was unable to change. Then Mom read a book about sensitive people and various coping methods, which she passed along to Iph and Orr. They made a game of it, spotting freak-outs before they erupted. They learned calming yoga poses. They meditated. They all learned to be kinder, gentler. Even Dad. But instead of laughing, he would go silent. Instead of meditating, he escaped to his den and shut the door.

As Orr got older and started running, he freaked out less often. Now he hardly ever does. But when he was little, it happened almost daily. Mom protected him, but for important things—things Orr needed to learn no matter how hard they seemed—his mother endured.

Whatever happened, Mom knew what to do. When kids called him a girl for his long hair, she took him to the mall to get a tiny gold earring. When his father complained, she brought home romance novels from the grocery store with long-haired, muscular, earringed men on the covers to put on Dad's bedside table. Mom knew Orr's hair was important. He needed its weight against his back, its rosewater curtain of protection around him wherever he went.

Mom taught him everything he knows about love. About being good. So he knew what to say when the letter came, inviting her to a prestigious residency in California to finish the epic dance piece she'd been working on since he and Iph were toddlers. Iph kicked him under the dinner table to make sure he said congratulations like he meant it.

Leading up to the residency, Orr tried to tell himself it would be like her other trips, just longer. In the past, he'd made it through by reading a book a day and buying and rationing a party-size bag of M&M'S. Doable, if just.

This time, she would be gone for three months.

That was ninety books. Eighteen jumbo bags of M&M'S.

Mom was worried, too, so she made lists and printed them out at Dad's office. A daily schedule with reminders and little jokes. She thought it would help, but it didn't.

Orr is sobbing now, his stress level rising fast. Tears run down the sides of his face and sting his nicked scalp. He reaches to rub them away and finds that his wrists are still bound with plastic ties. His body seems to exist in parts. Are his legs even attached? A wiggle of his toes tells him they are. Now that his eyes have adjusted to the dark, he sees the shape of the tent around him: small, too short to stand in. In the corner, there is a pile of something soft—his hair!—and in it, a small breathing something.

He crawls to the foot of the mattress and lies on his stomach. A mouse has made good use of his shorn hair, tucking her brood of children into the silky pile. Orr smiles and thinks of the *Red-wall* books with their poetry and ale-loving rodents. He makes the tiny sounds his neighbor's guinea pig, Estelle, prefers, but a little softer in deference to the mouse's smaller stature.

The mouse mother meets his gaze. She rises from the pile of nursing children and comes closer. She is a brown mouse, proof that *mouse-brown* should never be used as an insult. Her coat is the color of softness. Of late afternoon. Of small, warm safety.

Orr holds his breath.

On her hind legs, she sniffs the zip ties on his wrists and looks at him again. With her tiny hands braced on either side of Orr's right wrist, the mouse begins to nibble.

Orr thought Mom was the one who had a way with animals. The family of feral cats that live on the wooded edges of their half-acre yard allow her alone to pet them. Last fall, they found an injured falcon on the highway. Mom was the only one who could go near him. She's saved countless songbirds and more than one baby squirrel. Dad calls her a wood witch. The Lady of Beasts. Now it seems that Orr has some of her magic.

Orr smiles at the feel of mouse breath on his sensitive inner wrist. The mouse mother makes quick work of the right tie and moves to the left. She's so careful, he never once feels teeth.

The metal-on-metal sound of the tent zipper makes the metal in Orr's fillings ache. It's cold outside. Mountain cold. One more clue about where he is.

The lights are out in the building that houses the boys. The row of cabins under the stand of firs is also dark. He holds very still.

Even though Orr is fifteen, he doesn't often go places alone. In fact, the only places he's ever gone without Mom or Iph are the country roads around their subdivision. But of course he recognizes the white cap of the mountain behind him. Out-of-town business associates of his father's always *ooh* and *ahh* at the postcard perfection of Mount Hood, visible from the city on clear days. Iph always scoffed at it. "A little much, don't you think? Like it knows everyone's looking."

This always made Dad laugh. "A mountain can't be conceited."

"Umm, tell that to poor Mount Saint Helens," Iph said, pointing to the mountain's cropped top, her peak flattened when the volcano inside her bubbled to the surface.

Orr swears he remembers the day it happened, even though he wasn't quite two. They'd woken to a pale dusting of ash over everything. *Fairy snow*, Iph had called it, padding to the deck in her footie pajamas.

The mountain is much closer now, less a postcard than a sentinel. Meadowbrook must be in the forest at its feet. If Orr walks with the snowcap at his back, he will eventually find his way home.

The thought stops him.

Home.

His heart races, his breath a warm cloud in the air.

Home. To Dad. The person who'd authorized his kidnapping, his shearing, who was probably paying a lot of money to transform Orr into someone he wanted to call his son.

Orr is dizzy. He feels for pockets, but his pajamas don't have them. No vial of homeopathic anxiety medicine. No EpiPen.

He opens his mouth to call out . . . to who? Mom, all the way in California? Iph, who's probably so freaked out she's snagged one of Mom's sleeping pills?

There is no one.

He falls to his knees.

He lies down on the ground.

Pine needles lisp above him, mocking the tic of his grade school years.

He closes his eyes and gropes for the hologram of home that he carries inside himself. It's something he made to sustain him on the long days at school before Mom decided to keep him home. It never changes in his hologram world—always summer, always twilight, that perfect moment five minutes before nightfall when the sky turns indigo, a color his mother calls "our blue" because she and Orr love it equally.

Sobs gather in Orr's belly. The hologram can't help him. Nothing can.

Something cold touches his face, then something warm.

A nose, he guesses. A tongue.

He opens his eyes. Amber gleams down into his brown. Moonlight shines in a mouthful of teeth.

He sits up.

The coyote sits down.

If Orr had been raised by someone besides Mom, he might have been afraid.

The coyote whines, a high, soft sound. Orr searches her face, marked as if with makeup—dark liner around the eyes and a black star on a pale gold forehead. She moves a step closer and stops, sits, lowers her head.

Orr reaches out slowly, slowly, to touch the fur on her chest. Softer than he expected.

A heart beats under his hand, steady.

The animal is not afraid.

His own heart steadies.

The coyote rises, looks back at Orr, and trots west, away from the camp. Pulling his hood up to cover his shorn head, Orr follows her down the mountain.

5

STAGE
CHARM

George parks the bike under an awning around the corner from the hotel entrance and looks Iph up and down. Not checking her out or anything, but Iph blushes.

"We should clean you up a little."

Scout whines in the bag.

George shushes her but lets her out, setting the bag on the bike rack. "Okay if I get some of the smudges off?"

"Sure," Iph says.

From a pocket, George produces an actual handkerchief, clean and white and neatly folded. Very Prince Charming. "Close your eyes."

The cotton is soft and comforting. Iph realizes how tired she is. Her eyes fly open when the cleanup moves to her grime-splashed ankles and shoes. George is kneeling in front of her, intent on the work at hand. So gallant!

Rummaging in one of the messenger bag's outside pockets, George comes up with two tubes of lipstick. The red one is opened, discarded. George shows Iph a medium pink.

"Not mine," George says. There's a story in those two words. Maybe more than one. "My friend always brings both. She says pink is for innocent but classy. This might be a little light on you, though." George leans in close to apply the lipstick. It smells like cotton candy. Iph holds still, mouth open slightly for the second coat. She has done this so many times for actors as part of the costume crew, but no one's ever put makeup on her.

George tucks a few stray curls back into Iph's updo and steps back. "Yeah, that'll work. I see what she meant about the pink for certain missions. It does something red just can't."

"Missions? I'm going in there to find my dad, not abscond with state secrets."

"Lady," George says, "no disrespect intended, but you look a little . . . undone? There are a lot of street kids around here. Scammers. You know."

Iph doesn't know. She's nervous now as George steps back and nods. "Just go in there like you own the place. I'm gonna wait out here."

"Oh." Iph had imagined them going in together.

"You're better off on your own in there. Trust me."

And maybe she's an idiot for the second time tonight, but she doesn't think so—she does trust George.

"Thank you," Iph says, bending to touch Scout's silky head for luck. "Both of you. I'll be right back, whether he's in there or not. Will you wait?"

"I will if you're really coming back." Something crosses George's face—there and gone, like lights from a passing car. Iph wonders again about the bow and arrows, the index-card list. She reaches into her memories of *The Tempest* and whips out some Ariel.

> *My lord it shall be done!*
> *I drink the air before me, and return*
> *Or ere your pulse twice beat.*

"Excuse me," Iph says to the person at the front desk. "I'm looking for someone?" She'd blown easily past the doorman in his incongruous British tower guard uniform and large-brimmed, rose-wreathed hat. But this clerk seems like the kind of person Mom calls Born Skeptical. He's young, with longish droopy hair and an unsuccessful mustache. He looks up from his newspaper, eyebrows raised.

"He's tall," Iph says. "With dark hair. Was here earlier for the Theodore Velos party?"

"I can't help you, miss. There are no events happening now." His tone is smug and final.

"Did someone turn in a gold-beaded clutch purse?" Then, at least, Iph would have some money to make a call. "And a pair of glasses?"

She finally has the man's attention. He looks her up and down, and not in the concerned way George did. "Why don't you try finding your party at the bar?"

There is something condescending about the way he says *bar*. That and the disdainful look. Iph tries to flip her vision, see herself with his eyes. A little montage—the tight cocktail dress, Dad's horrified look, George's insistence on pink lipstick over red. Suddenly, she gets it. This man has added up the cut of her dress and her smudged eye makeup and rain-frizzed curls and decided she's a call girl. Rude! And so what if she *was* a call girl? This guy's clearly a jerk who needs a taste of his own snotty medicine.

Iph lets her eyes go wide and puts a tiny wobble in her voice, a teaspoon of angry in a cup of seriously offended. "The bar? How old do you think I am?"

The clerk looks confused.

"I'll tell you how old. Seventeen. So the bar isn't an option. But how about you go in there and find my party for me? And tell him his daughter is waiting for him."

"Oh, I see. I'm sorry, miss. What event did you say it was?"

"Velos Design."

"And you are?"

"Iphigenia Santos Velos." She actually taps her foot. She's having too much fun altogether, considering the situation.

The clerk magically notices the note his co-worker left at the desk and hands it to Iph. Dad's scrawl. *Looked everywhere. Worried sick. Call home* makes her ache for the warmth of his car, the dark of her room. She will fix this. Persuade him to go get Orr. Everything will be okay.

Her "Can I use the phone?" is met with a fast "Of course," but all Iph gets is a busy signal. She tries again and again. "I can't imagine who he's talking to," she says after the fourth try.

Her stomach drops. What if it's Mom? Iph imagines her in the big wooden common house in the Santa Cruz Mountains, pacing back and forth with the phone, twisting her long hair around her finger until it turns blue as Dad confesses.

"Call the operator," the clerk suggests. "Ask for an emergency breakthrough."

"You can do that?"

The clerk smiles, and the world shifts back into place. Iph is a kid, the clerk an indulgent grown-up. But the reason that's happening is because Dad left the note. What if he hadn't?

"Here, write down the number and I'll do it." The clerk speaks to the operator. No one is on the line. The phone is off the hook. Iph's eyes fill with tears.

"Is there someone else you can call?"

Iph shakes her head. She has no real friends at school. Not anymore. Mom has no family—at least no one she speaks to. Dad's family is all back east or in Greece. The only number Iph has memorized besides the video store and pizza place is their neighbor Mindy's. But Mindy and her family are out of town until next week.

"No," Iph says. "My dad and I had an argument. I ran off and got lost. I left my purse. My glasses. Everything."

"You can keep trying." The clerk's voice is gentle now. His eyes have gone kind, like maybe he understands problems with parents. That's the thing with people. They're both sour and sweet. Like Dad. In his misguided, messed-up way, he was trying to do the right thing. Iph calls again. He has to notice the phone sooner or later. "Maybe he'll turn up back here. Why don't you have a seat? We can call again in a few."

"Thank you so much." The plush sofas look like heaven. Except, there's George. Iph finds what she hopes is the right smile. "I ran into a friend who helped me find the way back here. I'm completely lost without my glasses." Iph does her best to channel innocent, nearsighted Marilyn in *How to Marry a Millionaire* without being too over the top. "Would you mind if we waited in here together? Just for a little while?"

The clerk's brow furrows. "Where is this friend?"

"Right outside." She opens her eyes a little wider.

Iph sees him weighing her boobs, his own sympathy, her father's status, his customer service training against some loitering rule, and she feels a little sorry for him. He's just here for the paycheck, biding his time to put food on the table. That's what Mom always says about cranky service workers. Still, Iph promised George.

He sighs and rolls his eyes. "Just for a few minutes," he says.

6

CHARACTERS
AND TYPES

Iph and George had been waiting together in the lobby with Scout concealed in George's bag for all of ten minutes when the manager walked in, took one look at George, and booted them all. Iph batted her eyes at the clerk, but he just shrugged. Now if Iph's dad got upset, it was on his boss's head, not his. This is the kind of thing that makes Mom say, *Capitalism wrecks everything*, and makes Dad call her his little Bolshevik and kiss her, which in turn makes Iph and Orr chorus *Gross* when what they mean is, *Our parents love each other and that feels good.*

Out on the street, the rain is finished and the sky is completely clear. "I'm sorry," George is saying as they head back to the bike, locked to the metal security door of a men's haberdashery half a block up. Before they get there, the doorman in the ridiculous outfit is calling them back.

"Hey," he says. Something about him suggests *Alice in Wonderland*—and not just the big floppy rose-crowned hat that is part of the hotel uniform. He's holding a cardboard box. "Sorry about that. It's the manager. He has it in for teenagers. But here—you can look for your stuff in the lost and found." He hands Iph the box and motions to the large doorway of the closed shop next to the hotel, set back from the street. There's someone sleeping in the other end of the alcove.

"We should be quiet," Iph whispers.

"He can't hear us," George says. "Takes his hearing aids out when he sleeps."

"You know him?"

"Everybody down here knows him." George kneels and hunts through the box so Iph doesn't have to bend over, which is a good thing because she's pretty sure she can't. Her dress dried out completely in the hotel and is now as stiff as paper. Apparently, there's a reason for the DRY CLEAN ONLY tag.

"Sorry," George says. "No purse."

The doorman ushers a handsome older couple into a cab, then ambles over on huge feet. "No luck? It's okay—take whatever you need. No one ever comes back for that stuff. Here"—he pulls out a huge Portland Trail Blazers hoodie from the box—"I almost took this myself, but the sleeves are too short. They had to order my uniform special." He sticks his long arms out like Frankenstein's monster and grins. He has braces, complete with an elaborate lacing of rubber bands.

"Thanks," Iph says. She puts on the hoodie and it's heaven. Soft and clean-smelling and warm.

"Thanks, man." George slaps his arm like maybe they know each other, then sorts the contents of the box methodically, taking a pair of leather gloves, a yellow Walkman, and a pair of pink fuzzy socks with the tag still on them. Last are a pair of round gold-framed glasses and a heavy black old-man pair. "Either of these yours?"

Iph shakes her head.

"Wanna try them on anyway? Maybe one of them's close enough to help."

The gold John Lennon glasses are crazy—bifocals, it turns out. The doorman tries them on after Iph. She's gotten used to the uniform, but the addition of the glasses skews it late sixties, very Sgt. Pepper's. He strikes a pose, surprisingly graceful.

"Do you dance?" Iph asks.

"Basketball," he says.

Iph tries the black glasses. Stronger than her regular prescription, but pretty good. She turns to the others. "What do you think?"

"Punky," the doorman says.

"Very cute. And look!" Two quarters shine in George's hand. "Okay if we take these, too?"

"Totally," the doorman says.

"Where's the best pay phone, do you think? 7-Eleven?"

"That one's always gross. Try up at PSU."

"Thanks," Iph says. "And thank the desk guy for sending out the box!"

"No problem. Take it sleazy!" The doorman flashes them a peace sign and hurries the lost and found box back inside.

IPH AND GEORGE ARE alone again, and the street is quiet. No people, except for the old man sleeping in the alcove. No cars. Iph feels a sudden vertigo. Everything is too sharp with the new glasses. Too clear.

"Milady?" George bows again.

"Are you sure? You've done so much already. Maybe I should . . ." But Iph doesn't know how to finish the sentence.

"I don't abandon my missions," George says. "Let's go find that pay phone."

THE PORTLAND STATE CAMPUS is quiet. A few people pass as Iph calls home, but the phone's still busy. What's Dad's deal? Why hasn't he tried calling the hotel? Why did he leave in the first place? "I still can't believe he went home." Iph says. "If that's where he even is. I mean, I don't know. I think I would've waited."

"Me, too," George says. "If it was my kid? I'd have waited all night."

"Well, in his defense, I was kind of horrible."

Iph's chest aches. She yelled and cried. Made such a scene. Heat rises from her clenched stomach to her face. Her feet throb. She sits on a wet bench, hoping her dress won't rip. At least the rain has stopped. Scout leaps up between Iph and George, settling her head in Iph's lap. The wind blows the big trees in the park that runs through the city campus. The sound is soothing. Like being at home.

"He sent my little brother away to a boot camp," Iph finally says. "He had him taken against his will. Orr . . . isn't a boot-camp sort of kid. If anyone is."

"Those places can be rough. I think some parents don't get what they're like."

"Have you ever . . . seen one?"

"Not boot camp," George says, "but something similar."

George gets up and leads Scout a few paces away for a bathroom break. Iph compares the buildings on either side of the bank of phones. One is a concrete structure designed in what Dad calls the "prison-yard school of architecture." The other is an old white Renaissance Revival hall, sturdy and elegant, the way a college building should look.

"Okay, here's the deal," George says, coming back to sit by Iph. Scout leaps back to her spot on the bench between them. Her ears feel like the silk lining of Iph's lost purse. "I have kind of a weird living situation. An apartment—but it's a secret. No one can know I live there."

"All right, but . . . I mean, how old are you?"

"Seventeen," George says. Iph's age. And living alone? "My mom's gone, my stepdad's out of the country. I was supposed to stay with my cousin, but that didn't work out. I decided to do some urban camping till he gets back and everything is sorted."

"Like squatting?" Mom has some great stories about her year squatting in Amsterdam.

"It's more like . . . haunting? It's my nana's old place. I come in late at night when I'm sure the neighbors are asleep, and I leave after they go to work. Sometimes I have to stay in all day on the weekends because they never leave. Then I'm up all night 'cause I've been cooped up so long."

"And that's when you ride around rescuing lost maidens?"

George grins. "Exactly."

"So are you inviting me to stay at your top-secret hideout?"

"I am."

"Is there a phone there?"

"Sorry, no." George takes out a pocket watch and studies it. "We can try stopping at pay phones along the way. We should jet, though. Downtown's dicey after midnight."

IMAGINATION

The sign on the building is shaped like a curvy bull, midnight blue, with a starry flank and horns like crescent moons. Under golden hooves, TAURUS TRUCKING is lettered in faded retro script with the ghost of an *F* over the *T*, a bad joke someone made and someone else scrubbed away.

"Your nana was a trucker?"

George laughs. "I mean, yeah. I guess you could say she was. Drove Ethel till she was in her seventies."

"Ethel?"

"Her tow truck," George says. "By the end, it was Ethel the Fourth."

They're on Division Street now, in Southeast, the sleepier part of the city. To get here, George and Iph rode over the fairy-lit Hawthorne Bridge, stopping at four Plaid Pantries along the way, but the phone was busy every time. Iph takes the street in, opening all her senses as wide as she can. The sidewalk is clean and smells of summer rain. The street is lined with shabby little houses with overgrown yards and weedy parking strips planted with sunflowers and rosemary and lamb's ears that spill over onto the sidewalks. Roses are everywhere, climbing the telephone poles and clinging to fences and front porches cluttered with gardening shoes, children's toys, and boxes of recycling. The odd little stores across the street seem barely plausible as businesses—a washing machine repair shop, barbecue supply outlet, and a barber shop with a sheet of plywood over a broken window and an actual barber's pole out front.

It seems fitting that if Orr must be alone in a new world, so should she. Cut off from her family and home, this little neighborhood is Iph's whole reality. George, a stranger two hours ago, is the only person she knows. The thought is a little revolution. Iph's chest expands, lets in so much air she's a little dizzy. Something akin to relief runs like a feather down her arms. Guilt follows, right on cue.

They enter through a side door. Iph feels the dark container of the garage around her. An old game she and Orr used to play was listing their three favorite darknesses. Whoever had the best answers won. Currently, Iph loves the fur of panthers, Maybelline black eyeliner, and the black velvet coat with black satin lining she stole from the costume closet at school but is afraid to wear anywhere but alone in her room at night. The darkness in Taurus Trucking is excellent, soft and deep, with bits of light wavering in like she and George are inside some massive underwater animal. The square building's giant metal garage door and concrete walls distort the sounds of the neighborhood outside.

Iph thinks of Orr's favorite childhood version of *Pinocchio*, the illustrations done with photographs of puppets. In the scene where the puppet maker/father figure, Geppetto, is stranded inside a whale, there is a whole living room. A table. A lamp. There, he mourns the loss of Pinocchio. Maybe Dad is doing that now—drinking whiskey, the empty house sighing around him.

"Sit tight," George says, a little louder but still conscious of volume. Scout's nails click against the floor. Iph peels off her shoes: pain, then pleasure. Or maybe just relief. They are so similar, she thinks, in the same way pain is caught up with want. Scout is at her feet sniffing her injuries, offering a soft lick. George is moving around the room. Spots of light bloom in the darkness as George turns on a series of flashlights that beam toward the high ceiling, tracing the shape of the empty garage.

"No trucks?"

"Not anymore," George says. "Sold to pay the property tax. My nana left this place to me. Some people in my family think that isn't fair. They want to, like, 'help out' and 'run the business' till I'm an adult." George's air quotes say it all. "My stepdad's in charge of the estate. Tells you something that it wasn't anyone blood-related. Anyway, he mostly got them off my case before he went back to Iraq. Now I'm sitting here waiting to turn eighteen."

George is like Mom, Iph realizes. A complicated history and a lot under lock and key. The flip side to this amazing place is that George lives here alone and in secret with no adults around to help—and still rides around at night, helping other people. Iph's stomach does a disappointed-in-herself drop. That's the problem with being young. You're immature, insufferable. And then you realize it and think, *Why? How could I be that self-absorbed?*

"So, um . . . welcome to my humble abode?" George says.

There's a hay bale with a canvas bull's-eye target stuck to it in the corner and a tire swing hooked to the rafters by a stout rope. In the other corner is a hammock. "Scored it on the street," George says. "And uh, maybe you want to turn around. One sec, I'll grab you a flashlight."

Iph turns back to the garage door. It's completely covered in painted images. "Oh!" She covers her mouth as the syllable bounces around the room, her flashlight illuminating a nearly life-size painting of George as both twins in Gemini, one with waist-length hair, the other with a short-cropped buzz. There are birds and flowers and animals, mythical and real. Trees. Constellations.

Iph moves closer to the Gemini twins, tracing the clasped hands of the two figures with her index finger. "It reminds me of this painting . . ."

"*The Two Fridas?*"

"Yes! I love Frida Kahlo," Iph says.

"Me, too. I call mine George and Georgina."

Touching the long-haired figure, Iph wonders if this is how George once looked. "Are you still both?" Iph asks, hoping it's not the wrong thing to say. "Or just George?"

"Good question," George says.

Iph moves the flashlight across the art-covered walls. There's a sort of cubist rendering of Scout chasing a squirrel that makes her laugh. A bear as high as the warehouse ceiling with its arms open to catch a school of starry fish. A figure—half man, half badger—holding a machine gun. An old woman in a sky-colored kimono flying with a great blue heron. Iph pauses again, this time at a large portrait of a naked blonde girl holding a golden apple. "Who's this?"

"This?" The word is a soliloquy of unrequited feeling. It is a perfect example of Iph's favorite thing: a true reveal. It's a Santos Velos term, something Mom and Dad made up to describe their favorite element in all kinds of art. A building could have a reveal. Or a dance, a play. A song. It starts with a particular kind of noticing. This heightened attention, Dad says, is performed by the noticer but initiated by the art itself, like a siren song calling you to see it. The true reveal is the moment you heed the call and slip into the artist's secret world.

Iph's brain goes where it usually does—she's onstage in London playing Antigone and whips out the sound of longing George has jammed into the tiny throwaway word about the girl in the painting. The theater is silent and electric, but . . . no. Iph shakes it off. The play dissolves. She might write a play with a moment like that, even direct one, but star in one? Not likely.

Last year, when she fired all her fake theater friends, she resolved to stop wanting the things she'd never get. The world is what it is, and Iph is what she is—medium height, medium brown with bombshell boobs and a butt that hasn't fit into a single-digit dress size since she was eleven. Since puberty, she has been the girl with "such a pretty face," a red pouty mouth and big brown eyes and Mom's skin and Dad's ridiculous lashes. Even she can admit to liking her freckles, and her cheekbones are legitimately great. Sometimes, if she is brave, she lets herself look in the mirror after a candlelit bath and see herself as beautiful. If this were the Renaissance and she could learn to sit still, she'd have a promising career as an artist's model. But it's not. Models today look like the girl on the garage door—slender, with high breasts and sculpted abs and thin, waifish limbs. She traces the golden apple with her finger. "I thought it was the snake who tempted Eve, not the other way around."

"Oh!" George's eyes open wide. "I never knew why I painted her like that. You might be onto something."

Iph is silent, waiting for more about the girl. It doesn't come. "So," she asks, "what are the rules of this lost-boy hideout, please?"

George grins. "The governing principle is to avoid detection."

"Who's detecting us?"

"Pirates. Grown-ups. The tricks are few. We come in late and leave when the neighbors aren't around. We don't use flashlights upstairs except for navigation—too many windows."

"Upstairs?"

"There's a whole apartment up top," George says. "We'll sleep up there. It gets cold in here at night and super hot in the morning. Upstairs is insulated."

Iph follows the beam of George's flashlight up a narrow staircase.

"We have water. The city never turned it off. But it's cold. The bathroom window has a shade that's pretty tight, so we can use a little light up there if we're careful. C'mon, Tinkerbell. I do think we should go up and take a better look at those feet."

Upstairs is shadowy, but Iph's eyes adjust. The streetlight seeps between the cracks in the drapes. Kitschy fifties paneling lines one wall of an oddly situated living room. The other wall is a muddy green. They pass a scratchy-looking plaid sofa and matching La-Z-Boy recliner, both a little big for the room. Iph follows George to a narrow elephant-themed bathroom.

"It's like a time capsule," Iph says. There's even a pink elephant soap dish and matching cotton-ball canister.

"Nana redecorated in 1964. After that, she said why mess with perfection."

"That's valid," Iph says, touching the shiny wallpaper with its pattern of champagne glasses and round, tipsy elephants.

"Sit." George puts the pink fluff-covered toilet lid down, grabs something from the medicine cabinet, and squats in front of her, reaching for her ankle. She allows this without protest, even though her feet are truly gross, crook-toed and bony. Iph sighs as her feet are washed with a cold cloth and dried with a soft towel, and antibiotic ointment and Band-Aids are expertly applied, along with the fuzzy socks from the hotel lost and found box. She is already used to George taking care of her.

"You could be a doctor," Iph says.

"I want to be a nurse."

"You'd be awesome at it."

"I'm also pretty good with a hot plate. Want some SpaghettiOs?"

8

MOON-FROTH
COVERED HER FACE

The coyote leads Orr down the mountain. The night has turned clear. He shivers, ears painfully exposed without his hair. Aside from the quarterly trims Mom did in the kitchen, always during a full moon because she said it was good luck, his hair had never been cut. All these years it worked, shielding him from germs and sounds and, lately, from the aliens haunting his dreams, beaming him to their glaring spaceships and returning him home, unable to place the tracker in his neck as they did with Agent Scully.

Mom is dead, he keeps thinking. He knows that's not true, but she *feels* dead, unreachable hundreds of miles away in the Santa Cruz Mountains.

Before she left, she showed him pictures so he could imagine her there—the cottage where she'd sleep, the dance studio with its meadow-flung windows and shiny wood floors, the sprawling wooden common house with the fireplace in the kitchen where she would hang out and eat with other artists—but the moment she drove away, the pictures began to fade. After five days, they were gray in his mind, like newsprint left in the rain. After a week, they were gone.

At first, she called every other day, but her voice sounded wrong, and Orr began to worry she'd been replaced by someone else. It was a weird thing to think. He knew that. He told her calling once a week was better. He told her he was completely fine. It was his first truly successful lie.

After that, he trudged through the motions of summer. Video marathons—sci-fi when he chose, Marilyn and musicals when Iph did. Brunch competitions with Iph and their neighbor Mindy, a Dungeons & Dragons–playing twelve-year-old aspiring chef. At his age, he was supposed to be considerate. Self-sufficient. But every night he tossed and turned until dawn, and every day it was harder to get out of bed.

Now he follows the coyote, probably a mother herself, to a dirt road that eventually leads to Highway 26.

Orr loves maps. Because of that, he knows this road. He walks it for a long time. Hours. He isn't sure how many. As the sky begins to purple, he looks back and sees how thick the forest is, how lost he might have been without the coyote's help. But she's brought him straight to this road that leads, fork after fork, mile after mile, right to his own tree-lined street. To his long gravel drive and the wood and glass house his father built his mother to get her to marry him.

Orr goes there in his mind as his body trudges the roadside. Inside the rustic-planked doors are soft, bright Mexican carpets in the colors his mother loves: magenta, cherry, gold, and parrot green. There are seventeen light switches with plates he and Mom and Iph had collaged using animal images from the Audubon calendar. There are forty windows, all looking out on something beautiful and green. There are fifteen stairs to the upstairs hall, where a window frames a fig tree named Fiona, her large fruit lusted after by his mother's favorite troupe of cedar waxwings— Bowie birds, she calls them, because of their Ziggy Stardust hair and makeup and their love of getting high on fermented fruit. At the height of the fig frenzy, some of them eat so much they fall off the tree, too drunk to perch. Iph and Orr used to collect the stunned party birds and place them carefully in towel-lined shoe-box drunk tanks, waiting for them to sleep it off.

At the top of the stairs is the family room, an open, octagonal space jutting over the living room like the crow's nest in a ship. This is where movies are watched, board games played. Down the hall are the bedrooms. The third door on the left is Orr's.

His room is sanctuary blue. His bed is narrow and canopied with an Indian tapestry of leaping deer that Mom used as a bed-spread when she lived in New York. Orr can smell the just-right scent of the lavender sachets his mother places in his drawers. It's as if he's come back from an early-morning trip to the bathroom. He sees it all so clearly—the droppers of flower essence tinctures in their perfect line on his bedside table: Rock Rose for bad dreams, Cherry Plum for depression, Rescue Remedy for freak-outs.

He's imagining climbing into bed when he realizes the coyote has stopped. She's sitting a few feet away, patient.

She waits for him to catch up to the truth.

Home is a thing of the past. As long as his father is there, Orr can never go back.

The coyote crinkles her furry lids to comfort him.

He trembles so hard, he thinks maybe it's the earth. A quake? The landing of a spacecraft so large it's shaking the snow off the mountain?

But no. Only him. Him and the first hint of birdsong and the fur-jacketed lady coyote who blinks at him, waiting for him to do the thing humans are supposed to do—think.

Orr could call his mother. If he were home, he would. The number is written in Sharpie on the notepad by the telephone in the entryway. Maybe he could find the number some other way. Information. 411. He could tell them the name of the residency. All he needs is to find a phone.

He thinks of his calendar, the X'd-out days until his mother comes home. Sixteen down, seventy-three to go.

There's no way he can survive in the woods for even a week on his own. He's read *My Side of the Mountain*, about the boy who left home to live off the land in the Catskills, taming a peregrine falcon to hunt for him. But even with his coyote guide, Orr knows he's not tough enough. He has allergies. Gets headaches. Is vegetarian. Neither he nor Iph have ever eaten meat, although Dad sometimes used to dare them. "Fifty bucks," he would say when they drove past a McDonald's.

Satisfied that Orr knows what is what, the coyote scratches and gets up, trotting to where the road widens. In the light, he can see she is shedding, fur rising in unkempt tufts on her rusty haunches. She glances down the road toward a sign: REST STOP. She and Orr walk side by side until they reach it.

A water faucet, a bench, a bathroom . . . and a phone! Orr picks it up, but there's no dial tone. He turns to look for the coyote, but she is already trotting off into the tree line beyond the parking lot.

Orr panics. But then he stops. He is alone. More alone than he's ever been. He can't rely on Mom or Iph, only himself.

He laps water at the faucet, a little at a time, until he feels better. He goes into the bathroom. The women's, he realizes when he sees the tampon machine. But it doesn't matter. No one is here. He uses the hand dryer to warm himself even though the roar hurts his ears.

Outside, the sky is paling and the birds are waking up. Orr walks the way the coyote had. The trees open to a rocky beach along a river. A scrub jay caws from a tree and flies downstream. Orr follows until the beach widens. Ahead is a large canvas tent, the bigger version of the place where he'd woken up with his hands tied and hair shorn. In front of the tent is a campfire, and tending the fire is a young woman with a cigarette in one hand and a hot dog on a stick in the other.

Orr stops and the woman looks up. For a moment, he thinks the coyote is back. That's what her surprised face seems to say. But it's Orr she is staring at.

"Hey there," she calls, as raspy as Orr's Greek grandmother. "Where'd you come from?"

"I escaped from some kidnappers," Orr says.

"No shit?" The girl blinks. "Seriously. Are you shitting me? 'Cause I'm a little hungover for boyish pranks."

"I'm not shitting," Orr says. He likes her swearing. It reminds him of Mom.

"Were you hitchhiking? I know you're a dude, but it's still not safe. Pervs are pervs, babe. You gotta watch out."

"I don't think they were pervs," Orr says. "It was a boot-camp place. They came to my house and put a hood over my head and put me in a van and took me there." He points toward the mountain.

"You escaped from Meadowdouche? What are you, like, a boy wizard?"

"I had some help." Orr grins. Why is he smiling at this strange woman? He only does that with family. And Mindy, their neighbor.

"You okay?"

"I'm hungry," Orr says.

"Here," she says, holding out the hot dog. Orr's mouth literally waters. Not a figure of speech after all, he realizes.

"I shouldn't," Orr says.

The girl laughs. "I don't bite." This is another expression Orr had needed to parse when he was little—just a joke, and no one expected other people to bite them. Except when it came to Iph, who was known to bite when provoked and occasionally when she was overcome with love.

"I'm a vegetarian," Orr says.

"Well then." The girl stands up and walks toward Orr with legs that are not in long pants as Orr first thought, but in cutoff shorts and covered in tattoos. "It's your lucky day. This is prime tofu wiener, my friend. Burned to a perfect crisp." She grins, showing a gap between her two large front teeth.

Orr's smile widens.

"C'mon, kid," she says, turning back to the fire. "Have a seat. We've got five packs of these puppies—I'll get us some ketchup. You want a beer?"

9

DICTION
AND SINGING

ph can't sleep. At home, there's a Jacuzzi tub for this in the pink bathroom attached to her bedroom, lined with vanilla-scented candles and lavender salts. There's her stereo and the pile of sleep mixes she and Orr trade to battle their insomnia, plus the guided meditations they borrowed from the library for their summer project of learning how to lucid dream. There's the stash of sleeping pills she's pilfered carefully from Mom and the vibrator—marketed as a neck massager—she shoplifted when her "friends" ditched her in Walgreens last year and took the bus to the mall without her. In winter, there's the rain on the roof, and now, in summer, there are crickets and tree frogs and the grove of plum trees behind the house, full of sleeping birds.

Here, there's the occasional car, the buzz of the streetlight, and a too-soft mattress that is an odd size between a double and a twin and smells faintly of menthol cigarettes. Her bed at home is a queen, a present for her tenth birthday with a headboard and footboard that Dad made himself, with hand-carved roses and gilded thorns like something out of *Sleeping Beauty*. "For my princess," he said.

This was before the fissures had formed, before it had become

her and Mom and Orr against Dad, a truth none of them wanted
to admit.

"What's this?" she asked Orr about the brochure on his desk—
when was that? Last night? The night before? It feels as if days
have passed.

"Boot camp for Bonzo," Orr answered, making a monkey
sound.

"Oh, you're definitely a menace," she said, flopping onto his
bed. "All those *Redwall* books and the classical music. Not to mention the chess."

"Dad's having buyer's remorse," Orr said, scooting his foot
away from hers.

When they were little, Iph used to tease that he'd never be able
to get married if he couldn't stand a little footsie. Orr maintained
that foot-to-foot contact was vile. Iph still finds it funny to push
it a little, scooting her always-cold feet toward his always-warm
ones.

"He thinks he can send me back to the factory and exchange
me for a real boy."

"Real boys are overrated," Iph said, getting up and grabbing
fresh Walkman batteries from his desk recharger. "Want me to talk
to him?"

Orr didn't reply. Since he was a toddler, he simply ignored the
things he wouldn't consider doing. You knew by his silence what
was a no-go. But Dad has been blown off one too many times.
And now Orr is paying for it. They all are.

"I'm telling Mom," Iph yelled at Dad mid–Frank Sinatra. She
hadn't raised her voice to him since she was four. It was about
Orr that time, too, the first and only time Dad had ever tried to
spank him. She didn't just yell back then. She bit, right on the
spanking arm.

"We have to go get him," she said, pulling Dad from the dance
floor. "Right now!"

But Dad shook his head with maddening calm.

It was then that Iph pushed him, pushed her *father*, pushed away the image of Orr being touched by strange hands, Orr without his Walkman and headphones, without his EpiPen, his anxiety pills, his special pillow. She pushed him and yelled, "What were you thinking?"

"Lower your voice," he said. He never yelled anymore. Not even at home. He'd taken classes for that.

"How could you?" Iph cried. She always cried. He wasn't looking at her, but over her head at the cluster of wives watching them. He sent them a look that said, *Teenagers—what can you do?* with his tan handsome face. The look he got in return made Iph want to barf. Women were always like that with Dad. Not that it did them any good. They could be as shiny blonde and jazzercised as humanly possible and Dad would never give them a second glance, because none of them were Mom.

That was Iph's thought when he asked her to the party. She'd go in Mom's place, a worthy understudy. In the dress, she really felt the part. What was that saying Mom hated? *Pride goeth before a fall?* There was a babysitter at some point, an after-school lady so Mom could take a dance class in Portland, who said stuff like that all the time and tried to teach Iph and Orr stories from the Bible. Mom fired her after four-year-old Orr started rambling about Adam's rib and the curse of Ham and pride before falls.

"Pride is good," Mom said, raising Orr's little fist.

"Brown power!" she said.

"Brown power!" Iph and Orr had chorused.

"Brown power!" Dad said in solidarity.

That's the thing with Dad. Iph knows he wants to do what's right. But sometimes, his version of right seems so wrong to the rest of them. The truth is, things have mostly been done Mom's way: no spanking, no yelling, no forced eating of hated foods. Mom grew up in a controlling religious family. Iph and Orr have pieced that much together. She was determined to do things differently with her own children. Iph felt sorry for Dad. Sometimes it felt like he was only along for the ride. Seems like he finally got sick of it.

After Mom left for Santa Cruz, when Orr stopped talking, Iph tried to explain it to Dad: Orr needed some time. She should have tried harder. And tonight—what if she hadn't flipped out? Maybe she and Dad would be in the car right now, speeding to Orr's rescue.

As it is, she's the one who's been rescued, and Orr is someplace far away in the care of adults whose job it is to kidnap and institutionalize unwilling teenagers.

Iph is sick with the wrongness of it. It goes against everything her family is supposed to be about—they are antiwar, feminist, democratic. Iph shakes her head even though there's no one there to see it. She balls her fists and presses them to her stomach. How could Dad betray them? Had he wanted a different family all this time? Normal kids, a regular wife? The kind of family who went to sporting events and knew all the words to the national anthem?

Iph remembers a fight her parents had years ago, before couples therapy taught them to disagree instead of battle. As always, the fight was about Orr.

"You sound like my father," Mom said in the coldest voice Iph had ever heard her use with Dad. "Don't you have any compassion?"

Dad's bitter laugh ran through her, even now. Karma for listening—she still wishes she never heard this fight. "Sometimes I feel like you don't even see me," he said. "Like all you see is the past."

Iph doesn't remember Mom's response.

Her throat clenches. For a second, she's worried she needs her inhaler, far away in the jumble of her nightstand drawer at home. Then she realizes it's not her asthma at all. It's that her family is falling apart.

Iph is standing. How did that happen?

She has to get to a phone. There has to be a way to fix this.

She fumbles for the thick-framed glasses. It's so dark in the hallway, Iph lets her hand trail the wall. The textured wallpaper is sticky in places, rough in others. She turns the corner to the main room. It's dark, too, but there are windows. A streetlight does its best to get in through the blinds. Everything, even the light, takes on a furtive feel.

George is on the sofa, covers kicked off. Scout is splayed on the rug, paws in the air, snoring. Iph takes the flashlight from the coffee table and walks backward into the bedroom.

The nightie she's wearing was Nana's. It's thin and a little pilled, see-through even in the dim apartment, but it will have to do. Iph finds her bra and hunts in the closet for shoes. She finds a neat row of canvas sneakers, all sized for the tiniest feet. Right as she's giving up, she notices a backpack in the corner, a beat-up green JanSport like the ones most kids use for school. Inside is a copy of *Shakespeare's Sonnets* and a pair of boots. The flashlight shines a *ta-da* light on the miracle of them—Doc Martens, size eight, black, adorned with hand-painted roses. Iph is a seven and half, but with the fuzzy socks, they feel great. Her blisters only hurt a little. She's sure George won't mind. A long crocheted cardigan completes the outfit. In the mirror on the closet door, she looks greenish and strange in her getup, with her wild curls and rose combat boots and old-man glasses.

She tiptoes past George and Scout, down the stairs and out. It's a little before daybreak, a time of day Iph knows well as an insomniac, though it's different being outdoors on her own. *These boots are made for walking.* The song repeats in Iph's head as she picks a direction that feels right. It's a favorite of Mom's, one that appears on most of her housework mixes. The tune of it marches Iph down the empty street. The rain has come and gone again. Everything is clean. It's dark, but the sky is showing signs of morning around the edges. Here and there, an early bird chirps, then quiets.

She passes a few houses, inhaling the sweetness of their jasmine-clotted porches. There is a Japanese restaurant and a few empty storefronts. A hardware store. An incongruous adult theater next to a new-looking coffee shop. Finally, the corner of a large street with the occasional car and a gas station. A pay phone! She still has the quarters from the lost and found, taken from the kitchen counter and slipped into Nana's nightgown pocket.

She's shaky as she puts the coin in its slot. She needs to keep it together. To find the magic words that will make Dad relent. The phone rings. The answering machine clicks on. It's Dad's deep voice instead of Mom's usual greeting.

"Hello, you've reached the Santos Velos household. If this is Iph, sit tight and leave a number where I can reach you. I'll call as soon as I can. Anyone else, please leave a message."

She imagines the night that led up to this—Dad trying to act normal at the party, then finally giving in to his worry and heading out to look for her. Yanking his tie loose in a familiar pissed-off gesture that says, *You kids never face the consequences of your actions.* She imagines him giving up, heading home, thinking maybe Iph got a ride with someone from his office, speeding toward Forest Lake half-ironically praying to whichever Greek Orthodox saint keeps you safe from getting a ticket. At home alone, he'd last an hour, maybe two, his leg jiggling as he tried to distract himself with *Star Trek* reruns. Finally, he'd discover the off-the-hook phone, call the hotel, and learn she'd been there and gone—and totally freak out. He's probably downtown right now. Or at a police station.

Iph can't remember how long it's been since the answering machine beeped. She has no phone number and even if she knew the address, she can't have Dad bursting into George's secret hideout. She hangs up and instantly regrets it—yet another instance where she acts before she thinks. When will she stop being such a drama queen? She should at least let him know she's safe, that she'll call again in a few hours.

She goes to slide her last quarter into the slot, but misses. It drops and rolls under an ice machine, totally out of reach. She's furious. Predictably, she starts to cry.

A little bark stops her.

"How did you know I was here?" Iph crouches and holds out her hand.

The dog's eyes are the exact color of maple syrup. Her coat is a mix of mink brown and ink black. She tilts her head as if she intends to speak.

"What?" Iph says.

Scout play-bows, circles three times, and trots over to the ice machine. Flattening into a small brindle pancake, she does an awkward scoot like something a seal might do on land and pushes herself underneath. She grunts as she scoots back, a movement she seems to manage with her whole body at once, and emerges, clearly pleased with herself, popping up like a jack-in-the-box to reveal Iph's lost quarter under her chin.

"You're a genius," Iph says. She's dropped any kind of dumbing-down she was doing before for the dog's sake. "Thank you so much."

She bends to pick up the coin and gets a surprise kiss attack. Scout seems determined to lick up all traces of her tears. After leaving a semi-sane-sounding message on her home answering machine, Iph takes a second to breathe. The sky is rosy pink and feels a little closer to earth than it does at home.

Scout's shoulders twitch as she trots up the block in a different direction than Iph came. Iph follows. They walk less than half a block up Southeast 39th and turn onto a narrow street crammed with tiny houses and outrageously lush gardens. What kind of story would you set in a place like this? What would her story be like if she'd grown up here, with neighbors so close you'd have to close the curtains to get dressed and whisper if you wanted to talk about them?

Scout zigs, then zags, taking them in what feels like the direction of Taurus Trucking with a few detours so they can see the best yards. The birds are in full morning mode. Chickadees sing their names to each other from the tops of wide-hipped maples with leaves as big as Iph's head. A hummingbird dives face-first into a fat purple flower. Iph wants to dive with her, to taste what the tiny bird tastes.

From a house ahead, a small stucco bungalow covered in pink climbing roses, piano music spills from an open window. Iph stops in the middle of the street to listen. A line of crows bob above her. Scout dances around her ankles. Iph is still, trying to will the peace of this morning, the joy of this music through the ether to Orr. She's crying a little and laughing a little at the crows because it seems like they're laughing at her. "Tell Orr I'm coming," she tells them softly. "Don't forget!" she calls as they caw at her and fly away like maybe they understand.

The piano music swells. A jazz standard, something familiar. A window down the street slams shut—not a morning person, perhaps.

Who plays the piano this early? Probably an insomniac like her who sleeps best at sunrise. Iph knows that if she lived here on this narrow street in one of these dollhouses—maybe the cream one on the corner with peeling paint and a tilting porch that seems to be held up by thick vines of passionflower and clematis—she would never be angry at the early-morning music. She'd let it slip into her sleep. Let it move her, change her, the way art is supposed to.

10

UNITS AND
OBJECTIVES

George is waiting, sitting at the top of a staircase leading directly to the apartment, when Iph follows Scout up a side street to the small parking lot behind Taurus Trucking. There is no mention of Iph leaving or Scout bringing her back, just a quick glance down at the boots she borrowed and a brief nod.

"They're never up this early on weekends," George whispers, nodding at the small house that shares a back fence with the lot. "Normally, I use the side door closer to the street." It takes Iph a minute to remember about the neighbors and the need for secrecy. "C'mon." George motions her inside.

There are three phone books on the kitchen table beside a piece of binder paper and a pen. George and Iph search for Meadowbrook in the cool light seeping through the yellowed window shades. Either Iph isn't remembering the name on the brochure correctly or the place isn't listed in metropolitan Portland. In any case, George woke up with a plan, and the phone book is only phase one.

It's too early for phase two, so they doze on the sofa, Scout between them, and wake up in the heat of early afternoon. It's so hot a cold shower feels good. George has given Iph the okay to

raid Nana's wardrobe. She finds a pair of overalls good enough
to fight for if someone else tried to nab them at a thrift store. The
denim is worn soft and paper-thin. The legs are loose and hit
Iph at the ankle. With an undershirt of George's, her hair piled
in a bun on top of her head and secured with a pair of take-out
chopsticks, and the clunky black glasses, Iph has managed to be
both on the lam and actually cute. Not that it matters. She shakes
her head at herself in Nana's vanity. *Pretty is as pretty does,* she
tells herself. Or maybe Nana's telling her that, because it's not a
thought she remembers having before.

The wait for the neighbors to leave is a metal-on-metal grind
Iph feels in her intestines and back teeth. What is Orr doing at
boot camp? Surely he's been up for hours. Maybe the place isn't
so bad. Maybe they're hiking or trying to force Orr to do crafts.
Maybe they will let him do a trail run. He loves to run through
the forest.

The street below Taurus Trucking is quiet. The businesses in
the neighborhood don't seem like they've ever been very busy.
It's the back neighbors George worries about, a nice family of four
who might be concerned about a lone teenager squatting at the
vacant tow truck place. So they wait, George narrating the family's exodus.

"They load the kids up first. Mom will get in and remember
the stuff she forgot. This happens between one and four times
before she's good to go. The dad blasts the tunes on his way home
from work in the evening, so when the mom turns the car on in
the morning, it's like a rock concert—Red Hots, Bad Brains, Fish-
bone. The mom turns it down and switches it to NPR, but the kids
make her change it back so they can sing. They know all the words.
It's pretty cute."

Iph laughs, watching Scout's ears telegraph the steps a second
before they happen. Kids in, a mumbled swear from the mom,
screen door slamming open, screen door slamming shut. The
music blast—Nirvana this time. Iph misses Orr even more hearing the kids scream-singing the words to "Smells Like Teen Spirit"

out the open windows as their mom drives away. Nirvana was Orr's first independently discovered teenager thing. Iph sort of misses the owlish little classical music snob he used to be.

In the bright heat, Taurus Trucking shows her age: blue paint faded to white in places, duct tape over the cracks in a window, rust on the metal garage door. Gripping the seat while George stands to pedal is easier since Iph ditched her party dress and can straddle the bike with these Rosie the Riveter overalls. She's getting used to the Orr-shaped pain in her stomach, and the hunger, too. George offered her Cheerios with bananas and soy milk, but Iph could barely manage a few bites.

Southeast Portland is thick with crows and roses and families out walking their dogs and toddlers. They fly down side streets and over the Hawthorne Bridge, pacing the seagulls, the river sparkling summer blue below. Iph puts a hand on the messenger bag to feel Scout's solid body. Downtown, they stop, and Iph hops off a second before George does, almost graceful.

They walk together, pace for pace. Today George wears jeans cut off at the knees, a short-sleeved shirt buttoned all the way up, and a mustard cardigan, even in the heat. Iph recognizes Pioneer Square. Once at Christmas, they'd come to Portland, all four of them, to see the massive tree lit up and have dinner at a restaurant at the top of a bank building.

Today the square is empty except for a group of ragged shirtless hacky-sack boys and some shopgirls drinking iced coffees on their cigarette break. Even without the bow and arrow, George heads into the square like someone who patrols the streets at night to protect wayward girls. Scout whines to be let out of the messenger bag and runs over to a black lab Iph hadn't noticed dozing in the shade. The two frolic with the boys, who play their game around them, a laughing mass of dog and boy and summer.

One of the players waves when they get closer and lobs the hacky sack to his friend, pulling a shirt from the pile and yanking it over his head, not seeming to notice it's inside out. He bows to George, then to Iph, doffing an imaginary top hat.

"Hey." George grins. "Iph, this is Josh. Josh, this is my friend Iph."

"If?" Josh says. He leaps to the bandstand, still set up from some weekend festival, and falls to his knees, clutching his heart.

O! if, I say, you look upon this verse,
When I perhaps compounded am with clay,
Do not so much as my poor name rehearse;
But let your love even with my life decay.

George snorts and Iph applauds. "From one of the sonnets?"

"Seventy-one," he says, getting up to take a bow.

"Bravo!" Iph laughs.

"If you go in for that sort of thing," George says like it's an old joke between them. How do these two know each other? And why do they both quote Shakespeare? "My man," George says, "we're here on business. Iph's brother got nabbed."

"Cops?" Josh leaps off the stage easy as a cat.

"Boot-camp mercenaries," George says. "A place called Meadowbrook, she thinks, but we can't find it in the phone book. Iph needs to call them and check in on him."

"Won't talk to her. Parents only. And they're all named like that—faux-wholesome nature-sounding crap. I've been in several." Iph looks closer at him. Pretty, sandy hair, hazel eyes. Something around the bridge of his nose, the memory of a fist or a rock—but Iph is probably imagining that. It happens sometimes, the outlandish image of some detail from a stranger's life. "Overactive imagination," her dad had said when, as a little girl, she worried that someone was hurting her third-grade teacher.

"It's Meadowbrook," Iph says. "I'm pretty sure. I saw the brochure."

Josh shakes his head. "Not ringing a bell. But wait—" He takes Iph's hand gently in his, running a finger over her long, glossy gold-painted nails, freshly manicured a lifetime ago. "A *lady*, I see," he says in his decent English accent. "So . . . are we talking Ritz-Carlton rehab? Is there money involved?"

Iph nods slowly. Her family *does* have money. Dad has been very successful. "Yeah. It would be expensive."

"I'm not your gent, then. It's institutions for the likes of me. But our friend Georgie knows someone who might be able to help." Josh drapes an arm around George, who shrugs it off, but not in an angry way. These two are playing their roles at full stage strength. For Iph? Another game with Orr is people as ice cream flavors. Together, these two are definitely Lost Boy Ripple.

"I could take her there, old chap, if it's too much for you." Josh says in the English accent again, and Iph imagines him dressed in jewels and a fur cape, like pictures she's seen of Oscar Wilde. But wait—is George pawning her off on this boy? He seems nice enough, but George and Iph are a team. At least, she thought they were after yesterday. This always happens. Why is she such a side-kick? Ever since preschool she's glommed on to a more outgoing or capable friend, usually an alpha girl who undid her elaborate braids at recess and insisted she do embarrassing or servile things to prove her loyalty. Last year, when Iph renounced this practice and gave up on the limited stock of potential friends at her small school, she glommed on to Mom. And now, on her own for the first time ever, she's immediately glommed on to George.

Iph sighs as George gestures to the side of the bandstand and pulls her over.

"There is someone who can probably help us."

Iph can't help it—she smiles a little at the *us.*

"She might not be thrilled to see me. But I'm worried your dad isn't picking up. Something feels off. We can at least use her phone."

"You've done so much already. Are you sure it's not too weird?"

Iph leaves the real question—*Why is it weird?*—unspoken. It's a Mom trick, and like always, it works.

"Cait . . . is my ex. It ended because of me. I cheated."

This is certainly a new data point in George's backstory. And a confirmation. George dates girls.

"You know how I was kind of weird for a second this morning?"

Iph nods. When Iph got back from the gas station with Scout, there was a moment—something about the boots. It's interesting that George noticed Iph noticing. George looks down at the flowered Docs Iph borrowed. "They . . . belonged to the girl I cheated with. I painted them for her. She's the reason I go out with my bow at night. Why I know what it's like to need to find someone."

"Oh."

"But it's okay. Cait and I are all right now, pretty much. And she'll definitely want to help you with this."

When they go back to Josh, he's sitting on the steps with a love-crazed Scout wriggling belly-up in his lap. "It's settled, then? You're taking your chances with the queen?"

George grunts and opens the messenger bag. A little girl in a pink leotard and leopard-print rain boots trailing her quick-stepping Birkenstocked mother sees Scout's leap and claps.

Josh gives George a quick, back-slapping hug and takes Iph's hand again, briefly kissing it. Close up, he smells like the boys' locker room. Iph knows because she'd had to go in there more than once to collect a melting Orr in middle school before Mom, to Iph's enormous relief, decided to keep him home.

The smell is strong, but backing away seems impolite. For all his charm and prettiness, Josh looks like the kids Iph used to see panhandling outside Powell's, the ones Mom always made sure to give whatever cash was in her wallet. He's probably homeless, Iph realizes. And without the secret hideout at Taurus Trucking, maybe George would be, too. They both know boot camps. Institutions. Maybe if Orr is lucky, he'll find a few kids like these at Meadowbrook, kind and wise in a way he and Iph have never had to be.

Gripping Josh's hand, Iph steps back into a curtsy, full prima ballerina. Pre-blood and boobs, Iph had been set on being a dancer like Mom. Her moves can still impress a layperson. Josh

and George are wide-eyed in a way Iph likes, and again she's confused by the pleasure-pain of this day and last night and all the
things that have happened since Orr was kidnapped and she ran
away.

"Farewell, milady," Josh says. It's nice on his lips. George
scowls and Josh grins.

Are they . . . competing? Over her?

"Farewell," Iph says. "And thank you."

11

THE SEAGULL

The bus climbs into the hills above the hospital. Iph has been to this part of Portland countless times for Orr's quarterly appointments with his psychiatrist. The medicine was a blessing. Before it, there were times when Orr's body went so rigid with tension, he would worry his limbs had turned to wood. The same doctor treated Iph last year during the worst of her existential crisis. She took the pills for several months until she felt stable enough to stop.

Iph notes the change in neighborhood as they climb. As the kid of an architect and a socialist kitchen witch, she perceives a city by its building style, garden aesthetic, class dissection, and degree of magic. Iph used to wonder what other parents talked about while driving their kids around.

This area was developed later than the tiny Victorian cottages, English Tudor revivals, and Craftsman bungalows in the other parts of Portland—probably constructed in the sixties or seventies, clean-lined geometric houses built for doctors and lawyers when everyone was talking about space travel, modern art, and the future. Ugly, but made of quality materials with at least some aesthetic in mind, they are her least favorite sort of Portland house. Some of her earliest memories are of Dad driving around the West Hills showing her examples of midcentury architecture or into Northeast to find a perfect example of an Old Portland foursquare.

The bus slows on a curving road that borders the city forest. They pass a familiar stretch that leads to a trailhead. Mom used to bring Orr here before his appointments so he'd burn enough energy to sit still. Iph would walk in the pagan cathedral of the trees slowly enough to lose sight of them, loving the illusion of being alone.

"Is Forest Lake like this?" George asks, speaking for the first time in a while. Maybe worried about the ex.

"Kind of. Not so wild. There's lots of trees, but they're more spread out and intentional looking. My mom always tells people it's east of the sun and west of Boring."

"Next door to the troll princess?" She and George clearly read the same books when they were kids.

"Just a type A, twelve-year-old aspiring chef," Iph says. "And more trees. And Republicans."

"I'm an Idaho kid myself. Or, was. I lived there when I was little. I'll never forget the day I learned Boring, Oregon, was a real place." In the light of day, Iph notices how crooked George's bottom teeth are. She commands herself not to stare. In her world, crooked teeth are quickly straightened.

At the top of the hill, they get off the bus and turn the corner. Iph pants up a tall set of cement stairs. The day has settled into true summer, in the high eighties at least. The entry of the glass-fronted house looks more like an office building than someone's actual home.

Our house could have been like this, Iph realizes. Her dad is into modern architecture and worships Frank Lloyd Wright, but instead of a cold, angular box, their house has a feel Dad calls organic, its tall sides clad in shingles faded to the sheened gray of lamb's ears in late summer. There were magazine profiles of it when it was first finished. The best was headlined, MODERN

BOHEMIA: WUNDERKIND ARCHITECT AND FLOWER-CHILD BRIDE MAKE FIRST HOME IN ELEGANT PORTLAND SUBURB. A framed photo of the cover shows Iph's parents, Mom barefoot and bangled with silver earrings and a white sundress and shaggy-haired Dad in jeans and sneakers, standing in the entry, backlit by sun streaming in through a line of slatted windows in the high ceiling—what Orr always called the house's gills. "It breathes sunlight," he'd insisted.

This had bothered Iph. "What happens at night, then?" she'd asked.

His answer hadn't made her feel any better. "At night it holds its breath."

Iph pulls the stray hair off her neck and knots it on the top of her head, repinning the chopsticks. The doorbell's echo hints at an even bigger house than the imposing façade suggests. George is suddenly a stranger beside her.

The girl who answers the door makes her feel both worse and better. Harmless, probably, but so fine-featured, blonde, and thin Iph has to fight the impulse to turn around and walk away. Suddenly, Nana's overalls are too snug. The not-quite-right glasses press a headache into her temples.

The girl tries to keep a straight face but smiles at George anyway, little lightning bolts of sun flying off her perfect cheekbones. "You're like a million hours too late, man. The party's over," she says. "The cleaners left half an hour ago. I'm locking it down. My parents will be home at four."

"Cleaners? Really?" George is smiling, too, and Iph feels the spark between them. Suddenly it's like every other day, demoted from principal to chorus girl just like that.

"Leave no trace," the girl says. Her golden hair falls over her eye, and she makes no move to shift it. Iph notes for future reference: in the truly beautiful, there is no such thing as a misstep or malfunction. Everything falls as it should.

"We aren't here for revels, milady. We come to request a boon." George bows low and turns on the charm, the same British schtick as Josh.

"You can take a shower," she says like it's grudging. "I have that shampoo you like." Cait moves aside for George, still not addressing Iph. Well, she's used to that treatment from pretty girls. *Conventionally pretty white girls*, she hears Mom correct. At school, Iph sometimes feels like she can smell the fear seeping out from under their deodorant, their worry that Iph's soft belly and thick thighs are contagious. Cait hugs herself, cupping the sharp tips of her elbows in her delicate hands. Black nail polish, chipped. Silver rings on every finger, even her thumbs.

"I'm the reason we're here," Iph says. "My brother is in trouble. George thinks you can help."

"He got nabbed," George says. Iph shivers at the fairy-tale finality of the word. "I wanted to ask you—what were the names of the first few places they put your sister? The outdoorsy ones?"

The look on Cait's face tells the missing part of this story. Iph thinks about that—how one look, one reaction, can say more than hours of dialogue.

"They kidnapped him," Iph tells her, looking her right in the eyes. "Last night."

The girl's eyes widen and change from pale blue to watery gray, and Iph knows that whatever monster is after Orr has already taken this beautiful girl's sister.

"Please," Iph says, "can you help me?"

12

LIKE METAL
IN ROADS

Another day, another van ride. The Columbia flows by on the right. The gorge is a dream landscape of forest and rock formations and spinning raptors and the wide powerful river.

There are two girls—women?—in front, and Orr and the tattooed tofu wiener girl are riding in back. Jane? He thinks it's Jane. She looks like a Jane. They stopped for breakfast at a diner that served perfect fried eggs over medium and almost-perfect pancakes because, as the girl driving said, "Woman cannot live on wieners alone." Now it's three in the afternoon, and they're headed for Portland.

Orr holds his hands over his ears. Probably-Jane snores on the bench seat beside him, sleeping through the mix blasting out of the low-quality speakers.

At a stoplight in the outskirts of the city, Jane wakes up. "Don't like Dead Moon?" she yells.

"I like it," he yells back. "It's just loud. And these speakers suck. No offense!" he remembers to add.

"Huh." She grunts and leans into the front seat, practically in the lap of the girl on the passenger side, a medium-tall, plump redhead. Orr has always loved red hair, even the dyed-red kind like hers. Not love-love. Orr isn't sure where he stands in that department. His mother asks him a few times a year, making sure he knows it's totally okay to be gay or bi or something else altogether that is specific to him. But at fifteen, Orr can't decide.

He knows a few things. He likes looking at certain parts of certain people—a boy's slender, long-fingered hands, a girl's high-arched feet and seashell ears. He prefers plumpness to thinness and darker skin like Iph's and Mom's and the girl driving the van's to lighter skin like Jane's, which is as white as binder paper under her colorful tattoos. He has always been able to tell Iph honestly that the shape of her body is good, fine. A valid shape for a body to be. He knows, of course, that the Overall Messaging for girls is particularly harsh on these attributes. They've talked about it, he and Iph and Mom. Although Mom is slimmer than Iph, she was told when she was young that her body was too sturdy for ballet, her breasts too big for Broadway. She tells Iph this when Iph feels bad about herself. Because of the patriarchy, they hear this story a lot.

Orr's own body is slim to bony and requires a lot of movement. He runs every morning at dawn because he must. It's been this way since he was eleven and the world began its slow press inward, like the trash compactor in the Death Star in the first *Star Wars* movie.

Mom went running with him at first because back then he was still prone to getting lost. But it was hard to wake her some mornings after she'd had wine or a sleeping pill the night before. So Orr studied maps. First his street and neighborhood, then the suburbs and freeways, then the streets of Portland and the surrounding mountains to the east and the coast to the west. When he knew he wouldn't get lost, he ran by himself. Not tethered to Mom's lesser stamina and slower pace, Orr galloped the surrounding country roads. His arms and legs, exposed in the tank top and running shorts Mom got him along with his running shoes, had turned the golden brown of Dad's Mediterranean skin in summer. He found a long, circular route, almost ten miles total. He ran it every morning and sometimes again before bed. Probably part of why he was able to keep up with the coyote, he realizes. Almost as if he's been training for this.

"Here, kid," Jane says, placing a small plastic bag in his hand. Inside are two little foam blobs, orange as safety cones. Orr can't decipher their purpose.

"Dude. They're earplugs." Jane laughs, opens the bag, takes one out. "Take your hands away, babe. One at a time." Orr likes clear, direct instruction. He likes being called babe. He does as she says.

The blobs are squishy and glove-compartment hot going into Orr's ears, but once there, he can hear the music without pain. The scratchy speaker noise and road sounds are gone.

The next song is from a band he hasn't heard before, all jangled and falling apart with a husky girl singer. The song goes perfectly with the big rattly van and the gray city outskirts and the summer-blue sky.

"How do you like this one?" the redhead yells from the front.

"It's great," Orr says. "Who is it?"

"It's us!" the girl driving says. "The Furies."

"The Furies rock," Orr says.

He grins at Jane.

Jane grins back.

13

TOWARD A PHYSICAL CHARACTERIZATION

The phone in Cait's room is pale blue to match the wildflower wallpaper peeking out between pages torn from magazines, postcards, photographs, and band posters. Cait has surprising taste—mostly seventies punk with some Björk and Tori Amos thrown in, and a vintage poster of Janis Joplin with a frame of dried marigolds pinned carefully to its edges that squeezes Iph's heart.

Dammit. Why isn't this girl more hateable?

Iph almost forgets to care about acting when she imagines directing someone like this. Cait doesn't even bother to put her body in character, as Iph surely would have had to do to make the phone call she's making. This girl is used to being obeyed. A fan of brochures filched from a filing cabinet in her mother's study sits on the bed next to her. None match the exact one Iph saw in Orr's room, but these are all from a few years ago, the font sort of hokey and the kids' clothes a little outdated. Iph is sure it's Meadowbrook, though. The lodge looks right, the position of the mountain in the background the same as in the brochure on Orr's desk. Cait tries it first.

Draped across her king-size canopy bed in baggy sweats and

a cropped Hello Kitty tee and smoking a clove cigarette, she sounds like the world's most bougie Euro-mom. "I'd like a progress report on my son. Orestes Santos Velos," she demands in a clipped, sexy growl. The rationale behind the accent is clear when she says Orr's not-American-sounding name. In Cait's mouth, it communicates "diplomatic corps" and "Spanish aristocracy" and "owns a Greek Island"—a strange opposite to Mom's California lilt and occasional Spanglish, which used to make people wonder if she was Iph and Orr's babysitter.

"What?" Cait's accent almost drops. She sits up. "Are you joking?"

Something is wrong.

"Has his father been informed?" she sputters as if genuinely affronted, the accent thicker now. Iph can hear the faint hiss of words on the other end of the phone. Cait nods and puts the receiver down in its cradle.

14

THE PERIOD
OF EMOTIONAL
EXPERIENCE

Iph tries Dad every ten minutes until they have to go.

"You could stay and keep trying," Cait says. "It's just George. Persona non grata. My parents would have a fit."

"No worries." Iph meets Cait's eye easily now. They are definitely going to be friends.

Iph picks up a photo on the nightstand: two blonde girls in swimsuits at the beach. There's so little margin between where Iph is now and where Cait lives every day as an only child. She may have supermodel cheekbones and mile-long legs, but her sister—her *sister*—is dead.

Cait rummages through her purse. Vintage Coach, simple with a brass lock. A smaller version of Mom's favorite bag, one she bought new in the early seventies with her first paycheck from an off-Broadway show.

"Here," Cait says. "Take my phone card. Run it up all you want. My dad's accountant pays it; my parents will never see the bill." She slips it into the front pocket of Iph's overalls with a packet of travel tissues.

At the bus stop, she and George are silent. The heat feels good after the air-conditioning at Cait's. It's when Iph goes to blow her nose, stuffy from crying, that she discovers the twenty-dollar bills Cait tucked in her pocket. They get off the bus on Hawthorne in front of Burgerville. Iph tries Dad. He doesn't pick up, and the machine is full.

After a Gardenburger Iph can barely swallow, she tries again while George stays in the cool restaurant with Scout. Like most people, the manager is a Scout fan and allows her to sit discreetly in a corner booth lapping water from a cup while George feeds her a child-size burger and fries.

It's boiling at the pay phone. Iph remembers why she hates summer. This time, Dad picks up on the first ring.

"Iph." Dad sounds like he's swimming underwater.

"Did you find him?"

"There was a search team," Dad says. "With dogs. Wait, how'd you know he was gone?"

"Is he okay?" The last time they went camping, Orr had to go to the emergency room for a wasp sting. Without help, he could have died.

"He's fine, sweetie. I know he is."

"You had him kidnapped. Now they've lost him. That doesn't sound fine."

"There's a waitress who swears she saw him yesterday with a bunch of tattooed girls."

"Dad! That doesn't sound like Orr."

"Eggs over medium, extra hash browns, add cheddar."

"Sub pancakes for toast," Iph whispers.

"Hot chocolate, lukewarm." Dad's voice breaks. "It was him. He must have hitched a ride."

Iph's mouth is hanging open. She shuts it and closes her eyes.

"The waitress said the girls looked like punkers from Portland."

Iph stands up straighter. He knows *punkers* is outdated. The cute dorky Dad routine isn't going to work. "Good thing there are so few tattooed girls in Portland. Finding him should be a breeze."

"Iph, come on. Where are you?"

"Don't worry about me. I'm fine."

"That's not what I asked." There it is—Dad's *I'm an Olympian god and you're a peon mortal* voice. "Iph?"

"Portland," Iph says. "With friends." Mom would have jumped right on this—she knows Iph's friends, if you could call them that, and none of them live in the city. "What about you? I called like a thousand times."

"How kind of you," Dad says. "That really helped when I was out scouring the streets."

"I came back to the hotel. You were gone."

Dad exhales. Iph feels him letting go of the rope. That's what he and Mom call it when one person realizes a fight is going nowhere. "When I got back, someone said Bill's daughter left early. I thought you must have gotten a ride with her."

"You thought I was with Mackenzie? Our last sleepover was in second grade. She thinks Phyllis Schlafly is a feminist icon. We've hated each other for years."

"I assumed you hated me more." Dad's gone quiet. Like Iph, his temper rises quickly and falls as fast. "I went to call you over there when you didn't come home. The phone was off the hook."

"I know," Iph says. "The hotel guy called the operator for me."

"That guy!" Iph can picture Dad shaking his head. "Couldn't answer a simple question. I had to lean on him pretty hard. A big tip helped. Apparently, you left with some boy."

There is a beat. A weighted silence.

"Dad, I told you. I'm perfectly fine."

Another beat. She can hear him shifting in his seat. "I called the police. They told me to call back if you were gone more than three days. I got home at four in the morning, and a few minutes later, Meadowbrook called. I drove straight there." Dad stops, takes a drink of something. "Iph," he finally says, "are you sure you're all right?"

"Dad. I just ate a Gardenburger."

"Really? That's good. You left your purse, so I was worried." He exhales like a horse, a thing Iph used to love when she was little enough to ride on his shoulders. "I still can't believe it. Your brother ran away."

Is that *pride* in Dad's voice? Running away is exactly the sort of thing he would admire. He's always telling stories about his adventures with his brother—pranks and misdemeanors, outsmarting neighborhood bullies. It would be just like him to spin Orr's disappearance into some sort of Huck Finn adventure. The fact that this is the only kind of bravery Dad can see is the whole problem. He's always underestimated Orr.

A group of squealing toddlers swarm the outside tables. Iph plugs her free ear.

"Did you call Mom?"

He hesitates. "I want to find him first."

Iph has never considered the possibility of her parents breaking up. They aren't just married. They're in love. They walk hand in hand. Stay up late talking politics and art. It's a common occurrence to enter a room and find them holding each other silently and breathing like they are each other's air. But if anything could break them apart, it's this.

"Dad, why? What were you thinking?"

"I'm his father." Iph hears ice cubes clinking in a glass. Is Dad drinking? That was a thing when Iph and Orr were little, Dad drinking a little too much every night.

"It's iced coffee," he says. As much as he blows off Iph's intuition, he's the other one in the family who seems to share it. "I know things are a mess, Iph. I'm not resting until I figure this out. I'm sure he'll call home soon. He hates sleeping away . . ." Dad trails off, perhaps stopped short by his own hypocrisy. Mom was going to have his guts for garters.

Iph shivers. *Someone walked over your grave.* That's what Mom always says about those weird spasms. The shiver and the saying became a part of her dance piece. She spent hours in the studio behind the house working variation after variation of it—that moment of cold or premonition or possession.

The working title of Mom's three-part modern ballet is *El*

Mundo Bueno/El Mundo Malo, from a favorite book of hers—*The Fifth Sacred Thing*, a utopian alternative history by an ecofeminist witch. *The good reality and the bad reality exist side by side,* Mom wrote in her application for the residency, *imperceptibly separate, like the scrim between waking and sleep. The trick is knowing where you are. Is the bad reality a dream that you only need to wake up from? Is the good reality lost in a single moment, like falling asleep at the wheel?*

Iph wonders now if the two worlds are not separate, but simultaneous. Or what if there is a space between them, a no-man's-land where things are good and bad all at once? Orr at boot camp and now lost is a living nightmare—but this otherworld she's found in Portland is the stuff of impossible dreams.

In just two days these strangers feel more like friends than the kids she grew up with. Even though they have every right to judge her, pickled as she is in her spoiled suburban childhood, they've been nothing but accepting and kind. Maybe time in *El Mundo Malo* marks you. Maybe George and Josh and Cait saw it before she did—that her life will never be the same.

Dad's ice clicks like he's draining the coffee. "Iph? Are you still there?"

"I'm here."

"I did a lot of research. Visited several places. Your mom and I talked about it last year, but she didn't think it was a good idea. He was just so depressed with her gone. I wanted to help him find his power."

"Waiting for Mom to come back without freaking out *was* Orr exercising his power. He needs to shut down sometimes. If you were ever around, you'd know that. But you're always at work or in your study or out on a date with your precious wife. You don't even know your own kids. I hope you're happy."

There is a hiss of breath—the sound of Dad expelling his own monster, the temper she'd inherited. In and out, three times. Then, "The camp has an investigator who's on it. The police will start looking if they don't find him by tomorrow."

"The police? Dad, oh my god." Iph will never forget the day

she found Mom doubled over in the kitchen, a copy of some magazine at her feet. There was an article about a kid who sounded a little like Orr, a brown-skinned boy who was melting down. There were cops and a gun and it was too close to home. "Dad, we don't need the cops. There's no way he'd sleep on the street. And if he's in the city, he's definitely not lost. Every time we're in Portland, Mom tests him, asks which way to go and he always knows. And I mean, at least it's girls who have him. They sound like kids, right?"

"College age," Dad says. "The waitress said they were rowdy but harmless. Talked about music and castrating rapists." There's a little uptick in Dad's tone. He's all about that Greek-tragedy level of revenge. Told Iph when she was ten that if any guy even tried to touch her against her will, kicking him in the balls was her birthright. "And you're right," he says. "We'll find him. Come home, *kuklamu.*"

Kukla. Dad's special nickname for her—"little doll" in Greek. Iph gets a wave of Dad: his bear-deep singing voice and cedar aftershave and honey shampoo. The world quiets, and it's him and Iph on a silent stage, their fast-beating hearts pounding over the sound system.

Dad needs help. Needs her. And yes, of course Iph wants to go home to her obscenely soft bed and enormous bathtub and full refrigerator and house that is shined weekly by a team of housekeepers. But can she?

Suddenly, she's not mad anymore. "Where are you?" she asks. "The deck?"

His voice catches as he says, "Treehouse." Orr's treehouse. The special place Dad made for him in the days when he was still trying to have an actual relationship with his son. He installed a phone up there, extending the landline from the second floor to the majestic linden at the bottom of their property where Orr retreated when things were too much. He could be alone there with Mom just a phone call away.

Dad sniffs. Is he crying?

"Let's go find him, Dad. Let's find him together."

"I'll come get you."

I'll stay if you come back. That's what George said when Iph went into the hotel.

Now, after all they've been through, Iph can't just say goodbye at this Burgerville. There has to be something more she can do. Some small way to pay George back for saving her. She'll have to be crafty. George was not happy when Iph discovered the twenties from Cait.

"She knows not to pull that with me," George said. "Unless Scout's going hungry, I won't take a handout. Of course, she left the larder open on purpose, knowing I don't mind nicking a few things from her robber-baron parents."

"Who says *larder*?" Iph laughed. "Who says *robber baron* and *nick*?" Then she saw what was in the backpack—a full bottle of gin and a six-pack of tonic water, several limes, and a carton of cigarettes. "And who needs all this?"

George quoted Shakespeare again, this time from *King Lear*. "*This cold night will turn us all to fools and madmen.*"

"Dad? Are you still there?"

"I'm here."

"We need to make flyers," Iph says. "My friend here is an artist who could totally make one. Like those police sketches." Maybe George will let Dad pay for that, like a commission. It's worth a shot, and maybe a better option than the few outdated snapshots they have of Orr, who hates being photographed. "I'm in Southeast. There's not a phone, but I can meet you—"

"Iph?" Dad's tone is suddenly cautious. "There's something else. Before you make a flyer." Dad clears his throat. "Honey, they cut Orr's hair." There is a beat that goes on a breath too long. "They shaved his head."

Anger has always been fleeting for Iph, there and gone faster than an ice cream headache. What she feels now is something else. It's muscled and clear-eyed and huge. *This tiger-footed rage.* Padding, soft, calculating. She shakes with it.

Her father is forgotten. She is nowhere, no place at all. Or someplace between atoms, some other dimension, sent away in a Hail Mary play to save life on earth because she's about to explode, and it will be nuclear.

Something is hot. Metal. The outside of the phone booth. She stumbles forward. There is a wall. She manages a pivot, the stucco rising to meet her back. She slides down to the hot pavement and clamps her hands over her face, not wanting anyone to hear the sound she is going to make. She weeps until she's sick with it. As if it is work she is being forced to do.

She gasps for breath and opens her eyes. The women herding the birthday party toddlers are making a quick exit, careful not to look at her.

She wipes her face. Finds one of the tissues from Cait. Blows her nose. The phone dangles on its metal cord like the Hanged Man in Mom's deck of tarot cards. She will get up any moment to hang it up. Sever her connection with Dad. She presses her back into the burning wall. She closes her eyes.

Scout pushes her sleek head under Iph's hand and presses her body into Iph's lap. Iph holds her. George reaches out a hand to help her up. Iph thinks of Mom, how she always wants to talk through every little thing, and for the first time ever she's glad to be away from her. The world is large and airy without her parents and their epic love affair and beautiful house and worry for Orr.

She and George walk into the quiet of Ladd's Addition, a neighborhood right off Hawthorne laid out around traffic circles full of roses. The Craftsman homes here are stately and square, made for large prosperous families. The massive trees—oaks and maples and cherries, the same vintage as the houses—touch fingers in the middle of the street like a line of couples waiting for a minuet to begin.

Scout scampers ahead to sniff, then waits for them to catch up. Iph likes the feel of George's hand in hers. She doesn't remember when it got there, but they're walking together like they do this every day. They emerge from Ladd's Addition at Division, and

Iph is pretty sure if they go left, they'll be back at Taurus Trucking. But even though they're tired, they can't go back, not yet. It's the weekend, so the neighbors could come home anytime.

They cross Division and walk aimlessly, changing sides of the street to follow the shade. Iph likes this modest neighborhood even more than grand Ladd's, with its mix of smaller bungalows and low-slung fifties garden apartment buildings and varied yards, some with unwatered lawns the color of toast, others psychedelic with bloom. They pass a house with a porch dressed in yellow roses that look and smell like cupcakes. There are two rust-flecked red tricycles and a pair of muddy clogs on the porch. Another house has dandelions gone to seed, a resplendent passionflower vine, and a peeling porch flanked by jasmine and purple hydrangea lounged upon by five fat cats.

"Come on," George says, turning the corner and breaking into a run. Scout darts to catch George, then shoots back to Iph, who does not run unless she is made to, and only then if she is wearing a sports bra over a very supportive underwire in a temperature below fifty degrees.

This street is shaded with lindens and cherries framing houses that are set up from the street with sidewalk-chalked cement staircases leading to their wide front porches. More cats. More kids' toys. And in the middle of the block, a little oasis of a park. "Scout's favorite," George says. "A pocket park for a pocket pit."

There is tender grass and glorious shade. In the center is a little elevated playground, bordered by a low brick wall, pungent with fresh cedar chips and shiny clean from yesterday's rain. George has already climbed to the top of the slide with Scout.

Iph sinks into the grass. A giggle, children's voices. The lovely rise and fall of George's voice directing Scout through her repertoire of tricks. The calliope sound of an ice cream truck in the distance. Iph closes her eyes, too exhausted to worry about anything.

She wakes at sunset to a melted-popsicle sky. George and Scout are crashed out beside her, both of them softly snoring. The air is still, and the playground is empty of children who are surely being put to bed, upset because it's still light outside.

Iph wanders toward the play structure. She sits on a swing, languid at first, then pumping her legs. Now she's flying alone in the sky. Crows roost in the tallest trees. Streetlights come on a few at a time.

Iph feels for Orr, imagines him swinging next to her. For years they've been honing their psychic powers, practicing ESP and, since last spring, lucid dreaming. They'd always treated it like it was a game, but maybe it wasn't. Maybe somehow, they knew something would happen and were training for this separation.

The rhythm of the swing is perfect for self-hypnosis.

How do my hands feel when Orr is swinging next to me?
How do my legs feel when we do the thing where we sync
the swings and pump in time?
How can my heartbeat match Orr's heartbeat?
How can my breath mirror his breath?

Iph slits her eyes and sees a small blue window high in a wall, the indigo moment right before dark. The exact color Orr and Mom have claimed as their own. A square, closet-size room. A velvet nap of dark hair on a delicate egg of a head on a faded zebra-striped pillow. It's probably just a comforting daydream. But sometimes, these weird daydreams of hers turn out to be true.

Clairvoyant is what Mom's New Age New York chorus-girl friend pronounced Iph when she predicted who was calling when the phone rang three times in two days. Dad says it's coincidence, especially when he does it, and maybe it is. It's never anything big. What's for dinner, what color someone will be wearing. Who's about to call. And usually no more than a few minutes into the future. Close enough that they've always laughed it off. Except sometimes, it's something bigger. Like when Iph had a nightmare that Yai-Yai fell on the ice. Or when Mom applied to the residency and Iph knew she would get it. So there is a chance that somewhere in this city a few minutes from now when the sun has just set, Orr will be snuggled in some safe zebra-cushioned nest, fast asleep.

She sends him a hug, her love. Pumps harder, swings higher.

Now George is beside her, swinging in rhythm.

In sync, they slow down.

Iph holds out a hand. George takes it.

Together, hands clasped, they jump.

15

MOTHER,
MY MOTHER

Orr wakes as the streetlights come on outside. The last thing he remembers is sitting on the sofa with a coverless copy of *Dragonsong*, lent to him by Mika—not reading, just listening to the comforting sound of the Furies' whispered talk and the almost-silence of their bare feet as they padded around the cluttered house. Now they are in their rooms. Allison, Mika, and Jane. Music and TV and cigarette smoke seep out from under the cracks of their three doors and sneak down the stairs.

Orr is so tired. He curls into himself, but the living room is too open, the door unseeable behind the cat-smelling sofa's back. Where is this cat? Orr barely remembers Dad's famous Maine coon, Agamemnon. Even though they all love animals, they haven't had a pet since then. It's too hard for Dad, Mom says. Their shorter life spans. The loss.

This sofa smells like several cats and, if he's honest, something like Mindy's house, where there are four guinea pigs, three indoor Abyssinians, and a rude parrot that reminds Orr of Iph when she has PMS.

Iph. He's barely thought of her since his escape. Can only stand to do it now for a minute or two. He usually thinks of her often. When he reads, he notes things to tell her. When he runs, he arranges playlists or new songs he will learn on the cello to stump her in their games of Name That Tune. So what's going on now? Memory erasure? Mind control? Orr indexes *X-Files* episodes, cross-referenced with *Star Trek*. Maybe the people at the boot camp were aliens in disguise. Or humans working for aliens. Or for the government. Maybe they put a tracker in his neck like they had with beautiful, badass Agent Scully.

He touches his head. Could his hair have already grown back a little? How many months would it take to reach its former length? And even if it did, would it ever be the same?

There is a story he tells himself at night. His hair features prominently. That, like so much else, will have to change. Not even in fantasy can Orr have long hair anymore. Its taking was too brutal, his transformation too extreme.

In the old story, Orr was a hero in his own personal X-File. Because his hair shielded him, he was able to sneak into the spaceship, sabotage the aliens' experiments, and free the people who'd been abducted, helping them recover their memories and heal from the violation of being taken unknowing from their beds every night for months, or in some cases, years. In the end, both Agents Mulder and Scully fell in love with him. Orr could never decide which one to kiss.

Now, will anyone ever want to kiss him? Like Jo March in *Little Women*, he considered his hair to be the one thing that made him beautiful. He still hasn't looked in a mirror to see if that's changed. Tomorrow, he promises himself. Standing before the mirror is a practice of his. The boy in his reflection is his old friend—himself, but not him. A boy trapped in the room inside the mirror. It's a silly game from when he was very small, but still. Routines are grounding. Ritual makes daily life sacred, according to Mom. She told him that when she was packing for the residency. She'd been trying to get him to write out a daily schedule for himself for when she was gone.

"Ritual creates boundaries," she said, holding a red dress against herself in the mirror.

"Bring it," Orr said. "It's one of your best."

"Boundaries are containers." Mom folded the dress into her suitcase. "Like a glass jar. Nothing special—till you think about what they can contain. All sorts of ambient intangibles."

Ambient Intangibles is the name Orr gave an imaginary paranormal investigative agency in a series of stories he was writing last winter. The whole family adopted it as shorthand for the inexplicable or vast—space, time, consciousness, the afterlife.

"I keep imagining a big invisible spider I'm trying to trap in a mason jar so I can take him outside," Orr said, fiddling with the zipper on Mom's suitcase.

"Sorry." Mom touched his hair, running a strand of it between her two fingers from his temple to where it ended below his shoulder blade. "But maybe it's not a spider. Or maybe it's a nice one."

"Maybe."

Mom stopped in front of him with a pair of socks in her hand. "Actually, I think the metaphor is good. Like, what if this ambient intangible gets out of control? Invisible spiders running rampant in your bedroom. Then what do you do?"

"Freak out?" Orr was kidding but also serious.

Mom laughed. "That's right, *mijo*. You freak the fuck out. And then you have to learn. You need a procedure. I'm asking you to think about what intangibles create chaos in your life. And what rituals could you create to contain them?"

Orr understood a little, but not all the way. "Bring this," he said, holding up one of Mom's most prized concert tees, thin now and faded from red to pink, from the second ever Bread and Roses Festival. They'd driven all the way to Berkeley for the three days of concerts. Iph says it's her first memory—the sound of Joni Mitchell's voice under the moon.

Orr remembers none of it but loves to hear Mom and Dad tell the story of that trip—camping on the Rogue River on the way down, staying with a friend of Dad's in Berkeley and an old hotel in the redwoods on the way home. All of them cozy in the car together. Mom and Dad realizing they could still have adventures even though they had kids.

Mom took the shirt, squinted at the pinholes along the hem, rolled it up, and tucked it inside a chunky brown ankle boot wedged in the corner of her suitcase.

"Three months is a long time," Orr said.

"That's what I'm trying to tell you, love. Think of it like beads on a necklace. Each chunk of time is a bead you string on the wire of the day. Be aware of this and you will calm down—"

"—because repetition is inherently calming." Orr finishes for her. They both know repetition's power from direct experience, Orr from music and Mom from dancing. They tried an experiment once: Orr wrote a song and Mom made a dance where nothing repeated. Neither piece worked.

Mom's eyes go darker and brighter. "When you slow down and make these daily activities conscious, you begin to see the beads differently. They start out plain. Boring. It's more about accumulation at that stage, like checking off days on a calendar or doing pliés at the bar. But after a while, the beads get shiny. Like by touching them again and again, you polish them into gems. That's when you know you're getting close."

"Close to what?"

"*El Mundo Bueno*. Life as art."

"How do you know all this?"

"I learned it the hard way, *mi amor*. The way I do everything." She was laughing, but there was also sadness.

"Why?" Orr was pushing now. "I mean, I learn this stuff from you. Didn't your parents teach you?"

Mom was silent at first, matching pairs of socks. Orr thought she was, as usual, blowing him off. Then she said, "There has to be trust for that, *mijo*. But I did learn things from my parents. I learned who not to be and what not to do. And that's something, right?"

She folded her second-best jeans in half, then rolled them

up. Orr didn't like to see them tucked away. Mom was quiet again. Orr saw her trying to decide what to tell him. She did that a lot. With Dad, the stories flowed. They'd heard about his childhood exploits hundreds of times. With Mom, they came out very rarely, like deer in the yard in winter.

She took a breath. "I was a little lost when I first had Iph. Then you came along so soon after. I was overwhelmed for a while. Your dad had to do everything. For a little while I even stopped nursing you. He fed you bottles. I stayed in bed. Then one day he burst in with a kid under each arm and plopped you both down next to me and stalked to the bathroom to take a shower."

Orr can see Dad doing this. And Mom still gets sad like that sometimes, but usually only for a day or two.

Mom patted Orr's hand and smiled. "You two were staring at me with your big black eyes in your creepy alien baby heads like *What now?* So I brought you down to the kitchen and put you in the playpen. You were standing in there with your hands on the bars like little jailbirds in your white onesies and sticking-up hair. I went to make some tea, but the kitchen was disgusting. That's how you know your dad was losing it.

"I don't know why I thought to do it, but I set the egg timer for ten minutes and tidied till it dinged. Then I went to the hall bathroom and washed my face. A pair of earrings was there on the shelf. I hadn't worn dangly earrings since I'd had Iph. The midwife told me I'd have to give them up because babies pull on them. I can't believe I listened to that. As you know, I might as well be naked without earrings."

He knew. Mom went nowhere without jewelry. It was her armor.

"So I put them on and kept doing that every day after washing my face. Then I'd go downstairs and set the timer for ten minutes. Then I'd have my tea. Like a little ritual—see where I'm going with this? If one of you interrupted the routine, I started where I left off. That timer was my lifeline, *mijo*. A little container of time. It wasn't fast, but after a while I learned to string the beads together like spells—dishes, garden, dance class, carpool. They all became sacred."

"Why are you leaving, then?"

"You know I'm coming back, right?"

"That's not what I asked."

Mom sighed and spoke to her reflection in the mirror, head cocked to one side. "I have to work again, my love. You and your sister are growing up. I need to grow, too."

She handed him the packet then, printed and comb-bound at Dad's office. Each day, a list. Little notes from her. Reading it, he became aware of a growing sensation of cold.

He stood up. "This isn't for me," he told Mom. "It's for you."

"I thought it would help. Just little reminders . . ."

"This isn't about me," he said. "Just admit it."

"You don't have to use it." Mom's face was red. She looked like she might cry.

"I won't," Orr said. And he took the little book and pulled it apart, ripping out its guts like a wild animal.

"Orr!" Mom's voice was hard. "You don't have to use it, but don't be an ass."

"I'm an ass?" Orr was shouting. "Me? You do so many things that are supposed to help me, but really, they just help you. Headphones? Great, now I don't flip out and embarrass you at the store. Telling me my hair is pretty? Good, now I'll take a bath so people don't say your kid stinks when you take him to school. This is the same. You did this so you don't have to worry. How about this? Just don't worry at all. Just go there and forget us for the summer. We'll be right back here when you come home. Just like always!"

Orr shakes to remember what he did next.

The things from the suitcase went everywhere.

Something small and hard—maybe Mom's green box full of earrings—flew out and hit Mom under her eye. But Orr did not stop.

The Bread and Roses shirt was thin from so many washings.

It ripped easily, right down the center.

Orr threw it in Mom's face and ran out of the room.
Climbed up to the treehouse.
Didn't come out until everyone was asleep.

A MOTORCYCLE WITH A terrible muffler zooms past the Furies'
house. Orr wipes his eyes. He sits up. The wood floor is gritty
under his bare feet. He flops back on the cat-smelling sofa.
Maps the house on his bare right leg. Allison lent him loose
basketball shorts and a Bikini Kill T-shirt. Iph loves Bikini Kill,
but Orr prefers Nirvana. Their music is almost painful to listen
to, but it's a good, productive sort of pain, like having sore
muscles from running. More memories rise—Mom coming in
to kiss him before she left for the airport. The silence of the
house when everyone left. Orr presses hard on the stop but-
ton to end the memory. "No more," he says out loud, his voice
small in the quiet house. He rolls on his back and hums "Come
as You Are" softly to himself.

Kurt Cobain is another one that's confusing—does Orr want
to kiss Kurt or *be* him? He starts from the beginning and goes
through the A side of *Nevermind* and feels a little better. The truth
is, there's no way he's going to be able to sleep on this sofa. And if
he doesn't sleep, he can't function. He tiptoes to the hall, less for
quiet than because he doesn't want to place his entire foot on the
floor. Even when surfaces are clean, Orr doesn't like much skin-
to-skin contact with the floors of other people's houses.

In the hall by the front door is a closet. Orr has to pull hard
to open it. As he suspected from the footprint of the house, it is
large and square. The small high window is a nice surprise. It's
later than Orr thought, early evening. The closet is full of junk, a
sediment of coats and shoes. On arrival, he noticed some boards
leaning in the corner of the porch, sharp with tacks. He removes
them using the nail clippers he found on the coffee table under
a pile of *Willamette Week* newspapers and Burgerville wrappers.
This works surprisingly well on the soft wood. A hunt with a
flashlight in the backyard unearths a few cinder blocks. There are

crickets here, like at home, but too faint to hear from inside the house. There is jasmine and some other night-blooming flower that smells like lemons. Orr is barefoot. *Outside*. He shakes his head and puts his feet out of his mind. His blisters are too bad for sneakers. The whole thing is outlandish. He doubts anything could surprise him now.

He excavates the closet until he finds floor, the same scarred, narrow oak as in the living room. The coats and impractical shoes are not as numerous as they seemed. In the entryway, he uses the boards and blocks to set up a shelf for the shoes, arranging them by size and color and heel height. He rummages for a hammer but can't find one. A hard-soled leopard-print platform sandal his mom and Iph would have loved works fine to bang the nails from the wood scraps in a straight row. A nail for each coat, four more for guests.

After sweeping out the now-empty closet with a broom he found in the questionable space between the refrigerator and kitchen wall, which is also stuffed with paper grocery bags, he takes the slippery cushions from the sofa and lines his nest. The cat smell is stronger here. He puts the cushions back and remembers the camping gear the girls dumped in a pile on the front porch. Out again, his feet cringing on the splintery wood, it takes three trips to bring it all inside.

He finds the first aid kit Mika used for his feet, an old Converse shoebox with Band-Aids, rubbing alcohol, and ointment. He disinfects the blow hole on the Therm-a-Rests and blows up all three. They fit almost perfectly into the square space of the closet. He opens two sleeping bags and puts them over the camping pads and snuggles into the woodsmoke and girl smell. His heart pounds the first notes of the fear song. Orr is always anxious before sleep.

He thinks of Iph, asleep in her rosy bedroom, her pedicured foot peeking out from the pile of light down quilts.

Thinking about someone causes missing.

Missing causes crying.

Orr isn't brainwashed; he's smart, rationing the things he can't control.

He girds himself and reaches for his sister now, mind-to-mind, a trick they've been practicing for years. A game, really. But maybe this time it will work.

He follows the bread-crumb trail of memory—first her face, her voice, then deeper, down to the ghost in him. Mom used to correct him. "I think you mean your soul, *mijo*." But he means more than a soul.

He'd gotten the idea from a song Mom used to play a lot from an old mixtape Dad made her. He could almost see his ghost with his eyes closed tight, a soft mist of a thing like shower steam or cotton candy. Iph has one, too—a ripe, bright yellow that feels the way an oven-fresh lemon bar both tingles and is sweet on your tongue after a glass of ice-cold water.

He settles in now to call Iph's ghost, a process he and Iph call *tuning*, where you think of the other person while checking your body one part at a time. All summer, they'd been using this to try and contact one another in dreams, and so far had come up with similar imagery seven nights out of twenty, according to Orr's detailed notes. Maybe the missing ingredient had been necessity. Orr needs his sister. Needs her to know he is safe.

He rolls to his back. The window is bluing, almost his favorite shade but not quite.

Hello, feet. If Iph were here, how would you feel?

"Scared," his feet say. "Scared of her gross clammy toes."

Hi, knees. How do you feel when your sister is with you?

"Soft," say his knees. "Less achy."

Hands, remember how you feel when Iph is beside you watching a movie?

"Worried," say his hands. "She'll steal the popcorn if we aren't careful."

Nose, what do you smell when Iph is around?

This one is easy—vanilla, sugar, amber. "You are what you

eat," Mindy always said to get Orr to eat more of her baking. Iph needed no encouragement to eat sweet or spicy things.

He checks in with his neck. His ears and eyes.

At his scalp, he has to stop and start over again.

His missing hair is still so hard to integrate. What does his head even feel like? He has no idea. It's like they cut his whole head off with his hair.

His heart is pounding, and his head feels hot.

Hot! That's how his head feels. Like a ball of fire.

That's what he imagines it looks like now—a burned meadow, the only thing left an inch of charred grass.

He feels like crying again. From sadness, but also relief. Like a Nirvana song.

Somehow, he got away from Meadowbrook and found these kind girls.

The moon rises in the window, smaller here—the window and the moon—than at home. Mom is under the moon. Dad, too. *Fucking Dad*. And Iph.

Orr's eyes are heavy.

He is so tired.

He sleeps and dreams.

Iph, flying through the evening sky in unfamiliar boots.

Iph, laughing. A boy in a yellow sweater holds her hand.

A tiger in miniature.

Anger, a phrase. Tiger-footed rage.

A dangling pay phone.

A crucified man.

Tarot cards falling from the trees like rain.

Iph, flying higher,

A crow winging past

The tops of trees,

Dollhouses golden with bedtime.

Tiny cats out to prowl the blue twilight.

Iph flies higher and higher.

Then she jumps!

16

ATTEMPTS
IN OPERETTAS

The pillow tastes like mothballs, but Iph keeps it shoved against her mouth because she can't stop laughing. Scout whines, nosing around to find her face.

"I have to smoke," George says. "Because drinking."

"Don't leave me!" Iph giggles. "You have to stay with me, George." Gin is her drink. The perfect alcohol. She sees now why Mom told her she wouldn't like it. Reverse psychology, because Iph more than likes this buzz. She is crushed out on it. On everything. Even herself. And, of course, George. Dapper, beautiful George with those crow-black eyes and perfect rose macaron mouth.

"Iph! I'll be right back. I don't want to give you asthma." George, impressively, stands up straight.

"You're a good drinker," Iph says, and they both laugh again, stuffing pillows into their faces, George kneeling. When did that happen? Wait—now George is up again, so easy. Standing, pulling Iph up.

"Come with me then." They are face to face, but the kiss doesn't happen.

George looks down and away.

"You're thinking about the lost girl, right?" She should be bummed, but the gin takes away the sting.

"Yes," George says, grabbing the big flashlight.

Iph stops herself short of rolling her eyes and stomping her foot. It's not George's fault for being in love. "Ugh," she says. "Fine. Let's go down to the garage. You can tell me all about her."

Downstairs, the cement floor is cool under Iph's feet. She plops into a rusty lawn chair with a faded floral cushion. "So, what's her name?"

George settles onto the tire swing and lights the cigarette, careful to blow the smoke away from Iph. "Lorna."

"In real life, is she strawberry blonde? With pale-blue eyes?" In George's painting, her hair is lavender and her eyes are gold.

"How did you know?"

"I don't know," Iph says. "It's how I imagine her. Delicate-looking, like in your painting, but tough in person. A little bit of a mean girl? But not all the way through."

George stops swaying around on the tire swing and shines the flashlight beam at the painting of Lorna with lavender hair and gold earrings and the Gustav Klimt–like suggestion of a halo. "Wow. Yeah, that's Lorna. You're exactly right." George sucks on the filter hard, blows the smoke out in a quick hot puff. Iph likes the smell. It reminds her of Mom.

"Hmmm," Iph says. She has a big crush on George, of course, but the gin seems to leave little room for being maudlin about it. "Let's have another gin and tonic, darling," Iph says in her best flapper voice. "But first, tell me the sad part."

"Oof." George mimes taking a hit to the gut and falls to the floor. When Iph offers a hand up, she's pulled down instead. The concrete is stained, but relatively clean. Deliciously cool.

"Well," George says, lying back, eyes closed. "It's all sad, if you want to know. I heard something on the street one night. It was Lorna. Someone was attacking her."

"Is that when you used your bow?"

"Yeah," George says. "I was too late. The damage was already done."

"Whoa," Iph says. "I'm so sorry. That's horrible."

"Yeah."

"So you rescued her and fell in love?"

"Something like that," George says.

They're quiet. A dog barks somewhere in the neighborhood. Scout's hackles rise.

"Leave it," George says.

They lie still, their hands a few inches apart. Iph can feel the heat coming off George's skin. She inches her pinkie closer. She pulls it back.

"C'mon," she says. On her feet she sways a little and holds out her hands to pull George up. Static sparks between them, the result of some explainable phenomenon that Dad has tried to teach her about on many occasions to absolutely no avail.

George's hand snaps away. "Whoa!" Then, with much heart clutching, "*My drops of tears I'll turn to sparks of fire.*"

Stop it. Stop being so adorable, Iph thinks. Her brow furrows. *Sparks of fire* . . . What play *is* that from? She sticks her tongue out at George.

"Queen Katherine," George says. "*Henry the Eighth*. Duh."

"Who knows that play? Who even reads the histories?" Iph's consonants are mushy, authentically drunk-sounding, something that is surprisingly hard to act. She turns on her mental tape recorder and hopes for the best. "How did you learn all this Shakespeare, anyway?"

"Shakespeare in the Shelter, milady. They had it at Outside In. Anyone could do it. You didn't have to live there," George adds quickly.

"Is that how you know Josh?"

"Yep," George says. "And Cait. She was a volunteer."

Cait. Lorna. George is way out of Iph's league.

Upstairs is still sweltering, the godlike effect of the gin is wearing off, and Iph feels like crap about Lorna and Cait and all the girls with leading roles. More gin doesn't help, partly because the bag of ice they put in the kitchen sink has melted away, and warm gin and tonic isn't nearly as nice as cold. But also, Iph is basically a monster, because Orr is gone and needs to be found, but all she seems to care about is George's stable of exes. Then again, maybe sitting in her personal lovelorn drama is easier than contemplating the spectacular fall of her own once-perfect family.

Lovelorn. Love Lorna.

Oh well. This is familiar, at least.

"You're tripping," George says, tapping Iph's forehead. "I see you in there."

Iph's eyes narrow. "Um, no. You see girls like Cait. And Lorna. And whatever other *Sassy* magazine models you hang around with."

George groans and leans forward in the plaid recliner, head in hands—the same pose Dad assumes at the start of a fight with Mom. This new alternate reality has such odd moments of symmetry to life at home. Same shapes, same sadness.

Are she and George fighting now? Iph used to think her temper was an essential part of her character, like hating watermelon or loving books, but lately she sees it as a habit, exhausting and so stupid. She can almost grasp this other, better version of herself that keeps her temper and does the right thing, but almost doesn't count. She's always apologizing. Another familiar thing. What's one more?

"I'm sorry," she says. "Please ignore me. I don't care about your girlfriends. I'm upset about my brother."

"Dude, no. It's me. I'm toxic. For real. Like . . . contagious." George is bright red. Takes the bottle and swigs. "Girls totally love me. I'm not being conceited. They've always loved me. You know that nursery rhyme? Well, it's basically my life."

Nursery rhyme? Iph scrunches her face. She sees her *Mother Goose* book like it's right in front of her. What's that damn rhyme? She needs to lie down. Nana's green shag carpet is dusty and smells a little like feet. Her own feet still hurt, so she puts them up on the sofa. The breeze wafts in, jasmine and mock orange. "You have to tell me. It's driving me crazy."

"Don't make me say it," George says, plopping down on the sofa with the bottle of gin, knees an inch from Iph's feet. "And don't you say it, either. I hate that thing."

"Tell me," Iph says. "It's killing me. It's on the tip of my brain."

George laughs. "Your brain has no tip. You mean your tongue."

The word *tongue* shuts them both up for a second. And then Iph has it. *Georgie Porgie, pudding and pie. Kissed the girls and made them cry.* She sits up slowly.

"Oh my god. I mean . . . wow. It's like destiny. Like, did your name make you a Lothario? Or is there some inherent quality from birth that causes a parent to name their kid George? A quality that, later in life, manifests in rampant, dramatic love affairs?"

"Whoa. Way to get it on the nose." George sits up and passes the gin to Iph.

"I know," Iph says. "I'm very good with summation." And she is. She feels good again. She's a seer, Mom says. A noticer. And lately, there are moments when she almost sees herself. As a woman, she may well be appreciated. A pretty face, a body that looks like it can make babies or fill out a fifties wiggle dress the way the Goddess intended. Womanly stuff. But now, it's girlishness that's wanted. The girls who look like kids the longest— waifish, like runway models—are always considered prettiest. All that was over for Iph by sixth grade. She's had a woman's body since she was twelve. It's what she's got. Who she is. For now, being smart will do. "At least I have my brain, right?"

"Shut up," George says. "I mean, my god, Iph. Look at yourself. Total Gina Lollobrigida."

"Sorry, but I know my movie stars, and she was totally skinny—just had big boobs. Plus, she's Italian, which I'm not. But whatever!"

"To be honest, I don't really know what Gina Lollobrigida looks like. Just, you know, voluptuous. And hot. I like the name. It rolls off the tongue."

That word again.

"Anyway," George says, "what I meant to say is, you look like a fifties screen siren. Especially in that white dress you were wearing."

"Whatever." Iph lies back again.

"Are you mad?"

"I don't think so. But you never know. Either I flip out right away or it happens a few days later. Ask me Wednesday."

"Don't be mad. You have star power, that's all I meant."

"George. I'm not fishing for compliments. But I don't really believe you. I go to this school with a big theater department. They're famous for it. I know I'm as good as some of the girls who get leads, but I can barely get cast as a maid or somebody's mother. I don't look like an ingenue. I don't fit into the costumes."

"Can't they, like, sew?"

"*I* sew! I could make it myself, if that's the issue. When I finally asked my drama teacher, do you know what he said? 'It's the way of world, dear. Some of us aren't leading ladies.' I get it. I'm supposed to, like, be a good sport and not be jealous and accept the things I can't change—but I don't. I can't! I hate it."

"Your drama teacher is an ass," George says. "But I get the jealousy. For me, it's more an envy. I wish I had certain things, you know? Like what you and Cait have. I know money can't buy love or anything, but I've always wished I had it."

Iph wants to say she's not like Cait, but the truth is, she is on the Cait continuum. Goes to a private school. Lives in a big house.

"Is it weird I said that?" George is on the sofa next to her.

"Not at all," Iph says. "I wish you had money, too. I wish everyone did. But I think we're alike in one way."

"What's that?" George meets her eyes. For a second Iph imagines herself leaning in, but she doesn't. She leans away, scoots to the edge of the sofa.

"Work," she says. "We both like a project. Systems. Rules for things. Like here. Most people would have blown it the first week and had a kegger, but you're good at this. You're a planner. A hard worker. I am, too. Everyone thinks I'm lazy, but I'm not. There just isn't anything real for me to do most of the time."

"Wow," George says. "I've been trying to think how to explain the good parts about living like this. That's it! It's real. Not the busywork you're supposed to waste your life on till the magical day you turn eighteen."

"Totally. And George? We're going to be hungover tomorrow, but we need to work anyway. Will you help me find my brother? Be the Ned to my Nancy?"

"I think you mean the Sid to your Nancy. Although I don't know if Sid Vicious was generally known for getting things done."

"No, no! Not Nancy Spungen—Nancy Drew!"

"That's her last name? Like a sponge?"

"My mom knew her," Iph says. "They worked together in New York."

"Wow. But wait, what were you saying? Hangover, work, something, something something?"

"George. You're drunk." Iph giggles. "I said be the Ned to my Nancy. I'm talking about NANCY DREW, for crying out loud."

"Um, is Ned the boyfriend?"

"That's not the point," Iph says. "I'm saying we need to sleuth. There's something afoot, my friend."

"Afoot?" George wiggles a foot in the air.

"George! Focus! My brother is hiding out somewhere in this city. We've gotta figure it out. I wish I had an apropos Shakespeare passage right now, but I don't."

"Is Lothario from Shakespeare?"

"I don't know," Iph says. They're quiet, and then George is laughing again, so hard there are tears.

"What?"

George is gasping and Iph is giggling. Finally, George comes up for air and grabs Iph by the shoulders. "Lothario? Oh my god, woman. Who even says that?"

"If the shoe fits—"

"I'm not wearing shoes." She sees it now. George does want to kiss her.

"I'm already crying," Iph says, "about my messed-up family. So it won't be your fault."

"It will," George says.

After a while George gets up and brings them both big glasses of water. It's late enough that they can drink them on the back steps.

The stars twinkle in a clear sky. It's going to be hot again tomorrow.

"You said you're Greek on your dad's side," George says. "What else?"

"Are you asking me what I am?"

"Well, when I tried to tell you what reminded me of, you got a little miffed. Which I get because I hate that myself. So yes. I am asking."

"Greek from my dad, Mexican from my mom. Hot-tempered and anxious from both."

"I'm Japanese and white on my mom's side and who-knows-what-because-my-mom-won't-say on my dad's."

Iph downs her water. "How about Scout?"

"Scout," George says, "is a pound puppy wonder dog."

At the sound of her name, Scout rallies, whining very quietly to go for a walk.

"Not now, little beast," George says. "Now it's time to sleep."

17

THE BOY
SHOUTED BACK

O rr is awake at dawn, starving. The girls' kitchen is the filthiest space he has ever seen. The weak light through grease-spattered windows turns the dish-piled whitish Formica counters the color of urine. The refrigerator is Chernobyl. An old model from a former era with the bins inside missing. In their place are desiccated carrots, an empty plastic tub labeled MIKA, and several cans of beer. On the top shelf are two boxes of Chinese takeout smeared radioactive red, a jar of honey mustard, a jar of cocktail olives, and a carton of milk screaming *go to hell* to the entire world with its sour-death smell.

He tries to remember the last time he ate. The night before. Pizza. Normally, he can handle an entire medium pie himself, but he remembered what Mom always said about making sure there was enough for everyone in group dining situations. The etiquette training seemed ludicrous then, but he's gone by many of her axioms since he took up with the Furies. After pizza, the girls had band practice. That had been the best part of the night. He didn't think about Mom or Dad or Iph or the polar ice caps. He didn't think about sex or his brain or how it would feel to contract a horrible disease. All that was in his head were

Mika's drums and Allison's bass and Jane's caterwauling over her badass guitar.

Yesterday, Orr had loved the Furies and their ramshackle pink house. WELCOME TO THE PUSSY PALACE, a sign on the door read in gold. A stylized sixties cat in an odd shade of green looked over its shoulder under the loopy cursive.

"That's your house's name?" Orr had looked back to ask Jane, but it was tiny Mika with the shaved head who answered.

"Yeah, but we usually call her Penelope."

Last night, Orr appreciated Penelope's quirks—the front door you had to slam to make it shut, the windows you had to prop open with moldy encyclopedias. He delighted in the number and variety of things on the dining room bookshelf alone: the encyclopedia set, a bunch of wilted daisies in a Slurpee cup, a discolored glass bong, a green glass ashtray stuffed with matchbooks, an aloe vera plant in a plastic pot, a set of jacks, a framed photo of the band onstage, a rusted metal Slinky, a Raggedy Ann doll with fishnet ankle socks and safety pin earrings, a pack of American Spirit cigarettes, a plastic tub of Red Vines (stale, but Orr eats three), a stack of feminist zines, and five books: *Blood and Guts in High School*, *SCUM Manifesto*, *Bastard Out of Carolina*, *Parable of the Sower*, and *This Bridge Called My Back*, which Orr recognizes from Mom's bookshelf.

Now, in the daylight, the house feels different. Stale, ugly. Sinister. Orr goes to the bathroom and thinks about a shower. The bath mat is soaked and smells like mildew. He curls his toes away and slits his eyes, tiptoeing out.

Back in the kitchen, sitting in the corner by the window in an easy chair with loose stuffing and a not-right pillow, Orr tries to get the feeling from last night back. All his usual ways of coping— hot food, hot shower, dark bedroom, clean clothes, even a run— are lost to him here. His feet are still blistered from the sockless hike. He nursed them the best he could last night, but had a hard time getting the Scooby-Doo Band-Aids to stick after putting on the antibiotic ointment Mika gave him. "I'm always scraping my knuckles on the rim of my drums," she said. "This shit works."

Orr likes Mika with her gruff words and high, gentle voice. He likes Allison's soft body and red hair and tough-guy attitude. He likes raspy, funny Jane the best. Yesterday, he didn't know any of them. Today, is he living at their house? Does he live anywhere? Orr is shaking. Mom did this experiment with him when he was younger, adding baking soda, spoonful by spoonful, into a glass of vinegar. It was a metaphor for meltdowns—meant to show that you needed to know how many spoonfuls of stress you could take before you started to bubble, how many more it would take to make you blow. At home, he knows exactly where he is in this process at any given moment. But here, he has no idea. He wants to go back to the coat closet but can't remember how. He wants to go *home*! He wants Mom! He needs the white oak outside his window, his Rescue Remedy tincture. He hears a buzzing—what if it's a bee? His EpiPen is miles away!

"Hey! Hey, you okay?"

A voice. It sounds . . . frightened. This makes Orr shake harder. Something, a hand, touching him. Orr flinches, his teeth aching like they do when he touches newsprint, like when he needs to get something out of his head. He puts his fist in his mouth to quiet the nerves in his gums. He knows he's crying too loud, but nothing can be done. He needs three hands: two for his ears, one for his mouth. Four hands, a long arm, octopus limbs to wrap around himself tight.

The girl is saying something, but he can't remember her name right now. All he can do is squeeze himself with his nontentacled arms and wait for Mom to come. He rocks and rolls. Mom calls it that. She plays him Jimmy Page, who can howl almost as loud as Orr.

The kitchen is loud. Led Zeppelin loud. He forgets where the volume control is in his brain. Pinocchio is never never never going to be a real boy. Never never never never never—

Orr gasps.

Gasps!

He's wet!

"I'm wet!" It's his voice! Speaking words!

"Yep," Jane says. "Sorry, dude. I didn't know what else to do." She stands in front of him with an empty glass in her hand. She hands him a towel to wipe the water from his face.

"Janie." Mika says this.

Mika, Allison, Jane. Orr remembers.

"Jane . . ." Mika's eyes are filled with tears. Orr sits at the kitchen table. He knows that look. He's frightened her.

"Mika," he says. "I'm sorry."

"It's cool." Mika tries to smile.

"It was a meltdown," Orr says. "I used to have them all the time. My mom helped me get them under control. Tame them."

Jane grins. "I'm picturing your mom in, like, fishnets and a sparkly leotard and tailcoat. Holding a chair and a whip, you know?"

"Uhh, that sounds kinda wrong in the context of his mom, Jane," Allison says.

"My mom would wear that," Orr says. "She loves costumes. But it's me who needs to wear it. I have to be responsible for taming myself."

"Word," Allison says. She gets up and plugs in the coffee maker. "Look, dude, I don't want to talk behind your back, so I'm gonna say what we're all thinking here. We can't keep you around if you're going to be doing that. I mean, what's the plan here, Jane?"

"We already decided last night," Jane says in a *that's final* voice. She's the one who could tame lions.

"Keep him till his mom comes home?" Mika pulls out a box of cereal and a container of soy milk from a cupboard next to the basement door. "We could get in trouble. His dad could, like, prosecute."

"He wouldn't," Orr says.

"How do you know that?" Allison sits next to Orr. "Look what he did to you."

"That's different," Orr says. "He wants a real boy, not to sue an awesome rock band."

"You think we're awesome?" Allison is smiling now. Orr likes the chip in her front tooth.

"Oh my god," Mika says, plopping an empty cereal bowl in front of Orr. "Allison, you're such a compliment whore."

"We're not putting him out like a stray cat," Jane says, lighting a cigarette and pulling a beer from the fridge.

"Jane!" Mika groans and takes the beer away, replacing it with coffee.

"Fine," Jane says.

"None of us would put a cat out, either." Allison coughs and produces a cigarette from the pocket of her bathrobe. Jane lights it with her shiny silver lighter. It smells like the ones Great Aunt Lolly used to smoke—attic dust and breath mints. Mika frowns and opens the window, propping it up with three encyclopedias. They're silent while the coffee machine slurps like a very rude eater. Orr starts to laugh.

"Your coffee machine," he says between giggles. He's often punchy after a meltdown. "That sound!"

"Like a queef, am I right?" Allison says.

"What's a queef?" Orr asks. This sets them all off laughing. Orr keeps asking, but every time he says queef, they laugh more. Finally Jane sits up straight, folds her hands, and says, "A queef, young man, is like a fart."

"Only it comes out of your . . ." Allison is laughing again, a great sound peppered with little snorts. She's wearing a T-shirt that says PROPERTY OF SAN QUENTIN and fuzzy slippers shaped like Oscar the Grouch.

"I like your slippers," Orr says.

The laughter calms down. Mika gestures for Orr to pour himself some cereal. Cheerios, not cornflakes, but he complies. Soy milk is a Mom food, not preferred but acceptable.

"Do you have any honey?"

"Above the stove," Jane says. Orr gets it down and honeys his Cheerios.

"Out of where?" he asks when they are all crunching their cereal. They look at him askance, as Iph would say. "A queef is a fart that comes out of . . . ?" he reminds them.

"Persistent," Allison mutters.

"Fine," Mika says. "Fine. A queef is a fart that comes out of your . . . Penelope." She bursts out laughing. Allison nearly spits out her coffee.

"You mean vagina?" Orr asks.

The Furies look at Orr like he's a cute stray cat. He grins back at them. Mom always taught him to use the proper words for body parts.

"What are we gonna do with you?" Jane says, stubbing out her cigarette and opening the cooler from yesterday. She gets out the last pack of tofu wieners and stabs one with a fork. Holding it over the open flame on the gas stove, she looks at Orr like he knows things.

"Keep me?" Orr says. "Maybe till my mom gets home?"

ACT II

Whoever drinks from me will become a wolf

1

THE FIRST JOURNEY
TO PETROGRAD

ph's first act as a profoundly hungover girl detective is to drag
herself to the gas station and call the diner in Sandy. The waitress isn't there, but the guy answering the phone claims he was
out having a smoke when the group of them—three girls and a
boy with a shaved head that had to be Orr—left. "I asked if they
were a gang. They said no, they were a rock band."

It's been oddly easy between Iph and George from the moment
they woke up back to back on the carpet, heads pounding and
parched in the stuffy apartment. Iph couldn't face the bumpy ride
on the bike rack. She had bruises, she finally admitted. Black and
blue and green ones. So they walked.

Now, at a little vegan diner on Belmont, they share veggie biscuits and gravy and the free weekly paper, reading each other's
horoscopes.

"Okay, Gemini," Iph reads, "*It's time to regain the focus you
need for the massively ambitious work of the next few years. Review all
commitments and connections, especially your closest ones.*" Iph wonders—does that mean Cait and Lorna? Or her?

"Don't look at me like that," George says, taking the paper
and reading Cancer to Iph. "*There's power in what you say and hear*

now. This week brings a flurry of messages and ideas, pushing important pending matters (including relationship decisions) decidedly forward."

"Hmm," is all Iph says, taking the paper back in the spirit of leaving no clue unturned to read Virgo for Orr.

Focus on gaining the momentum where you can, Virgo, without resorting to road rage. The opportunity here is to become more structurally sound. Relationships are challenged now; you might even feel trapped. Some of this alleviates next week, after the full moon.

She reads it twice but can't find anything useful. The thought of Orr feeling trapped is scary, but maybe the horoscope is referring to Meadowbrook?

Fed and properly caffeinated, they begin part two of George's plan. They hit Showcase Music and Portland Music, asking if people know a band who meets the diner guy's description, with no luck. They also tried Music Millennium, a record store where bands would definitely advertise their shows.

"We still need to make a flyer," Iph says. "Maybe later could you draw Orr for me?" She tenses her body for the blow that comes with imagining his shaved head, but she is stronger today. It feels good to have a plan.

All morning, George has been lugging around a huge backpack full of clothes to sell, including Iph's shoes of pain. Her feet are better now. Have they healed quickly? How many days has she been in Portland? Time feels so strange. It's hard to remember a life before this one.

At 6th and Burnside, Scout runs up to a door and barks. The shabby storefront doesn't look like the sort of place with air-conditioning, but anything is sure to be better than the naked sun. The sign on the door is lettered in pink duct tape:

SHINY DANCER
FINERY FOR THE FINE

A woman in cutoffs and a turquoise tank top is sitting on the counter, acid-green platforms dangling in time with the *toot-toot beep-beep* of Donna Summer's "Bad Girls." She drops to the floor at the sight of Scout, allowing herself to be flagrantly kissed. "Who's my baby?" she asks Scout. "Who's the best girl?"

"Wow," George says. "My dog is such a slut."

"She's come to the right place then," the woman says. After another kiss and then one more, she holds out a hand to be helped up. "Hey, Georgie. And Georgie's cute friend," she says.

"This is Iph," George says. "Iph, meet Glow. She runs this joint."

"Hi," Iph says. The walls are pink and peppermint, and the floors are stenciled with stars in gold and baby blue. "I love this shop! Great feminist reclaiming of pink."

"See?" Glow sticks her hip out at George.

"You're a pinkist?" Iph puts her hands on her hips, too. Glow might be a fellow Latina, by the look of her—light-brown skin and big brown eyes, hair dyed honey blonde.

"Look," George says, "I have a complicated relationship with pink. My mom dressed me like a Polly Pocket until I staged a coup when I was nine."

"Pink was a boy's color till the twenties," Iph says.

"Whoa. That's weird. I mean, it's not a bad color. Roses and girl parts and strawberry ice cream and bubble gum, all good stuff."

Girl parts? Iph closes her gaping mouth, also pink.

"Fair enough," Glow says, laughing. Turning a movie-star smile on Iph, she says, "Nice outfit, Georgie's friend Iph."

Iph is wearing another Nana ensemble, a muumuu printed with little hula girls and hibiscus flowers that hits mid-thigh and may have been originally intended to wear over a bathing suit at the beach. It's thin as onion skin and so light it feels a little indecent. The boots make it an outfit, even if they're basically functioning as foot ovens. Iph imagines her feet in Nana's white ankle socks, a pair of biscuits getting browner as they bake.

"I think I've discovered my new look," Iph says. "Nana chic."

"It's working for you. As for you and that big-ass bag," Glow tells George, "you know the rules, right? Iph, you listen up, too. Word on the street is I only take donations, so this is on the DL. I don't want people trying to sell me the clothes off their backs when they come in here for a health kit. However, since you're a Pippi Longstocking–level thing finder, Georgie my love, I will happily transact with you. But mum's the word. Yes?"

"Yes, ma'am!" George says. "And nice Pippi reference."

Iph eyes George. Another childhood book in common. She's smiling and realizes it when George goes, "What?" Flirting again. But under the flirting, there's always a hint of sadness. Lorna, maybe. Or something deeper, older. In every detective story, the partners getting to know each other's deep dark secrets is always Iph's favorite part.

"Quit mooning and show me your goods," Glow says, feeding Scout a tortilla chip.

While they do business, Iph wanders. Clothing carousels packed with magpie treasures are topped by displays with posters listing statistics illustrating the public health benefits of needle exchange programs, diagrams of how to properly put on a condom, and complimentary travel-size bottles of lube. Iph first encountered the concept of lube recently—and only then because of the terribly uncomfortable conversation she'd had with the nurse practitioner at Planned Parenthood the time Mom took her to get birth-control pills—not for sex, but to help her heavy periods and monster PMS. A sex-ed 101 lecture was the price she had to pay to slow her monthly deluge.

And then there was all the other stuff Mom—*oh god*—told her when she started high school. Lube was probably the only thing she forgot to mention.

"Eww," was all Iph could manage as Mom did a thing with a rubber and a banana. They'd been in the kitchen of all places on a rare Saturday afternoon when Orr had agreed to go on an errand with Dad.

"You need these anytime there's contact with fluids," Mom had said. "Even if it's just a blow job."

"MOM! There are no blow jobs in my near future, I can guarantee it."

"Safe sex is important with women, too."

"Like that's really going to happen in Forest Lake. Can we table this till college?"

"Sometimes you don't see it coming," Mom said.

Mom would certainly approve of Shiny Dancer with its glitter and sequins and high-heeled shoes and radical posters—everything you needed to look hot and be safe and get justice. Iph likes it, too. Except the dildos propped here and there in the displays. They're one of those things you hear about and think you can picture, and then the reality is so much worse. Some are oversize and grotesquely fleshy. Iph can barely look at them. Surely no real penis is that enormous? Even the not-especially-detailed ones in sparkly pink and green to match the walls do not bode well for the real thing. Just . . . *gross*. Maybe Iph is a straight-up lesbian after all.

The far wall of the shop is all shoes. Iph fingers a pair of pink flip-flops with little daisy toppers and wonders if she could use some of the money her shoes bring in to get them. She puts them back. They'd be cool on her toes but terrible for trekking around Portland. Another vestige of her pampered life—not having to worry about practical shoes because your mom will always give you a ride. Iph should have womaned up and gotten her license. This would all be so much faster with a car.

A magazine rack is at the back of the shop with issues of a neon pink zine, also called *Shiny Dancer*, with a blurry black-and-white picture of Glow and a short punk girl on the front, both wearing knee-high boots and feather boas. Above is a sign that says:

SHINY DANCER IS A NONPROFIT THAT PROVIDES INFORMA-
TION, SUPPLIES, AND ADVOCACY TO SEX INDUSTRY WORK-
ERS, DRUG USERS, AND OTHER MARGINALIZED MEMBERS
OF OUR COMMUNITY. OUR PROGRAMS INCLUDE NEEDLE
EXCHANGE; A THRIFT STORE AND COMMUNITY EDUCATION
CENTER; LOCAL, NATIONAL, AND INTERNATIONAL LABOR

AND PUBLIC HEALTH ADVOCACY FOR SEX WORKERS' RIGHTS
AND WELL-BEING; AND A QUARTERLY PUBLICATION. RACISM,
SEXISM, AND HOMOPHOBIA WILL NOT BE TOLERATED HERE.

The only other person Iph's heard use the term *sex worker* is Mom. Once, when Orr had first learned to read, they'd seen the word WHORE tagged on the wall of a parking garage. When he asked what it meant, Mom said, "*Whore* is a mean way of saying *prostitute*, honey."

"What's a prostitute?" Orr had asked.

Mom didn't hesitate. "A nice lady who has sex with people for money."

Iph flips through the zine. She has a small zine collection herself, things she's picked up from Powell's and others she's written away for. There is a body positivity one she especially loves called *I'm So Fucking Beautiful* that has helped her feel better about her big hips and belly and thighs—or to at least question why she feels so awful about them. She also loves the more personal zines—more like illustrated diaries—like the one about a girl and her cat and a deeply sad illustrated memoir by a girl who was abused by her dad. Iph will never forget the look she saw on Mom's face when she picked it up from Iph's bedroom floor and read a little. Mom won't talk about her past, but Iph has always known some sort of abuse was there. She feels it. The more she learns about the way things can go wrong for kids, for brown people, for girls, the surer she is that something really bad happened to Mom when she was younger.

Iph's way of finding things out is often like that—intuitive and roundabout. She always thinks of the bread-crumb trail in Hansel and Gretel. People forget that trail was their downfall. They used pebbles at first, a smart plan. The bread crumbs were what sunk them—birds and animals ate them up. How do you find your way then? You find the ghost of the thing, the echo of the trail, the little tells everyone has to show you who they are. That's theater done right. In her limited experience, it works for life, too.

Iph takes a copy of *Shiny Dancer* and sits on the pink faux-fur sofa. The low-quality fur prickles, but it's good to be off her feet. The zine is both serious and funny, with a mix of handwritten and typed articles and great cartoons. There are reviews of different strip clubs from the worker perspective, some poems, an article about what to tell your family about your job and how to form a childcare co-op with other sex workers to make sure your kids are in good hands while you're at work. In the back, there's a feature called the Bad Date Sheet. The scrubbed, simple language of it is stunning.

- *Anthony, white male, dark hair, gray beard, heavyset, at least six feet tall. Followed dancer home from Magic Gardens and rang her doorbell for three hours. Police called but never came. Became abusive when bouncers refused to let him into the club after the incident.*

- *White Ford pickup with dent in passenger side near door. White older male, bald, gold aviator glasses. Picked up worker from 82nd and Powell, took to a vacant lot on Columbia Blvd. and assaulted. Injuries required stitches.*

- *White older male. Black late model Cadillac sedan. Violent with male workers. Refuses to pay. Strands workers in remote areas.*

- *Younger male. Brown skin, dressed business casual. Newer Honda Civic with child seat in back. Raped worker.*

- *Kelly, fifteen years old, white, brown hair, green eyes. Missing since May 17th. Last seen in Old Town. Leave any information about whereabouts at Shiny Dancer, 6th and Burnside.*

The missing persons listing has a sketch of the girl, pretty and so young. Iph thinks of George's index card and the story about Lorna. She wonders how George knows Glow. On a table next to the rack is a sign on heavy cream paper with crisp lettering in front of a blue ceramic bowl.

ROSE CITY TRANSMUTATION

PUBLISHER OF FORGOTTEN POETS

HEALER SPECIALIZING IN

DREAMWORK, TRANSFORMATION, TRANSMOGRIFICATION

DISCOUNTS FOR SEX AND SERVICE WORKERS, ANIMAL HELPERS, STRAPPED

WITCHES, TEEN MOMS.

COME FIND US.

Come find us? There's no address. Iph giggles. She's been raised on Dad's old Monty Python reruns and appreciates the surreal. At the bottom of the sign is a stamped hand with a finger pointing down to the bowl with the words FREE POETRY.

The poetry is printed in matchbook-size volumes. Iph squints. The heavy-framed glasses are almost too clear for distance but make it oddly difficult to read close up. She takes them off. The front cover is a meticulously detailed watercolor of a forest. On the back cover is a tiny logo, the letters *RCT* made of climbing roses.

"Ready?" George says.

Iph startles. "Sure." She starts to take a copy of *Shiny Dancer* to the counter, but Mom isn't here with her credit card now. She puts it back but pockets the free matchbook poem.

At the front of the store, Scout is up on the counter eating chips with Glow.

"*Gracias por los tacones,*" Glow says, dangling the shoes in one hand and beckoning Iph to the counter with a twenty-dollar bill in the other. "These are so about to be my lucky work shoes. I can just see those hundreds raining down on the stage."

Ah! Iph had wondered if Glow was a sex worker herself. "You're welcome!" she says, leaning on the counter. Iph loves when people speak Spanish to her but hates that she never speaks it back. She sighs for the gold shoes a final time. No wonder Mom had them in a giveaway box. She and Iph share the same weird feet. Maybe Glow will have better luck.

"*No hablas español?*" Glow says, kicking off her platforms and setting the gold shoes reverently on the floor to be tried on.

"Ugh!" Iph hides her face in her hands. Scout, still happily up on the counter, whines and tries to pry them off with her muzzle. "Kind of? *Pero malo?* I spoke some when I was little. I had this *Sesame Street* book with Spanish words I loved. So, like, if you know any babies or Cookie Monster fans, I can talk to them."

"I learned after college when I lived in Peru—and Spanish was my freaking minor in undergrad. I'm super rusty now. I guess it was the shoes. They moved me."

"These shoes for sure speak Spanish. They used to be my mom's. I wouldn't part with them, but they totally chewed my feet up," Iph says, stroking a gold strap. "I think they run small. I knew when I tried them on, but they were so pretty."

"Hmmm." Glow takes a few steps. "Damn," she says. "Like, they fit, but I know with a little swelling it's gonna be all over. It's one spot right by my big toe. Oh well, some other lucky babe is gonna score. I'm charging an arm and leg for 'em, though. Fleet Week's coming up. High-end vintage is gonna move great." She puts the shoes on the counter next to Scout, who's sitting like a little Buddha propped against the huge antique cash register. She promptly licks each shoe in turn. "Yes, baby, kiss them goodbye," Glow says. Iph blows them a kiss, too.

"You women are crazy," George says. "Those things are little torture chambers."

"It's a deep femme mystery, Georgie my love," Glow says, waving a hand. "The lure of the high-heeled shoe. So, are you coming to see me tomorrow?" Where does she mean? Here? At the strip club? You have to be eighteen to go into those places, right? Or even twenty-one?

"And don't forget the benefit Saturday. I think it's all ages."

"I'll be at needle exchange for sure," George says. "And hopefully the benefit."

Glow hands George the now-empty backpack. "Maybe I'll see you, too, Iph?"

"Sure," Iph says. "I'm kind of just visiting, but if I'm still here . . ."

"Hey, wait a sec," George says. "I almost forgot to ask. We're looking for someone."

"Haven't seen her," Glow says. "And if I did see her at needle exchange or at work, I couldn't tell you."

"No," George says. "Not Lorna. I figured you'd say—if you could."

"But I can't," Glow says, no-nonsense. And wait . . . are they saying Lorna is a stripper like Glow? How old is this ex, anyway?

"Understood, boss. I know I was a pest in the past. Never again, I promise. This time it's actually important. We're looking for Iph's little brother."

They explain about Orr and boot camp and the girl band. "That sounds like this girl Mika's band."

"Do you know how to get in touch with her?" Maybe this is it!

"I met her a few months ago at a self-defense workshop and I've seen her play, but I don't have her number or anything. She seems like a righteous babe, though. Used to volunteer for needle exchange downtown and works at Powell's. I'm pretty sure she's the one who got them to carry our zine."

"What's the name of the band?" Iph's whole body is suddenly one pounding heart.

"The Furies," Glow says. "Rad, right?"

"Thank you so much!" Iph's mind is already outside racing toward Powell's.

"Thanks, Miss Glow," George says. "C'mon, Scoutie. No bag, but you gotta go on the leash."

"Bye, little burrito!" Glow calls to Scout. "You be good, Georgie. You, too, Georgie's cute friend. Hope you find your brother!"

2

UNWOUND HER
HEAVY KNOT OF HAIR

"**W**ake up, babe."

Orr startles. One eye, two eyes. Why is he asleep on the sofa and not in his closet? The last thing he remembers is sitting down to have some tea. The tea is there on the coffee table, cold. Meltdown recovery requires sleep. Usually he makes it to bed, though. Well, things are different at Penelope than they are at home, but—a novel thought!—maybe that's all right.

"C'mon," Jane says. "Get your shoes. We're going out."

He goes to the hall to get his sneakers off the shelf. His feet are better today. He puts on the pair of socks Jane lent him—the ankle kind people wear for sports but rainbow-striped and sparkly. A little small, but workable.

"Orr, dude. This situation is life-changingly rad." Jane is so psyched about his hall organization project. She couldn't stop saying "Dude!" and "Wow" when she first saw it. Mika and Allison like it, too.

Outside, Portland is hot but beautiful. Orr doesn't always think this about the city, but usually he's riding in a car with his headphones on. Today, he and Jane walk. Roses trade scent for sunlight. Lavender sways lightly in the wind. They cross a major street—Belmont, Orr notes. Mom got him a Portland map before she left. She wanted him to start thinking about taking the bus into the city for his cello lessons. "Just consider it," she said when she saw the look on Orr's face. "I'd say Iph could go with you, but honestly, you'd be better off blindfolded. No sense of direction, that girl."

Orr notes how Iph's name slips past his brain's sieve like a tiny minnow through a net. She's probably not even awake. In the summer Iph is almost completely nocturnal.

As for Mom's suggestion that he come into Portland on his own—it seemed absurd at the time, but maybe she was onto something after all. Orr pictures the booklet she made him. He only managed to read a few pages before freaking out. In addition to his daily routines, Mom listed some suggested activities—cleaning out closets full of outdated stuff, spending time outside, going places on his own. All stuff he's actually been doing.

The rest of the memory flares, this time from a different angle. Huh. He lets it play, sound off. Much less upsetting. This way, he sees that even though she'd been onto something about being more independent, he had been a little right, too. What Mom was trying to do defied the laws of physics. There was no way she could be two places at once. Now, instead of being mad at her for it, Orr feels sorry that she was so torn.

Jane is a surprisingly fast walker, given that she is also smoking a cigarette and drinking a Diet Coke. They pass the Bagdad Theater, a beautifully renovated 1920s movie house that serves pizza and the best strawberry lemonade in addition to popcorn to eat while you watch your movie. Iph and Orr love it, even though Dad thinks the place is hideous because it's made to look like a white person's idea of Egypt. "Not to steal your mom's catchphrase, but all I see is imperialism when I look at that place. I'd rather go to the movies in the mall."

Dad! Ugh. Thinking of him is exhausting. Or maybe it's the meltdown hangover. It's suddenly hard to keep his eyes open.

The neighborhood's big-boned Craftsman houses have such wide, inviting porches, like nice ladies with soft laps. A patch of sunlit grass in a side yard beckons. Orr lets them pass and dutifully follows Jane. She won't tell him where they're going or why, but Orr has lost any leeway for protest after this morning, and he knows it.

They finally stop at a once-green house, its paint flaking like the skin of some huge molting reptile. Jane bypasses the front door for a gate that leads to a narrow side yard. Orr runs his nail along a peeling green shingle, pretending the house is a dragon with an itch. The narrow path is dim and cool, a tunnel of faded jasmine with a hint of sweetness left.

Jane gives his arm a gentle pinch. "C'mon," she says. It's the first thing she's said since they left Penelope.

Around the corner the yard is bright with weeds and waist-high wildflowers. If there is a fence, it's invisible, covered in tall roses with wicked thorns that completely obscure the neighboring houses. The yard could go on for miles, Orr thinks, walking around a lacy gingko, like the rose hedge around the castle in *Sleeping Beauty*. A deck is built around the tree connecting the yard to the back of the house.

He follows Jane up the stairs to the back door. A hot tub is recessed into the far side of the deck, smaller than the redwood tub Dad installed for Mom's thirty-fifth birthday. The cover is off, propped awkwardly against the snakeskin siding. The sun is shining like a spotlight on the octagon of water, and first all Orr sees are flower petals and white light. The light resolves into fabric, and the fabric clings around the shape of a person. A girl floats in the tub in a white dress, eyes closed, covered in rose petals and jasmine blossoms, crowned in sunlight, a mane of crimson hair floating around her like blood in the water. Orr looks away. His mouth is suddenly so dry.

"Kids today," Jane says, shaking her head. She sits in a rickety Adirondack chair whose paint has worn away. Orr touches its arm, soft like the paper bags they rubbed together in kindergarten to make buckskin clothing for the Thanksgiving play. Mom had come to help that day and was livid when she read the script of the racist, historically inaccurate skit. The other kids' eyes were wide. They liked Orr's mom. All kids did. The teacher had no choice after she'd told the real story of Thanksgiving but to the change the script on the spot.

Orr is smiling now. Smiling makes him forget where he is, but when he notices again, he sees the girl, her eyes closed in the water, and worries she'll be frightened when she realizes they are there.

Jane lights another cigarette. Orr is suddenly parched, overtaken with the desire to fall to his knees and lap at the water in the tub like an animal. Would it taste like the rose tea Mom gets at her favorite café? Or would it be salty with the sweat of the girl?

Jane blows smoke toward the tub. The mermaid's nose wrinkles. She opens her eyes.

"Hi, Jane," she says, rising ungracefully and heaving herself out the tub. The fabric of the dress molds to her skin, and Orr feels a surprising flair of want—what, exactly, he doesn't know. Still thirsty, he watches her wring the water out of her hair, longer than even Orr's used to be. She has to pull its heavy wet mass over her shoulder to avoid sitting on it.

Settled in the sun on the bare wood of the splintery deck, which has needed to be sanded and refinished for many years now by the look of it, the girl finally turns to Orr.

"I'm Plum," she says. "Who are you?"

"I'm Orr."

"Huh." She takes her thick rope of hair in her hands and wrings it out again. Orr touches the moss-soft velvet of his own skull. His head is throbbing a little. Jane's cigarette, probably. Or the heat.

"I had a Jane's-coming inkling this morning when I woke up and smelled Irish whiskey in the bathroom," Plum says. "I thought it was premonition, but it turned out it was an open bottle someone left in the shower where the shampoo goes. Now I'm thinking the premonition still counts."

"Jimmy partying a lot?" Jane asks, a little frown between her brows.

"The usual," Plum says. "It's more the girlfriend and her friends. But she won't last."

"Well, you would be the one to know, Plum Jam."

Orr notes the look they share, the little nickname, and realizes Jane has known Plum for a long time.

"Jane was my mama's client," Plum says, like she can hear Orr's thoughts. "At Outside In. Then they became friends. She used to babysit me. She even lived with us to take care of Mama when she got sick."

"Your mom is sick?"

"Dead," Plum says gently, as if she doesn't want to scare Orr. But it's too late—Orr is scared. He thinks of Mom dying and cuts the thought short as fast as he can, erasing as he goes. He cannot think about losing Mom. And what about Iph? Why isn't he thinking of her more? She must know he's gone by now. Must've found out the other night when she and Dad got home from the party. She will be so worried. And so, so mad.

The world is spinning. Jane's cigarette, the hot-tub water, the heat. He needs to sit, to lie down, but his body stands there, head untethered in the vast universe, the blue sky stretching too wide above the spinning planet, its cloud countries unmappable.

Something clatters like the keys of a typewriter, and Orr opens his eyes and sees it's the girl, bluish with cold, chattering her teeth.

"Aren't hot tubs supposed to be hot?" he asks.

"Only if the heater works," Plum says.

"What were you doing in there?"

"Acting out a painting," she says. "Waterhouse. *Ophelia*."

"Ha!" Jane says. "This is what happens when you homeschool your children."

"I want to know how it feels to *be* them, okay?" Plum says.

"I'm homeschooled," Orr says.

"Of course you are." Jane puts her cigarette out in an old mason jar.

Plum holds her hand out to Orr from her sunny spot on the deck. "Help me up, fellow uneducated heathen. I need to change before I freeze."

He likes this, of course. Bossiness is one of his favorite qualities in a person. He takes her cold hand in his warm one and pulls.

On her feet, she is almost as tall as Orr.

"I'm off to check on Jimmy," Jane says. "Behave, you two."

"Plum," Orr says, wiping his hand on his jeans, then worrying she'll think it's about germs and not water. Honestly, it's a little bit of both, but Orr means no offense. Plum's face seems to say she hasn't taken any. Still, it's hard to know. "Can I use your phone?"

Plum leads Orr down the basement stairs and pushes through a beaded curtain. "This was my mom's office. I sleep down here now." The low-ceilinged room is dim, painted the color of clover honey. Green light slips past the lemon thyme that grows in front of the ground-level windows across the front of the basement. The air smells of incense and old books. The floor is covered in a pinkish, threadbare carpet that was probably red or purple once. A spinning wheel stands in a corner like a prop out of the illustrated fairy tales Iph used to read to him when he was small. In the center of the room is a table covered in a block-print cloth.

"My mom was an art therapist," Plum says. "She saw her clients here."

"I've done art therapy before," Orr says, remembering therapist number five. "We drew a map of my inner landscape."

"Cool," Plum says. "The phone is there." She points to a table next to a low-slung sofa. "I'm gonna go change."

Orr dials the number. He knows it by heart, of course, but has dialed it himself very few times. Usually, he is the one at home doing the answering.

Dad picks up on the first ring.

"It's me," Orr says.

"Orr!" Dad sounds weird in a way Orr can't place. Not business Dad. Not weekend-energy Dad. Not not-a-morning-person

Dad before coffee. Not headache Dad or date-night Dad. Not even tipsy Dad.

"Son," he says, and all Orr can picture is a desert. Nothing but sand and wind for miles.

"Not the one you want."

"Orr."

Why does Dad keep saying his name?

"Did you really go to Portland with a bunch of tattooed girls?"

"How do you know that?" Orr touches the back of his neck— maybe there's a tracker there after all.

"The waitress. At the diner. Your order was a dead giveaway."

Of course. He always has the same thing at any breakfast place. Still, wow. Orr didn't ever imagine that—a manhunt. Again, life is like an *X-Files* episode. "Did they scour the forest? Were there search and rescue dogs?"

"Yes," Dad says, and Orr knows he's smiling. "Two German Shepherds. Taiga and Tundra. Sisters, the handler said."

"Nice." Orr can't help it—he's softening to this throwback Dad who remembers smiling and shares his love of dogs. This is how Dad always wins. He turns on the warm tan handsome tall money-guy charm. The good-guy routine. You can see it then, why Mom married him. But Orr isn't Mom. He isn't even Iph.

"I'm not coming home, Dad," he says. "Not till Mom gets back."

"That's a long time to be away."

"What do you mean?"

Dad is silent.

"She doesn't know?" Orr had assumed Mom would come home the second she found out. That it was a matter of Dad getting in touch with her. There is no phone in Mom's cabin. She has to use the phone in the common house. Calling in, there's no guarantee someone will be around to pick up.

"I want her to have her residency, Orr. She deserves it."

"Maybe you shouldn't have had me kidnapped by fascists, then."

"Maybe not," Dad says. Orr knows he's thinking about Mom, about how angry she'll be when she finds out about Meadowbrook. "I'm hoping she'll decide to stay. If you're sure you're okay."

"Do you even care?"

The other end of the line goes silent. Have they been disconnected? Then Dad breathes, so ragged on the exhale, Orr wonders if he's crying. "I was worried about you. You were sleeping so much and not eating. You wouldn't talk to me. I found out about Meadowbrook from Oliver's wife. She's a school psychologist. She highly recommended it."

"I don't care," Orr says. "If it was so good, you should have convinced me. You didn't even try."

"I didn't think you'd listen."

They're silent together—one of the few traits they share. Mom and Iph have debates about who's more stubborn, Orr or Dad.

Finally, Dad says, "I'll come get you. What's the address?"

"What makes you think I would go anywhere with you?" Orr's voice is louder now. "I told you, I'm not coming home till Mom gets back. The girls say it's all good. They don't mind feeding me, because I clean."

"You clean?" There he is—the typical, more skeptical Dad. "Have they seen how much you eat?"

Wait. *Wait.* He's sitting here talking to Dad, but what about Iph? "Dad! Why aren't you telling Iph?" He's done it again—forgotten his sister. "Is she freaked out that I'm missing?"

Dad makes a weird noise. "Iph isn't here. She says she's in Portland. With a friend."

He's lying. Orr knows for a fact that Iph has no friends. Not even in Forest Lake, let alone all the way out in Portland. "Where did you send her? Dad, what did you do?"

"Nothing. God, Orr. Nothing, all right? It's all her—she's there looking for you, kid."

Dad sounds so strange. What is he feeling? What does he want?

"I told her about Meadowbrook. That night at the party. She

was furious. She took off. Left the hotel. I tried to find her. Looked all over. She left a message early Friday morning. I didn't get it because I was driving up to Mount Hood to search for you."

"You lost both your kids?"

"Father of the year," he says, but Orr doesn't feel sorry for him.

"Did she ever call back?" Orr is standing now, pacing, twisting the phone cord as he goes.

"She's fine," Dad says. "We talked yesterday. She won't come home, either. I guess you both think I'm a total bastard."

"Dad. Why did you send me there?"

"I thought it would help."

"Help what?"

"Help you feel stronger. Happier."

Orr stops. "Say that again."

"I thought Meadowbrook would make you feel stronger. And being stronger would make you happier."

Orr takes the words in through his nose, sniffing deep the way the coyote on the mountain had at a hole in the base of a tree. He swallows Dad's words. Listens to them in the hollow of his chest, lets them vibrate like strings on a cello, and now he is crying.

"You thought having me kidnapped would make me happy? Dad, they put a sack over my head and carried me out like executioners. They tied my wrists and stole my hair."

Dad is silent. Then he says, "It was a mistake. I don't know what I thought it was going to be like. I guess I didn't think about that—the means. I was focused on the end result."

"They were racist," Orr says. "Homophobic! It was a bad place." Orr takes a deep breath, all the way down to his tailbone, the way he does when he's getting ready to play a difficult piece. "But, Dad . . . getting away from there? Finding Jane and Allison and Mika and living in Portland? This is what's making me strong. *This* is making me happy. And it doesn't mean I forgive you," Orr says. "I don't know if I ever can."

Dad is silent again. Finally, he says, "Iph is looking for you, Orr. If she calls, can I give her your number?"

"I don't know it."

"Can't you ask?"

Plum is back, changed into leggings and a white button-down shirt that reaches her knees. Her rainbow-striped socks bunch at her ankles in the uncomfortable-looking way Iph always wears hers.

"Do you know the number for Penelope?" Orr asks her.

"Who's Penelope?" Dad asks. "I thought you said the punkers were Mika, Allison, and Jane."

Orr rolls his eyes. "No one says *punkers* anymore, Dad. And Penelope is the house."

"Then who are you talking to? Where are you?"

"I'm at Plum's house," Orr says. "I'm talking to Plum."

"Who is that? Another punker?" Dad's doing this on purpose to make Orr laugh, but it won't work.

"Plum's a friend of Jane's."

Plum grabs Orr's wrist. Her hand is dry now but still cold. She writes a phone number in purple Sharpie on the back of his hand. Orr repeats it for Dad.

"I'll give this to Iph," he says. "Now, how about the address?"

"I don't know it," Orr says and looks at Plum. She mouths *no*—she must be able to hear Dad through the receiver. It's a Dad thing, always being a little too loud on the phone. "I know where the house is. It's on Southeast 35th Street, off Belmont. The pink one on the east side of the street halfway down. I can give you the address later."

"I'd appreciate that."

"Dad, why aren't you trying to make me come home?"

"Because I believe you," Dad says. "I believe you're happy. You sound happy. You haven't been in bed with your headphones on, have you?"

"No. They're still at the house, anyway."

"Not banging your head or not eating?"

"No." Well, he could be eating more, but that's not Dad's problem. Not anymore.

"Is this Plum person nice?"

"She seems nice. Very pretty," Orr says. "She homeschools." Why is he telling this to Dad?

"Orr, I'm planning to tell your sister this next time we talk. I'm saying it now to you. I'm willing to evac you anytime for any reason, but if you come home, you stay home. If you stay in Portland, you're on your own."

"I'm not coming home."

"I won't ever send you back to Meadowbrook, Orr. I promise."

"I don't believe you."

"Fair enough. One more thing, though—I want you to call me. Once a week, okay? Every Sunday. No matter how much you hate me. And call me sooner with the exact address."

"I can do that."

"Thank you," Dad says. Orr is surprised by that. He's not sure why. "I love you."

Orr doesn't say it back and hangs up the phone.

Plum is there with a little frown on her forehead, but the rest of her face is smiling. Her skin is speckled like a sparrow's egg. Even her lavender eyelids are freckled. The hair around her face escapes the top of her bun in corkscrews—curly like Iph's and Mom's now that it is drying.

"So," Plum says, "you think I'm pretty?"

3

THE OPERA

ph doesn't need a mirror to know her cheeks are red and her hair is crazy. Waiting to cross the street to the movie theater, she puffs out Nana's muumuu for air and gets another whiff of minty smoke. She imagines herself lighting up a skinny white cigarette, enjoying every puff. George said Nana smoked Pall Malls. The dress, it seems, is a little haunted.

She and George hit Powell's downtown and the one on Hawthorne before calling it quits. Glow had been right—Mika does work at the bookstore, but the information desk guy wouldn't tell them which location she worked at or when she would be in next. There was nothing to do but try again tomorrow.

For dinner, they had slices of pizza and endless free cups of water. She wanted to split a salad, but she wanted air-conditioning more, so she and George are going to the dollar movies.

They're early enough that the line is short. The cute green-haired girl in the ticket booth seems to know George and won't take any money. George winks at Iph and waves an extra ticket, pink instead of the red ones for admission. "Free popcorn and a Coke!" George crows.

"I have to pee," Iph says. "I'll see you in there."

The restroom is oddly situated, up a narrow flight of stairs carpeted in a color you never see anymore, the pinkish-gray of end-of-summer hydrangeas and faded velvet sofas. Inside the restroom is an anteroom, an actual place to rest, with a love seat and small tufted stools in front of a mirrored counter. A girl is there putting on lipstick. She is mouse-boned with delicate hands, her vertebrae a dollhouse staircase in her back-baring halter dress. In the mirror, she looks Iph up and down—and down again. She turns and asks, "Why are you wearing my boots?"

Iph rubs her temples where the lost-and-found glasses pinch. Takes in the girl's familiar waifish supermodel brand of pretty.

Of course. The mystery girl in George's painting.

"You're Lorna," Iph says.

"I know who I am," the girl says. "The question is, who are you?"

"I'm Iph. I'm in town for few days," Iph says. Why did she say that?

"Do I look like I care about your itinerary?" Lorna stands, taller than Iph would have guessed. Iph looks her up and down and down again. Gold strappy sandals with a chunky forties heel.

"Why are you wearing *my* shoes?" Iph says.

"These are . . ." Lorna's huffiness disappears. She drops back down to her seat. "Wait," she says. "You're the cute friend. And George, I presume, is here?"

"And you bought those from Shiny Dancer today, didn't you?"

Lorna holds one foot out, tilting the shoe to catch the light like it's a diamond engagement ring at the end of her hand. Her feet are daintily shaped, with red toenails and high arches that mold to the shoes' own curves. She'll probably be able to walk ten miles and then dance all night in them without a single blister.

"George has been looking all over for you." Iph says it like she and Lorna are friends, aiming for disarmament. As much as she'd like to instigate some soap-opera-style manipulation to keep Lorna and George apart, she won't. For whatever reason, it's not in her.

"Georgie Porgie, pudding and pie. Kissed the girls and made them cry," Lorna says. "You crying yet?"

"Did George do something to you?"

Lorna's forehead is high and her eyes are blue, but she's a little more like a real person and a little less like Kate Moss than she was in Iph's head last night. Still, just a little.

"No," Lorna says. "Georgie's fine. It was me." Lorna pinches the bridge of her nose like she's a forty-year-old French woman having problems with her lover. Like someone who talks about the people she's dating using that word. *Lover*—eww. It's probably uncalled-for to hate Lorna for something Iph only imagines she's guilty of, but there is a too-muchness about this girl. And an odd vulnerability.

"Please," Lorna says, "don't tell George you saw me." She meets Iph's eyes, and there it is—the beleaguered heroine. Iph would cast her as Nora in *A Doll's House*. As Queen Anne in *Richard the Third*. As Norma Jean in the play about Marilyn Monroe in high school that Iph is supposed to be secretly writing in her spare time.

"Please," she says again. The lipstick is still in her hand. She puts it in her purse. How old is she, anyway? Her eyes have faint creases at their tips. Her under-eyes are bruised crescents. World-weary, that's how she looks.

"I know it's none of my business, but . . . would it be so bad to go say hi?"

Lorna looks up and to the left—a gesture to access memory. Iph sees her love story with George in that look. Is she about to cry?

Suddenly, Iph is willing to cede any sort of claim she might have on George. It's always this way for her—she's jealous and possessive until the moment she's not. In the end, competition doesn't make sense. Whoever wants the thing more should get it. She wonders, though, does Lorna want it more, or is she just good at looking heartbroken?

"George and I are just friends," Iph says. "If that helps at all."

"For now." Lorna puts away her lipstick. "You are so Georgie's type."

"I think that's more you," Iph says. "Have you seen the painting?"

Lorna nods. Slowly, like the painting is a lot. Which it is. You might think you want that kind of attention thrown your way, but Iph sees it on Lorna's face—that kind of love can be a burden.

"Here's the thing," Lorna says. "Georgie loves to be in love."

"So it was a one-way street?"

"No! I mean, George is amazing. But . . . kind of? I don't know, George made me feel safe. For a while." Lorna looks down at her hands, clasped like she's holding a tiny animal between them. Like she's praying. A tear drops and disappears into the folds of her fingers.

Iph reaches out her own hand like Lorna is a child she's about to help across a busy street. Lorna takes it. They're quiet. The moment is weirdly intimate. Iph's theater brain strains to be let free, to take notes, but something else in her shushes it.

"Maybe I used George." Lorna's grip tightens. "It's hard to know how much you like someone when you need a place to sleep." She looks straight at Iph and takes her hand back.

"That makes sense," Iph says. And for once she knows it's true, not because she has a great imagination, but because she's been there herself. *Is* there herself. But honestly, even if she were riding high right now, Iph would still like George. She's never met anyone she's liked even half as much.

"Be careful." Lorna's eyes are wide open now and pale as a husky's. "George is easy to love."

"I can see that."

Iph can just as easily see how to fall in love with Lorna—just look into her eyes. So big and blue. So much saving to do. Irresistible for a knight like George.

Lorna looks back at the mirror. Takes out a brush and pulls it through her silky hair, then zips up her purse and stands. Awkward, yet elegant. Like Audrey in *Funny Face*. Or Jean Seberg in anything.

"Those boots look better on you than on me," she says. "Just keep them. I'm gonna take off. I've seen this movie a hundred times anyway."

4

LIFE FROM
THE FLOWERS

P eople crowd the sidewalk in front of the theater. The line
snakes around the corner. It's seven P.M. and eighty-seven
degrees in the shade, but at least the light is softer now that
the sun is lower in the sky.

Even here on busy Hawthorne Street, Orr smells roses from
people's yards and the sunscreen everyone uses on children that
is synonymous with summer. Most days, he tries to hold sensory
input at bay, taking in a little at a time. Not tonight. He wants
every possible detail of popcorn smell and snatches of car-radio
music and kids bickering and cawing crows to stay in his memory
so he never forgets this feeling of waiting in line for the movies on
a summer night with such a beautiful girl.

When it comes to looking straight at Plum, though, Orr has
decided to pace himself. Out here in the gold-lit world, she is
bright as a parrot in a yellow dress that makes her dark red hair
look almost magenta. These are Mom's colors in the house, the
walls of their living and dining rooms. Here, they are Plum's
alone. She wears white rubber flip-flops, and her toenails have
chipped purple polish. Her feet are very nice. She originally
intended to leave the house barefoot, but to Orr's immense relief,

when her dad and Jane found out they were going to the movies, they both insisted she wear shoes.

"Fine." Plum has a way of saying it that sounds like, *You're an idiot, but I'll humor you.* Iph's *fine* is also loaded, but hers is more like, *Screw you.* Orr wonders if this is a universal teenage girl thing.

Now, they wait. Jane gave Orr the dollar for the movies, but Plum has money for popcorn and candy, and Orr, as always, is starving. He wonders if they will give him a free cup of water. He feels like he could drink a river. A lake. A sea.

"Have you seen this yet?" Plum points her fox chin at the marquee. THE SECRET OF ROAN INISH.

"I haven't," Orr says. "Have you?"

"Ten times. It's the only thing that ever plays at this theater. It's, like, a thing this summer. I think it's doing something to the city."

"Something good?"

"Something magical."

"You sound like my mom," Orr says. "She's witchy, too."

"All women are," Plum says. "But not all of us know it."

"What about men?"

"Men . . . oy." Plum rolls her eyes. "Men have magic. Look at little boys! But you squish it down young. You know how in physics, pressure changes things? Like, makes carbon into diamonds? Men's magic is like that. Then they sell the diamonds for something else. That's what ruins it for you guys, I think. The whole alpha-male status trip."

"I'm not like that," Orr says.

Plum cocks her head. What kind of animal *is* she, anyway? A fox, probably. Or a cat. That's an Iph game, figuring out what kind of animals people are. She learned it for acting, to help her get into character. She decided to play Hermia as a standard poodle for a monologue at school. When she practiced it for Orr, she was suddenly not Iph at all, but a completely different girl. It almost frightened him.

Orr sends his sibling tentacles out into the city but feels

nothing. Dad says Iph is here, that she's looking for him. He imagines seeing her in line for the movie. She'd run up to him, jump on him, squeeze him way too tight. He always complained, but really, he liked it. She knew that. But now his body curls away from the image like a poked pill bug. He doesn't want to see Iph. He doesn't even want to see Mom. The only person he wants to see right now is Plum.

5

ADAPTATION

It's stifling in the apartment. The rule is windows closed till the neighbor's house goes dark, but it's too hot to bear. They've taken a risk already, coming home so early. They didn't stay for the movie. George was too upset. Now they have to keep their voices low.

Iph is lying on the scratchy carpet like a starfish, trying to maximize her surface area to catch any hope of a breeze. George is on the sofa. Scout has ditched them for the cooler kitchen linoleum.

"Did she tell you about how she disappeared one day?"

"No," Iph says.

"She's stripping now. Did she tell you that?"

"You sort of did. At Shiny Dancer." It had been hypothetical then. The reality of it is hard to connect with the actual girl. "How old is she?"

"Eighteen as of two weeks ago. She used her stepsister's ID when she started. They probably didn't even look at it."

"Well . . . I don't know. In a perfect world, she'd be taken care of by nice adults, but that doesn't seem like it's happening. I mean, how does she feel about her job? Does she like it?"

"Iph. She takes her clothes off in front of creeps for money."

Iph feels Mom's training rise but sets it aside for now. "Did you two fight about it?"

George groans.

"I mean, I'm sure she has her reasons. Did she tell you why she first decided to strip?"

"Why does anyone?" George flops facedown on the sofa. "Kill me now."

"You don't seem to have a problem with Glow's work," Iph says, rolling over and stretching up into a cobra pose, trying to relieve what riding on the bike rack has done to her lower back.

"That's different. Glow's older. And I don't know—she doesn't seem like she has Lorna's history. I told you how Lorna and I met. I can't believe she'd get naked for strangers after that. It doesn't make sense."

"I don't know. Maybe it's not perfect logic, but I bet it makes sense. Everyone has their reasons," Iph says. "Or maybe you're right and it's self-destructive. But George . . . it's kind of up to her, you know?"

"I drove her away. She wanted to stay here," George says into the mossy deep of Nana's couch cushions. "She kept bringing home weed and Thai food. Kept buying me stuff."

"Sounds terrible."

"It *was* terrible," George says rolling to face the back of the sofa. "I couldn't accept her ill-gotten gains."

Iph sits up and props her back against the sofa. She's trying not to laugh. George slides off the sofa to sit next to her and is smiling a little, too, because it's hard to be melodramatic in a hundred-degree apartment.

Iph shoves George a little with her shoulder. "Ill-gotten gains?" She giggles and George giggles, and it's suddenly more of a slumber party and less of a funeral, but it's so hot that even party-girl Scout just thumps her tail from the next room.

When the laughing is over, they're sitting cross-legged, face to face like they're preparing to do the hand-clapping game Iph loved as a little girl. *Say, say, oh playmate. Come out and play with me.*

Iph leans in and kisses George—a short press of Iph's chapped lips to George's smooth ones.

"It's fine," Iph whispers, "that you still love Lorna. You can love her and like me at the same time. If that's what's happening."

George's eyes glow. "I think that's what's happening."

Iph leans in again, and the kiss is deeper this time. She's never done this before, but already she knows she's good at it. With practice, she'll be really good. An alternative future spools away from the lonely dorm-room microwave-brownie scenario Iph has been inching toward since high school disappointed her. There is sex in her future if she wants it.

George—who is also good at this, whether inherently or from practice—seems lost in the kiss. Iph touches the baby hairs on George's neck with her fingertips. Moves her lips down to those beautiful collarbones. Brushes her eyelashes against George's cheek. Blows cool air on George's sweaty forehead. Lightly bites George's ear. Stops. Looks into George's eyes. Sees herself there, yes. But Lorna's there, too.

"So," she says. "Tell me more."

"About?"

Iph laughs at the look on George's face. "About Lorna. You're thinking about her, right?"

"You're a little scary with your mind reading."

Iph smiles. Everything feels . . . fine.

She reaches out for Orr wherever he is in the city. *Safe* thrums back to her.

Nothing is how it's supposed to be, but everything is all right.

6

OVER THE POOL

Movies are often overwhelming for Orr. *The Secret of Roan Inish* is no exception. There are moments he needs to cover his ears—not because the soundtrack is loud, but because the emotions are so intense. The selkie woman is too lovely, the tiny child in the cradle boat too brave, too alone. The wistful sister longing for her lost baby brother nearly undoes him. It's all too close to home.

And then there's Plum in the seat next to him. Orr is grateful for her contained energy. She seems to expect nothing of him. The first time he put his head down and covered his ears, he felt her noticing. After that, she seemed to get that some parts were a little too much and handed him the tub of popcorn or moved a little to let him know it was safe to emerge. Now that the movie is over, she waits with him till most of the people are out of the theater, almost as if she knows that's the way he likes to do things.

Should he have held Plum's hand during the movie? Should he hold it now? But she is walking in front of him, hands in the pockets of her sundress, hair swishing back and forth behind her like a goldfish tail. Orr hurries to catch up with her.

They are mostly quiet on the way home. The night is still warm, but it's nice after the air-conditioned theater. The scent of night-blooming flowers flavors the air like syrup in an Italian soda. A few blocks from her house, Plum asks, "What was your favorite part?"

"That the boy didn't come home easily," Orr says. "He wouldn't have in real life. He was scared, but his sister knew how to call him. She understood him even after they'd been apart so long."

"Do you miss your sister?" Plum asks, her voice very soft like Orr is the feral little boy in the movie, living with the seals in his cradle of a ship, naked out at sea.

Orr nods. "Do you miss your mom?"

Plum says, "I always cry when Jamie goes back to his family. It's the right ending, I know. But there's a part of me that's a little resentful. It's like the movie version of my favorite book. This girl's dad dies, and she has to overcome it and keep living. But in the movie, it's all a mistake. He's not dead after all. It's like, give us the real story, you know?"

They're quiet for the rest of the walk. When they get back to Plum's, the house is dark. There's a note on the refrigerator door from Jane held by the same wizard magnet that's on Orr's refrigerator at home, a free gift from a box of herbal tea. Jane's out grocery shopping with Plum's dad, the note says. Orr can wait at Plum's or go back to Penelope.

"That's good," Plum says. "Most days, he doesn't leave the house." She must mean her dad. "So, wanna stay and hang out? I'm going to make tea and read. You can join me if you want."

"I'm tired," Orr says. He knows it's from the movie.

"I'll make you a map." She draws a diagram of how to get back to Penelope on the back of an envelope that reads *Environment Oregon*.

Orr prowls the living room, restless and ready to be alone. Plum's house is messy at first glance, full of books and newspapers and empty beer and soda bottles and board games and musical instruments, but clean underneath. Like the Furies' house is now that Orr has moved in.

On the front porch, Plum says goodbye. She does this with a hug and then a funny thing—a head press, her forehead to his. How had she known his head was hot and a little achy? Plum has powers, like Iph.

He finger-traces the map and the digits of Plum's phone number, written on the other side of the envelope, then puts it in the pocket of Allison's basketball shorts. He knows the way. He starts to run, and when he starts, he doesn't want to stop. He flies past Penelope, blocks and blocks. He smells green. He is so fast. His body makes wind that cools his face. Ahead, massive trees touch the black velvet sky where the brightest stars are visible—such a different sky from the one at home, where even a few miles from the city the light pollution is so much less.

Orr remembers his hair, the way his ponytail flowed out behind him when he ran. He is so light now without it. So much faster. How can a good thing come from such a violation? This night would never have happened without Meadowbrook. Orr thinks about the dark theater hour spent shoulder-to-shoulder with Plum and the way fairy tales are sometimes true.

He runs toward the trees, past a playground, and into a park. He senses water before he's even close to the big oval pond. The rancid mossy green surely reeks—but tonight the strong smell is enticing. He thinks of Plum floating in the hot tub, surrounded by flowered water. Here, there are no flowers. Only a neon scrim of algae over black water. Still, he kneels at the water's muddy edge.

On the center island, the ducks murmur. Surely if he drinks here, he will be sick. The moon is so bright, a few days away from full. There are turtles sleeping on a log in the center of the pond. How does he know that? It's a smell or maybe a sound, slow amphibian blood. He cocks his head to hear the roosting herons. Crows sleep tucked in high branches in a stand of Douglas firs around the pond. Little fish swim deep below. The water wears moonlight the way Plum wore her Ophelia dress. Orr's mouth is so dry. His hands are in the water now.

A sound startles him. A growl. A big lab's quick bark rebukes his aberrant behavior. The dog strains on the leash held by a small, hurrying woman. Orr smells their fear, both the woman's and the dog's.

Why is he here at the edge of this pond? The gravel cuts into his knees. Without even drinking, he knows how the water will taste—of pleasure and relief.

But Orr stands and backs away. Listens to the lap of the pond against the shore. Smells pot smoke. Hears voices from the far end of the park. A bat passes under a streetlamp. Orr turns his back to the pond.

You can have all the water you want at the house, he tells this new, thirsty part of himself. After one final look at the moonlit water, Orr trots back to Penelope.

7

HIS FOUR
BLACK HOOVES

There is a man in the kitchen. He is stinking drunk—another supposed euphemism proven. He makes the entire house rank with beer and pee and gross BO. Orr stands over him, cast-iron skillet poised.

"Who the hell *are* you?" The guy has asked this seven or eight times. The emphasis had switched at around the fourth query from "Who the hell are *you*?" to the way it is now, less belligerent and more bemused. "Dude, let me up, man. I wanna get my stuff."

"You don't live here," Orr says. His heart is beating so hard. Like always, he is thirsty. "Will you stay down while I get a drink?"

"These chicks are straight-edge, bro. It's like the Bible Belt up in here."

Orr has no idea what the man is talking about. All he wants is a glass of water.

"We're not straight-edge, asswipe," a voice says. "We hide our stuff from you. Our cash, our smokes. Definitely our beer. We lock our bedroom doors." Mika stands fierce in her tank top and boys' underwear with dinosaurs on it. She told Orr she shops in the kids' department where clothes are cheaper—usually the boys' section, because she prefers the prints. She touches Orr's elbow, and he sets down the pan. It's funny how long he was able to hold it without shaking. His bicep is a small hillock of rock—when did that happen?

The guy shifts like he's going to stand, but Mika puts up a hand. "Don't move." She grabs her camera from the counter and snaps. "For posterity," she says. "Now get out, or I'm getting Allison."

"Jane," the guy shouts.

"Shut up!" Mika says. "She's not here."

"Janie!" the guy yells, lumbering to his feet. "JANE." Mika starts kicking him, but her feet are bare. She gets in a few good ones, but he just laughs. He's so drunk. Orr has never seen someone this intoxicated in real life. "*JANE!*"

Mika gets a dish towel and goes to stuff it in the guy's mouth as he tries and fails to stand up, singing as he stiff-arms Mika with one hand and snatches the dish towel away with the other. Orr knows the song—"Kung Fu Fighting." Mika makes a little shriek and pulls back her arm to sock him. Then Jane is there, pulling Mika off and pulling the guy up. Once he's standing, she shoves him and bursts into tears. Then he's holding her.

Orr doesn't like this one bit. "Jane, who is this guy?" he asks. But Jane isn't listening.

"Come on," Mika says and pulls Orr into the living room. Jane is still crying, and the guy is slurring something.

"I can't watch this," Mika says. "Porch?"

Outside is cool and perfect. The wind slides over the trees like a loose-strung bow. "Want to go for a run?" Orr asks Mika. But Mika is resting her head on her knees.

"I hate that guy," she says. "He's awful for Jane."

Orr thinks of Dad. Is he bad for Mom? Are he and Iph bad for her? Part of the reason she needed the residency was because of her sadness. It's why Dad encouraged her to dance more, to go into Portland for the classes that left them eating pizza three nights a week. And the way Orr acted when she left . . . no wonder she wanted to go away for so long.

"Awful how?" Orr asks Mika.

"In every way possible," Mika says. "I can't deal with this. Not again." There's a note in Mika's voice that makes Orr understand how temporary his own stay at Penelope will be.

"That song," Orr says.

"Racist dickhead."

Orr is shaking. It must have started before, when he thought the guy was there to kill the Furies in their sleep. He sits on his hands. That stupid song is stuck in his head now.

"Why's Jane with him?"

"They went through some hard stuff together when they were young. Jane got over it, but Red never did."

They're quiet enough that the background sounds of the neighborhood move to the front. Voices rise and fall in the house. The crickets sing and the neighbors across the street laugh at something they're watching on TV. Someone next door turns on a shower. A baby cries, then quiets. Unlike his neighborhood at home, the houses in Southeast Portland are close together and no one seems to have an air conditioner—hence all the open windows. A car passes, then a trio of laughing bearded guys on bikes.

"People always teased me for being Asian when I was a kid," Orr says.

Mika looks closely at Orr. "Huh."

"I'm not Asian," Orr says. "They didn't know what I was, so they guessed."

"They knew you were something," Mika says. "So, uh . . . where are you *from*?"

The way she says it makes Orr laugh out loud. "My mom hates that."

"Don't you hate it?"

"Oh, no," Orr says. "I love it. I get to tell them I'm from the galaxy QRT 9987 in the Orion sector. Or sometimes I say I'm a fugitive surfing the space-time continuum. Or, you know, keep it simple. Say I'm from Mars."

Mika is smiling now. The grin makes her face into a pointy triangle like the face of a cat. "Can I borrow that?"

"Are you a Martian, too?"

"I'm thinking more like a vengeful time-traveling demigod."

"People will definitely believe that," Orr says. "Especially if they ever hear you drum."

Mika turns red when he says it, and that makes Orr blush, too. They're quiet again. Mika punches him softly on the arm. "Wait here. I'll be right back."

The door makes the tiniest squeak as Mika opens it. Orr inhales deeply. Something sweet blooms on Penelope's street at night. Mika returns with both their sneakers. She plops Orr's on the porch and sits on the top step to lace up her own.

He pulls on his shoes over bare feet. It doesn't even bother him now not to have socks.

"Race you to the cemetery!" she says and takes off.

Mika is faster, but Orr's legs are much longer. They are both straining in the final blocks, bursting past the cemetery gates neck and neck. At the last second something gathers in the muscles of Orr's legs and rockets him past Mika. He's halfway down the path before he can stop.

Mika trots up, laughing. "You're a freaking centaur, boy! I thought you had hooves for a second there."

They stagger to a moonlit patch of grass and collapse.

8

FAITH AND A
SENSE OF TRUTH

The heat is an asshole. Iph misses the rain. She's gone through all of Nana's clothes, and the only clean things are a huge boxy T-shirt with a sea lion on the front from the Newport Aquarium and some unflattering, baggy shorts. Just lovely with her undereye circles and frizzed-out curls.

George woke up quiet and distant, and Iph the bohemian adventuress of the night before was gone like yesterday's makeup, leaving her in the familiar Land of Almost. Almost pretty. Almost cool. A party guest earnestly mumbling *peas and carrots* in the chorus.

Being a protagonist is infinitely better.

There is a thing Orr always said about the kids who were nice to him at school. That he was their "human credential." Like, *Look, I'm so kind and open-minded, I'm friends with the boy who meows in class when he's bored.* It was like that with Iph's friends, too, although it took her longer to realize it. She knew how to make herself socially useful in a way Orr never figured out. But by sophomore year, Iph got tired of it. She experimented with eating lunch alone in the library and not calling anyone for a week. After a month without diminishing herself to fit in, she was stronger.

She boxed the sporty, brightly colored clothes she'd never liked and had Mom take them to the women's shelter.

She'd decided on her new uniform and started wearing it: old dress shirts of Dad's, knotted at the waist. Straight-legged jeans and men's white tees and vintage penny loafers. Pencil skirts and sweater sets. She offset the classic fifties coed vibe with Yai-Yai's loud costume jewelry, mixed with little things she made from party favors from the toy store—mismatched earrings and bracelets made of tiny plastic animals and a growing collection of Barbie shoes. She was never without lipstick, dark red or hot pink with nails to match. A sort of method-acting, student-era Marilyn Monroe going to a rave. A few of her old friends had been interested in her transformation—at first. A few boys seemed to notice, too—but that meant nothing unless she was down for clandestine sex. There would be no actual dating in high school for Iph. Teen coupling was all about status, and Iph's body type and brownness counted her out, at least in Forest Lake.

"Ugh," George says, pulling the bike out. "Portland is not supposed to be this hot."

"Does she have a name?" Iph asks about the bike as they wait for Scout to do her business.

"Ethelette," George says. "I'm a dork, okay?"

"No," she says, straddling the bike rack. "That's perfect."

As crappy and insecure as she feels this morning, she'd rather be here than anywhere else. Bouncing on the back of the ten-speed is what Iph does now. George has even fastened a throw pillow to the rack with a bungee cord in deference to Iph's bruised butt.

Last night, post-kiss, George had been chivalrous, offering Iph Nana's room like crashing in a pile on the sofa together suddenly wasn't proper. Except neither of them wanted to separate. They'd stayed up talking till four in the morning instead and took Scout for a pre-sunrise walk. It was dawn when they went to bed and three in the afternoon when they finally woke up. Now the bones of the Hawthorne Bridge tower above them. George's calves are glorious as they push the bike through the hottest part of the afternoon.

George is busy today. A stop in Old Town. A stop in Southeast. Then meeting Glow at her needle exchange site. After Old Town, Iph will be dropped off at Powell's to wait like a child.

You're a detective, she tells herself, *looking for Glow's friend Mika.* But before the thought is complete, she shuts it down. The whole girl-detective thing is a game. She can't actually find Orr. Is she even trying? What about flyers? Ads in the paper? If she was serious, she'd go back to Dad and get his credit card and plaster every telephone pole in Portland with images of her brother. She'd make Dad hire a real investigator. Use her supposed psychic powers to find him herself.

Once off the bridge, they veer right and cross Burnside, passing under the red lion-guarded gate to Chinatown. George gave her the downtown tour the day before, and surprisingly she's retained some of it. It's different exploring without a car. Slow enough for her brain to catch up with her body.

George locks the bike kitty-corner from an old hotel called the Gentry, telling her it's known as the Entry on the street. "It's a joke," George says. "Gallows humor. The Entry is like a portal. Once you go through, it's hard to find your way back."

Iph has never been on this street. Its narrowness and the age of the buildings hint at earlier eras of white settlement. She always wonders what it was like for the indigenous people who lived here before colonization. There are so few traces left of that world. When people talk about Portland history, they tell you which settlers the streets are named after and how the city almost washed away in the 1894 flood. Some of the bars around here probably still have basements that lead to the so-called Shanghai tunnels below the city that were used for shipping and as speakeasies during Prohibition. There were even rumors that poor white sailors and racial minorities were kidnapped and kept there to be indentured to ships' captains when they came into port.

Then and now, the population in Portland is mostly white.

Mom used to supplement the history they learned at school. It was from her, not the teachers, that Iph learned Oregon was the only state to explicitly exclude Black people at its founding. Even though that law eventually changed, the sentiment is baked into the city's segregated neighborhoods. It's a regret of her parents' now, that they settled in a place with so few Black and brown people.

"You should probably wait outside with Scout," George says, checking and rechecking the bike lock. Iph rolls her shoulders back and knots her hair on the top of her head. If she had a pair of scissors, she'd cut her T-shirt into a tank top right here on the street. Even Scout looks cranky.

"Stay close—I'll be quick." George hands Scout's leash to Iph. Maybe George is getting sick of her. They've spent almost every moment of the past four days together.

The street smells like pee, and Scout is very busy checking it out. A man is having an angry conversation with himself. He passes Iph and turns a red face to her. He is clearly in pain, his head fiery with things he sees and she doesn't. But he's also scary, filthy in a layered, long-term way, with filmy, unfocused eyes. Iph thinks of the word *unhinged* and how this describes not just his possible mental state, but the way he's holding his body. His arms are too loose, his knees too mobile. Maybe he's drunk, but Iph doesn't think so.

"GO AWAY!" he roars. Iph steps back. Sweat drips from her forehead to her nose. Her glasses fog. She wipes them, puts them back on. Like the first time she wore them, everything looks too bright.

"GO AWAY."

This time, he is roaring at her.

Scout moves between Iph and the man and bristles.

An insect halo is swarming the man's head. It's not really there . . . is it? He swats around his ears. He's stomping now. People cross the street to get away from him. "GO. AWAY." He's in tears. The insects buzz louder.

Iph wipes her glasses clean again with her T-shirt. She can see them now. Winged red ants with little angry human faces and mouths full of pointed teeth.

"Hey!" Iph says. "Hold on for a second." Scout barks to get the man's attention, ready to go along with Iph's improv. The man stills. Listens. "I have some insecticide in my bag." She gestures to a bag that's not there. "You'll have to close your eyes to protect them. Maybe you should cover your face, too."

The man is startled. "The bugs?"

"Yes, those red ants. They're awful. Let me get them."

He tenses, afraid, she realizes.

"I'm going to stay back and spray from here. It's a strong propellent, so it should work all right."

His eyes widen. "Give me some warning," he says. "Count to three."

"Okay! Here goes." She braces herself and pretends to pull out a heavy can of bug spray. She feels the efficacy of the spray will depend completely on her commitment to its reality. She uncaps the canister and puts the cap in the bag. She shakes it and holds out her arm. "Here it comes," she says. "One, two, three!" She presses the nozzle, making the *shhhhh*-ing sound of liquid spraying out.

"Keep your eyes closed! They're dropping," Iph says. "I'm gonna spray the ones on the ground to be sure."

When Iph stops spraying, he opens his eyes one at a time. He turns in a circle, nodding as he goes. He presses his hands together like he's going to pray, bows a little in Iph's direction, then walks away, still nodding.

Iph rubs her temples, the sweaty back of her neck. She feels drained now and a little like crying. The door to the Gentry opens, and a crusty older version of one of the Pioneer Square boys emerges. His energy is sticky as ground fruit, sweet and false. There is violence there. Iph shivers in the heat. Steps back. She's raw from the red-ant man, she realizes, too open.

She used to get headaches from going out in crowds when she

was younger. Mom said she was like a sponge and taught her to close her receptors. "Like a little psychic raincoat," she said.

Iph's been spongey all day. Skinless. Maybe kissing George has opened her up. And that, of course, is the danger of sex. The reason why there might be less of it in her future than last night's flagrant kissing promised. She is exposed now. Fatigued from seeing and being seen.

"You going in?" the guy asks. Before she can say no, Scout shoots through the open door, dragging Iph inside. Scout may be tiny, but she's strong enough to pull a sled.

INSIDE, IPH LOOKS FOR a sofa to rest on, but it's not that kind of hotel. There doesn't even seem to be air-conditioning. The desk clerk is a head and torso in a plexiglass box, like those animatronic fortune-tellers they had in the awesome pizza place in downtown Forest Lake before it was torn down to build a Wal-Mart.

Scout barks a sharp little hello.

"Scout!" The lady adjusts her Dolly Parton wig and slips a bejeweled hand out of a slot in the plexiglass, wiggling two manicured fingers. Scout hops up to lick them, then sits for a treat. The lady obliges with a cackle, tossing it out the slot into Scout's jaws.

"George is on the third floor. Take the stairs, sweetheart. There's a mess in the elevator. If it opens, hold your nose."

Iph follows the extended red claw to a door that reads STAIRS and climbs. Can the elevator smell worse than this? She wills her nose shut and follows a perfectly cheerful Scout up two flights.

The third floor smells better, but still not remotely good. There's a cafeteria scent mixed with wet gymnasium and some sort of toxic cleaning solution. Iph hesitates, but Scout pulls her down the hall. There's a weird vibe in the place that Iph can't quite pin down.

Scout tugs her onward and stops at the final door on the left. She scratches and whines until it opens. "Sorry," Iph says when she sees George's face. "There was a guy. Scout brought me here—"

"It's all right, doll," someone says. "Come on in." It's a woman. White, older, hard to say how old. She's wearing a pink kimono trimmed in balding ostrich feathers, and her hennaed hair is piled high on her head and stuck through with three red chopsticks. Another woman leans against the headboard, eyes closed. This one is light brown, graying and handsome, eyelids fluttering like she's in the middle of an intense dream. Iph turns away, trying not to stare. The woman is high, Iph realizes. Probably on heroin.

"This is Velma," George says. A rotating fan clicks in the corner like a metronome. Iph turns her face to meet the breeze.

"I'm Iphigenia." Iph smiles. Something about this woman's old-timey glamour makes Iph want to give her full name.

Velma's eyebrows raise. Maybe she knows her Greek tragedy. "Well, hello there," she says like they're all in a forties comedy and there isn't someone nodding out right next to her. "George tells me you're an actor. And clearly quite the dish."

"Why, thank you," Iph says, smiling like a silver-screen ingenue. It's nice being referred to as an actor. And it's the first time anyone's ever called her a dish.

"Don't mind Pete," Velma says.

"I'm so sorry for barging in." Iph's eyes have adjusted, and she sees that Velma is older than she thought. She has great skin, but her hands, absently stroking Pete's arm, are wrinkled. Her neck is, too. She's probably at least sixty. That explains the name. No one is called Velma anymore.

"Velma's a poet," George says. "Pete's a jazz man."

He, Iph mentally corrects herself in relation to Pete. "I love poetry," she says. "And my dad's a big jazz guy."

"What poets do you like?" Velma leans forward like she's dying to know.

"Anne Sexton," Iph says. "Theodore Roethke. Sylvia Plath. Emily Dickinson. Shakespeare. Tennyson. Sappho. Blake."

"That's an excellent list. It's so nice to see young people still read," Velma says. "Shakespeare certainly improved George. You should have seen the hell-raising before the bard came along."

"Velma!" George shakes a finger and Scout dances as Velma laughs.

"I won't keep you kids." Velma rubs the cuff of Pete's white shirt, a long-sleeved button-up that's surprising in this heat. "And George, if they have anything in the van for Pete's leg—"

"Velma"—George's voice lowers—"you might want to get over to the ER. I'm worried. I think it's got to be lanced."

Velma's eyes fill. "Pete won't," she says. "Not after the way they treated us last time."

George exhales, short and fierce. Sometimes Iph sees the ghost of the bow and arrow even when George isn't wearing it.

"So lovely to meet you," Velma says. Her voice is soft and slow. Is she high, too? Iph has never considered this—older people addicted to drugs. But of course it happens.

"You, too," Iph says. "I love your kimono."

"Oh, this old thing?" Velma smiles, winking like a showgirl. "You two be good, now."

In the hall, Iph stops. Something's pulling her back into the room. She looks at the door. For a second, she sees water flowing out from under it, a wave on the beach of worn brown carpet.

"George, what's wrong with Pete's leg?"

George sighs. "An abscess. Probably an infected injection site. I wish Glow was here. She knows how to lance them."

"How do you know Glow, anyway?"

"I lived around the corner from the needle exchange site a few years ago. I'd go bug her over there, asking to help out."

There are so many things left out of what George shares. Iph is getting used to that. She imagines what's missing. The dark apartment. The missing-in-action mom. Lonely George with long braids like the ones in the painting at Taurus Trucking.

"Why weren't you more freaked out in there?" George asks. "It's pretty intense."

They've started toward the stairwell. Iph stops again. "I don't know. My mom, maybe? She had a friend, her best friend Rob, that died of an overdose. I've heard a lot of stories. Mom was kind of wild back in the day."

"How wild are we talking?"

"Like, *lived at the Chelsea Hotel with a rock star* wild," Iph says. "Like, there are famous naked pictures of her in photography books that this woman took when she lived there."

"What rock star?" George is hooked. Everyone loves Mom's stories. Everyone loves Mom.

"She won't say. Says it's for Dad's benefit, so it doesn't wreck the guy's music for him. Dad says she's making it up to make him jealous. I'm not sure, but I think it might have been Jimi Hendrix."

They're quiet for a moment. Then George says, "Can we go back and try to help Pete? I think I could probably deal with her leg with what I've got in my bag."

Her, then. Good to know.

"I can't look, but I can keep Velma distracted. I'm squeamish."

"Definitely don't look. And I'm going to open a window before I start. There might be a smell."

"No problem. I'm very good at turning my nose off when necessary. I babysit."

"Of course you do." George takes her hand and squeezes, and together they walk back down the hall.

9

EMOTION MEMORY

Velma and Pete's bathroom is small and stuffed with beauty products. A sticky layer of what is probably hairspray covers the sink and mirror and walls. There's a thing Velma said while George worked on Pete's wound that Iph can't get out of her head.

"They treated us like dirt last time Pete went to the clinic with an abscess. The nurse was so rough. When I asked her to be gentle, she made this sound—I swear to God, honey, it was like a wicked witch cackle with a little snort at the end—and said maybe next time, Pete would learn her lesson."

"Do they treat smokers with lung cancer like that?" Iph asked, squeezing Velma's hand.

"That's a good point, sweetie," Velma said, wiping her eyes.

What George did for Pete was amazing. Not just the skill of it, but the bedside manner. Shame and fear drained from the wound. Like a day in endless Portland January when the sun comes out and everyone feels awake for the first time in weeks. Now Pete is laughing in the other room at some story George is telling. Velma is singing jazz standards to Scout.

Iph puts the toilet lid down and pulls the phone cord taut.

She is procrastinating. It was George who suggested she use the phone to call Dad, and Velma who sent her to the bathroom for privacy. She dials.

"Iph!" How does he know it's her? It really must be Dad she gets that intuition from. "He called me!"

Everything seeps out of her till she is boneless. She grabs the side of the tub for support.

"Let me talk to him." Iph is shaking. From the next room, she hears Pete laughing again.

"He's not here," Dad says. "He decided to stay in Portland."

"What . . . do you mean?" Iph is dizzy—probably needs to eat. Dad is saying something. The world has changed so fast. Without the gravity of Mom, they've all spun off so quickly.

"He's having a good time with the punk chicks. Jane and Allison and . . ."

"Mika," Iph says. "I think the third one is Mika."

"You found him, too?"

"Almost," Iph says.

"He met a girl," Dad says. "Said she was pretty, so maybe he likes her. I told him he can come home whenever he wants. All he has to do is say the word. But once he's back, he's back for good. The same goes for you."

Iph is silent. Dad as the villain has shifted into some other thing that is still sneaky, but also a little brilliant.

"Do you want his phone number?"

"Yes," Iph says. "And the address. I can't believe this." She cradles the phone against her shoulder and turns on the cold tap. Lets it run over her hot, sticky hands.

"I don't have an address. He didn't know it. He called me from the girl's house. Some kid who's a friend of the band. They're called the Furies. Which is . . . well, kind of perfect. The house is in Southeast Portland off Belmont, and they call it Penelope. You should call him and go see for yourself. I bet he'll be happy to hear from you."

"He's really okay?"

"More than okay. He sounded great."

Dad sounds smug. Why didn't he make Orr give him the exact address? Iph slurps a little water from her cupped hand and dries it on her shorts. There is a stack of brown paper towels by the sink. Iph grabs one and an eyeliner pencil and writes down the number.

There's a silence. Dad is fiddling with something. He never could stay still.

"Iph," Dad says. "I'm sorry."

"For what?"

"You were right. I underestimated him."

"Yeah," Iph says. "You did. I'm assuming you haven't told Mom." Iph imagines her mother flying home from Santa Cruz, Wicked Witch of the West style. She's glad she won't be around for that fight.

"Not yet," Dad says. "I'm going to try and convince her to stay. Can I have her call you? She'll want to hear your voice herself."

"My friend doesn't have a phone," Iph says, basically daring Dad to freak out with the deadpan way she says it.

But he stays cool. If his blasé attitude is part of some overall strategy, Iph can't figure out what he's planning. "That's okay. Not everyone can afford one. I remember those days. Is there somewhere I can leave a message? In case I need to reach you?"

Iph thinks. "There's a store. Shiny Dancer. On East Burnside. You could probably call there. I'm assuming it's in the phone book." Iph wonders what, exactly, the Yellow Pages listing for Shiny Dancer will show. Will there be an ad with a little cartoon stripper?

"Thank you," Dad says. "Will they let you use the phone sometimes? Or can you get to a pay phone once a week? I told Orr he has to call in on Sundays. Would you do that, too?"

"Sure," Iph says, suddenly missing him. "I'll talk to you soon."

"I love you, Iph."

Iph opens her mouth to say it back, but the words won't come. She puts the phone in its cradle and folds the paper towel into a small, thick rectangle, feeling . . . what?

This part of the story is so unexpected, so surreal. Orr, living with a punk band in Southeast Portland. Iph . . . here, in this seedy hotel that feels normal in a way school never has. She's at home in this world of George's. Why does she feel this way?

She taps the phone with her index finger. The polish is still intact, a relic from another world. She knows she should call Orr. But she's not going to. She doesn't know why, or if it's right or wrong. Their trajectories have fractured. Their lives are suddenly separate. Iph rips the paper towel into little pieces and confettis the toilet bowl with them, a celebration of something. Then she opens the bathroom door to George and Velma and Scout and Pete.

"This is for you, doll." Velma is sitting at a book-piled desk with a slim volume open to the title page, fountain pen in hand. "Spelled like Agamemnon's daughter in *The Iliad*?"

"Just like that," Iph says. Not many people catch the reference. "Is this your book?"

"It's so good," George says.

"I didn't know you read poetry," Iph says. "You've been holding out on me."

"Writes it, too." Velma winks. "Damn fine poetry, if you ask me. The one time I got to read it."

"That was a fluke. I don't write much anymore."

"Hmm," Pete says, "that notebook you keep in your back pocket tells me otherwise, my friend."

Huh. Come to the think of it, Iph *has* seen a little notebook tucked under George's wallet and keys on the kitchen counter at Taurus Trucking. She's noted how George always puts it in the same place, right after coming in the door. Dad is like that. Orr, too. Good at regularity and habits. Iph and Mom are another story, always losing their keys and never able to find the mate for a sock or shoe or earring.

"Here you go, sweetheart." Velma hands Iph her book. It's a thin, elegant volume with a matte cream cover and a foiled circle—or no, it's a snake. A silver-green snake eating its tail. The title reads: *Ouroboros*.

"What does it mean?"

"It's the name of the snake symbol. It came from Egypt and spread to the alchemists in Alexandria and ancient Greece. It's an image of wholeness, of the way we transform and circle back into ourselves. It's also a fertility symbol, but self-contained. How we self-create, how we contain the parts we need to be whole."

Iph turns the book over. A familiar symbol—*RCT*, in rose vines. Like the little matchbook poetry book she found at Shiny Dancer.

"I've seen this before," Iph says. "RCT Editions."

"Rose City Transmutation. They do great work," Pete says. "All kinds of stuff. Poetry collections. Experimental theater and little one-off matchbooks with out-of-print poems. I met the publisher at one of my shows. She was there looking for Velma. Had an old collection of hers. Wanted to see if she had anything new. That's how the book came be." Pete is an old-school looker, with thick cropped hair, huge dark eyes, a soft wide mouth, and a smoky voice with a mild Southern accent. The wound Iph saw from the corner of her eye—she tried to give Pete a little privacy, even in the small room—was a devastation, a screaming plea from Pete's body for relief. There must be a reason for it, Pete and Velma's addiction. Some reason, some solution. It's the kid part of her that's begging for this, she realizes. The same part that used to think if Mom told her about her past, Iph could find a way to fix it. Like with Mom, there probably isn't an answer here. Not a simple one, anyway. Most things are like this, she is beginning to understand. Most things and most people.

Iph smiles at Pete and Velma, at George and at Scout, snuggled into Velma's lap like she's never planning to leave. "Thanks for the book. And for inviting me in. It's been great to meet you both. Pete, maybe sometime I'll get to hear you play."

"I'd like that," Pete says. George's smile is sunlight in the dim room.

"Hold your horses, you two." Velma is rummaging in the room's small closet. She appears with a large slouchy rose velvet shoulder bag, something that would work as well for a play set in the 1620s or the 1920s.

"Be right back," she sings, heading for the bathroom.

When she returns with the bag, she presents it to Iph with a flourish. "I've tucked in a few goodies. You can look later."

She ushers them to the door like they're leaving a grand apartment, not a stuffy run-down SRO. She takes Iph's fingers in hers, an old-fashioned ladylike farewell handshake Iph finds brilliant. "Charmed," she says, then leans over to kiss George on the cheek. "Off you go now, sweet young things."

Iph wonders if she'll ever see Pete and Velma again.

"You're a good egg, Iphigenia Santos Velos," George says, grabbing Iph's hand and holding it tight until they reach the stairs.

In front of the Gentry, Iph feels like crying but won't. She hasn't told George about finding Orr. She's not ready for this to end. There's more for her here—she can feel it.

"It's too hot to bike," George says. "I'm gonna leave Ethelette locked up here. You sure you don't want to bus over to needle exchange with me? We can still go to Powell's after and check for Mika then."

Iph surprises herself by saying, "I think I'm gonna head to Powell's on my own. I need a nice bookstore visit. And air-conditioning."

"Fair enough. They have free water in the café," George says. "You were pretty great in there. Pete and Velma are crazy about you. You should have heard them when you were in the bathroom."

"I did nothing," Iph says. "That was all you."

"You did the most important thing," George says. "You didn't judge."

"I didn't—but I did wonder. Why are they doing that? Can they stop? Don't they want to?"

"They've tried. I hope they'll try again. Even with all the stuff they're dealing with, they really helped me when I was losing it,"

George says. "Pete's the only person I've ever met who's like me. I mean, none of the words feel quite right. Queer? Sure. But there's something else. Butch sort of gets at it, but then . . . I don't know. Pete's the same way. Says we're peas in a pod. Plus, dude, such a style icon."

"They both are."

Iph closes her eyes and sees a Japanese mother that looks like George alongside a stocky white man. Sees George with a freshly buzzed head and a red puffy face. Sees the stuffed backpack and rolled-up sleeping bag. Sees George at a bus stop, all alone. Iph knows she's probably making it up, imagining a story to fill in the blank spots George isn't ready to share. But another part of her knows these images are close to the truth. She takes off her glasses. They actually feel like hers now. She wipes them clear.

George leans in and kisses her forehead. Marking it, like Glinda the Good. "You know how to get to Powell's, right?"

"No." Iph laughs. "I would lie to save face, but it's too hot to get lost again."

"Let us walk you," George says. "I'll catch the bus from there."

O rr sits on the sofa tuning Jane's acoustic guitar while the band fights in the kitchen.

"For fork's sake, Allison!" Jane is angry because Allison broke her hand and can't play bass until she gets the cast off. They've also decided to not to swear so much in front of young Orr. A joke, considering who raised him. "Why'd you have to hit him so hard?"

"I don't do dick in the wild," Allison says. "He, like, whipped it out of nowhere. I didn't think—I just clocked him."

"You should've kicked him in the balls," Mika says. Her high voice and small body make her look as young as Orr. In reality, Jane, Allison, and Mika are all twenty-four. The age Mom was when she had Iph.

Mom. It's weird thinking about her here in this living room with its wallpaper of band flyers and postcards and rough wood floors prickly with staples the girls didn't bother to remove when they pulled the carpet up after one too many cat accidents. Orr still hasn't seen the cat that made them.

"He's a lounger agent," Allison told him when he asked about the housemate responsible for the smell. Finally, he realizes who she sounds like—the girl from *Clueless*, one of Iph's favorite movies. It makes sense. Allison says she's a real-life Valley girl, born and raised in LA.

"He's for sure some sort of spy," Mika says. "Does nothing but lie around for weeks, then goes off on some secret mission out of nowhere. Clearly, it's when his handlers activate him. Comes home dirty and exhausted and sleeps for days."

"Either that, or he gets locked in people's garages. He's a little . . . decorative," Jane says. "Not the brightest kitty in the caboodle, if you know what I mean."

The girls deny you can still smell the cat pee, but they've let Orr scrub every floor in the run-down, hundred-year-old house, happy to buy him the Murphy Oil Soap he asked for and watch as he dumped pail after pail of black water into the backyard to quench the summer-dry jasmine.

"The issue remains," Jane says, carrying two Slurpee cups full of iced tea into the living room—one for her and one for Orr— and settling beside him on the sofa, which Orr has covered with a paisley tapestry he found in the basement. "We finally have a chance at a decent gig, and now we can't even do it. I mean, you guys, Dead Moon! And it's a benefit for the hos!"

"I know that girl—from Shiny Dancer? Kind of a babe," Mika says.

"It sucks that the Meow-Meows broke up." Allison lights up a cigarette. Mika instantly jumps up and opens a window. "But dudes, their loss has got to be our gain. We can't afford to pass this up."

"You don't mind if someone else plays bass?" Mika says. "Be honest."

"I mean, ego-wise, a little. But band first. I mean, I can at least shake a tambourine while I do my vocals."

The girls start making lists of possible substitute bass players. Orr tunes out, noodling around on the guitar. He plays a chord progression—something vaguely familiar. He slides into something else—a version of a song he heard the band play over and over again the night before, when Allison still had the use of both her hands. He sets the guitar on its end like it's a cello or a tiny upright bass, thinking about Mom and Iph and Dad and what it felt like when they used to go camping and why, even if he tries, he still doesn't feel homesick. When he finally looks up the girls are frozen and staring straight at him.

Jane is the first one to thaw. "What the hell was that?"

"What?" Orr looks behind him toward the white-flowered tree in the yard framed by the large front window, sparkling after Orr cleaned it that morning with newspaper and white vinegar.

"Play that again," Jane says.

Orr does.

"You know our songs?" Allison's mouth makes a perfect cartoon *O*.

Of course he knows them. The Furies have been rehearsing every night since he arrived—he's heard their set at least twenty times.

"Come." Jane's pulling him down to the basement. The girls follow. Jane turns on some equipment, and Mika gets behind the drums.

"Here." Allison puts the strap of her bass guitar over Orr's head. "Do you know how to use this?" Orr shakes his head no. The basement isn't his favorite place, with its lack of windows and mildew smell. Allison flips a switch on the bass's side and shows Orr the volume and effects knobs.

When everyone's ready, Jane gets on the mic. Then she stops, smacks her forehead with her hand, and tears up the stairs, returning with Orr's orange earplugs. He squishes them into his ears. Jane grins at him, and Orr grins back. She gets him.

Back at the microphone, Jane cocks her hip the way singers do on MTV, and Mika counts off the beat.

"One, two—one two three four!"

11

SWALLOW
THE WELL

Orr is in his closet warding off the start of a headache. Last night, he managed to decouple the little window from the layers of old paint that stuck it to the sash. Now, the closet is perfect, blissfully cool and comfy since Allison brought him a thick piece of foam from her boyfriend's recording studio. It was being used for sound absorption but makes an excellent bed.

In the other room, voices rise and fall, a gentle chirping like the tree frogs outside his bedroom window at home.

His neck is sore from banging his head in a way that always looked so affected when he saw guitarists do it on MTV but turned out to be a natural movement in the context of actual rock and roll. Maybe that's what's causing the headache. He's so tired, but his body is tense the way it gets when he needs a run. There are simply too many things to process from playing with the Furies. And then there's Plum.

At the thought of her, heat surges through his body, but there's no erection. He hasn't had one since he left home and wonders if it has something to do with his hair being cut.

At the beginning of the summer, constant arousal plagued him. The desire was never directed at or stimulated by another person. When he lay in bed and touched himself, he thought of running through beautiful terrain, places he'd seen in the pages of *National Geographic* or even the woods that bordered their town. Sometimes, the feeling built up as he ran. He'd sprint home and climb into the treehouse, feeling a little resentful afterward about the strength of his body's call. The pleasure was almost a pain, too intense.

When he was younger, he imagined that desire would bring him close to another person, help him find some reason to get to know someone besides Iph and Mom, but the confusing power of it had isolated him further. When he turned twelve, Dad tried to talk with him about girls. Finally, he even tried talking about boys. Orr was silent for both, and Dad seemed happy enough to give up.

But the other day, when he called home from Plum's house, there was something in Dad's voice. Almost . . . satisfaction. Maybe even approval. Are these the kinds of adventures he always wanted for his son? Midnight escapes, van rides with punk bands, a redheaded girl who looks like a painting? Orr thinks yes, they probably are. Even so, Dad didn't even try to imagine a life like this for Orr. All he could think of was a place like Meadowbrook.

Late afternoon sounds drift past Penelope. Kids rolling down the sidewalk on skateboards and scooters. Cars driving by, windows down and radios on. Orr knows he is crying because the shaking hurts his head. He is weeping like a puppet might, limbs floppy, torso jerking up and down with the rhythm of this unidentifiable emotion. Panic rises, but he sends it a song—something in Spanish Mom used to sing.

Whatever this feeling is, it's linked somehow with memory. He shudders to recall his childhood foolishness. So many misunderstandings. Outbursts he couldn't control, rules he could never intuit. The tsunami of stimulation from the other children—their smells and colors and accessories and, worst of all, their energies. It was like living in a vat of primary-colored poster paint. All the edges were hard and the textures unpleasant. But these are old memories, situations already cried over and gone. What's left is this strange . . . sorrow.

Orr weeps for the boy who wanted his mother to stay so badly he overturned her suitcase and ripped her favorite shirt. For the boy who was stolen in sleep, innocent in a way he will never be again. He weeps for Dad, maybe most of all. At heart, Dad is admirable. Like a TV dad, he is wise in so many ways. But what he's done, this level of his betrayal—handing his son over to bigots. Having him kidnapped from his own bed. Orr can't ever forget. Dad found and lost his son in the wrong order. Can it ever be right between them again?

Orr's headache is getting worse. He rubs his temples. Sleep is the thing that will stop it from turning into a migraine. He hums Mom's lullaby to himself.

Ai, ai, ai, ai! Canta y no llores. Sing, don't cry.

12

WHEN ACTING
IS AN ART

ph drops a dime into the violin case of the busker outside Powell's, sorry it isn't more. The temperature inside the bookstore is deliciously just right, not over-air-conditioned like the mall, where Iph always ends up with a summer cold. Just cool enough for the relief-pleasure loop to activate.

And then there are the books. A whole city block of them. Room after room. Floors and floors. Iph and Orr used to fantasize about being locked in Powell's overnight, their version of the brother and sister in *From the Mixed-Up Files of Mrs. Basil E. Frankweiler*. They'd strategize about how they would hide, but more importantly, how they would spend the precious hours between the store's 11 P.M. closing time and when it opened again at 9 A.M.

As always, Iph starts in the Blue Room at the drama shelf. Today, she finds a sweet old edition of *An Actor Prepares*. Stanislavski was the Russian creator of "the Method" and mentor to Lee Strasberg, who passed along this physical/psychological approach to Broadway and Hollywood actors. Iph had learned about Stanislavski because of her favorite version of Marilyn Monroe, all dressed-down and bespectacled in her New York acting student days. When Iph had asked about method acting in her high school drama class, she was told it was old-fashioned and too complex for high schoolers.

So she studied it herself, learning the techniques in secret and trying them out in class. Some were good, basic tune-ups for an essentially physical art. Some of the exercises felt clunky, more academic than useful—like the sense memory technique where you recalled physical details of something in the past to evoke the emotion called for in a scene.

Iph's approach is more visceral, like a dancer's. In dance, the movement and music should be enough to evoke the feeling. Iph feels like the text and relationships should do the same in a play, at least when you're onstage. But before that, during preparation, Stanislavski is very useful. She grabs *An Actor Prepares*, which at this point is a comfort read, and heads to the café for a nice sit and several gallons of free water.

There are ghost prints of Iph's childhood everywhere in this place. On the maps they offer at the big info desk, she can trace her own development from the toddler-size tables in the picture book section of the Rose Room to the middle-reader stacks she haunted and adored until she got the theater bug and became a professional lurker in her special section of the Blue Room.

Ever devoted to his *Redwall* books, Orr had stayed in the Rose Room until last year, when he started making forays into the Gold Room for fantasy and sci-fi. Iph closes her eyes against tears for the millionth time today. She must be premenstrual. What had she been thinking, ripping up Orr's number and flushing it away? If she had it right now, she'd be outside at the pay phone with her second-to-last quarter.

Clearly, Powell's has undone her. She misses Orr. And Mom. Even Dad. But how can she go back? Even with the sweetness of their shared language and familiar bodies and beloved faces, she can't imagine the old life being anything but suffocating after her days in the real world with George.

Her heart beats hard. A sign of dehydration. The tables in the café are all occupied. Tourists with stacks of books and shopping bags. Moms with little kids. Street people drinking the free water like she is—except she can't forget, for her this is a choice. She gulps a final cup of the cold water and heads for the bathroom. It's when she's alone in the stall that she remembers Velma's velvet bag slung over her shoulder.

She reaches inside. Silk chiffon. Her fingers know without looking. She pulls the fabric gently from the bag. A scarf? No, a dress. An antique treasure that surely Velma should have kept. Its provenance is likely late twenties or early thirties, with a painterly scattering of wildflowers on a ballet-pink background. It has short, barely-there sleeves, a low ruffled surplice neckline, and a flowing bias-cut skirt. Iph's chest burns with disappointment. With want. This is exactly the sort of dress she wears in her leading-lady daydreams, but, as always, there is no way it will fit in real life. The best vintage clothes, like so many other things Iph covets, are made for the slight and slender. So sweet of Velma, though. She folds the dress carefully and slips it back in the bag, pees, and heads out of the café for a favorite bench of hers next to the section for small-press poetry and zines. Maybe when Mom comes home, she will give the dress to her.

Before she sits to read, Iph looks for books by Velma Smith and finds nothing. She checks big-press poetry, too, but no luck. She settles on the bench and wishes hard for five bucks. Iced tea and a chocolate croissant sound like heaven. After that, a nap. Iph looks around. The section is empty. She lies back on the bench and closes her eyes.

Pssst.

She sits up too fast. Dizzy. Now that she's cooled off, she feels how hungry she is. She lowers her head between her legs like she does when she's worried she might faint.

Psst.

She looks up. Is someone talking to her? Is she imagining things?

Psst.

The sound seems to be coming from a cylindrical rack of books. There is a sign on the rounder: PORTLAND PRESSES.

A deep-green hardbound book seems to be emitting some sort of glow. It's often like this at a bookstore, where a title seems to call to you from its place on the shelf.

Keep telling yourself that, says a little voice in Iph's head. (It *is* in her head, right?)

She gets up and walks to the rounder. Picks up the shiny green book. The source of light is the book itself—a figure on the cover embossed in gold, a riot grrrl mohawked Artemis with a bow and arrow and a dog at her heels. Basically, the patron saint of George. There is no title.

The first page reads, *Stratagems, Poetry, Plans.*

It's a journal. Each page has faint bronze lines on one side, with a blank page opposite. The perfect thing for a Renaissance artist like George. Poetry on one side, sketches on the other. Iph thinks of the beat-up spiral-bound notebook and the way George's energy flickered when Velma mentioned writing. George deserves a book like this. Maybe even needs it.

Iph fingers the smooth spine. Sniffs the pages—fresh paper and fir trees.

She turns it over. Stamped in the same gold as the front cover are the initials *RCT* with its vine climbing the *R* and *C*. This time, there are little wings sprouting from the top of the *T* in *Rose City Transmutation.*

The price tag reads $9.99. It might as well be a hundred. Iph puts the book back. Rejoins Stanislavski on the bench. The section remains empty, so she risks lying back again and closes her eyes.

What would the book's patient teacher, Tortsov, a stand-in for Stanislavski himself, advise in this situation? If it were an acting exercise, what would Iph do?

She wants to give this journal to George. But how to obtain it? In the theater and out in the world, a character's trajectory is never perfectly smooth. In every play, even every scene, there must be an obstacle. Here, the obstacle is money. How can Iph get some? She relaxes, lets her body melt into the part of Girl Who Wants to Buy a Present for Her Sweetheart.

She lets her mind wander. A song peeks out like a rabbit in the underbrush. A jig played on a fiddle.

Iph sits up. She hides the journal behind another book to prevent anyone else from buying it. All the water she's had in the café has gone right through her, so she stops at the bathroom on the way to the exit. Drying her hands after washing them and splashing water on her face, Iph feels around in the bag, almost like she's worried the dress will be gone. She pulls it out again.

In the larger space of the empty ladies' room, she notices that there is no zipper. It's a wrap dress, an adjustable style that often works for curves. She also remembers how oddly stretchy silk can be when it's cut on the bias. How many times has she succumbed to a beautiful vintage dress's siren song only to crash into the rocks in the dressing room when she realizes she can't get the thing past her neck?

Girding herself, she sets the velvet bag on the metal ledge above the sink, checks under the stalls for feet, then whips off her shirt and slips on the dress. It goes around her, at least. Under the cover of the skirt, she turns her back to the mirror and takes off Nana's baggy shorts and stuffs them into the bag. The skirt has a sewn-in slip of smooth silk that's cool against her legs. Her bra is totally visible in the front, but untying, adjusting, and retying the dress at her waist actually fixes that. She turns slowly, not ready to believe. But, oh! The mirror reveals the truth. Velma is a sorceress.

The dress is perfect. Iph is both voluptuous and somehow light. A girl of summer, sylphlike and young. An ingenue. A leading lady.

Rearranging her shorts and bulky T-shirt so they fit in the velvet shoulder bag, Iph finds a little packet at the bottom. An envelope of rice-paper blotters, a sweet old-fashioned beauty trick. Iph uses one on her face. There is a small sample lipstick, the kind in a fingernail-size pink tube from Avon. Mindy's mom used to sell these and let Mindy and Iph have all the unused samples. Iph puts on the berry-pink shade and pulls her hair up off her neck. This whole situation seems to call for an updo. Of course, there's an ivory hair comb in the bag. And finally, a pair of delicate gold chandelier earrings. Looking at the entire ensemble, Iph smiles. She's always been the kind of actor who comes to life in costume. Her plan is totally going to work.

THE FIDDLE PLAYER HAS moved around the corner from the entrance, following the shade. What now? She remembers her training and takes a beat, leaning against the building a respectable distance away. He finishes the song and takes a break to drink some water.

Iph's intention is to persuade—but maybe she needs a better verb. What she wants is to join forces with this guy.

"Hey," she says. "Thanks for the music."

"Anytime!" He grins. He's actually kind of gorgeous, with dark shoulder-length hair and elegant wrists covered in jade bracelets. "It's been so slow. It's the heat, you know? I keep thinking if I figure out the right song, it'll shake loose. It's like that sometimes—you get a few tips and then the rest rolls in." He plays a few notes of a mournful flamenco.

"I have an idea," Iph says. "And it's totally fine if the answer is no. But I think people may need something unexpected in this ridiculous heat. And to be honest, I could use a little cash."

"Do you sing?" The guy looks excited.

"A little," Iph says. She can carry a tune, but that's not what she has in mind. "I'm more of an actor. And I was thinking a little Shakespeare accompanied by music could be just the thing."

He looks at her, and maybe he thinks she's flirting. Guys usually don't interest her, but this one's exceptionally pretty. Besides, her objective must be achieved! They will join forces.

"I'm Iph," she says.

"Simon." He puts his hand out. Iph takes it, knowing she's won. "What should I play?"

"Anything you want. I'm going to start with Emilia from *Othello*. She has an excellent feminist rant in Act Four in defense of cheating wives. That should stir things up!"

"Sounds good. Just wait one sec, though. The lights are about to turn red, and then all those people will be a captive audience while they wait."

"Pro advice. You got it."

The violin begins a few moments before the light changes, priming people to listen and look. Iph takes a step away from the building into the sun.

For a moment, she is lost. She knows the words to the monologue but has forgotten whatever preparation she did before performing it last year in class. Besides, this isn't a stage, and these strangers haven't signed up to watch a show. She steps back, then realizes. She will join forces with *them*.

Diaphragm engaged, Iph begins.

> *But I do think it is their husbands' faults*
> *If wives do fall.*

People are stopping, smiling. They definitely want to hear what these errant husbands have done.

> *Say that they slack their duties,*
> *And pour our treasures into foreign laps,*
> *Or else break out in peevish jealousies,*
> *Throwing restraint upon us; or say they strike us,*
> *Or scant our former having in despite;*
> *Why, we have galls, and though we have some grace,*
> *Yet have we some revenge.*

A crowd has gathered. The fiddle is underscoring her delivery perfectly, egging her on and adding an edge of humor that is perfect for Iph's objective.

> *Let husbands know*
> *Their wives have sense like them: they see and smell*
> *And have their palates both for sweet and sour,*
> *As husbands have. What is it that they do*
> *When they change us for others? Is it sport?*
> *I think it is: and doth affection breed it?*
> *I think it doth: is't frailty that thus errs?*
> *It is so too: and have not we affections,*
> *Desires for sport, and frailty, as men have?*
> *Then let them use us well: else let them know,*
> *The ills we do, their ills instruct us so.*

Iph concludes to a huge round of applause and a bark. George and Scout! How did they get back from needle exchange so quickly? Several people have dropped money in the open violin case, but the crowd hasn't dispersed. To Simon, she whispers, "Play something romantic."

Looking straight at George and then away, she begins the balcony scene from *Romeo and Juliet*. After swearing that a rose by any other name would be as sweet, she has a quick wonder about her objective here. But then she knows. It is beguilement. She slows for the final lines of the monologue.

> *Romeo, doff thy name*
> *And for that name which is no part of thee*
> *Take all myself.*

From the audience, George answers, striding forward.

> *I take thee at thy word:*
> *Call me but love, and I'll be new baptized;*
> *Henceforth I never will be Romeo.*

The crowd goes crazy as George moves to the open sidewalk and falls to a knee, kissing Iph's hand. She pulls George to stand, and they finish the scene, hands clasped, Scout gazing up at them like a trained dog actor.

Money floods the violin case, and people head around the corner to Powell's thanking and complimenting the trio as they go.

"Here," Simon says, handing Iph a wad of cash. "That was badass. Can I call you sometime? Both of you," he rushes to add, looking sideways at George, who is giving him the evil eye. "I'd love to try that at Saturday Market."

"Can I grab your number instead?" Iph says. "I'm not quite settled right now." Saying that is weird, like Iph is channeling a future self that might have the sort of bohemian situation her answer suggests.

He hands her a slip of paper with his number and packs up his case. "Time for a beer," he says. "Thanks, Iph. And you, too."

"It's George."

"Yeah, man. Thanks."

George turns to Iph with a face like fairy lights.

"Wait here!" Iph says.

"Iph!" George calls. "*Parting is such sweet sorrow.*"

"That's my line," Iph says.

13

COMMUNION

Iph and George leave Powell's at dusk with the crows. They cross the river with a tailwind and hit all the green lights on Hawthorne. Flying past Mount Tabor, they blow a kiss to Pele, goddess of volcanos, because that's what Mount Tabor is—a little volcano in the center of Portland. Orr did a report on it in the third grade.

George stops at an apartment building called the Lindy Sue. It's baby-shit brown and a little run-down with those Brillo-pad evergreen shrubs with the chalky blue poisonous berries people planted by the thousands in the seventies. Dad considers them a scourge. Scout hops down and swaggers up the stairs to the second-floor apartments.

"Scout really can pull off Big Pit when she wants to," George says. "Like, any ne'er-do-well would think twice, even though she's the size of a piece of sushi."

"Don't even say the word *sushi*!" After she bought the journal, they took what was left of their share of the busking money to gorge at the Sushi Train. "And also—who says ne'er-do-well? Tell me that."

George laughs and pulls Iph up the cement staircase with a rusted wrought-iron railing. The night ahead thickens between

them. A whole long, beautiful night. It's cooling off, and Iph wonders if they can spare fifty cents for a bag of ice for the rest of
Cait's gin.

George's cousin Julie opens the door. You can tell she was once
as pretty as George described her, but now her beauty is faded—
no, more than that. It's drained.

"Hey." Julie's voice wobbles like a tape deck in a bumpy car.
She does not look pleased to see Iph.

"Just dropping something off for you," George says. Clean
needles, alcohol wipes, little metal containers Iph thought were
some sort of portable votive candleholders when she looked in
the brown paper bag at the sushi place. Really, they are used for
cooking heroin. And maybe other drugs? Iph isn't sure of the procedure. The thought of it makes her a little faint.

"This is Iph—the girl I told you about. I'm actually wondering
if you'd loan her your bike." Julie believes George is staying with a
girl and her roommates in Northeast Portland. Iph is to play the girl.

Julie smiles and steps aside to let them in. That smile changes
everything. She's clearly related to George, with thick-lashed dark
eyes and long silky hair. Iph recognizes her now from a photo collage in the upstairs hall at Taurus Trucking.

Inside, the apartment smells like garbage. George gathers the
trash, takes it out to the dumpster. Scout is kissing Julie's face on
the sofa, trying to make her laugh. "Come sit down," Julie says,
patting the seat next to her.

"Thanks," Iph says. The living room isn't so bad. Cluttered, but
there was clearly a recent attempt at tidying. There are pictures on
the wall. A black-and-white photo of a wolf. An Ansel Adams print
and a framed drawing of a mermaid that looks a lot like Julie.

"Did George do that?"

"The family genius." Julie smiles, clearly proud of her cousin.
Her nails are painted a deep blue, perfectly done and pretty against
her pale skin. "It's cool of you to let George stay with you," she
says, right as George comes back with the empty trash can.

"Yep," George says. "I'm lucky she isn't sick of me yet."

"George isn't so bad," Iph tells Julie. "Makes a mean can of SpaghettiOs. And this one"—she reaches over to pet Scout—"is a sweet little angel muffin." Scout enjoys baby talk, even though it drives George nuts.

"Yes, she is!" Julie joins in. Her laugh is light and young, even though her smile is a little sad. George says she has a terrible boyfriend.

"How are you?" George perches on the arm of a ripped gray chair, leg jiggling—not comfortable here, Iph realizes, but pretending it's all okay.

"I'm good," Julie says.

"Liar."

"I'm getting there. Like Nana used to say, it's not over till it's over. But when it's over, run." They say this last line together and laugh.

"Seriously, Jules. I worry about you."

"Soon," Julie says. "I'll be done soon." Are they talking about the drugs or the guy? Maybe both.

They're silent for a minute. Iph has kind of missed TV. Julie's watching a nature show for kids, Scout splayed out like a tiny beached hippo in her lap.

"I'm sorry," Julie finally says, meeting George's eyes. For what? Maybe picking the drugs and the guy over George.

"Here," George says, handing Julie a brown bag. "I put in a flyer with some resources, too. Don't be mad."

"George, you know I can't have that around here."

"I'll put it in the pile with the bills," George says. "I know he never looks there."

"Oh, he's interested in my mail these days," Julie says. "Ever since Dale sent me a birthday card. He thinks we're running away together." To Iph she says, "Dale was my first boyfriend."

"Dale was nice. Maybe you should write back," George says.

"Maybe." Julie stands and pulls George in for a hug. Iph sees the love. Thinks of her own family. Their first story together is over. What will the next one be?

14

THE SECOND REVOLUTION

The wind molds Velma's dress to Iph's legs. Julie's purple ten-speed is a perfect fit. She imagines Velma in the dress, pear-shaped and pink-cheeked, riding a bike in some European city, a loaf of bread in the handlebar basket and Pete on a bike ahead.

It's been years since Iph has ridden. What happened to the happy days of flying around the lake on her princess-pink Schwinn, pumping hard to keep up with Dad? When does the past become the past? It can happen slowly, the way her childhood has faded, the way the daylight is fading now. Or it can happen so fast, the way it has for her family.

She pedals harder, lungs so generous in this life. Maybe her asthma lives back in Forest Lake with the unkissed version of herself. Maybe, like in a fairy tale, George's kiss has cured her.

George signals left, and Iph follows, coasting down the hill to Plaid Pantry. The guy there knows George and gives them ice and two candy bars for free.

They pedal lazily now. Apartments give way to houses, snug little sun-faded family homes with sensible cars parked outside and children's toys in the yards. They turn onto Southeast

Division and swoosh up to Taurus Trucking. There is a light on in the basement of the neighbor's house. George shrugs, and they risk it, golden and untouchable.

Nana's apartment is reasonably cool. George gives the bag of ice to Iph. From the kitchen, Iph hears music. Ella Fitzgerald on very low, a splurge of expensive battery use. A song about beaming smiles that could so easily be about George. Iph runs cold water over her wrists and splashes her face and heads to Nana's room.

She carefully takes off Velma's dress and hangs it on a padded satin hanger. There is some rose water in a mister on the dresser. The droplets are deliciously cool on her skin. Riffling through the drawers, she spots a slip she's overlooked. It's tight—probably something from Nana's younger days. The white cotton is moony in the dark room. Iph's curls spill onto her temples and around her forehead. She tamps down the impulse to turn sideways and chide her stomach for not being flat. She won't allow a single despairing look at her ass. She smooths the slip with her hands, the thin fabric soft against her softness.

In the living room, George has bathed early—wet hair, scrubbed face. Their drinks are on the coffee table, and Iph can feel the ghost of Nana and her third and favorite husband on a hot summer night dancing cheek to cheek in the space between the window and dinette.

They sit and rest and drink their drinks. Ella sings on. George stands and offers a hand. Iph accepts. She is shaking; this is different than before. She has seen George's secrets. They slow dance like they're in a movie. Of course, George can actually lead. Iph goes loose, follows the press of the hand on her back, the knees against her knees. They're belly to belly now. Iph instinctively shrinks, always trying to hide this part of her, but George tells her it's okay with a gentle press on her back. They dance until the tape clicks off.

Iph steps away, reaches for her drink. Takes a sip for courage. George does the same. They move together again, no music but breath.

Scout whines. Runs around the room. They pull apart. Laugh. Come back together in their silent dance. George is kissing her neck, pulling down the strap of her slip. There is a sound, and George jumps back as the door that leads from the garage below opens. Iph expects a meth-loaded relative, but it's so much worse than that.

"Sorry," Lorna says. "I still have my key—"

She stops. Sees Iph. And George. Together.

"Well," she says, setting down a duffel bag that surely contains her work outfits, "let the crying begin."

15

SCATTER
HIS BONES

Someone is sobbing. Orr stands up in his closet before he's even awake. He ducks when his scalp connects with one of the brass hooks near the door. Too late. It throbs. He's walking before he sees the blood from his head on his hand. The sounds are getting worse, deep and ugly. Is this how it feels for people to hear him melt down?

There's a light in the kitchen. It bounces off the freshly waxed avocado linoleum and turns the whole room green. Even Jane looks green kneeling there on the floor.

Orr knows he should hide before he knows why. He crouches in the dark hall to see Jane better. She doesn't see him. She's looking at Red.

Jane reaches for Red's belt buckle. He smacks her hand away. "Get off, bitch." His voice is incinerating. Orr looks for the imprint of Jane's charred skeleton in the air. *Dragon man. Evil Wyrm.*

Orr stands and walks in. "Get of here," he says.

"What the hell?"

"Leave!" Orr yells.

Red says something but all Orr hears is Jane. She's back to life, furious. *Furious.* With . . . with him?

"Orr," she says, standing. "Get out. Now."

Red smirks. His face is pale as a pancaked clown's, his red-dyed mohawk an ugly joke.

"Get out, Orr," Red mimics in a high, silly voice.

Orr hates that. Hates mimicking so much. When he and Iph were kids, it was the one thing she could do that made him lose his cool. That and her icy feet.

"Get out now!" Red says again. His stupid cartoon voice is nothing like Jane's.

Orr steps between Red and Jane. "You called her a name. You made her cry. *You* need to go."

Red moves closer. So close, Orr can smell him. He smells like sex, Orr thinks. How does he know this? There's a movie Mom loves, *The Unbearable Lightness of Being*. The wife smells another woman on her cheating husband's face, in his hair. That's what this fight is about.

"You lied to her," Orr says. "You're a cheater."

Red pushes. Orr stands his ground.

Red lunges. Orr's fist shoots out. Red is on him. A fist to his face. Spit in his eyes. Orr's hands balled up, hitting back. Not stopping.

Hands clawing, pulling at his back. Orr shrugs the weight off his shoulders, a heavy cape of fur. His forehead throbs in twin points of pain. He bucks, turns, pushes. Jane! It's Jane. She flies across the kitchen, lands at Mika's feet.

"Get out." Jane is crying. She's not talking to Red, who is doubled over by the refrigerator. She's talking to Orr. She's rubbing her head, cradling her arm.

She is hurt.

Orr has hurt her.

"*Leave*, Orr. And don't come back."

16

MY GRAVEYARD ANTLERS

Orr is Jane on the ground, the buckle on Red's belt, Red's spit running down his own face. He is the word *bitch*. He is his fist against the bone of Red's skull. He is his own skull beating like a heart, and his bone-hard bare feet hitting the sidewalk stride after stride, running away from Penelope.

He flees to the cemetery to hide among the graves.

The moon reserves judgment.

The grass is cool.

His sister is somewhere in the city.

His sister.

His mother.

He lowers to all fours and retches.

He curls in a ball and rocks. Shame has fallen on his house, and now he is houseless.

Dad.

Fucking Dad.

Red.

Orr presses his head to the flat stone marker, its marble as cold as the moon.

He rubs his cheek back and forth on the gravestone as his

breath slows. He bangs his head there, too, but gently. He sits. He aches but can't cry. This pain is not for him, but for Jane. For the wrongness of her groveling before such an inferior person.

Jane on her knees.

The image is attached like a leech, somewhere loathsomely deep inside his body.

He sits up and braces his back against the headstone.

He reaches for something real. Digs his fingers into the grass. Planting himself.

The trees of Lone Fir Cemetery hum.

They hold him in a lattice of root and dirt.

They acknowledge him, a fellow soul, breathing in the summer night.

Animal, boy.

Animal boy.

Animal desire.

Arousal like hunger.

Like the thirst Orr has for the wrong things: pond water and hot tubs, the droplets on the pink tiles of the bathroom at Penelope after one of the Furies has taken a shower.

Like being vegetarian, you can choose the right thing and reject what's wrong. After a while, even the thought of meat will choke you. If he can suppress this want long enough, maybe it will go away.

But Orr is thirsty. And so, so hungry.

Just today, he's eaten half a loaf of bread and the remaining peanut butter at Penelope and slurped a quart of chocolate milk. Even if Jane forgives him, it's wrong to ask for more. He sees that now, what they've all given up to take care of him.

The trees whisper their approval. They know that sometimes a sacrifice is needed.

He reads the gravestone where he's lying: ANNE JEANNE TINGRY-LE COZ. She died in 1885.

"I'm sorry," he tells her and lies with the damp grass under his back, hands folded like hers might have been in her coffin. Unlike

Anne Jeanne, Orr can look up and see the sky. He tries to see it for both of them.

His eyelids grow heavy. He will sleep here with the moon and the dead.

He will send his soul to comfort them instead of dreaming.

He will wake in the morning and call his father.

He will go home.

17

THE OPERA STUDIO

"Truth or dare?" Lorna calls from the kitchen.

"I'm not playing," George says.

Lorna comes back into the living room with two gin and tonics. She sets them on the table and goes back for the third. How she's seized power by serving them is something Iph is going to have to study later. Right now, she's still stuck in the perfection of half an hour ago, no Lorna, slow dancing with George. At least the genius of Stanislavski's sense memory technique is finally obvious. It's all about having good enough physical memories. The feel of George's hand on her back, the shiver of hip against hip—that could fuel an extended run on Broadway with even a lukewarm leading man.

Lorna settles on the floor on the other side of the coffee table with Scout in her lap. She is such a slut. Not Lorna! Iph is a feminist, even in jealousy. It's Scout who spreads herself around like peanut butter on crackers. Not that there's anything wrong with that. Certainly some people would say Iph is a slut. She's known George for—how many days now? If Lorna hadn't come in, who knows what they'd be doing?

"How about you, Iph? Truth or dare?" Lorna's face is freshly scrubbed, and she's wearing a white baby tee, pink shorts, the gold shoes, and a ponytail. She looks like a fourteen-year-old runway model.

"Truth." It's what Iph always says—the only way to survive this game, which should rightly be called Sex & Misdemeanors.

"Hmmm." Lorna is pretending to think. It's true: when you're that pretty, you don't have to be able to act.

Me-ow, Iph thinks. *So much for my inner feminist.*

"Lorna, no," George says. "Come on. Don't be like this."

"I'm playing. Trying to, you know, make the moment less awkward. But I can go now." She stands. Iph would bet her last ten bucks from busking that Lorna is bluffing. "Sorry for the interruption." Lorna says *interruption* like it's the title of a porno.

"I didn't say you had to go," George says. "I'm just not in the mood for games."

Go, Iph thinks. *Go, go, go!*

Lorna's face slides from femme fatale straight into girl next door. Maybe she can act after all. "You're right. I'm sorry. I barged in. I came to talk, but if it's a bad time . . ."

Is she being honest or manipulative? And when is she going to leave? Not that they'll ever get the mood back. One look at George is all Iph needs to see that.

"We can talk . . . we'll go have one cigarette, okay?"

Iph's body fills with poisonous gas. She will expel it and kill them all. Except, of course, because of the patriarchy and her own passive personality, she won't kill anyone. She will swallow it. Swallow the poison, her own tongue, until her stomach balloons. Her eye whites will turn saffron, and her skin will follow. And no, she doesn't think this is overdramatic.

Iph stands. "Don't leave on my account," she says. "I'm going to bed."

"Iph!" George stands, too, as if suddenly remembering she's there.

Iph wills her face to be still. Wills her body to the bedroom. Except she isn't going. Her face is contorting. Her eyes sting.

NO!

No no no no no no no.

She's crying.

In front of George. In front of *Lorna.*

"Oh my god!" Lorna says. Yet again, her face is different. This one seems closer to the real girl. "I'm such a dick. Wouldn't you know? It was me, not George! I'm the one who made you cry."

"Not just you," George says, grabbing Iph's hand and pulling her back to the sofa. Everyone breathes and drinks and listens to the bus clacking along outside.

"Things have been so weird since that night I met you at the movies," Lorna finally says. "It almost feels like it's the shoes. I keep wanting to go to the train station to visit my mom in Tacoma, except we're not speaking. I left work early tonight and started walking to the opposite side of Burnside. I didn't even know where I was going. I figured it out when I got off the bus and starting walking toward Division. And here"—she hands George a key—"I should have left it when I bailed."

George takes it. More silence. Iph sniffs. There's Kleenex in a mother-of-pearl tissue holder that is one of Iph's favorite things in Nana's house. It's such a sweetness, to make this thing used for colds and crying a pretty part of the decor. She takes a tissue and blows her nose, not worrying herself about dainty Lorna.

"I kept thinking about you," Lorna is saying. Wait—she's talking to Iph. "How nice you were. How decent. I could tell how much you liked Georgie. You could have done ten different things besides try to get me to go down and patch it up. But you didn't."

"If you and George want to be together, that's what you should do," Iph says. "I'm going home soon anyway."

"You are?" George's eyes are wide.

"Orr called my dad. He's fine."

"So wait, you're leaving, then?"

"I can leave now. Or I can stay. My dad doesn't care what I do." That's not quite true, but Iph can't stop her own pity party. There's one way to be sure of the outcome here, and that's to beat them to the punch. She folds her arms and refuses to look at either of them.

"All right, that's it." Lorna is surprisingly versatile. In this mode, she could easily be cast as the older sister or a young mom. "George, come on. You're totally over me and into Iph, right? Be honest! I can take it."

George's open mouth is classic. It's weird how responses considered cliché onstage feel natural in real life. "You want to talk about this now?"

"Yes," Lorna says. "I think it's only fair."

"Fair to who?" Iph is surprised to hear herself asking.

"To you," Lorna says to Iph, wrinkling her adorable nose like that's the obvious answer. "I mean, I came in drama-ready. You were an innocent bystander."

"I guess some things never change." It could have been an insult, but George says it like it's the opposite. These two have some serious history.

Lorna smiles for real, and of course she has dimples. "So, out with it, George. Just how over me are you?"

George laughs outright. Iph finds herself . . . smiling. The whole thing is oddly not embarrassing. Just interesting. Her kingdom for a notepad. Or a video camera.

"Last week, it was hovering at fifty percent. But the last few days . . . I have to admit, it's closer to ninety. Maybe eighty-five. I might always love you a little, okay? But I see how I put a lot on you. We didn't even know each other that well. We never really talked that much."

"Oh my god, you guys. I don't need to hear about your sex life." Iph can't believe she's joking now, but every time she tries to buy into the drama of this love triangle, something else happens instead.

Lorna is laughing. George is laughing, red. Iph is laughing so hard she sneezes. Lora hands her another tissue.

They all reach for their gins and sip on cue.

"So, Lorna," Iph says. "Truth or dare?"

18

IF I WERE
TO GO BACK

Orr can't fall asleep in the graveyard. The dead are buried too deep to be any company, and the moon has traveled somewhere behind the trees. He's waited as long as he can for something to happen, an *X-Files*–worthy brush with aliens or the occult, but there is only a pair of fat raccoons.

Orr has been thinking about the baby squirrel Mom found last year. They first saw it sitting preternaturally still on the driveway down to their house. Mom stopped the car and jumped out, knelt, held out her hand. "I don't know how," Mom had said, "but I knew she'd trust me."

They called the Audubon Society, but the person on the phone decided that because it was born so late in the season, it must be a red squirrel, not native, and therefore ineligible for rescue.

Undaunted, Mom called the library information line, where the librarians would look things up for you on their computer. A squirrel rescue was found. The lady there knew exactly what to do. She held out her cupped hand and took the little thing, stroking it with her finger until it stretched with pleasure. "This is no red squirrel," she said. "This is a Douglas pine squirrel. It has every right to be here in Oregon. *Every right!*"

They'd all loved that so much. Even Dad. Every once in a while, one of them would say it out of nowhere. "This is a Douglas pine squirrel! It has every right to be in Oregon. *Every right!*"

Would they ever say it again?

That squirrel lady was so much like Jane, so calm and assured and easy to relax around. But unlike that little squirrel, Orr is no orphan, and his right to be at Penelope is tenuous at best. Even though he was trying to protect Jane, there's something off about what happened. In what he did. He wishes he could figure out what.

Mom always says love is complicated—usually when he bugs her for stories about her family. There is something bad in Mom's past, a love there she doesn't think she should feel. And a terrible, destroying hurt. She cries sometimes, and Dad holds her. Once, Orr saw her curled up in Dad's lap like she was child. He rocked her back and forth the way he used to with Orr before the meltdowns and freak-outs hollowed out the love between them.

That's what Jane needs. Someone who loves her the way Dad loves Mom. But Orr can't make her hold out for that. Maybe it's something she needs to figure out for herself.

And then there is the violence. Orr knows he needs to think about that. Once is an anomaly. Now there is a pattern.

The worst was the thing that happened when Mom was packing. The way he pushed her suitcase off the bed. The way the green silk earring box flew out and hit her below the eye. Orr never meant to hurt her, but the box left a mark. Orr saw it when she came to say goodbye.

Tonight, it was Jane he hurt, even if he hadn't meant to. But Red—he'd meant to hurt him. Orr had never used his fists that way before, not on a person. It was a little like a meltdown, a sort of fugue state. The worst part is that Orr liked it—being stronger than Red. Making him fall. Defeating him.

Orr gets up and brushes off his butt. Why his bare feet aren't killing him is a mystery, but they feel normal. Portland has toughened them.

It's close to sunrise, and he knows where to go. He stretches and begins a slow trot. Out of the corner of his eye, a white flash of something. A ghost? No, ghosts probably aren't so cliché. He runs again, a little faster.

Again, a flash. He stops. Nothing. Starts. Stops.

Finally, he sees them. A slinky white dog, tall as a wolfhound with the legs of a gazelle, and a smaller pure-white wolf dog about the size of Orr's friend, the lady coyote, running together on the far side of the graveyard. Orr crouches. They bow. Orr bows back. They charge, stopping a few feet away from him, tails wagging.

The big one approaches first, sniffing Orr in an almost maternal way. Her cool nose on his forehead erases the last of the throbbing headache. The smaller dog, her protégé by the look of things, bounds over, unable to wait any longer. This one must still be a pup. Orr romps with him in the grass, then races the ghost dogs out of the cemetery. They pace him to the exit and trot alongside as he heads down Stark Street toward Plum's house. At Southeast 30th, they part ways. Orr's trot falters. He's tired now. And very hungry.

Two blocks away, he tastes Plum on the air—dandelion greens, hot sauce, and honey. He also smells a cigarette. Closer, he sees the red glow on Plum's porch.

It's Jane, sitting on the front steps.

He slows to a walk. Stands on the sidewalk—looking respectful, he hopes. He waits for her to say something first.

"Orr." Jane's face is all worry and mascara. "I'm so sorry."

"I'm sorry," he says. "I've never done that before. Never hit anyone."

"Whoa," Jane says. "You cleaned Red's clock, babe. He'll certainly think twice before pissing off the next skinny fifteen-year-old."

Orr is shaking, so relieved it tells him how scared he was. Jane pats the step beside her. He sits, close but not too close.

"Jane," he says, "you deserve someone good."

Jane closes her eyes. "Red used to be different."

"Different how?"

Jane cocks her head and looks at Orr. "I'm trying to think." She laughs. "Actually, he was drunk then, too. We met in a train yard. He showed me how to ride the rails."

"Like a Woody Guthrie song?" This is stuff Dad likes, Depression-era old-timey freight-riding troubadour stuff. That and Sinatra.

"More like don't get killed, don't get raped. Traveling with a guy was smart."

"Red doesn't seem smart, Jane." Orr lets a twinkle show in his eyes so Jane knows he's teasing her.

"Nope. That hasn't changed, that's for sure." She sucks on her cigarette and blows some feeling out with the smoke. Sitting up straighter, she says, "If I'm honest, nothing about him has. He wasn't different back then. I was. Now he's just a bad habit. One I gotta break."

"I have those, too. I think that's why my dad wanted to send me somewhere."

"Some people think you need to break to heal. Not me, man. I think that's bullshit. I think joy is what heals you."

"Me, too," Orr says. "You helped me so much, Jane. I wanted to help you back."

"Oh, you did!" Jane says. "Tonight was the last straw, kid. Mika and Allison told me I'm the one getting kicked out if I let Red in again. They're making me pay to change the locks."

"I don't want them to kick you out!"

"No—babe. They're messing with me. We had a good talk. Those girls, the band, it's the first time I've felt part of something real. I got kinda messed up after Plum's mom died. She meant a lot to me."

The sky is turning to roses. A snore sounds from somewhere on the porch. Orr stands and pads up the stairs toward it.

Plum is lying across the porch swing like a drooping poppy in a yellow nightgown, her hair in a pile on the blue floor. She opens her eyes.

"I told Jane," she says. "I knew you'd come here."

"Are you playing a painting again?"

Plum stretches, laughs. "No, crazy man cub. I'm sleeping."

"If I'm the man cub," Orr says, loving the *Jungle Book* reference, "then which one are you?"

"Me?" Plum thinks. "Definitely Kaa," she hisses, making her eyes snakelike.

"You're not Kaa." Orr is thinking about the girl at the end of the Disney version. The beauty who lures Mowgli to the village.

"I'm not that girl." Apparently Plum is reading his mind again. "I'm not any of them. Just a girl cub you met in the jungle."

"Hey," Jane says, coming up onto the porch. "Does the Paradox Café still open at six? I'd roll a nun for some vegan biscuits and gravy about now."

"I'm pretty sure," Plum says. "Maybe you should go see if my dad's up. Just yell from the bottom of the stairs. My goal is getting him out of the house at least three times a week. Remind him of the cornmeal pancakes."

Jane leaves and Orr sits next to Plum on the porch swing.

"I'm going home after tomorrow night," he says. "But it's not far—will you ever visit me?"

"I might." Plum says it like it's a yes.

The sky is hibiscus tea and honey now. The wisteria climbing the purple trim on the lizard-green house stretches all the way to the porch roof.

"You did look like a painting when you were asleep, you know," Orr tells her. "It's called *Flaming June*. It's in one of my dad's art history books. There's a beautiful redhaired lady sleeping in a long orange dress sort of half sitting, half lying down with her hair flowing down to the floor."

"Orr?" Plum says like she's going to laugh. "Are you doing it again?"

"Doing what?"

"Calling me beautiful."

"Yes," Orr says. "I am."

19

FIRST EXPERIENCE
AS A DIRECTOR

"**D**are," Lorna says.

Iph takes her time. Something is happening here—or maybe something needs to happen. There's a space for change. She thinks about her drama teacher's litany: *Make the most dramatic choice.*

"I dare you," Iph says, "to show us your favorite move from work."

George's mouth hangs open again. Mission accomplished.

The one virtue of this stupid game is that it's good for airing certain truths. Iph shouldn't hate it so much. It was Truth or Dare that helped her realize she liked girls when it devolved, as it always did, into a directive brand of spin the bottle.

Lorna laughs. "I mean, we don't have a pole, so—"

"You said you were no good at pole tricks." George's tone is petulant, trying for a fight.

"Practice makes perfect, right?" Iph says. Her light tone is both a dare and a rescue. She's seen Mom remind people of their manners this way before. Like, *Are you going to make this situation worse with your bad behavior? Or are you going to save face and grab this rope and pretend you were joking?*

"Well, in that case, I guess Lorna's probably going to win an award, considering she spends all her time at that disgusting place." Clearly, no. The rope has been bypassed, and George is going full-on jealous ex. So much for that eighty-five to ninety percent. George is not over Lorna at all.

"Wow," Iph says. "That was rude."

"I'll say." The calm in Lorna's voice belies her tense posture, the way a cat is silent before it pounces and rips your face off.

Iph giggles, not because it's funny, but because she's nervous, and also because it reminds her of four-year-old Orr's confusion about the term *spitting mad*. He thought it meant that instead of yelling, a person would literally act like a cat to show displeasure—growling, spitting, arching their back. The family had been pretty confused when he whipped that out to protest bedtime.

"Is this funny to you?" George asks Iph.

"No! No, not at all. I'm remembering this thing from when my brother was little. He didn't get euphemistic language—"

"What does that mean?" Lorna asks.

Ugh. The game is doing its evil. With one word, she's exposed her life in a house full of books with a family who enjoys Scrabble tournaments and the *New York Times* crossword puzzle every Sunday. Her vocabulary was something she used to get teased about. Other kids thought she was being stuck-up when she used archaic words from the old-fashioned books she preferred. She felt powerless then. Later, when Mom helped someone in the store who didn't speak English or a classmate couldn't make heads or tails of Shakespeare, she realized language was a route to power. And now she's made Lorna feel stupid.

"It just means, like, a metaphor. Like, right now, you look spitting mad. My brother used to take stuff like that literally—he really expected people to spit."

"I can't make any promises," Lorna says with a look Iph can't decode.

George looks down. Everything is off.

"Well," Lorna says, getting up. "Here you go."

"You don't have to." George says it like a plea.

Lorna takes a chair from the dinette and places it in the center of the small living room. The moon is her spotlight. Her hair glows with it. She walks deliberately to the tape deck, takes out the Ella Fitzgerald, and pops in another cassette in its place. It's Billie Holiday. "Ain't Nobody's Business." *Ha!* After being so judgy about Lorna's business, it's totally the song George deserves.

Lorna stalks a circle around the chair, her hand running along its back like it's the jacket of a man in a three-piece suit. She flips her hair, arches into a spin, and sits, crossing her legs into a pose worthy of a fifties pinup.

"Wow!" Iph says. The move is very Bob Fosse, something straight out of *Cabaret*.

"Why do you wanna do that?" George says. "For those gross perverts?"

"They're not all like that."

"So you actually like the table dances, Lorna?"

"We've all done things we don't love to get by," Lorna says. "Including both of us."

George folds up like a broken-down cardboard box. Iph's glasses are acting up. She takes them off, wipes them. Back on, it's clearer—George isn't breaking down, but squaring up to fight.

Lorna is sitting in her chair, holding her pose, face tight. There is something so familiar about her locked-together knees, the way her spirit seems to have left her body. And then Iph sees it. Lorna is like Mom. The pieces click into place like a Rubik's Cube she's been trying to solve her entire life.

This is why Mom gives money to homeless kids every chance she gets, making sure to get cash from the ATM in Forest Lake before they drive into the city. This is why she knows to say *sex worker* instead of *prostitute* or *whore*. Why she's always made sure her kids knew not to judge. Mom was that kid, once. On the street, alone. Doing what she had to in order to survive. Like Lorna. Like George.

Iph gathers her mother's secret life into her body like a treasure.

She will hold it there and never say a single word unless Mom wants to talk. But she's right. She knows it. And even though there's nothing she can do for teenage runaway Mom, maybe it's enough to help these two.

"Can I ask something? What are you guys really fighting about?"

George glares at Iph. "Why did you ask her to do that?"

"I'll tell you what we're fighting about," Lorna says. She walks over to the sofa and sits, owning the room. She must make so much money at the strip club. "George is judging me. We can't all rise to your level of moral perfection, okay?"

"What are you talking about? I'm not perfect." George's eyes close, and Iph sees how perfect George wants to be. How perfection is George's way of surviving, no better or worse than living as Lorna does, this girl equivalent of a Siamese cat.

"I'm not like you." Lorna hugs her knees to her chest. "I don't like urban camping. I don't find it charming or fun. I don't like having to sneak around and worry all the time. You know what happened to me on the street. You're the one who picked up the pieces. But I have an apartment now, George. Did you even wonder where I was staying?"

"I assumed with some guy."

Lorna heaves a pillow at George and misses. "Go to hell." She takes a breath. "After living here, I needed space. I live by myself, you self-righteous little pill."

Scout whines into the silence. Wags hopefully at George and Lorna and Iph. Iph pulls her close and comforts her.

"What's your apartment like?" Iph asks. "Is it nice?"

"It's just a dinky studio in one of those old buildings near the library."

"One of the ones from the twenties? With those medallion things on the roofline?"

"Kind of," Lorna says. "I think it might be older than that. The kitchen and bathroom have that black-and-white tile, like a checkerboard. And there's these ledge things over all the windows and doors. There's no reason for them—they're just pretty. I hung Christmas lights on them."

"Crown molding," Iph says. To Lorna's raised eyebrow, she says, "My dad's an architect."

"My bed is right under the windows—what are they called? When three windows meet and are, like, pushed out from the front of the building?"

"Huh. I don't know. Picture windows? That doesn't sound right."

"No, I think that's it. Anyway, they're super tall, so I bought these long white lace curtains at Fred Meyer, and it's so pretty with the wind blowing in. I love to just lie there with windows open. I feel like a girl in a book."

"I'd love an apartment like that."

"I mean, it's nothing special," Lorna says. Iph knows this need to downplay; if you shine too much, the gods might get jealous and take it all away. "But I've got my routine—go to work, come home. Make food. I actually cook! I have a wok. I drink tea at night. There's this herbal tea that's supposed to be relaxing. With the bear on the front?"

"Sleepytime," Iph says.

"Yes! I make that and run a bath. I put on music. I thought I'd get a TV right away, but I love it without. Life at Taurus Trucking taught me to entertain myself." She looks at George, who is staring down at the floor. "I'm starting at PCC in the fall. I took all the placement tests and applied for financial aid."

"That's amazing," George says, finally looking at Lorna. "I want you to have all that. I just wish you didn't have to do this to get it."

"Maybe I'm not supposed to admit this, but I like my job." Lorna sits up straighter. "I like performing. I love the other dancers. Even the mean ones. The unstable cuckoo ones are kind of my favorite. I've made friends. I feel . . . at home there."

"Maybe that's not healthy, Lorna. Did you ever think about that?" George's voice is low, already defeated.

"I'm not working at another restaurant, George. I've had enough grease in my hair to last a lifetime. Enough minimum wage. And what about all the times I've had to do stuff for free? Take a number I don't want, smile on the street so I don't get harassed. It feels good to get paid. At least at the club, there's a bouncer. There are rules. I leave with what I used to make in a week in one night. Tell me that isn't better."

"Those guys don't deserve you."

Lorna rolls her eyes. To Iph she says, "Ever wonder what a Gemini with a Taurus moon *and* a Taurus rising looks like? Here it is!"

"George?" Iph touches her foot to George's. Even with all this drama, there's still a little spark. "Have you thought about what Lorna deserves? She sounds happy."

"I am." Lorna gets up and heads for the gin in the kitchen. She brings back the bottle and sits back down on her chair.

They're all quiet. Scout makes the rounds to each of their laps in turn as they finish off the gin.

"So," Lorna says. "Now you, Iph. Truth or dare?"

"Dare," Iph says like a crazy person.

"Ha!" Lorna sits back in her chair like she's not onstage but in an audience. "Excellent choice."

There is a pause, but Iph knows what Lorna's going to say.

"I dare you," she says, "to do what you were doing five minutes before I barged in here."

TIME STOPS AS IT always does when the game turns transgressive. Iph knows how this plays out—she and George kiss. Then Lorna and George. And finally, Lorna and Iph. Maybe Lorna's been wanting to do that since she first saw Iph at the Roan Inish theater. Maybe Iph thought about it then, too, or earlier, when she first saw the painting. Maybe George wants this, although that's the least likely possibility. It will end with someone crying, Iph or Lorna. Odds are it will be Iph, sitting there, waiting for George and Lorna to stop, for the game to continue. But it won't, and Iph will run off like she did at the hotel with Dad.

"No," Iph says. "We have to stop."

"What? I did your dare."

"Lorna. You just want to compare our chemistry to yours. That's still us competing for George. And I'm probably going to lose. But either way, this is beneath us."

Lorna's face is blank for a second, but she finds her footing quickly. "Oh, I'm so sorry, do they not play truth or dare in the West Hills?"

"Lorna," Iph says, "do you want George back?"

The room is silent and still, down to Scout. "Does it even matter?"

Now George breathes out, an exhale that's almost a whinny. On the back of the bike, Iph enjoyed thinking about how like a centaur George was. Lorna and George finally lock eyes. Iph's chest aches as she watches. What are they acting out, and why?

It's not simple teenage relationship drama; that much she knows for sure. It's deeper, about their parents and their child-hoods and the things they've seen too young. These two will do this over and over again, Iph realizes, until they've hurt each other so badly there's nothing left to salvage. Something has to change.

"I dare you both," Iph says, "to do exactly what I say right now."

Lorna laughs. "Now who's the boss?" she asks Scout.

"Fine," George says. "But I'm drinking the rest of my gin first."

"No more gin," Iph says. "Stand up, both of you."

Lorna looks surprised but does it. George obeys only when Iph holds out her hand.

"Close your eyes."

First, Iph moves George a little closer to Lorna. Then she moves Lorna into George, as close as Iph was an hour before. Their hip bones collide. Iph adjusts Lorna until they fit together. They stand like that, arms at their sides. "I want you to be aware of your body right now," Iph says. "Focus on your breath, your heartbeat."

She turns on the tape. She places George's hand on the small of Lorna's back and Lorna's on George's shoulder. "Listen to the music. Open your senses wide. What do you smell? Do you still

taste the gin? How do your legs feel? Is there tension in your face?"
She waits, watching them both pretend to follow her instructions
at first, then fall into the tasks. "Breathe," she reminds them. She
fits Lorna's free hand into George's. "Now dance."

The two sway and stumble. Feet are an issue. And shoulders.
And knees. "Lorna, lean your head on George's shoulder and take
a deep breath. What's the first thing you notice?"

"Rose soap," Lorna says. "George washed up for you."

"What else?"

"The breeze on my neck feels good."

"And?"

Lorna stops swaying. "I feel . . . sad."

"How about you, George?"

"For the last three months, this was all I wanted," George says,
eyes open and on Iph. "But now it feels weird. I'm worried about
you."

"George? I don't want to know how you feel about your
breakup with Lorna or anything about me. I want you to tell me
how you feel right now, in this moment. And close your eyes!"

After a beat or two, George says, "I'm sad, too."

Iph lets them dance for a while. "Spin her," she says. And,
"Don't forget to breathe."

The two of them dance to the end of "My Man" and through
"Stormy Weather," gliding around the living room gracefully
now, eyes open. The song changes to "Don't Get Around Much
Anymore," and they're looking at each other once in a while,
smiling now. If this were a play, Iph would start the scene here:
they're both so present, in sync with each other, simultaneously
happy and sad. They stop. Step back a foot, no longer touching.

"We're done, aren't we?" says George.

"Yeah," Lorna says. "We are."

They hug as Scout dances around their feet, and then they stop
and open their circle to Iph. She hesitates.

"We're friends now," Lorna says. "All of us. Promise me,
you guys. I don't have too many people I can be real with. I

think that's why I was so scared to lose George. Why I couldn't let go."

George nods. "You know that stuff you said when we had that fight on Hawthorne?"

"I said a lot of things."

"Well, at least one of them was true. It's sort of a life mission of mine—to be someone's person. Their protector."

"I said that?"

"You said I loved being in love," George says.

"That's what she told me in the bathroom at the movie theater," Iph says, stepping back.

Lorna laughs and plops to the floor, pulling them both down with her. They're in a circle now, cross-legged, knee to knee.

"Is that what it is with us?" Iph asks George. "A rescue drama? The prince and the maiden?"

"Iph." George gives her a look she doesn't understand. "Let's talk about this later."

"What do you mean, later?" She knows she's whining, but it doesn't stop her.

George laughs. "How old are you right now?"

"I feel about thirteen," Lorna says. "Also, forty-five."

"I meant Iph," George says.

"Huh," Iph says to Lorna. "That's what I thought when I first saw you. You have a spooky old-young thing going on."

"I do," Lorna says. "But tonight, dancing with George, I felt my age. Like the age I was at that very second. It was wild."

"That's presence," Iph says. "It's what actors do. You're good at it. I think you could act if you wanted."

"You think?"

"Um, yeah," George says. "But Iph? So can you. You're so smart and shiny." George presses a shoulder into Iph's.

"So is it later now?" Iph is teasing, but she's also human. The director in her has left the building and all she wants to know is if George still likes her.

"What I am," George says, dark eyes wide, *"and what I would,*

are as secret as maidenhead; to your ears, divinity, to any other's, profa-
nation."

Iph's whole body contracts. She sees George seeing it, lips parting into a pretty *O*.

"That's what?" Lorna says. "Shakespeare again?"

"Ask Iph," George says.

"I don't know what it's from." Iph wonders if she's blushing.

"Twelfth Night," George says.

"All I know is *Romeo and Juliet*," Lorna says. "And you're perfect for that. Noble family, super smart. All bright-eyed and pretty."

"You really think so?" It's like Iph is ten years old, maybe eleven, at an epic sleepover.

Lorna looks at Iph like she's a problem that needs solving. "Are you still in high school?"

"I'll be a senior," Iph says.

"Well, I'm sure you're headed off to college or Broadway or whatever after that, but if you ever needed the cash, you would clean up at my club."

"Really?"

"Oh my god, yes, and I'm not even into girly-girls. Plus, say all you want about the strip club, but high school is seriously toxic." Lorna winks at her.

"Hey!" George says. "Don't put that idea in her head."

"Don't worry," Lorna says. "She's not going to take me up on it. No offense, Iph, but I have the feeling girls like you do internships and summer jobs abroad."

"None taken," Iph says, thinking about Mom and the daughter Lorna might someday have. About money and healing and love.

THE SKY IS ITS earliest-morning pale, and the neighborhood is hushed. Not a car or person in sight. They walk in a hip-and-shoulder-bumping mass toward Clinton Street and end up at Piccolo Park. Scout races off-leash in the cool grass as George easily crosses the monkey bars. They converge at the swings, three in a row with Iph in the middle, pumping in unison into the rosy sky.

"When does Cup and Saucer open?" Lorna calls from her swing.

"We're broke," George says. "We blew our busking money on sushi and presents."

"It's on me, dummy," Lorna calls.

"I don't want your ill-gotten gains, woman," George says.

"Oh, George," Lorna says. "I made a stupid amount of money last night. Let me spend it on you two."

"Do they have French toast?" Iph's mouth is already watering.

"Yes," Lorna says. "It's excellent."

"Let's jump off together," Iph says. "On three!"

They grab hands, and together, they fly into the dew-dropped summer morning.

Lorna's hand slips from Iph's, but Iph and George land together, feet on the tan bark, hands clasped.

20

THE CHERRY
ORCHARD

Iph rubs the crust from her eyes and stretches out on the sofa. She's been curled tight into herself, too crashed to realize she needed a blanket. The apartment is chilly, and the sky is pinking. Dusk or dawn?

She sits up. George is on the floor, snoring lightly. Kicked-off covers reveal curves of breast and hip that are usually hidden. Mink lashes skim delicate cheekbones. Scout is cuddled at George's feet.

After breakfast with Lorna, on their own again on the walk back to Taurus Trucking, George told Iph Nana's story—how her father came to Oregon to work the railroads and how her grandmother had been a picture bride from Japan. When Nana was fifteen, her family was uprooted and sent to a Japanese American internment camp in Minidoka, Idaho. George stopped at that part—stood still, eyes down. "She told me before she died. From what she said, it was like a prison. Growing up, my mom barely knew about it. Like, she knew it happened, but not anything else. My great-aunts don't talk about it, either. Like they're ashamed. Like it was their fault."

"I never heard about it in school," Iph said. "I only know because of my parents."

"I got like one paragraph in middle school," George said. "I don't know why, but I didn't connect it with my own family."

"What happened after the war?"

"She stayed in Idaho a while, got married to a louse at seventeen who left her after two years, then a nice but boring guy who died six months later. After that, she swore off husbands and became a truck mechanic—the one woman in her trade-school class. That was how she met her true love. She helped him fix a stubborn carburetor."

George said Nana wore orange lipstick with her grease-covered overalls and got a manicure every Friday after work, even though it was usually wrecked by Monday night. Nana's third husband, George's grandpa, was also called George. Nana and Grandpa George had George's mom, an only child. There was a typical George-style silence at this part. "My mom won't tell me who my dad is. She married my stepdad when I was three. Her drinking got bad when he deployed. In rehab, she found Jesus. Met husband number two. And suddenly, it was clear who my dad must have been."

They'd gotten home by that point and were in the bathroom together, brushing their teeth. How had that become a thing? "Wait, who's your dad?"

"Well, if I'm as evil and degenerate as my mom seems to believe, it can only be one man . . . "

"Ah, Satan! I see." They laughed the way you laugh about abortion protesters and Republicans who think condoms in schools make kids into sex fiends. But George didn't bother to hide the hurt there, the bitterness.

Now Iph has to pee. She tiptoes around George and peeks out the window—it's evening, not morning. And there is an ugly brown pickup pulling into the Taurus Trucking parking lot.

"George!"

George bolts up and is at the window in an instant. Car doors slam shut. Feet pound up the unused back stairs.

George pulls jeans and a T-shirt over heart-printed boxers. Voices bounce up through the open windows. A woman's. A man's. Too late, Iph remembers that she, too, should get dressed, but the door is opening. She grabs the afghan from the floor.

"Georgina Marie!" The woman is shorter than George and almost as pretty, with dark bobbed hair and a pink cardigan—total PTA president. Or based on what George said last night, the church-lady equivalent.

The man is wearing cowboy boots, a baseball cap, and a gross mustache. Iph is certain there is a combed-over bald spot under the Oakland Raiders cap and a Bush-Quayle sticker on his over-compensatingly large truck.

"What are you doing here?" George says. Scout is on edge, doing her big-pit routine.

The man notices Iph. George's mom turns to her a split second after. When you ask people what the most important element of a play is, most will say writing or acting. Yes, those are essential. The set, too. But more than all of this, Iph has always been a firm believer in the power of costume.

If she were to set a scene where she wanted to show two worlds colliding in the most disturbing way, she would have dressed George's mom and stepdad exactly the way they are dressed and put herself, the surprise element, in the thin white slip that is so much more transparent in daylight than it was in last night's dark apartment. She would have styled her curls into a wanton mess. Even Iph's bare feet somehow scream *lesbian sex*—even though she and George only talked before falling asleep that morning in separate nests.

"Hi," Iph says, channeling one of her favorite characters from the dated collection of plays on her drama teacher's bookshelf—the free-spirited hippie Jill from the sixties dramedy *Butterflies Are Free*. She bats her eyes and smiles.

George shoots her a look. Panic retreats. Understanding dawns. This is their show. They can direct it. Iph has George's back.

"Georgina, did you break into Nana's apartment?"

"It's *my* apartment, Brenda. Remember the will?" George's tone is even. So far so good.

"That will is still being contested," George's mom says.

The man is leaning in the doorjamb with his armpit exposed. It's a pose that says *I'm releasing my stink on all of you, and there's nothing you can do about it.* "Your nana was a little senile there at the end," he says.

"No, Gary. She wasn't. And I'd appreciate it if you'd both leave."

"So you can party all night in poor Nana's house doing God knows what?" George's mom stares at the empty gin bottle like she might set it on fire with her eyes.

"Brenda," George says, "that's pretty rich coming from you. But whatever. You still need to go."

The husband pushes past Brenda and George with a leave-the-women-to-fight-it-out look and heads purposefully toward the door leading down to the garage.

"What do you think you're doing?" Scout's accompanying growl tells Iph all she needs to know about how pissed George is.

The man doesn't answer but goes on his way.

"Why are you here?" All of George's untold stories are distilled in the question that is actually a warning.

Brenda tucks her hair behind her ears and shifts in her pristine white mules. "Bob wanted to borrow a few tools from downstairs, is all. To work on the truck."

"Did he lose his job again?" George's voice is a notch softer.

Iph knows from growing up with her dad that tools are worth a lot of money and easy to sell secondhand.

Brenda picks up the gin bottle from the coffee table. Sets it down again. "I can't believe you'd desecrate Nana's home." In the movie version of this, Brenda's tone would be nasty. Here, it's shaky, sad, and afraid. Then her eyes slide to Iph, and there it is—judgment. Maybe even disdain?

Iph's breath catches. Being branded with a scarlet *A* is both awful and strangely exhilarating. Hester Prynne is a role that's always interested her.

"Get out." George's voice has taken the register of Scout's low growl. It's a new side of George, a little scary. "Brenda, you don't want to mess with me. I promise. I still know things Gary doesn't."

Brenda pales and backs away before turning to head out the door, her steps clicking like animal claws down the wooden stairs. George watches the parking lot. Iph hears a car door slam.

"Go get dressed, but stay up here," George says. "I'm going down to deal with Gary. He's not taking my tools—*Nana's* tools—because he lost his temper and got fired from another shady car lot."

"Just a second." Iph grabs a Nana sweater from the recliner and shoves her bare feet into her boots. "You're not going down there alone." But George doesn't wait. Iph struggles with the laces, then the arm of the sweater. She pounds down the narrow staircase. The light in the garage is diffuse. Gary is fumbling in a toolbox, his back to the stairs.

George is standing, feet apart, bow and arrow ready, waiting for him to notice.

Iph opens her mouth to say something. Physical violence was not part of the danger she considered here. But looking at George, at Scout, even the way Brenda left and got in the truck, violence has always been a part of this scene. It's come to Taurus Trucking with this man.

Gary glances up and goes straight back to digging. There's already a pile of tools on the workbench.

"Gary, get off this property. I'm warning you."

"Shoot me and you'll go straight to juvie. Maybe even grown-up lady jail. Or wait, I guess they have to send you in with the men, *George.* The rest of the guys are gonna love you."

He turns, neck out, head cocked, like this is the wittiest thing in the world. Scout barks . . . and lunges for the asshole's ankles. Before Iph or George can move to grab her, the man has pushed Scout away with his boot and then, though she doesn't lunge again, kicks her across the room.

Iph is there a moment before Scout lands, or is it the moment after? The timeline is scrambling and she's both holding the dog and running toward her, unsure how badly she's hurt. Scout's high-pitched scream of pain bounces off the walls for longer than it seems like it should. Like there are multiple keening animals in the room. The sound mixes with the man's profanity—ostensibly English, but Iph can't understand it; she can only perceive the singe of Scout's pain and her own fear for all of them. In less than the space of a breath, Iph understands why George goes around with the bow and arrows.

Scout is in her arms, and she turns just in time to see it—the muscles in George's back flexing like wings, the arrow flying in slow motion through the dim garage, the sound like scissors cutting hair when the arrow pierces the Oakland Raiders cap and pins it to the wall.

The head is balder than anticipated. Blood trickles down. A nick.

Everything stills.

Then, all at once: movement. Scout wriggles out of Iph's arms and is at George's side again, barking. Gary is shouting. Iph understands the words now. A river of acid—the most misogynistic, hateful rant she's ever encountered. The sound bounces off the painted metal walls. The side door to the garage unlocks and opens.

A woman stands in the doorway with a toddler on her hip and a baseball bat in her hand. It's the neighbor lady. A man holding a newspaper follows her in, trailed by a little girl.

"Oooh!" the girl says, seeing the painted walls. The *oohs* turn to squeals when she sees Scout.

"Is there a problem here?" The man moves his daughter behind him. She peeks out around his legs.

"Just a family disagreement," Gary says. George is pale. Iph knows exactly what to do. What Mom would do. She ignores Gary and speaks to the neighbors.

"This man is here uninvited and attempting to take tools that don't belong to him." Iph lowers her voice so that the daughter, who's being licked all over by Scout, doesn't hear the next part. "He kicked my friend's dog. He needs to leave. We don't have a phone here. Can we use yours to call the police?"

"Iph," George hisses. Iph ignores it. The mom of this family is like her mom. These people are not on Gary's side.

"This building belonged to my wife's mother. I came over here to check on things and found these kids. They must have broken in."

"That's not how I understand it," the mom says. "I'm Ellie Crawford Ford, by the way. Civil rights attorney and mother."

"John Crawford Ford," her husband says. "Public defender. And, uh, dad to these hooligans." He smiles toward his kids and extends a hand to George. "A family friend of yours, Kyle Murphy, asked us to keep an eye on this place while he was out of the country. Said it was willed to his stepkid and some relatives weren't happy about that. Gave us this extra set of keys in case."

"Murphy did that?" George is shaking.

"Yep." The woman smiles. Laugh lines form around her dark eyes. The toddler pulls on her cornrows and puts the beaded end of one braid in his mouth.

"Kid's underage," Gary tries.

"I'm almost eighteen," George says.

"It's a gray area." Ellie Crawford Ford smiles. "You, however, have no legal right to be on the premises. And I have to say"—she hands the baby to her white, long-haired, spectacled husband—"I didn't like the language I heard coming in my kitchen window a few minutes ago. I was concerned an assault was taking place over here. Which is why I brought my bat." She swings it lightly. Her bicep is impressive. George is grinning now. "This one is such a quiet neighbor. We never hear a peep. So you can imagine how worried we were."

The man looks at all of them now, and Iph sees it click. This interracial lawyer couple and their kids. George and Iph and Scout. They're what he's afraid of. The change he goes to church and the rifle range to keep at bay.

He shakes his head in a fake-pious, *I'll pray for you but you're going to hell* way and takes his time walking out.

The air in the room brightens. Or maybe it's Iph's glasses, which she's taken off and cleaned with Nana's sweater.

The little girl hugs Scout around the neck. "I don't like that man," she says.

"Me neither." Iph smiles at her.

"Smart kid," George says.

"You knew I was here?" George asks the Crawford Fords.

"Were we not supposed to know?" Ellie furrows her brow. "Wait, have you been living here?"

George takes an unconscious step back. John steps in to stanch the fear in the room. "It's fine," he says. "Murphy said you were staying with a relative, but this is your place. I don't see why you shouldn't stay here."

"When do you turn eighteen?" Ellie puts a hand on George's shoulder. Iph suddenly realizes George is still holding the bow.

"May." George looks down. "Almost a year from now."

"Well, you could have a great case for becoming legally emancipated. I'm not sure if that would secure you the right to manage your inheritance—that's not my area. But I have a friend I could hook you up with. They owe me one—I'll make sure it's pro bono."

"Wow," George says. "Thank you. Should I . . . come by and ask about that later?"

"Sure," she says. "Or I'll stop by when I find out."

"Are you like Robin Hood?" the little girl asks, looking up at George with wide excited eyes.

"Yes," Iph says before George can answer. "Just like Robin Hood."

21

LIKE A
WILD ORCHID

Orr wakes in his little closet from a dream of running with the ghost dogs. Today is cooler, and because of that, he has slept a little too long. His forehead aches like two beating hearts. There are bumps now, one on each side. He hoped he was done with the head thing. It upsets everyone so much. But he's not trying to harm himself. It's something he needs to do to readjust. To process what has happened and figure out what to do next.

As always these days, he is hungry and thirsty. And a weird mix of bouncy and tired. When Orr was little, this mood boded poorly for his coming day at school. He'd do the wrong thing, either accidentally or on purpose. Either way, it had been exhausting for the entire family. What a relief it had been to leave that behind and stay home with Mom.

But this past year, even at home, he's had the bouncy-tired feeling most days, and there's been nothing to do about it except run and sleep. He's even fibbed to Mom sometimes about how he spends his days when she takes classes in Portland or spends hours out in her studio. Most of it was watching *X-Files* episodes he'd taped on the VCR, living a life of purpose as an FBI agent investigating the paranormal through Mulder and Scully. It was almost enough.

In the living room, Mika is doing push-ups. On the coffee table is a stack of the zines she made to pass out at tonight's show. The cover is a blown-up picture of Red's face. Mika wasn't kidding when she said she'd plaster Portland with it. It's titled THE FURIES. And below that is the excellent subtitle: Assholes to Avoid: Portland's Worst Boyfriends.

"You know it's funny you guys are the Furies, right?"

"Huh?" Mika puffs out the final set. She is such a badass.

"In Greek mythology, the Furies are after Orestes. They want to kill him."

"Why?"

"Well, you know—Greek tragedy stuff. He killed his mom because she killed his dad because he killed their daughter, Iphigenia. Same name as Iph. Only the daughter didn't die. She got a last-minute save from Artemis."

"Whoa. That's twisted. Why'd your parents name you guys after such a bloodthirsty family?"

"I don't think they're bloodthirsty. Just tragic. The names are from Dad's side of the family. His brother, who died young, was Orestes. And his grandmother, who was, like, his favorite person in the world, was Iphigenia. He and Mom decided the real people were more powerful than the mythical ones."

"Orestes—that's what Orr is short for? I thought it was iron ore or something volcanic, since you said your mom's kind of a hippie." Mika sits up and stretches. She has a whole preshow workout. "The Furies did try to catch up with you last night, you know. You should run track. I left maybe twenty seconds after you bailed, but you totally smoked me."

"I did?"

"Yeah. And Allison went after you in the van."

"Oh."

"Orr. You're a great kid. If I had a little brother, you're the one I'd want. We all would."

Orr looks away and fights the urge to walk over to Mika and press his head into her shoulder. She's not big on physical affection. "I am someone's little brother," he says softly. "But it's like my sister and I both forgot."

"I'm a twin," Mika says. "My sister and I go weeks without talking. We used to be together all the time. When she went away to college, I was devastated for, like, months. But then I started making zines and got into playing drums. Last year I met Allison and Jane. Now I love my life. And I don't know if I would've found it if Layla hadn't made the break for both of us."

There's something so true in this. For the whole family, maybe—him and Iph and Mom and Dad. "When do we leave for the show?"

"Like, now."

"Already? I need to eat first, but then I'm ready. Sorry, though. About eating so much. I'm always hungry."

"Consider tonight's bass service payment in full. Also, you're not ready. Plum's styling us. We were supposed to be at her house twenty minutes ago."

Orr stuffs down a PBJ and drinks the last of the soy milk. Mika's already on the front porch. "Wanna run there?" she says. "Race you!"

JANE AND ALLISON ARE in Plum's basement, looking like great and terrible goddesses in blood-red togas and fishnet stockings and big chunky boots. Allison's hair is braided into a thick crown around her head with several plastic snakes woven through it. Jane is wearing an ivy crown with a wine-colored band of paint across her eyes and the same color on her lips. "Mika, yours is in the bathroom," Plum says, taking a pin from her mouth. "It's the sturdiest one. I didn't want you busting out of it like She-Hulk the second you hit the drums." Jane stays very still as Plum removes the rest of her pins. "I have to sew them onto you guys," she tells Orr. "It's the only way we can make it stay. Next time, please tell me you want costumes before the day of the show."

"But we didn't know until you had the idea at breakfast," Jane says.

"And anyway, Plum, you're totally pulling it off," Allison says. "You're a wizard."

"That's witch to you," Plum says. She is wearing her white men's shirt again, this time belted as a dress. Her legs are long and beautifully freckled. There's a delicate silver chain around her left ankle with woodland animal charms hanging off it—a skunk, a rabbit, a deer. Plum catches Orr looking. "It's from Disneyland," she says. "From my mom. Bambi was her favorite . . . I know"— Plum stabs the pins into a tomato-shaped pincushion—"Bambi's mom and all. Ironic. But back then, we didn't know." Plum's basement is a riot of costume supplies. "Take your shirt off and stand still."

Orr hesitates.

"Chill," Plum says. "I'm a professional." She takes a red length of fabric and pins it on him, then sews the pinned spots to secure them. "It will rip if you take it off, so there's no going back. But it should be fine for the show. And here." She hands him red-and-black striped leggings. "These are mine, but you'll wanna wear them to be decent. I only had enough fabric for a short toga for you." She stands back and observes him. The basement is cool and green, with garden light through the open door and ground-level windows. Plum takes his hand in hers. He wants to lick it. *It will be salty,* he thinks. *It will be sweet.* She sits him in a chair to do his makeup.

"You're so blinky," she says. Then, gently, "I know this feels weird. Raise your eyebrows like you're surprised and make your face sort of stiff."

Plum's breath smells like lemons and sends quivers down his back every time she exhales. If they were alone, Orr might kiss her.

Her lips are pursed as she tickles his face with a large fluffy makeup brush. She touches the bumps on his head with a fingertip. "Did this happen last night?" She's talking about the fight with Red, but Orr nods. "Do they hurt?" Orr shakes his head, but Plum kisses both spots anyway, so quickly it could have been a moth flying by. When she smooths color onto his lips with her fingers, Orr pulls away. Even good things can sometimes be too much.

She steps back. There's a feeling growing between them like the wisteria vines on her porch. Orr watches her know what he knows. Her cheeks turn pink and her freckles darken.

"You're fabulous," she says. "Let me put your crown on, then you can go change into your leggings and report back."

ORR STANDS IN FRONT of the bathroom mirror for several minutes. The boy in front of him seems to know him, maybe better than Orr knows himself.

He tilts his head to see how he looks from different angles. The ring of black around his eyes makes them bigger and darker. The red lipstick gives him the look of a classical cupid. The wreath of fresh roses around his head makes him look like some sort of god. All he has for shoes are his sneakers. Plum was adamant in her veto of them. He will be barefoot onstage.

"Come out," Jane says behind the bathroom door. "Plum insists on painting your nails."

ACT III

Whoever drinks from me will become a roe

1

GIVEN
CIRCUMSTANCES

The bus huffs and puffs down Burnside. It's after eight, but the day gleams on with its buttery light, still and hot. Iph rests her head on George's shoulder. They pass Music Millennium, the Laurelhurst Theater, and Shiny Dancer, heading for the bridge. Iph hums something soft and low to Scout, who has her head out of the messenger bag for pets. Iph smiles, realizing what she's singing—a lullaby she and Orr used to call *"Ai, ai, ai"* for the first line of the chorus. *"Cielito Lindo"* is its real name. Pretty Little Heaven.

The river is full of sailboats. At the end of the bridge the neon stag rises from the Portland sign like it's leaping away from Old Town into the blue-green Willamette. Mom's husky voice floats through Iph's head. *Ai, ai, ai, ai. Canta y no llores.* Sing, don't cry. After everything that's happened, the timing is right. Iph is ready to find her brother.

They have John Crawford Ford to thank for this confluence. Clearly an agent of fate, he left the weekly paper on the workbench at Taurus Trucking, open to the live music listings. And there it was, in big block letters:

FRIDAY NIGHT AT THE X-RAY CAFÉ
DEAD MOON
CAUSTIC SODA
THE FURIES
WITH A SPECIAL BUCK MOON INVOCATION
BY THE SCARLET LETTER PERFORMANCE COLLECTIVE
3 DOLLARS
ALL AGES
NO ONE TURNED AWAY FOR LACK OF FUNDS.
PROCEEDS TO BENEFIT SHINY DANCER

IPH FEELS CUTE IN Nana's minidress muumuu, worn this time with drugstore fishnets and a ninety-nine cent red lipstick. In the bathroom drawer of Taurus Trucking, she found the stubby end of an eyeliner pencil and revived it the way Mom taught her, by holding the freshly sharpened tip to a lit match. George liked her smoky eyes, red lips, and fishnets so much it led to kissing, then painting each other's nails with silver glitter polish. On the way to the bus, George poached some pink roses and tucked them here and there into Iph's tied-up curls. Iph plucked a daisy to thread through the buttonhole in the chest pocket of George's crisp white shirt and two more for Scout's collar.

Because the moon is full and it's a perfect kind of night, the first person they see is Lorna rocking a sixties-inspired Twiggy ensemble with mile-long lashes, white go-go boots, and an ugly-cute loud floral shorts-and-halter set—most likely once a swimsuit—that turns her eyes green. She pulls Iph and George into her spot in line and hugs them. Even though they're cutting, no one seems to mind.

The sidewalk in front the X-Ray Café is packed with every kind of kid. A pair of lipsticked boys in metallic leggings, feather boas, and hair like the guy from the Cure stand behind raccoon-eyed rocker girls in fishnets, cutoffs, and knee-high boots. Unshowered grunge kids in new Converse and holey flannels lean against the building next to too-skinny street kids with the occasional sock poking through their beat-up sneakers, scarfing falafels provided by one of the grunge guys. He's older than the others and looks sort of familiar—like maybe he's in a band Iph's seen on MTV.

A gang of buzz-cut vegan punks with safety pins in their faces, home-Sharpied MEAT IS MURDER T-shirts, and those World Wildlife Fund panda-bear patches on their jean jackets pass around a single clove cigarette. A boy in a top hat rides up on a unicycle so tall the seat is level with the street signs. He dismounts with surprising grace to perform a complicated lock-up and is greeted by a mohawked girl on a normal bike with a pink-haired toddler strapped into the baby seat behind her. The unicyclist swoops the toddler onto his shoulders, and the three of them head for the back of the line. George raises an eyebrow at Iph, like *cute* but also *whoa*. Iph nods. Those parents look about their age.

A trio of tween girls in kindergarten dresses and plastic barrettes coo at the toddler and flirt with skater boys doing tricks at the curb. Interspersed like sparrows among Bowie birds are a surprising number of normal-looking teenagers who might've come straight from the library or soccer practice—or even, like Iph, from Forest Lake.

The line moves fast. Inside is dim and smelly but buzzing with energy. Sitting at tables with the posture of regulars are a mixed-age group of what Dad would call career misfits for their well-marinated quirkiness. Some look like they're in their twenties. Others are older, maybe even her parents' age. In a corner in the back, Iph spots the guy who had ants buzzing around his head that day outside the Gentry. He looks better today, showered and in clean clothes with clear eyes and a relaxed face. He's younger than Iph thought. He sees her and gives her a thumbs-up.

"What was that about?" Lorna asks, blowing bubblegum breath in Iph's ear.

"Nothing," Iph says. "Just a friend."

UP FRONT THE DIN is fantastic. George is swamped by a pack of kids who've spotted Scout in the messenger bag, and the pink-haired toddler climbs onto the stage and jumps off into her dad's arms. Baby Orr would have been a howling puddle after five minutes here. Even Iph has to fight the urge to cover her ears. It's not the volume so much as the chaos—thrash punk over the house speakers mixed with talking-yelling-laughing and someone onstage doing a sound check that involves an unreasonable amount of screaming feedback. Then, all at once, the X-Ray quiets.

A *sssss* starts somewhere in the back of the room, and the Scarlet Letter moon priestesses begin their snaking procession through the small, packed space. Their silver outfits and metallic kohl-lined eyes are a knockout combination of silent film goddess and science fiction robot queen. They wear identical black Cleopatra wigs, chain-metal bras, low-riding liquid-silver harem pants, and space-age moon-phase headpieces. One of them, at the head of the sinuous line, has a fat albino boa constrictor draped over her shoulders and around her waist. All of them are tattooed: mushrooms and mermaids, waves and fire, flowers, birds, foxes, bats. One of the few brown priestesses looks a little like Mom with a machine-gun Guadalupe on her forearm and what looks like a vintage educational chart of all the kinds of sacred hearts on her back: hearts on fire, hearts with wings. Knife-, arrow-, and sword-pierced hearts. Hearts wreathed in roses and golden light. Broken hearts wrapped in garlands of thorn.

"I heard about them at work," Lorna whispers to Iph. "They're a coven of sex worker poets. They came up from San Francisco."

A ritual cup passes, lip to lip. "Magic mushrooms," Lorna says, drinking. Iph takes the vessel and sips the bitter forest tea. George passes it along, not drinking.

Iph has never taken psychedelics before, but both her parents have. "It was the seventies," they used to say when Orr, who's never seen the point of drugs of any kind, not even caffeine, scolded them for it. It's how her parents met, at an East Village party thrown by Dad's musician brother. Mom knew the punch was spiked, but poor straightlaced Dad, visiting from college in Oregon, did not. According to family lore, Mom found him wide-eyed and freaked out, hiding in the bathroom. They spent all night talking on the roof, a conversation that's still going.

George pulls Iph close as the procession speeds up. Scout peeks her head out of the bag to give Iph a tentative lick. She's not sure about these priestess-snake-women. "It's okay," Iph says. "We've got you, girl."

The hissing line resolves to a linked circle in the center of the crowd. Hearts pound. Drums beat. Or is it rain in an ancient grove? Maybe it's both—drums calling rain from the clear summer sky. *Sympathetic magic* is what Dad calls it, Mom's religion of tarot cards and candles and feathers and pine cones and stones. What exactly are these witches calling?

As the rhythm reaches an apex, the snake grows arms, a bejeweled kraken rising from the deep to partner the crowd in a dance. As if instructed, everyone joins hands to move in a spiral, chaos to order, like the folk reels Iph learned in preschool. She and George are linked for a moment, but George's hand is jostled away and another takes its place, calloused, belonging to a woman whose round, high-cheekboned face changes age in the flickering light—twenty, fifty, twelve. The hissing thickens as tongues kiss teeth throughout the room. On the stage is a large bowl full of gleaming coals. One by one, the priestesses peel away from the crowd and drop branches of rosemary onto the fire. The smoke curls through the air, another kind of snaking, and the spiral slithers faster.

Then, in marvelous unison, the collective snake of them stops. The hiss sheds its skin, becomes song. An elfin blonde onstage is singing to the moon. She plays a strange instrument, a gold electronic-looking box with an antenna sticking up from either side. Moving her hands between the two metal poles, she seems to bend space into sound. The word *theremin* forms in typeface in Iph's mind. The woman's head tilts, almost as if she was the one who sent it.

"Who is that?" Iph asks George, whose rose-soap sweetness is somehow extra thrilling in this crowd where only Iph really knows it. Well, Lorna knows it, too. And did Iph see Cait back near the door? She flashes back to the ticket girl at the movies. Probably there are more of George's exes here. It's that kind of crowd. She leans in close to hear George's answer, inhaling.

"Are you smelling me?"

"Yes."

George moves closer, lips to Iph's neck. "What were you saying?"

"The singer." Iph is grinning. Ridiculously crushed out.

"Right," George says. "She's from some San Francisco band. Why can't I think of the name? You're distracting me, woman."

"I'm just standing here," Iph says.

"You guys are gross," says Lorna, reappearing from wherever the dance landed her. "She's from Lady Frieda. They're in town for a big show. Oh, she's from the same band." Lorna gestures toward a woman with blue mermaid curls and light-brown eyes who has joined the theremin player. They sing together, their harmony breaking the room like an egg.

"Swoon in moonlight," they sing. *"Fall into the arms of fate."*

Iph closes her eyes, giving into the woodland magic of the tea.

In the still moment of synchronized breath after the song is over, Iph feels him.

Orr.

Her brother is very near.

2

SPOKE TO THE
SONGBIRDS

There isn't really a dressing room, but there is a patchwork curtain at the back of the stage and a small space behind it with a few folding chairs. After one look at Orr when they first walked in, Jane led him here, handed him a fresh set of safety-orange earplugs, and said to wait while the girls went and smoked and the witches did their thing.

It's taken him the better part of half an hour to calm down, but now that his heart's stopped racing and he's used to the noise, it's kind of great. Iph is so right: backstage darkness is one of the best kinds, even though in this case the stage is more a platform in the middle of a café and its darkness is broken by tiny beams of light coming in through the curtain's irregular seams.

The hairs raise on Orr's arms when the hissing in the café stops and changes to a weird wordless song that sounds like an old record Dad has of singing humpback whales. There is also music. What instrument? Orr could get up and look but doesn't. The words morph from sound to language.

"*Compass your blood to your desires,*" a witch sings. "*Swoon into the arms of the moon.*"

Orr pulls Allison's bass onto his lap. If his family knew about this, they would be here, cheering in the front row. He closes his eyes and tries to feel them, but all he sees are Jane and Mika and Allison—or really, mental portraits of them in their red costumes with golden auras around their heads like the saint candles on Mom's altar.

"Classic transference." Iph said this when he was eleven and fell in love with his third therapist. Or wait, had Thao been the fourth? Either way, what he's done is clear—substituted Jane for Mom and the girls for Iph. And in this version of mathematics, people aren't important beyond meeting Orr's needs. Maybe Portland has changed him into some sort of monster. Or no, it's the same kind of beast he's always been. The one who made his mother cry the night before her residency started and pretended to be asleep when she left for the airport. In this way, he is like Red. Selfish, no self-control. A terrifying, giant man-baby-monster.

He tries to concentrate on this, teach himself to change, but as always, his thoughts turn to Plum. He doesn't even have to try to conjure every detail of her snapdragon hair and lake-colored eyes. She's always there, hovering like a swarm of honeybees, a constant buzz in the back of his brain. She'll be in the front row tonight. She promised. Even if he doesn't deserve her, Orr's heart gallops.

Coming offstage, a woman with white-blonde hair and a slight English accent is saying, "Someone was passing this around, and I have to say, I don't approve."

"Haven't they heard of germs in this town?" another woman says, laughing. "I think it's pretty weak. But yeah, not cool at an all-ages show."

"Oh," the small blonde one says, noticing Orr. "Hello. Are you in the opening band?"

"Yes," Orr says. He is!

"Stage fright?" The other woman sets a blue ceramic bowl the color of her curls on the graffitied head of a dented tom-tom that seems to function as a backstage table. "I still get it myself," she says. "It's all good—just energy. Your body getting ready for something big!"

He smiles at them. He likes the smaller woman's pointy ears with their many silver studs and the bluish-green curls and maple-syrup eyes of the curvy one who looks like a mermaid, and how they talk to one another like they're sisters.

"Have a great show!" the blonde woman says. "You look amazing, by the way. I love your toga."

"Love and luck!" says her blue-haired sister. They leave, and before Orr can think about what they've told him, the blue-haired one is back. "That bowl should be dumped out—like down the drain—but we have to go. Can you tell somebody?"

"What is it?"

"Mushroom tea," the woman says. "Don't get rid of it outside. I heard about someone doing that and feral cats getting to it. It really messed them up."

3

NEON GLITTER

"It's time," Jane says.

Orr's mouth is still contracted from the bitter tea in the blue bowl and Plum's strawberry lip gloss. He was thinking of her when the thirst came on, worse than ever before. Did the bowl really glow? Did the tea actually call to him? When Plum found him, he was licking the bitter dregs.

"Jane's on her way, crazy boy," Plum said. "I wanted to give you this for luck." Orr held out his hand, but Plum pushed it away, standing on tiptoe to kiss Orr on the mouth. His ears had filled, wings beating, hoofbeats, blood. When he opened his eyes, she was gone.

Now he follows Jane to the stage and waits at her heels. He can see the crowd from here. So many people!

Allison is on the mic brandishing her cast. "So he whips his dick out," she says. The crowd is roaring. "Who knew his dumb face would be so hard when I hit it?"

"Next time aim lower!" someone yells.

"That's what we told her," Jane yells back.

"All right, animals!" Allison says. "Simmer down. I wanna introduce my new friend Orr! This boy genius started playing the bass like five days ago, and he's already got me out of a job. Give him a warm Portland welcome!"

Jane pushes Orr up front and he feels it then: the forest swelling toward him, sweet pitch, wind in his face. He's supposed to be moving into his spot in front of the drum set, but he's standing there, staring at the crowd. Jane laughs and leads him to the amp. Allison plugs him in while Jane greets the audience. Then there's a fizzing moment of silence before Mika counts out the beat.

"One, two—one two three four!"

4

CHARISMA

The minor sparkle of the mushroom tea is nothing compared to this boy. Her brother.

Orr is stunning. The lead singer of the Furies, impressively tattooed and legitimately hot with a Joan-Jett-meets-an-avenging-goddess vibe, is reduced to a bit player, singing the words so Orr can bounce them back to her with effortless notes from the bass while he stands there in his eyeliner and red toga and rose crown, looking like a young god visiting from Olympus or Chichén Itzá.

"Your little brother is a total rock star," Lorna yells into Iph's ear.

All Iph can do is watch, mouth open like she's trying to drink the music. Like that will somehow explain this phenomenon. This human who she's bathed with, who slept in her bed until he was five, who's needed so much from her his entire life, is thriving without her. In this chaotic space, Orr has found balance. His rhythm is generous—steady and loyal, like he is. Iph is crying. She always cries. Love and loss mix and cleanse. The bread-crumb trail has finally led her back to Orr. Soon, this chapter of their story will be over.

"You okay?" George's mouth is on her ear. Iph turns her face to meet those lips. George pulls her closer. Tears, tongue, a hand to her neck. It's a light kiss that knows there are many more to come. Iph takes a deep breath and smiles to show George she's all right.

"I'm taking her out," George says.

Iph touches the messenger bag to feel Scout inside. Her little body is tense.

They talked about this earlier. That for Scout's sake, George would probably listen from outside. That they wouldn't leave without each other, no matter what happened with finding Orr. "I'll find you or you find me," George says, giving her one last kiss.

Iph turns to look for Lorna, but Lorna is gone.

Alone in the crowd, she imagines that Orr is gone as well. "The tea was strong after all," she'll say later to George as they sprawl upstairs together at Taurus Trucking. "Maybe we'll find him tomorrow." As the traitorous thoughts unspool, Iph tries to wind them back. But there are no do-overs here. The truth is, she's not quite ready to be anyone's big sister again.

"I abandoned him," she says out loud to no one in particular. "I abandoned my brother for lust."

The guitar solo eats her words and flings them back to her. There's no room for recrimination now. Lust is fine with this music. And if she abandoned Orr, look who picked him up! A pack of tween girls have commandeered the front of the stage and are dancing like dervishes. Little trails spark from the tips of their fingers and the ends of their hair as they spin. They crash into one another, laughing, drunk from the movement. Just like that, Iph lets go. Mind off.

And here is Lorna, shimmying around like a baby horse on her long graceful legs. She isn't slinky here, but awkward in a way that is a gorgeous contrast to her it-girl perfection. For a second, Lorna's just-rightness wraps around Iph, and every move she makes is glorious. A split second later, Iph sinks into herself, so heavy she can't move.

She will never be beautiful like that. Never so light and lithe.

So perfect. *Never*, her heart wails. *Never ever!* The mushroom tea plays cat's cradle with the string of thought. *Never. Never ever.*

Iph can usually tame these voices with Mom's rabid feminism or the wise words she's read in riot grrrl zines. But it takes energy. And so much precious time. It seems like it will never end.

The song is reaching a distorted crescendo. The audience screams. Iph screams with them and feels a little better.

The next song creeps in as the band is tuning up with a sneaky drumbeat and slow simple bass. The X-Ray Café inhales, a dumpster-dive creature made of glitter, trash, hormones, and magic markers. Jane whisper-sings into the mic.

> *Don't be sorry*
> *Don't say sorry*
> *Don't be sorry*
> *Don't say sorry*

Iph steps a few feet back from the stage because Jane is up there reading her mind. The music builds and the front-loaded chorus repeats, getting louder each time. Iph is singing with her now. The entire audience is.

> *Don't apologize*
> *Blood in his eyes*
> *I'm not sanitary*
> *Not your Virgin Mary*
> *Look at me*
> *A delicacy*
> *It's that time babe*
> *You can eat me*

Orr yells this last line with the rest of the band and the crowd yells it back, and someone pogos into Iph, and she's laughing and dancing. Orr is dancing, too, headbanging with Jane and Allison and the joy onstage is a slow-motion firework, sending tails of light out into the crowd.

The Furies are Iph's new favorite band, her brother her all-time favorite bass player. Their music is hard like punk but a little slower, with a bluesy feel that takes hips into account. The lyrics are total riot grrrl, personal and political. The songs pile up one after the other with almost no breathing room in between. After the friend breakup and abortion and period songs and a very short song the drummer dedicated to someone named Red that is basically the band playing the *Batman* theme but screaming *Fuck You* every time you'd normally say *Batman*, there are two longer songs. One is slow, about a friend dying—just Jane and her guitar and the rest of the band humming behind her, a container for her sorrow. Here Jane shines, and Iph can see the craft she's put into this lo-fi, seemingly thrown-together show. She is open-eyed and breathtakingly present. *This*, Iph thinks, *is how you do it.*

They wrap up with a surprising slow-funk seventies groove and announce that people can make an extra donation to Shiny Dancer at the table in the back. Glow comes onstage in a pink plastic raincoat and monster silver patent leather platforms and shares the mic with Jane to do an excellent rap about stripping.

She walks right up to those neon lights
Gonna make her rent in just one night
She's knows it's not her clothes or her smooth young skin
It's how she moves with what she's in
She shakes it hard, she's got a plan
You know that she knows what the men don't understand
You call her a slut, call her a ho
But she knows a little secret that you don't know

The audience is howling. The song ends, and Orr scans the crowd. Iph jumps up and waves. "Orr!" she shouts. But he's not looking her way.

No, her brother is looking stage left, smiling like a googly-eyed cartoon character. Iph follows his gaze. Dad mentioned a girl, and this has got to be her. The entire family has wondered for years if Orr would ever have a type, but if they'd just stepped back and pictured it, it totally would be someone like this—waist-length wavy dark-red hair worn with a Halloween devil-horn headband, a black leotard under a frayed denim miniskirt, black Converse, sparkly striped knee socks, and a furry blue Cookie Monster back-pack. Iph already loves her.

5

STAG OF THE STONE FOREST

Orr's playing is like breathing. One long breath sipped from Plum's lips, a radiating warmth, a sure path through a grove, a roving, ramping lust.

It is the belly of a bear. He is a beast being born.

His shorn head buzzes with a crown of bees, and Plum in the front of the crowd is the honey.

When the music finally pants to rest, he is sweating and thirsty, and the room is a mush of color and muffled sound. Then he sees the Furies. They are haloed as he imagined them before the show. Allison, Patron Saint of Knuckle Sandwiches, is holding him as they jump up and down together. Even Mika comes to join the hug. Jane waits for the others to step away.

"Babe," she says. She means, *You were good*. She means, *I am proud*. She hugs him.

People worm into their pack with more hugs and congratulations. The next band is setting up. The Furies scatter. Orr stands alone on the stage.

Where is Plum? She said she'd find him. Fear sprouts. His head twinges a migraine warning above each eye.

"Orr!"

He looks around the room, but there are too many possible sources.

"Orr!"

The stage tilts and begins to revolve, a slow orbit around the throbbing pulses in Orr's head. The singer for the next band, a slight pale girl with big dark eyes and curls like Iph's, comes over to adjust the height of a mic stand. He moves out of her way to stand at the edge of the stage. Where is he supposed to go now?

Then, somehow, with no warning at all, his sister is standing on the stage beside him.

Iph? Is his mouth moving? Did he say her name or think it? His heart is racing. "Iph, I'm kind of spinning."

She smiles. "You, too?" She puts her hands on his shoulders to steady him.

"Hi," she says.

"Hi," he says back.

Iph. It's Iph.

"You were beautiful up there." Her face is shining. Her curls are full of roses. She smells like herself but different.

"Iph?" Orr says. "Is the stage tilting?"

"Little brother," Iph says in a bad British accent that means he's stumbled onto one of their many private jokes. "Did you, by chance, drink any of that tea?"

"Iph," Orr says, "we're on drugs. Are you even here right now?"

She laughs and Orr's head stops pounding.

"We have to get off the stage," he says. "I need to find Plum."

"I'd be offended that finding some girl is all you can think about after this crazy week, but I have to find someone, too."

"A boy?" Orr asks. "A girl?"

"Yes," Iph says. "Named George. And a pocket pit named Scout. Now take my hand. We're gonna walk to the edge and jump off together."

Hand in hand, they're laughing like hyenas. That's what Dad always says when his children get started and can't stop.

They jump on the count of three. The distance is short, but time stretches and they land softly, like the floor of the club is a pile of September leaves.

When Orr looks up, Plum is there. He looks from her to Iph. He should say something out of politeness, blah blah blah. He's laughing again. Plum's face is slow-motion starting to frown. Iph saves him because she's his big sister.

"I'm Orr's sister," she says. "Iphigenia." Why is she giving her full name? Orr swats away the thought of alien abduction in favor of mushroom tea. Or maybe this week has changed Iph as much as it has changed him.

"I'm Plum," Plum says, and Orr can only think of kissing her again. "And that," she says to Orr, "was fantastic. FANFREAK-INGTASTIC. I'm almost mad at you, it was so good."

"Why mad?"

"Because you're a maniac rock-star man cub, that's why." Plum grabs his shoulders and shakes him a little. "How did you learn to do that?"

"Iph," Orr says, "we're not on TV." Iph is standing there staring, like she's watching *Bringing Up Baby* or *My So-Called Life*. She has that same smile.

"Sorry," Iph says. "Do you want to come outside and meet my friend George? And I'd love to meet the band—"

Feedback screeches, penetrating Orr's earplugs. Nails on a chalkboard amplified all the way up. *Up to eleven,* Orr thinks—Dad's dumb joke from some old movie. It squeals again, and the crowd seems to double. Orr remembers, something about the next two bands. They are popular, better known than the Furies. Iph is talking to Plum, who is pointing out Mika. Orr puts his hands over his ears. Where is backstage? Is there a quiet place here? Allison warned him about the bathroom—too gross even for her, she says.

Orr does a therapy technique, looks for the corners of the room. Velvet-painted Elvises and glamour girls stare back. A table of poker-playing dogs look suspicious as he tries to scan the room's perimeter. His head hurts. He needs air.

Then Plum is there, leading him outside, around the corner. "Your sister's going to meet us out here," she says. It's still loud, but quieter. The moon is high and the cool is good. Plum leans against the building. Orr looks down at her. When did he get so tall? He touches her hair, something he's longed to do. Bunches it in his hands.

She closes her eyes, lifts her face. They are kissing now. A real kiss. Plum is pulling him closer. A car speeds by, honking. He startles, pulls away. Plum laughs, but her face is distorted like she is underwater. Orr's head aches. It hurts so bad. He's holding it. He is so thirsty. He presses his forehead to the side of the building. The rough brick is a poultice. He's tapping now, rhythmic hits against the bricks. Plum is saying . . . something. Pulling at his arm. Everything is hushed except for the sound of his forehead hitting the wall.

"Orr!" Iph says. "Stop it!"

Your sister is in charge. That's what his parents always say when they go out. *Listen to your sister.*

"Stop it right now!"

Dad's voice.

No, it's Iph channeling Dad. And it's enough. He stops. Turns. Plum is crying.

Humiliation falls like poisoned rain. Or is he drenched in sweat? He won't look at Plum. Can't bear to. Can't even look at Iph as she pulls him away from the wall. Then he sees it in the glass of a shop window.

The boy in the mirror is gone, and so is Orr's pain.

In their place is a tall lanky creature with two small mossy horns peeking from his forehead.

He stomps his foot. Once, twice, three times.

This is not a place for him to be. Not anymore.

Orr steps back, clear of Iph and Plum. Then he runs.

6

INNER
PSYCHOLOGICAL
DRIVES

ph is in front of the X-Ray yelling her brother's name, but he is so fast. She wishes for George, for the bikes. She can barely see him now, already blocks away and still running down Burnside.

"Iph!"

She turns. Not George, but Josh—no Shakespeare now, all business.

"Cait's getting her car. I'm gonna run ahead and see if I can at least keep sight of him."

How are Josh and Cait here just when she needs them? She remembers hearing people call Portland a big small town. Josh takes off fast, but not as fast as Orr. Iph squints to see the red toga now. And where is George?

Plum takes her arm. "What can I do?"

A honking BMW sedan turns the corner. "My friend is here somewhere. George—with dark hair and a mohawk, carrying around a little pit named Scout."

"I saw them earlier! I'll tell George where you went," Plum says. "Do you want to meet somewhere later?"

"Back at Taurus Trucking," Iph says. "George will know."

CAIT PULLS UP IN front of the club. Iph climbs in the back seat. Somehow, Lorna is in the passenger seat. "Thank you, Plum," Iph calls out the open window. "Tell George I'm sorry!"

The car is silent as Cait drives down Burnside. Iph doesn't see Josh or her brother. Cait speeds up. There, on the corner in front of Powell's, is Josh, doubled over. Cait pulls into the bus stop, and he gets in the back with Iph.

"Your brother is hella fast," he says, panting. "He went that-away." Josh points past Powell's. "Down 12th."

"Thank you," Iph says. "I didn't even know you were at the show."

"I got there late. George heard your brother ran off and sent me." He leans forward, hands on the two front seats. "Greetings, George's exes."

"Shut up," Cait and Lorna say in unison.

Cait drives several blocks. They stop to ask a guy on a bicycle if he's seen a barefoot boy in a red toga running past. *Barefoot.* Iph has a moment of certainty that this is all a dream. There is no reality in which tender-footed, easily grossed-out Orr would walk barefoot anywhere, let alone run.

"He went up Lovejoy," the guy says. "Is he training for the Olympics or something?"

"Thank you," Cait says and takes off.

The streets in this part of the city behind Powell's are alpha-betical. Iph checks them off as they pass. On Lovejoy, Cait floors it. At Overton, she stops again to ask a group of smokers out-side a restaurant. "I saw him," a guy says. "He was headed that way." The man points toward Northwest 23rd.

They keep driving, but Orr is nowhere in sight. Cait pulls over to regroup. Iph's hand goes to her pocket. Matches? No, it's the little book of poetry she picked up at Shiny Dancer. The moon comes out from behind a cloud, illuminating the inside of the car. Iph opens the tiny cover. On the title page it says:

Fragment from Ferenc Juhász's
"The Boy Changed Into a Stag Clamors at the Gate of
Secrets"

On the next few tiny pages she reads:

He stoops over the pool
stares into the moonlit water—
a beech tree with the moon in its hair
shudders—the pool reflects a stag!

Iph can't breathe. She flashes for a panicked second on her inhaler, left in her nightstand drawer. Her quiet, empty, messy room. She needs air. Gets out of the car.

"You all right?" Lorna is beside her.

"I'm scared."

Lorna takes her hand. "Think about him. You know him. Where would he go?"

Iph hands Lorna the matchbook poem. Lorna nods as she reads it.

"Is there an entrance to Forest Park around here? Maybe a trail with a creek?" she asks through the car's open windows.

"On Thurman," Josh says. "The trail to the Witch's Castle."

7

JOURNEY TO
THE PROVINCES

Iph waits alone in the dark forest, sitting on the steps of the Witch's Castle. Cait, Josh, and Lorna offered to stay, but she sent them back to Taurus Trucking to update George. She has the flashlight and blanket from the trunk of Cait's car. The butterflies in her stomach—well, maybe bats, considering her location—tell her Orr is close by.

The air is sweet with the breath of trees who tower over the tumbledown stone house like whispering giants in fringed pine-needle party dresses, their limbs silvered in moonlight. The Witch's Castle was once part of an 1880s homestead, then a rest stop for hikers, Cait told them. Now it's a burned-out stone structure layered with graffiti and moss that glows highlighter bright in the beam of Iph's flashlight. She runs her hand over the springy stuff and tries to send a psychic message to Orr. He is in this forest; she knows he is.

She draws her knees up and makes herself small. The forest is singing its midnight litany of *swish* and *woosh* and *chirrup* and *snap*. Iph looks up, hoping for stars, but the branches are too thick above to see more than a few patches of sky, a grayer black than the forest's darkness. Iph leans against the mossy wall and closes her eyes.

SHE'S WALKING THROUGH THE *lavender light of the predawn forest. A lanky white hound, the sort of regal beast you'd see on a Medieval tapestry, is a bend ahead. Every time the path curves, Iph sees the feathery tail flick and disappear.*

The path follows a creek, which ends at a wide, deep pond. Iph must cross it. She undresses. Takes off the rose-painted boots. Wades into the pond, deeper and deeper. The cold is profound.

The still water ripples with her approach. A court of swans, moonwhite and black-beaked, surround her. She crouches until her chin grazes the water, digging her toes into the slime. She gathers herself and rises, winged now and powerful. She flies from the pond, wings spread over the wood, and lands in a meadow. The grass is dew-damp and sun-warm under her wide, webbed feet. She stretches like a fern unfurling—tall, then taller still, wings to forelegs, webbed feet thickening to large, razor-tipped paws. She ambles to a tree to scratch her back, fur against fir, like Baloo from the movie The Jungle Book. *She drops to the ground and shambles forward on all fours. Comes to a gate.*

Inside is a beehive, a siren on the rocks promising every sweet thing she could ever want. She rambles forward, works the gate handle, and reaches for the gold. Honey to tongue, throat to heart, and she is shrinking like Alice, folding into herself until she is a golden unit of pure desire. She flies over the meadow fragrant with wildflowers that glow psychedelic with sunrise.

A stone cottage peeks from behind a copse of trees. The flower world buzzes with morning work. Iph flies through a glittering cloud of pollen to land on a sunlit dais, velvet-draped with the scent of summer. Here, she sleeps.

Waking, she rises on her two feet again. Slowly, processionally, she makes her way toward the large dark shapes in the shady border where the meadow ends and the forest begins.

There, in the midst of a sleeping family of deer, is her brother.

The toga is gone. He is wearing a pair of torn red-and-black striped leggings and somehow still has the crown of roses he wore onstage. His head is leaning against the haunch of a large doe half-hidden in the trees' shadow.

Iph takes a step closer. The deer are awake. Have been since she began her approach. One step more, and the deer rise. Orr awakens. The stately animals walk slowly away, leaving Orr in the meadow, shirtless and barefoot, roses twined between his newly budded antlers.

8

WHERE THE BONE-BRANCHES BUDDED

"Iph, where are your clothes?" Orr's voice sounds different to him. He's surprised the words make sense when they come out. He touches his ears. The earplugs must have fallen out when he ran. The morning sun is so warm. He is so tired.

Iph spins in a circle. "I . . ." she says, scanning the meadow. "I'm sorry. I don't know what happened." She sits and pulls her knees to her chest, hiding her body.

"I don't care," Orr says. "Just pretend we're at the hot springs. Anyway, it's kind of the least of our worries." His ears twitch. As in, actually move. He feels for them. They're in the same location and the same shape as always—just keener and more mobile. He reaches up to touch his forehead, but he isn't ready. He knows this. Knows he must wait to confirm such an outlandish, impossible change.

At the far edge of the meadow is a flash of white. It moves closer. A single dog, the smaller companion to the leggy hound from the cemetery. Orr is certain it's the same animal—he knows it by smell. The thick-ruffed dog is a little larger than the coyote Orr met on the mountain, with a long snout and the golden eyes of a wolf. He—this is another thing Orr knows from the smell—is carrying a basket, handle in his mouth. He trots a respectful distance from Iph, sets the basket down, and bows, playfully wagging. Iph puts out her hand, and the dog comes eagerly forward, pressing his blocky head into her shoulder.

Orr picks up the basket and brings it to Iph. "My clothes!" She pulls out a dress and her underwear, bra, and socks. There is a blanket folded in the bottom of the basket. And a flashlight.

"This stuff looks like it came straight from the cleaner," she says, turning her back on Orr to dress.

The dog bows and bounds off, returning quickly with a pair of boots in his mouth. Dropping them at Iph's feet, he races around the meadow like a puppy, clearly pleased with himself, then speeds away again into the woods.

"Orr," Iph says. Her voice is shaking. "What happened last night?"

Orr stands, paces. Twitches again, the animal sounds around him distractingly loud. The squirrels scold. Birds forage for their fledglings. And the deer. The deer breathe a few bounds away, hidden in a cluster of salmonberry bushes inside the dark, fragrant grove.

Last night.

Last night.

How to even think about it?

Last night wasn't the ending he'd meant it to be—a graduation from this adventure and a way to take responsibility for himself. No longer a burden to the Furies. No longer hiding from his family. In that way, it had been an end. But in a vast and terrifying way—he can't explain it—it was also a beginning.

"I saw myself in the glass," he says to Iph. "I ran."

"Right," Iph says. "But Orr, those deer . . ."

Orr crouches in the dewy grass, clipped short by the deer who were sheltering him. "I don't know how, but I knew where to find the forest. I didn't stop until I came to that stone structure. I was panting and crying. I was so thirsty. Then I felt them, all around me. Quiet until they were close enough to touch. But I didn't move. I was scared! They're so big. Iph, they've been living right here. Animals in the city with us all this time."

"Right?" Iph says. "There are all kinds of things happening we never imagined tucked away in Forest Lake."

Orr is pacing again. "They have a hierarchy. The one in charge—her granddaughter came to inspect me first. Then her daughter. Then, finally, the oldest deer came over. Touched her nose to my nose. Then licked me." He stops, remembering the sweetness of it. "My headache . . . it went completely away. And now, I feel . . . right, but also not right."

Orr is shaking. He is so exhausted. He drops onto the grass beside his sister. Lies down. She folds the blanket into a pillow, and he rests his head in her lap.

She touches his shorn hair. It has grown into a short, thick pelt in the week since the men on the mountain sheared him. Her cool, strong fingers find the place on his neck where the migraines start. Her hands are as familiar as his mother's. Since the moment he took his first breath of air, Iph has been there. She was never a jealous sister, never a judgmental or rejecting one. She begged Mom and Dad for him. Lobbied for him. Loved him before he even existed. His first memories are of her holding him. Holding his hand as he toddled around the house. Holding his foot when he rode in his car seat. Memories so early he's not supposed to have them—but he does. Not of Mom. Not of nursing or riding in a sling. But of Iph, curled around him in their puppy pile of sister and brother.

Now she traces his forehead, fingers running over the substance that has mossed the skin there. "It's so soft," she whispers. "I'm going to press down a little—is that all right? I want to make sure you're not hurt."

Iph is always gentle with him.

"Orr," she says, "what do they feel like?"

"Before they came out, they felt achy, like a loose tooth. Now there's a little pressure, but it's sort of . . . a relief."

"Orr, these look like they're antler buds. I think they call this stuff around them velvet. They seem like they've grown since last night." Her words are calm, matter of fact. It's the same voice she uses to help him figure out the source of a meltdown. Orr has always appreciated her talent for being able to see the big picture and finding a way to talk about it that makes sense.

"I think you should touch them," she says. "Mostly for me. I want to be sure this is real."

Orr grabs Iph's hand so it covers his. This is how he learned to hold a crayon, then a pencil. He touches the velvet first. It is so soft and sensitive, the way the inner part of his forearm and earlobes are, but more. Then he touches the antlers, only single horn buds at present, one by one. The right is slightly larger than the left, but both are about two inches long. They are like teeth, he realizes, growing in the bed of velvet on his forehead like teeth grow in gums.

"I'm so scared, Iph. But also . . . I kind of love them."

9

CONCENTRATION
& ATTENTION

Stroking Orr's forehead, Iph is filled with purpose. The chaos last night after the mushroom tea is one thing. It is morning now, and they are here. Her brother is changing, and he needs help. Things could have gone so badly for her alone on the street that first night when she ran away from Dad. It was luck, maybe fate, that she met George when she did—but it was also Iph. She's learned to trust herself more over the past year.

She extricates herself gently and stands.

"Orr," she says. "Come on."

"Where are we going?"

"Over there." She points to the cottage.

THE PATH LEADS THROUGH the meadow and into the copse. Iph feels comforted among the trees. Last night's dream is still looping through her mind—swan, bear, bee. Lying on the path is a long, curved white feather. She picks it up and puts it in the basket, then continues out of the fir trees into a small grove of cherries with gnarled trunks and rustling leaves. At its heart is a bright cottage garden, meant to look wild but carefully tended. The garden path curves to reveal a small stone house, constructed similarly to the Witch's Castle, but as maintained and tidy as the castle is derelict.

Iph grabs Orr's hand. Together, they approach. The red-painted door is slightly ajar.

"Hello?" Iph calls. The place is silent and feels empty. But it's warm inside, and Iph is chilly after the walk through the dark grove. She pulls Orr in behind her.

Iph has always loved the sort of house Dad calls fairy-tale rustic. They often stayed in cabins or beach houses with a handmade whimsical feel when they traveled, but those all pale in comparison to this cottage. This is the real thing.

Inside, the entry is made of two miniature linden trees, white with blooms growing up through the stone floor to create an arched corridor, a miniature of the one Iph and George strolled through in Ladd's Addition. Farther inside is a large woodstove glowing with a crackling fire, a pillow-stuffed window seat, and several worktables.

At the longest table are a typewriter and three stacks of materials. The largest pile is made of various unopened envelopes, the middle one a stack of manuscripts, presumably unread, and the third pile, the smallest, is made of manuscripts marked in red and held together with large brass paper clips. In the typewriter is a blank piece of stationery with a familiar letterhead—*RCT*, vined with roses and shaped around the silhouette of a leggy white hound.

Iph steps back and keeps going until she's sitting on the window seat. There in the corner under the opposite window is a letterpress. In the middle of the room is a table piled with matchbooks—the source of the matchbook poetry Iph found at Shiny Dancer. At another table is a large embosser. Iph recognizes these archaic machines because Orr did a report on print methods for Mom as part of his homeschooling. He'd been obsessed with the *Terminator* movies and wanted to be prepared to foster the revolution after artificial intelligence took over and digital technology had to be abandoned.

"Orr, I know these books. I've been seeing them all over Portland." Iph gets up and runs her hand over the creamy paper in the typewriter. "Orr?"

Where is he? She rushes from the workroom through a dining room and a large living room into a hallway, longer than it should be given the footprint of the house. The third door on the left is open. Orr is there in a modest twin bed, snuggled under a feather comforter and patchwork quilt.

"I'm so sleepy," he says, then closes his eyes and starts to snore.

Iph backs away. Trapped in a fairy tale—well, she's not going to sleep. She will explore. She'll find the next clue. There has to be one. In stories like this, there always is.

She retraces her steps to the workroom. A dim corner opens into an alcove she didn't see before. She walks in and the lamps turn on. It's a library. She reaches for a random book.

Over here, says a very small voice.

She turns, but no one is there.

She moves closer to the shelves and sees they're labeled. FICTION, FAIRY TALE, POETRY, MYTH, MEMOIR, POLITICAL SCIENCE, MUSICOLOGY, SHAMANISM, RADICAL PSYCHOLOGY, PERFORMANCE STUDIES, ALCHEMY, etc. She yawns again.

Pssst, says the voice again.

Oh! Like at Powell's, a book is calling her.

Of course it is.

She takes a breath and listens. Touches a possible source of the call. No. She knows somehow. Not that one. She tries again, but it's for sport. Given the logic that is surely behind this situation, she knows her third choice will be the correct one. She pulls the book from the shelf.

Case Studies in Transmutation

What is that supposed to mean? A sound like a window closing draws her attention to a large dictionary on a stand, lit up by a perfectly placed sconce. The sound she'd heard must have been the book opening. She reads:

TRANSMUTATION, noun.
TRANSFORM, METAMORPHOSE, TRANSMUTE, CONVERT, TRANSMOGRIFY, TRANSFIGURE: *to change a thing into a different thing.* TRANSFORM *implies a major change in form, nature, or function ("transformed a pile of scraps and snippets into a book of poetry").* METAMORPHOSE *suggests an abrupt or startling change induced by or as if by magic or a supernatural power ("the silver-haired woman transformed into a tall, lanky hound").* TRANSMUTE *implies transforming into a higher element or thing ("the alchemist transmuted lead into gold").* CONVERT *implies a change fitting something for a new or different use or function ("converted the ruins of the cabin into a snug forest home").* TRANSMOGRIFY *suggests a strange or preposterous metamorphosis ("the boy was transmogrified into a deer").* TRANSFIGURE *implies a change that exalts or glorifies ("wonder transfigured her face").*

Well, then. Iph is definitely in the right quadrant of the enchanted forest. She opens to a page that reads:

Transmogrification has been reported to occur as the result of a curse or as an intentionally developed skill. We are not referring to either manifestation in this chapter, but rather the occurrence of temporary or permanent physical transformation as a result of psychological trauma.[1]

In such cases, the course may be reversed by enacting a psychonarrative change such that the affected person is able to release and/or incorporate the elements and/or experiences in such a way as to render the physical transfiguration unnecessary. This operation requires: [2]

1. *A willing subject*
2. *A trusted psychopomp*
3. *Trained ritual participants*

At the bottom of the page are footnotes:

1. See the tales "Tam Lin" and "The Girl Who Trod on the Loaf."
2. See ancient Greek dream theaters—*Asklepion*.

Iph knows "Tam Lin"—the story of Janet, whose lover is taken by the Fairy Queen. To get him back she must grab him and hold on no matter what as he morphs into a succession of terrifying beasts. The other one with the weird name she's never heard of. And what the hell is a psychopomp?

She needs paper, and of course there is a stack of index cards and a box of small, perfectly sharpened silver pencils at the end of the shelf—the enchanted cottage version of the scrap paper and golf pencils they keep by the lookup computers at the library and at Powell's. After writing down *The Girl Who Trod on the Loaf*, she goes to the dictionary, unsurprised to find it already opened to *P*.

PSYCHOPOMP, *noun*
plural noun: psychopomps; noun: psychopompos; plural noun: psycho-pompi (in Greek mythology) a guide of souls to the place of the dead.

The spiritual guide of a living person's soul ("a psychopomp who stays by her and walks in her dreams").

Iph thinks back to last night's dream—if that's even what it was—and the white dog who led her into the forest. Not the Malamute who brought her clothes to her, who is clearly a minion, but the regal moon-colored hound. Definitely a psychopomp.

She carries the book to the workroom window seat. On the wide sill is a cup of steaming black tea, flavored with roses and pale with the perfect amount of cream. She sits and reads.

She closes the book when she hears singing from the library, something that sounds vaguely like doo-wop or Motown. Iph finds several books with spines sticking out an inch or two, asking to be chosen. She takes her stack back to the window seat.

A Feminist Reimagining of Jodorowsky
The Theater of the Oppressed
Individuation in Fairy Tales
Flying Ointment: The Witch's Book of Depth Psychology
Women Who Run with the Wolves: Myths and Stories of
     the Wild Woman Archetype
Grimm's Fairy Tales with an Introduction by Carl Jung
The Pan Within: Transmuting the Masculine
Radical Intuition: Lessons from Baba Yaga
In My Mother's Garden: The Somatics of
     Intergenerational Trauma

There is too much to read. Too much to learn. The stakes are too high.

She puts her head down. There is a sound, little clicking hoof-beats. She looks up. Like a player piano, the typewriter is moving on its own.

The message reads: *Bibliomancy: foretelling the future by interpreting a randomly chosen passage from a book.*

As Iph reads the sentence, another forms.

You can do this.

There is a yellow legal pad Iph didn't notice before and a cup full of tall pencils, this time licorice black.

Back at the window seat is another steaming cup of tea and a plate—a golden grilled cheese and tomato sandwich, carrot sticks, and sliced strawberries. Now her throat aches, because this is Mom's special lunch for her. Her favorite. Maybe there's a phone in this house. Maybe she can call Mom. Get help. But what would she say? The ache turns to laughter. She must be hysterical—a word she hates, but if the laughing/crying/hyperventilating fits . . .

She looks around the room. Curtains embroidered with forest flora blow in the breeze. The creamy stucco walls are rough and peaked like meringue, covered in small paintings, etchings, and shadow-boxed objects—a little plastic doll, a spool of red thread and thimble, a rusty military medal on a purple ribbon, a shiny brass bullet casing and a playing card, the ace of hearts; a baby's white sock, a red-capped mushroom, a pressed pansy, a diminutive silver spoon. Ordinary, sentimental objects that somehow in this context don't seem ordinary at all. This whole thing is both magical and surreal. Like the Brothers Grimm meets Theater of the Absurd.

What Iph needs now is fairy-tale logic. She is desperate for her mother. She tries to imagine her now, in her residency studio surrounded by redwoods. Iph suddenly wishes she could see the sky.

A CROW CAWS OUTSIDE the window. *They know things,* Mom always says. Iph heads to the back door she noticed earlier in the kitchen. Outside is a creek crisscrossed with bridges. The most delightful things! Little replicas of Portland's bridges across the Willamette. Iph is drawn to them—but which to cross? The familiar Hawthorne? The industrial beauty of the group, the Steel Bridge? Over the Burnside Bridge replica is a miniature of the famous Portland sign with its retro neon leaping stag. This seems like the most likely candidate until she walks toward the creek and sees it around a short bend: the St. John's Bridge, Portland's pale jade empress. Memories of summers past wash over her—the years they had the boat, before Dad started working so much. They would sail down the river from the Forest Lake boat club all the way to Cathedral Park, right under this bridge, Dad's favorite.

Iph crosses in a few steps and walks down a narrow path to the tallest tree she's seen outside California.

The redwood is as thick around as the linked arms of at least ten children playing ring-around-the-rosy and so tall she can't see the top. She approaches slowly and touches the bark. The comfort is instant, like a hug from someone who loves her. She wraps her arms around the tree. She falls to her knees. The ground is spongy and sweet-smelling, dotted with mushrooms. She digs like an animal until she's buried her hands to the wrists. She lies on her side, fetal in the womb of the forest. *Mom*, she thinks, sending her thoughts to the roots of this tree, imagining it sending out a tendril to its neighbor, on and on through the forested lands of the West Coast to the redwoods in Santa Cruz, a kids' cup-and-string telephone-style SOS. *We need you. Help us!*

She closes her eyes and maybe even sleeps. After a while, she rises and turns back to the cottage. Behind the kitchen is a garden, fenced against deer. Beyond it, she sees large dark shapes moving in the trees. The wild animals who have cared for her brother. Her brother, asleep, his body changing in a way Mom's puberty talks and embarrassing illustrated books would never have anticipated.

Iph returns to her window seat. The grilled cheese still looks as if it came out of the pan and is almost too hot to touch. She eats the strawberries first. She'll save the carrots to munch as she reads. Eating and reading at the same time is a primary pleasure of hers, the ultimate comfort.

She looks down at the note, which she must have pulled from the typewriter because here it is, tucked inside *Artemis's Arrow: Performance Practice and the Reclamation of Wildness.*

Bibliomancy? Well, she'll try it. She opens to a page: *Instinct is the primary tool of the artist.*

She takes up the next book, *Ritual for the Modern Witch*, and opens to: *The drum is ritual's heartbeat.*

She sips and reads and makes her notes on every book in the stack. There is a rhythm to her work, like creating a collage. An idea is forming, a plan where none seemed possible.

10

ONLY THE
VOICE OF A STAG

Orr's body is a castle with stained glass windows for eyes and jeweled caverns for intestines. His toes are secret coves at the edge of a warm blue sea.

Red-haired girls in yellow dresses dance on the sand, none of them Plum. They laugh and whisper and run away, looking back now and then as if daring him to follow. He shadows them to the entrance of a cave that is barnacled and covered with slime. A briny wind from deep inside the rock formation blows his hair behind him like the robe of a king. It is long again, longer than ever, all the way down to his waist. His walk slows, as befits his royalty, understanding the paradox of simultaneously walking into and *being* the stone castle, the cliff, the beach, the girls, even the sea.

The cave narrows for a long, dark stretch, then opens wide. He is not inside his own body now, but the body of a whale. A whale inside a book about a puppet inside a dream, like a Jungian Matryoshka doll.

The puppet maker's chair is empty and on the little table sit three frogs. One is Plum. Orr knows this. One is Iph. One is Mom. He must kiss them to find out who is who, but he can't bring himself to touch their green-brown warty skin. They croak, singing. Their frog song pitches higher, and the frogs are transforming. They are birds now, *little brown sparrows. They fly away and leave Orr alone. He weeps for them, all of them. But he knows: in this moment, none of them are the right choice.*

He sits in the chair and waits as his hair grows longer. He is restless. He moves around the little room. There is a dresser with three drawers. The first has a mirror inside it. The second, a pair of scissors, and the third, a fat carrot with a feathery green top.

Orr looks into the mirror. A three-eyed deer boy with tall antlers looks back. He blinks. Three eyes blink back. He takes the scissors. He cuts his hair, first in big chunks, and then in careful snips so it is close to his head. He gathers the hair and places it in a large pot filled with water on the round-bellied woodstove he now notices. He makes a fire. The pot boils, and the air smells of roses and patchouli and rotting leaves. He remembers the carrot. It is still there. He eats it, savoring the greens on top. Looking in the mirror now, his face is covered in a fine down, and his third eye is closed, concealed by furring.

The hair soup on the stove is singing like a kettle, but it's not a kettle. It's the woman from the X-Ray, the blond sylph. She rises with the steam and turns into a cloud. The cloud dissolves the whale cave, and Orr is on an island. His mother approaches from the end of the beach. "I'm coming," she says, but never gets any closer. "Wait for me!"

Orr is gazing at his reflection in a puddle collected in the smooth bowl of a boulder and sees himself, a long-haired boy waiting for his mother. His face tightens and shrinks. The hair grows down his forehead to cover his eyes, his nose, his mouth. He is mummified by hair.

He is back in his bed at home. He dreams of Plum and music and sex, but the world is too loud. He steps out of the boy in the bed and observes him.

He is onstage after the show at the X-Ray, looking for Plum.

The stage is revolving, turning him away from the people in the club, pointing him toward the forest.

He is running through the city, keenly aware of every danger with his mouth and nose and ears. His eyes work even faster than his legs, so well it's like he's able to speed up time. He always knows what's coming.

He reaches the forest and doesn't stop running until he sees the stone building. There is the long-legged white dog. No, it's a woman. Long-legged, white-haired, tall, and slender in silver earrings and a green sweater. She whistles a low call Orr feels in the newly hardened soles of his feet.

The deer come, crowding around him.

11

THE SUBCONSCIOUS
AND THE ACTOR'S
CREATIVE STATE

ph sleeps and dreams in black and white. A movie musical starring her and George. They meet and the dialogue sparkles. They dance and are light as air. They kiss and the sky opens, drenching them with rain. They bicker and make up. They are in danger and save each other. The movie ends and Iph rewinds.

12

THE UNFAMILIAR VOICE

When Orr wakes from his deep-dreaming slumber and stumbles into the main room of the cottage, Iph is asleep in the window seat. There is food on the table in the cheerful kitchen. Fruit and a salad of tomatoes and corn. Eating makes Orr want to move. As the sun sets into the blue hour, Orr hears them. Looking out the window, he sees them. Not the does who sheltered him the night before, but bucks with budding antlers and strong musks.

Orr itches to go outside, but memory stops him—playground children promising joy that always turned to cruelty or confusion. He closes the curtains. Closes his eyes.

A melody sounds from somewhere in the cottage. It is coming from the tree-arched entryway. From the front door? Then he sees that its source is the doorknob, shaped like a hare's head, with tall ears and a slender snout. The brass animal's mouth is open, and it is singing. The song is familiar. It takes Orr a while to figure out how he knows it. Finally, he connects the sweet, high voice of the surreal brass hare with the buzz-saw punk-rock anthem Iph blasted last year after she divorced her awful friends. She played it so loud and so often it drove the whole family crazy:

I will resist with all my breath
I will resist this psychic death

He didn't understand it back then. It sounded like noise. Now he gets it, and it gives him courage. He takes off the striped leggings that belonged to Plum and leaves them on the floor. He walks naked into the meadow. The ground is still warm underfoot from the just-set sun. The grass is sweet, with a lemon and ginger sharpness. Orr bends, pulls a blade from the ground. Puts it on his tongue. It tastes the way it smells. Better, even.

The largest buck snorts. Taps the ground with a gleaming hoof. The tails of the three others twitch. Their scent is heady and terrifying. The night glows so blue it blues Orr's skin. Or is it hair—hair or fur? The air is cool. The moon is rising huge and gold above the tree line. He looks down. His skin is brown. Skin or fur? He moves forward. Lowers his head and settles his shoulders into a posture of respect.

The lesser bucks snort as well. One dances. Orr's heels ache to dance back. He does it, a little three-step gambol. The largest buck meets his eyes, twitches his nose, and runs. Orr chases, muscles straining, body singing, foot to hoof to bone to antler into the dark wood.

13

THE SUPERTASK

Iph is on her knees on the porch of the cottage, Orr's striped leggings in her hands. She doesn't have to search the house to know that he has left to run with the deer. She buries her face in the gross leggings and lets loose. And suddenly, someone is nosing under her elbow. Someone is squirming into her lap. A wet nose pushes her hands away and a soft little tongue licks up her tears.

By some miracle, here is Scout. And George, who says nothing, just holds her, which is the exact right thing. Scout barks, and Iph looks up to see Lorna and Cait and Josh and Plum and the members of the Furies carrying their instruments through the gate.

"How?" Iph is laughing. The relief of them. The reality of them! If she is delusional, it's a shared hallucination. Introductions are made. Then explanations.

"It was this one," Jane says, scooping up Scout. "She started howling like a little werewolf."

"She totally did," George says. "Good thing we don't have to worry about being quiet anymore."

"She made us all get off our asses and get in the car," Josh says. "We figured she wanted to come find you."

"Dude," Allison says. "What is this place? We were on the

path, and then it was like the path was never there. I didn't even have any of that tea last night."

"Well, it's a fairy-tale cottage in an enchanted wood," Plum says. "I mean, obviously."

Everyone laughs at that and goes inside, exclaiming over the cottage. Plum hangs back, picks up the leggings.

"He was here?"

"Here and gone," Iph says. "He slept for a long time. I meant to watch him, but I fell asleep myself."

"Did you, like, touch the antlers?" Plum looks exhausted.

"They're really there," Iph says. "I mean, if you're losing it, I am, too."

"What should we do?"

"I have an idea, but he needs to come back first."

Plum nods. "I'm assuming there's an awesome bathroom in there?"

Iph laughs. "If you don't come out in an hour, I'll assume you decided to move in."

"I'm just going to pee," Plum says, oddly forthright. "I brought my tarot cards. I think I'd better take a look."

Iph sits still again, like maybe if she doesn't move Orr will come back.

Scout sidles into her lap, a warm dose of chamomile tea in dog form, nosing her and meeting her eyes. There is so much awareness there. Iph's been too busy mooning over George to notice.

George comes out of the house with a glass of water for each of them and a little bowl for Scout. They drink.

"I missed you," George says.

"I missed you, too." Iph runs her hand over the shaved part of George's head, which is nearly as soft as the velvet around Orr's antlers.

Orr's antlers.

Scout makes a playful little growl-bark and picks up the leggings in her mouth. She shakes them and drops them at Iph's feet. Iph gets it. "I don't want you going out there alone, girl."

George offers Iph a hand. So warm. Scout presses next to her on the other side. The pair of them make her strong enough to think this through. "She wants to go get him," Iph says.

"If anyone here can bring him back, it's probably her."

"Aren't you worried?"

George crouches down to look Scout in the eyes. "Are you sure?"

Scout whines, spins in a circle, and sits. Waiting for George's word.

George puts the leggings under Scout's nose once more. "This is him."

Scout inhales and sits again.

"Okay!" George says.

Before the word is out of George's mouth, Scout shoots out of the cottage and into the trees.

14

THE DRAMA
OF LIFE

As the night deepens, things happen on their own in the cottage. Lamps light. Windows open to let in the cool evening air. Fairy lights turn on in the garden. Plum discovers the laden table first.

"Everyone come out here!" she calls.

Mika looks up from a conversation with Lorna. Holds out her hand to help Lorna off the deep-cushioned sofa in the corner. Iph shoots a look at George and gets a raised eyebrow back. Jane and Allison are swearing their appreciation at the wooden table in the garden piled with food.

"Holy shit!"

"Hell yes!"

There are kebabs of grilled vegetables and tofu, shiny with olive oil and green with fresh rosemary. There is a salad of spinach, strawberries, and feta cheese. There is *elote*—corn on the cob Mexican-style, grilled with butter and chile and squash blossom enchiladas. There is seashell pasta, bright with moss-green pesto and studded with forest mushrooms and tiny yellow flowers. There is a bowl of whipped cream, a platter of blackberries, and five kinds of pie.

They sit and eat. Plum is next to Iph.

"I kind of wondered why he didn't talk much about you. I figured it was either because you guys were super close or not close at all."

A little bit of guilt drains away. Iph is always surprised how much she has stored in her well. The Furies' song plays in her head. *Don't say sorry. Don't be sorry.* She's trying.

"He's perfectly fine out there, you know," Plum says.

"Trust her." Jane has a kebab in one hand and *elote* in the other. She looks like Caesar, still dressed in her red toga from the show. "She's hella uncanny. Her mama was a fortune teller."

"It's true." Mika nods. Mika is also wearing the toga, but under the Trail Blazers hoodie Iph and George got from the Heathman's lost and found. It goes past her knees.

Iph likes Mika. She's a curious combination of reserved and a little shy without seeming insecure. And Iph isn't the only one who's curious. Lorna is across from Mika looking almost better after being up all night than she did in line for the show. She lowers her lashes at Mika, whose eyes widen.

"Are we talking séances? Should I be scared?" Cait asks. Iph notes her seating choice—right next to Mika. She's subtler than Lorna but possibly even more devastating. Her barely-there smile has everyone smiling back.

"Maybe a little," Mika says. "But I'm pretty sure Plum uses her powers only for good."

"How about you?" Lorna says, meeting and holding Mika's gaze. "Do you use your powers for good?"

Mika is bright red. She touches her cheeks. "It's the wine," she says, raising her glass to take another gulp.

"Did your mom have one of those Psychic Reading shops you see around?" Josh asks. He has been silent since they sat down to eat, already on seconds. He looks skinnier than he did a week ago. Iph wonders—where does he sleep? "My mom used to go to one when we lived in Oakland—" He stops. Iph can't tell if it's the mom or the psychic Josh doesn't want to talk about.

"No shop. My mom was a therapist," Plum says. "But also a great tarot reader. My deck used to be hers."

"Used to be?" Iph catches her eye. Plum is so pretty, with those gorgeous freckles and fox-fur brows. Orr has excellent taste—in girls, of all things! Iph's guess had been boys for her brother, but maybe she was projecting her own queerness onto him. Or maybe he likes boys, too.

"Cancer," Plum says. "Don't be sad, Janey." She reaches across the table for Jane's hand. "I've been feeling her lately, you know? She wants us to move on."

Jane wipes her eyes with the backs of her hands and presses her palms onto them, rose tattoos where her eyes were.

"Your eyes just turned into roses," Iph says. Maybe this place will change them all.

"How bad did they hurt when you got them?" George asks.

"A lot," Jane says. "But they're my favorites."

"So, Iph," Allison says, "what's going on? It seems like nothing has been the same since Orr found us that day. What's the story with your family?"

Iph tells the group their story: Mom and Dad meeting at the party, falling in love. Writing letters for two years while Dad finished college and secretly started building Mom their house. How the two of them shared a tiny trailer in the meadow until the house was finished, and how they got married under the hawthorn tree where Orr's treehouse is now, just the two of them and a pagan priestess in a white robe and motorcycle boots. How things got hard. How they went wrong.

"It sounds like you all really love each other," Plum says.

Iph sighs. "Love isn't the problem."

They're silent now, just eating and drinking and listening to the crickets.

Finally, Cait says, "Um, I keep wanting to ask this. If you guys knew someone." She looks at Mika, Allison, and Jane. "My sister was in a band a few years ago. In Olympia. The Athenas? Have you ever heard of them?"

Jane stands up, knocking a fork off the table. "Cait, is your sister Britta?"

"Yeah," Cait says, barely audible.

Jane sits. "I should have seen it the second I met you. You look just like her. I was in her band when they were the Grizzlies. Right before I moved back to Portland." To Plum, Jane says, "That was the friend who died right after your mom."

"That was a horrible year." Cait puts her fork down.

"I knew Britta," Mika says. "Just a little. She dated my roommate for a while when I lived in Seattle. I played at her memorial show."

"She was a kickass bass player," Allison says. "I was such a fan. Dude, you do look just like her."

"It's wild that you all knew her," Iph says.

Jane nods. "That's the music scene. Especially coming out of Olympia."

"Not many girls," Mika says. "We tend to know each other."

Lorna reaches across a plate of berries to touch Mika's hand. Josh puts an arm around Cait. George raises a wineglass. "To our beloved dead."

"To your nana," Mika says in the after-toast quiet. "I loved being at Taurus Trucking last night. It's so cool that she came back after internment and did something so badass. My family was first generation, all in Hood River. Half of them were sent to a camp in Idaho and half to California. Those two parts of the family don't really know each other now." Mika takes a long drink of water. "They had a fruit market, but it was taken from them. They never came back here."

"To Nana," Iph says. "And Mika's family."

The ruby liquid in their glasses is somewhere between wine and ambrosia, whatever that's supposed to taste like. It's cool going down Iph's throat but warm in her belly.

"To Britta," Josh says.

"And my mom," says Plum.

They raise their glasses and drink again.

There is a silence filled with the whispers of the dead, other losses too sore in their hearts to mention. Parts of themselves they buried long ago.

"To the ghosts in all of us," Iph says.

All glasses are raised.

They return to the food. The talk dissolves into twos and threes. People drift from the table.

"Plum," Iph says, "can we consult your tarot cards? Like, maybe just a three-card reading? I have an idea, but I need some sort of structure to start."

"Structure. Huh," Plum says. "That's a nice way of thinking about the tarot. Do you read?"

"My mom does," Iph says. "She uses it like this—that's what made me think of it. She's a choreographer and sometimes when she's stuck, she'll draw some cards to get her going again."

"My dad used to do that," Plum says. "When he played music. He has this weird deck from the seventies called *Oblique Strategies* by this musician guy—what's his name?"

"Brian Eno," Jane calls from across the room.

"Yes," Plum says. "Eno. I'll go get my backpack. I left it some-place around here."

To Josh and Cait and George, who are clustered around a firepit that is now burning brightly inside a circle of Adirondack chairs, Iph says, "Do you guys have any training in improv?"

"Yes!" Josh says.

"Yes, *and*." Cait laughs.

"Good answer," Iph says. "Sit tight. Plum and I have some witching to do."

15

BITS & TASKS

Indoors, the cottage flickers with candlelight. The workroom is rearranged with the tables pushed up against the walls, leaving an empty space in the center of the room. A large round carpet takes up most of the space with its forest pattern of red-capped mushrooms and stylized banana slugs on a background of deep green and pale gold. Iph and Plum sit in the center. Plum unties the moth's-wing silk scarf wrapped around her cards. These, too, are round, their colors and card backs echoing the carpet, the forest, the room's gold glow. Plum shuffles and hands the deck to Iph.

Iph grounds herself the way Mom taught her—rooting her energy down past the carpet, past the foundation of this old house and the worm-rich soil beneath it, deep down to the roots of the surrounding trees. *Orr*, she thinks. *What does he need?* She holds the deck. It feels good in her hands. She shuffles and chooses—once, twice, three times.

Plum turns over the first card. Death. "So," she says. "The way I read them, the cards tell a story. So Death is like the 'once upon a time' of the reading."

Iph must have a look on her face that betrays what's happening in her stomach, because Plum grabs her hand. "I know it's not literal," Iph says, squeezing back.

"It's about transformation." Plum's voice is high and sweet. It's an odd combination, this woman-level wisdom and forthright girlishness. "The snake in the foreground—that's about change and rebirth. The tree, too. Birches also shed their skin. The skeleton on the card—it's what we need to mourn to really change. Sometimes you have to let stuff go to make room for something new."

Orr *does* need to release something. And according to the books Iph just read, the only way to stop him from transforming so radically is to find the fork in his path that allows another choice.

Plum turns over the next card. "The Four of Discs," she says.

"Does that look a little like the inside of this house to you?" Iph squints to get a better look at the card. There's a woman in a white robe inside a cozy room with a fire and open beams along the roof. Art on the walls. She is holding on to the door—to open or close it, it's hard to tell which.

"It does!" Plum says. "It's about being in a safe place where you can decide something. We're at a pause point—a time where we can either open the door to something new or close it against something unwanted."

"What about the third card?"

"Another four—interesting. The fours are about the completion of a cycle. In the *I Ching*, the fourth hexagram is called Youthful Folly. In this deck they're having some sort of party. Plus, it's the Wands—power, energy, will, sex. To me, this says Rite of Passage. It says ritual. So yeah."

"That's good, right? It feels like we're on the right track. We need to do some sort of ritual, some rite to help him." There is a word for this from one of the books—a word that is a combination of ingesting and incorporating. Like a snake eating its own tail. Iph flashes on Velma's book of poetry, the snake image on the front. The title—*Ouroboros*. Integrate. That's it!

"He needs to integrate it—whatever energy he has right now that's manifesting as a deer. Then it can become a part of him without taking over. Does that sound right to you?"

Plum pauses and wrinkles her nose. Iph likes her more and more by the second. After a lifetime living alone with Orr on the island of misfit toys, it's still a shock that they're suddenly out here in the world, their lives webbing with others' lives, making the kind of friendships that vine and flower and last.

"I mean, yes," Plum says. "Integrate sounds right. But Iph—he needs our help to choose what's right for *him*. I mean, have you asked him what he wants? I see this ritual as more of a way to help him decide. Like, this could take him over before he realizes it's happening—and that's scary. He's very impulsive, you know."

Iph does know. She wraps her arms around the ache of it. *What if he doesn't come back?* It's what they're both thinking.

They sit, quiet, for several minutes as the fire crackles.

Plum sighs. "How long ago did Scout leave?"

Iph shakes her head. "Time is weird here. When did you arrive?"

"We left Taurus Trucking at around six, and it only takes about twenty minutes from there to the trailhead. But then we walked forever until Scout found the right trail. It's so dark now. It must be at least after ten." Plum yawns. "Sorry," she says, covering her mouth. "We were up all night." She folds the silk scarf back around her tarot cards. "Deer are crepuscular. Active mostly at dusk and dawn. I have a feeling he'll be back by sunrise. Unless Scout can get him." She gets up and stretches and heads to the window seat. "I'm gonna rest for a few minutes."

GEORGE AND JOSH AND Lorna and Cait and the Furies wander in a few at a time, talking softly. A delicious scent wafts from the kitchen. George goes in and comes back carrying a tray with nine cups of hot cocoa and a plate of fresh-baked almond cookies.

"I'm never leaving this place," Jane says. "Just so you guys know."

"This is the best cocoa I've ever had," Cait says.

"It's Mexican hot chocolate," Iph says. "With cinnamon. The kind my mom makes."

"Not mine," Josh says. "Mine is totally Swiss Miss from the packet with the little freeze-dried marshmallows—my all-time trailer park favorite."

"Mine's a ringer for the kind they make at Stumptown on Belmont," Mika says.

Jane's and Allison's are extra thick with a mint leaf on top— just like at brunch at the Cuban place in Northeast.

The fire crackles as they sip and talk a little, trailing off. Mika and Lorna are on the sofa, curled up together under a blanket. Jane and Allison and Josh and Cait have wandered into the bedrooms. Iph gets an extra blanket and throw pillows from the sofa and lies next to George, who is crashed out in front of the fire. She might rest her eyes, too. Just for a minute.

16

THE LITTLE
THEATER

CAIT IS COVERED IN trash. It sticks to her hair in slimy clumps. To her face. To her dress, which is pink as a piglet. Rotting vegetables and old Kleenex and clumps of dirt stick to her skin. And Cait is happy about it. She finds a pit of mud and rolls in it. She then rolls on the newly mowed lawn of her parents' country club. Dry grass sticks to the entire mess like she's one of those candies coated in chopped nuts. People—her parents, their colleagues from the law firm, her next-door neighbors, her orthodontist and pediatrician—are picnicking on the golf course. She stomps over their blankets to reach all eighteen holes. Inside each plastic cup, wedged into the sod, is a small animal. These she rescues and carries away in a basket. The birds and mice and chipmunks and frogs and little garter snakes all sit prettily together, taking great care not to upset one another with any sudden movement.

Now she is at the river. She sets the basket down. She sits in the mud at the river's edge, waiting. A person approaches. Britta. She holds out a hand. Together, they walk into the river. When the water reaches their shoulders, Britta dissolves but is still present. Cait's hair grows until it brushes her ankles. She begins to sing.

JOSH IS ON HIS knees, puking off a bridge. Luminescent fish flop from his mouth into the bay far below, one after the other. He sees them glowing in the black water as they swim toward the open sea. His body is bruised and bloody. He is finished with this life of cold sidewalks and winter shelters, sleeping with his shoes under his head so no one will steal them. Finished with the men in the cars and alleys and the pain in his jaw and the way his hair never ever feels clean. His face is swollen from being hit. His fists are hot from hitting back. He is strong for how skinny he is, for how hungry he is. He stands. The bridge is the color of Cait's nails—the orange of coral reefs, not golden. When did he hitchhike all the way back home? He is climbing the supports like the bridge is a ship and he is a sailor. The breeze throws his scent back at him, and he gags again. His wounds are already rotting.

Across the bay is the redwood forest. All he has to do is fall into the water and swim.

He hears singing in the bay below, down near Angel Island. The words are in a language he doesn't understand. He opens his own mouth and drinks in the sound. He exhales small green birds. His wounds begin to heal. His stomach feels full of wholesome food. His blood is clean, his skin is clear, his organs are unbruised. He stretches his arms out into the mist, and his hair whips behind him. He smells roses. He smells the sea. He climbs to edge of the support beam and leaps—not down, but up. Josh is flying. He reels and rolls and swoops and floats. Finally, he dives joyfully into the blue-black water.

JANE, MIKA, AND ALLISON are tending the garden in the back of Penelope. They are singing together. The sun shines down.

"What are you doing?" Red says from outside the fence.

"We're going on tour," Mika says. "We need to have enough food."

"We got a record deal," Allison says. "We need to get these tomatoes mulched."

"We're getting married," Jane says, smoothing the wedding dress down over her hips with her dirty hands. "We need wheat and berries for wedding cake."

Red shakes the gate.

The Furies laugh and sing louder.

Allison gets the hose and sprays Red until he disappears.

Jane twirls in her wedding dress, tattoo sleeves dark against the stark white skirt. She spins and spins. Mika and Allison join her. They twirl until the garden tilts and they all fall down onto the warm tilled earth.

Lorna has never danced *this well, every move more perfect than the last. All the dancers, the bouncers, the bartender, and every man in the audience are rapt. A customer approaches the rack and Lorna's breath catches. A tiger dressed in a three-piece suit places a hundred-dollar bill on the stage.*

Lorna is lying on hot rocks near a gentle sea in a state of perfect pleasure. The enormous sandpaper tongue slides slowly down her spine, down each leg all the way to the soles of her feet. She turns her face to see him—the tiger, no suit, but a patch over one eye, like a pirate. "Do you want to wear this?" the tiger asks. "To cover your wound?"

Lorna touches her face and there is . . . nothing. Nothing where her eye should be! Nothing! She screams, but no sound comes out of her mouth.

She's walking up the front steps to her dead grandma's house in Tacoma, wearing the good-luck gold shoes she got at Shiny Dancer, and they refuse to be quiet. "Go on!" they dare her. "Go on!"

"Screw you," Lorna hisses. But she keeps on going, one step at a time.

She feels for the key under the ceramic pig with the chipped snout and real rubber rain boots that once belonged to a doll of Lorna's named Bitty. The pig never got a name. Just Pig.

"If she's dead, she's dead," Lorna tells the shoes, unlocking the door.

The house smells like cat piss and garbage. Home sweet home.

The TV is on upstairs, so you know the power bill was paid and someone was once alive enough to turn the damn thing on. Lorna thinks about hiding the shoes. She knows her mother will try to take them. But when she faces the staircase with its moldy brown carpet, she decides to keep her shoes on and take her chances.

Mom is in bed.

Georgie always thought Lorna was sending letters to an old boyfriend in Tacoma, but this is infinitely worse.

This lady.

Her mom.

A boyfriend would be easier to leave.

Even Georgie, the best kisser in Portland, was easier to leave.

"Hey," Lorna says from the doorway.

Mom barely looks up. "Well, I'll be damned," she says like she's saying hi back. "How many days, Lorna? How many days has it been?"

"I don't know, Mama," Lorna says. "Why don't you tell me?"

PLUM IS IN A *Dublin pub, pregnant with her own grandmother. She drinks a glass of black beer and follows a familiar green coat out the door and around the back of the building. She is kissing a redheaded man for all she's worth. This man is not her husband.*

Plum is in labor in her bathtub in Portland. Her belly ripples as she bears down. It's early in the morning, and no one is awake. If she calls for her father, he won't come. Since her mother died, he needs whiskey to sleep. She crouches now, hands on either side of the tub, and pushes. A large, silver-scaled fish slides out of her body and into the bathwater. It bumps its blunt head against her leg—a greeting and a farewell—and narrows its body to swim down the drain.

GEORGE IS ON THE *back steps of Taurus Trucking with Nana. This is a lucid dream, George knows, downshifting time until it purrs along slow as a summer afternoon. George lifts Nana's beloved hand and kisses it. Nana is in workday mode with unpolished nails, a little grease in her cuticles. George squeezes, and Nana squeezes back. She is very strong.*

George holds close this stolen moment between the worlds, rolling in the warmth of Nana, the fit of George's head against her shoulder; the orange-sherbet-menthol-cigarette-green-tea scent of her. The way Nana's pointy chin presses into George's freshly buzzed scalp. They sit, content, grandmother and grandchild. Every detail gleams with precision, and George doesn't know if this is a visit to Nana's version of heaven or a relived moment from the past or random neurons sparking into a beautiful dream.

"Georgie," Nana says.

"Nana," George says back.

They are silent. Cars pass now and then. Chickadees sing their names from the pine tree in the corner of the parking lot, and crows hop around the asphalt, pecking for the bread Nana feeds them every morning. A baby cries and children laugh. The wind rustles the neighborhood trees.

17

THE CONSERVATORY

ph is backstage with a team of dressers. She holds her hands up and a garment slips over her head, covering her everywhere. A second skin.

She looks in the mirror, and she is her mother. She isn't Gracia, the girl her mom was on her birth certificate and during the childhood she won't talk about with anyone. She isn't Gracie, the straight-A high school sophomore who dropped out and ran away. She's not Callie, either—the name she says she got from her best friend, a boy she met when she first arrived in New York from California. She is Grace, the girl who came to New York alone at fifteen.

The curtain rises. Lights fade up on a playground.

Grace pulls her sweater tight, sliding lower against the wall. Up high in the little room made by the walls at the top of the slide, she is invisible from below. She knows because she propped her sweater up to her seated height earlier, slid down to the bottom of the twisty slide, and checked every angle.

She curls up and closes her eyes. She's almost asleep when she hears it: whistling. Someone's on the swings. Grace grins. It's a perfect rendition of the doot-do-doots in "Walk on The Wild Side." He whistles the entire song, then moves on to "The Low Spark of High Heeled Boys." She sits up and peeks over the edge of her playground fortress.

Just as she thought—it's the cute skinny blond boy she's been seeing around. No, Grace thinks, skinny is too generous a word. That boy is a swing-set calavero. *A skeleton whistling as he sways back and forth, a bottle dangling loosely from one bony hand.*

"I see you," the boy drawls. He sounds a little like the girl from Kentucky Grace met on the bus. "Saw you go up there. Thought I'd try a Pied Piper approach to get you out." He leaps off the swing, lands solid, and holds up the bottle. "Seems like a shame to drink it alone." His cowboy voice is soft, but it carries.

"You spent actual money on that? Instead of food and cigarettes?" Grace tries not to think about how empty she is now or the Automat cheese sandwich she ate yesterday morning or how she got the money for it. The taste of that is still bitter in her mouth.

"Girl, who says I spent money?" He pulls a salami and a loaf of bread from someplace in his trench coat and walks over to an empty park bench. The other person in the park is an old woman snoring under a layer of newspaper. He motions for Grace to sit. "I'll have you know, though—I am officially employed as of today. That's why we're celebrating."

"Where?"

"Strip joint around the corner. I'm the bouncer, ma'am."

"Who do they think you're gonna bounce? A bunch of rowdy kindergarteners?"

"I'm not questioning their judgment. I'm happy for the cash. Tomorrow night, it's gonna be a hotel room for your boy here. And a shower down the hall."

Grace sighs. She'll probably be in a room tomorrow night, too—she's getting to the point where she's going to have to try and pick someone up. Her hair is stringy. And her period is due any day—for that, she's going to need money for supplies.

"You could dance over there, I bet. You're pretty enough, that's for sure."

"No ID," Grace says.

"You think they're checking? Anyway, that's my job now. Can you dance?"

"That's what I came here to do," she says. She stands up on the bench

and does her prettiest ballet curtsy, then plops down beside him. The skeleton boy hands her a crusty piece of bread stuffed with salami. She picks up the sandwich and raises it in a toast. They clink and wolf down the food and trade gulps from the stolen bottle of Chianti.

"I'm as full as a queen," she says.

"You think you're the queen here?"

"Oh, you're a queen, all right. The queen of thieves!" Grace holds the bottle up in salute.

"I've been called worse. But my mom calls me Rob."

She holds out her hand. "I'm Grace."

"Grace? That sounds like somebody's great-aunt. Where are you from?"

"California," Grace says, chin out, daring him to ask her what she is. Although that doesn't happen much here in the city. Most people assume she's Puerto Rican.

"Hmmm," he says. "That's more like it. That's what I'm gonna call you from now on, so get used to it."

"Get used to what?" Grace laughs.

"Your name. California. Callie for short."

"If you call me Callie, I'm calling you Queen Rob."

"Oh, I insist," Rob says. He gets up and runs to the slide like they're kids at recess.

She runs after him, slides down . . .

. . . and down . . .

IPH IS IN A *windowless room. There is a baby on the floor—her mother. Tiny. Maybe under a year.* We are born with all our eggs, *Iph thinks. The eggs that will become her and Orr are here, dormant for now, inside this brown dark-haired baby in a dirty onesie and saggy diaper. Little gold hoops hang from her ears. She's playing with something on the floor. Behind her is a door. There are noises she doesn't like. A woman, crying. Gracia's mother?* Iph's abuela? *The dream pans closer, zeroes in on baby Gracia's toy. A severed finger! With a long, yellowed nail and a flaking gold-plated ring, the detached end caked with dried blood. Iph screams as Gracia lifts it toward her mouth.*

Iph takes the finger and puts it in the sink. Turns on the water, then flicks on the garbage disposal. Gracia cries for the finger, her only toy. Iph pats her pockets. She's wearing Nana's overalls. She pulls out a stick of eyeliner from one. Gracia reaches for the red pencil, pops it in her mouth. "No," says Iph, taking it away. Gracia screams. Iph's head is pounding. She reaches in her right pocket and pulls out a red-capped mushroom. This she eats herself to make sure the baby doesn't get it. "It's poison for you," she tells her nine-month-old mother.

Gracia reaches out her arms to be held. Iph picks her up, holds her close. The heaviness of the baby head on her shoulder is exhausting. She shifts her to a hip. A little hand reaches into the bib pocket of the overalls and pulls out a ring of golden keys. "Where there's a key, there must be a lock," Iph says. She searches the small room, but it is bare. She turns to the door, which has a cheap dented doorknob with no visible lock of any kind. She sets the baby down to search. As she runs her hands over every inch of the door, minuscule splinters penetrate her skin. Her palms burn. The pads of her fingers begin to bleed. The baby whimpers, then howls. Iph sits on the floor next to her, defeated. Then she sees it. There! On Gracia's pink tongue! A small golden keyhole! A door opens from the cave of her baby mouth, and water pours out. The room fills, faster and faster. Iph stretches Gracia high in the air, away from the water that pours from her eyes and ears, as well as her mouth. Soon, they are both engulfed.

IPH SEARCHES THE WATER, *frantic. Gracia is gone. She vomits, and out come the eels, brown and fanged and muscular. They crowd up into her throat, stampeding toward freedom. She gags until she is empty. Numb. She swims toward a light. A boy a little older than Orr is drifting here, long hair and love beads swaying like underwater flora. Iph touches his face. Dad's face! Dad?*

The boy isn't breathing. He is so heavy. The current pulls him away. Iph tries to follow, but the tide takes her to land.

Dad is there on his knees in the sand. His stomach heaves, but there is nothing left inside him. He doesn't see Iph. Doesn't feel her embrace. He is sobbing. The boy in the sea is his brother. His brother who died, who killed himself by jumping off a bridge.

Iph is lucid now and knows what to do. She reaches her hand into Dad's chest. She pulls out his heart and rinses it in the sea. Lifts it to the sun until it is warm as blood. Then she places it back in his chest, holding her hand over the wound to close it.

18

EACH LACE
FROND OF HORN

ome, she said. *Follow me!*

There was a moment in the woods when Orr truly thought the little dog meant to lead him home to Forest Lake. She'd found him after a run with the bucks, his body in an awkward state of almost-transformation, exhausted and alone. At the sight of the humble little brindled animal, a sweet and ordinary creature from the old world, he wanted nothing more than his room at home, with its line of flower-remedy tinctures on his neat bedside table and the sound of his parents laughing while they did the dishes together, listening to Mom's classic rock or Dad's cheesy jazz. Iph would be running the bath in the next room. He'd fall asleep without even the Walkman. He would wake up in his old life.

He wept then. It was the tears that called back his human form, his shape of sorrow. The dog had tenderly washed his face, licking at the spots of blood where the velvet had frayed after his dangerous frolic with the bucks. After a time, he'd become more oriented.

Now, approaching the familiar clearing, he sees that he is still in some enchanted corner of Forest Park. This dog must be Scout, the one who belongs to Iph's friend George—the person who made his sister blush and look so happy. He sits for a moment, and Scout waits at his side. His head is heavy. The antlers have grown. Soon, the velvet will drop from them, leaving the blood-stained bone exposed until the sun blanches it.

This time, the change was exultant and pitiless. Mulder would have loved it. "The Deer Boy"—a case for *The X-Files* if ever there was one.

They are in the clearing now.

Home is where your pack sleeps, Scout says without moving. Then she runs, as tired and paw-sore as she must be, body vibrating with joy at the prospect of reunion.

Orr follows her slowly into the cottage. Already its magic is ordinary, incorporated. Maybe because his own body has already shown him the magic of the impossible world. *I wonder*, he thinks, *did I cross over somewhere, or were things always this way and I didn't notice?*

Orr opens the arched door and stands at the flowery threshold. It's like looking into an enchanted snow globe. He feels large and distant but still deeply drawn to the action in the warm golden realm inside.

Inside, Scout is in George's arms.

Inside, Iph is offering George a small red pot of some sort of ointment. "Poor little paws," he hears Iph say.

Inside, Plum is sleeping. He knows by her smell. He finds Jane and Allison the same way. Mika is asleep on the sofa in the corner, huddled next to a girl who was in the audience at the show.

This is a place for him.

He knows. Most of him knows.

Home is where your people are.

But it feels wrong to enter.

"Orr!" Iph sees him. Grabs a blanket and rushes to put it around his shoulders. Opens her arms. He lets her hug him, because this he knows: his sister will always be able to show him the way home.

She leads him in, and he collapses on the carpet. "I'm so tired."

"I bet." Iph sits beside him. "Do you need food? A glass of water?"

He looks up at her. "I'm fine. I ate and drank with the bucks."

He watches her take that in. All the improv training has made her mind so flexible. Or no—she was always this way. Empathetic and curious. Her natural gift.

"I have an idea," she says. "First, I have to ask—do you want to stop this?"

Want. Orr hasn't considered it in the context of a decision. Want is what calls him to run alongside the herd. But tonight, after a while, even that want faded and changed. There was a time in a deep part of the forest where he made a bed of pine needles and rested alone. He dreamed the seasons changing—a thickening coat, bright leaves, the ground littered with apples. A secret place protected from rain and snow. The quickening spring. And . . . rest. A break from the world of talk and expectations.

"I don't know," he says. "It's lonely there. They let me stay with them. They're curious. But they know I'm different. Even if I change completely, I think they'll know. But Iph"—he takes her hand—"something about it also feels right."

"Maybe my plan can help you decide," Iph says. "That's what Plum thinks."

"Yes," Plum says. She has wandered over, rubbing sleep from her eyes. "Hey," she says to Orr. "How are you?"

"I don't know," Orr says. He is naked under the blanket, which would have embarrassed him once.

Plum settles cross-legged next to them as if this were a normal night and they're all getting ready to play a hand of Uno. Orr smiles. *Uno.* It's good he can still remember these things.

"I want to try a ritual," Iph says. "A kind of . . . psychodrama. It's a thing from ancient Greece—they would act out people's dreams as a type of medicine. I wonder if somewhere along the way, your narrative split. Like a whole part of you separated and went into this . . . other reality? Does that make sense?"

"I was thinking that." Orr nods. He almost topples backward, unbraced for the new weight there. He holds his ears to steady himself. They are softer than usual, beginning to fur. He pulls his hands away and sits on them.

"They must be so heavy," Iph says.

"But also . . . so beautiful," Plum says. Why is she blushing?

Iph laughs. "Oh my god, Plum, do you think my brother's hot as a deer?"

Plum hides her face in her hands. Scout dances over to push her head under Plum's fingers so she can lick her face. "You are so precious," Plum tells Scout in a way that makes Orr a little jealous.

"We need to get ahold of ourselves, people." It's Dad's voice again. Dad's phrase. Orr sits up straighter, stretches. His neck is sinewy in response to the new weight of his head. He has to forget about what's there, or the panic will keep whipping his insides like a black-ops helicopter landing in his stomach. What would Mulder do? Or no, forget Mulder—he needs to channel the smart one. What would Scully do? Or, wait! He smiles. In this scenario, Iph is Scully.

"What?" Iph says.

"You." Orr's smile widens. He feels almost normal.

"No, you!" Iph says.

"You guys are adorable." Plum's voice gets thin at the end.

"Why are you sad?" Orr wants to touch her hand but is suddenly very aware of how naked he is under the blanket.

"Why are you psychic?" Plum sticks her tongue out.

"Now who's adorable?" Iph says.

"Tell us the plan, Agent." Orr sits up very straight.

"That's what it was. I know I'm not Mulder here, so that means I'm the hot one!"

"The hot *smart* one," Orr says. "Yes. Tell me!"

"Fine, but go get dressed," Iph says. "I have a feeling there will be clothes for you in the room where you were sleeping."

19

THE TRANSITION
TO EMBODIMENT

The Furies circle with their instruments on the periphery of the carpet—Jane's two guitars, one shiny new, the other battered and plastered with stickers. Allison holds her tambourine, and Mika places the percussion instruments and hand drums she's gathered from the shelves of the cottage.

With Jane, Iph goes to the garden. They snip rosemary, a large basketful. They snip roses, peonies, daisies, lavender, and bright, old-fashioned flowers whose name Iph doesn't know.

"Thank you," Iph says as she and Jane head back to the cottage. "For taking care of him."

"It's been my pleasure," Jane says. "Your mom and dad must really be something."

"Why do you say that?"

"Just . . . with you two. I see it."

"They're all right," Iph says. "Even my dumb dad." She wonders—when will it be time to call them?

INSIDE, PLUM IS GIVING Lorna a tarot reading. Mika and Allison and Cait help Jane and Iph line the edge of the carpet with the rosemary and flowers. Iph keeps back a few stems for the fire.

George and Orr are laughing about something. Scout is crashed on the hearth. *This place*, Iph thinks, trying to reach for what it is or represents, but her thoughts are slippery, and she finds herself staring at the bright coals in the fireplace instead.

"Um, Iph," Jane says.

Iph looks up to find that the round rug has transformed into a woodland stage with moss for carpet and real mushrooms dotting the soft green. There are a few stumps and a rough carved step for entrances and exits. Really, the perfect set for a Shakespearean romp. If only this were *Midsummer* or *As You Like It*. Iph can't forget—the magic that's making all this happen is also swallowing her brother bit by bit. She takes a deep breath and gets to work.

Plum pulls a card from her tarot deck—The Wheel of Fortune. Noting the circular image on the circular card and the circular stage, Iph places Lorna, Josh, Cait, and George in the cardinal directions. Plum sits in the center with her tarot cards in her lap. In middle school they learned about a classic dramatic structure called Freytag's Pyramid. Diagrammed on the board and described, even seventh graders saw the embarrassing parallels in the formula—inciting incident, a series of rising actions, a big climax, and then falling back to rest with the denouement. A few of the boys illustrated with a pencil and exaggerated panting. Iph was incensed. Was there nothing the patriarchy hadn't tried to wreck? She argued that this was only one way for a play to operate. The teacher told her she was wrong. She said he was a misogynist and proposed a vaginal story arc. "What would that look like?" she demanded. "Something new, right? Not the same old play we've all seen a million times!" She may have actually stomped her foot. It was the only time she ever got sent to the principal.

What she sees here, now, is not a rise and fall, but a spiral—circles in circles in circles.

She asks them all to sit. To start by telling their dreams. "Furies," she says, "anytime the mood strikes you, play to the narrative."

"Iph?" Plum asks. "What about Orr?"

Iph planned to let him watch as the stories unspooled, but maybe Plum is right. "What do you think?" Iph asks her brother. "Do you want to sit in the middle with Plum?"

"I want to stay here for now," he says. Scout is in his lap. "If I need to join you, I will."

"I kind of want to sit on the side," Plum says. "If that's all right."

"You guys," Iph says. "This is devised theater. We're making the story together. If I say something, it's just a suggestion. We need everyone's intuition. Everyone's voice."

Allison has her bass in her lap. She plucks the lowest string with her good hand, and now they have a heartbeat.

Iph inhales and exhales. They mirror her, already starting to sync up. Mika's hand drum joins Allison's bass.

One after another, they speak their dreams aloud. There is a theme here Iph is trying to understand, something cathartic and elemental. Jane plays a harsh progression of chords on her electric guitar that resolves to melancholy, even bereavement. Loss is part of this story; that much Iph knows for sure.

Allison sings, her voice shockingly angelic, in a language Iph doesn't know. Maybe Allison doesn't even know it. Iph opens her mouth to take in the high notes; they taste like the purest water.

Something about Lorna's dream makes Iph think of banked coals or a dormant volcano. "You're holding our fire," Iph says to Lorna.

"What about your dream?" Lorna's voice is sharp, but she is fully present for this. Willing, Iph senses, to expose herself in a new way—but only if everyone else does.

Iph sits next to Orr, takes his hand, and tells him her dream of their parents.

"Whoa," Lorna says. "Your mom—I guess it explains the gold stripper shoes."

"Her mom was a stripper?" Allison's whisper to Jane carries like her soprano singing voice. "Sorry!" she says when heads turn. "I always used to get in trouble at church for loud-whispering.

But it wasn't a your-mom joke or anything. I was just curious—some of my best friends are sex workers."

"Our mom is a huge proponent of your-mom jokes," Orr says. "She's the queen of them. And I know your dream about Dad is right. His brother did die, but I didn't know it was suicide."

"It might not be a perfect interpretation of what happened, but I'm not sure that matters."

"Me neither," Orr says.

Jane picks the guitar up again. She hums a low, simple lullaby. Then the song changes to something familiar Iph can't place. Maybe it's not usually done on the acoustic guitar.

"Remember, babe?" Jane says in her ten-packs-a-day rasp. For a moment, Iph sees her and Allison as cigar-smoking old ladies.

"Nirvana," Orr says. He joins the circle with the musicians. Grabs Jane's acoustic guitar. They play together. Suddenly, Orr stops. Jane keeps playing, a song that gets soft and sad, like the wind blowing through an empty house.

"I'm going to tell you about the mountain," Orr says.

Iph rises. Brings Cait to the center. Is it cruel to cast her, with her lost sister, in this role? She asks Cait, "Are you okay?"

"I'm all in," Cait says.

Orr looks at her. These two haven't connected until now. "George told me about your sister," he says. "I'm sorry."

"I'm glad you got away from that place," Cait says. "Britta was a badass, but even she never managed to escape from the girls' side."

Orr directs them. "Lie down," he says to Cait. "The house is empty. You're in your bed. You're thinking about *The X-Files*."

Cait giggles and it's the cutest sound. Iph realizes it's the first time she's heard Cait laugh.

The others play the transport team. Someone fetches a pillowcase, and Iph says, "Scene!"

They go through the motions as Orr describes them: The abduction, the van ride. Arrival. When Orr reaches the part about running from the men, Cait explodes into fury, kicking and screaming and spitting like a wild animal.

Lorna stalks forward, hunching her shoulders to shape the Minotaur man who shaved Orr's head. George and Josh are the chair that holds Cait as Orr tells of the taking of his dark sentinel locks—his only protection.

He stops there. "Please, do it again."

They repeat.

"Again!" Orr says.

They are switching roles now, rotating until they come back to Cait.

"No, wait," Plum says. How did Iph forget about Plum? "I should do it."

"No," Orr says. "Not you. Maybe Josh can be me this time. You be the mouse."

Plum nods. Jane squeezes her hand.

Orr tells of waking in the tent. Of the mouse, played by Plum. Of the coyote, obviously George.

Iph doesn't have to direct them now; they are choosing their own roles perfectly.

When Orr gets off the mountain and meets Jane at the campfire, Iph signals for them to stop.

"Orr," she says. The music stops suddenly, too. It's as if they all know what she is thinking. "Orr, what about you? Can you do it?"

A bell chimes. Allison has amazing timing. Again, the bell. And again. A little voice calling Orr. Mika's heartbeat drumming resumes. Orr moves to the center, lies down, and pretends to be in bed. Jane is playing the guitar again, peanut-butter-thick blues. Where the movements were fast and raw before, they are now stylized and deliberate, more choreographed dance than theatrical improvisation.

Orr is deep in concentration, a look reserved for the cello. Something flickers at the edge of Iph's attention, but she releases it. She has to be here in every sense. She is the psychopomp. Orr's witness and guide.

Everything goes well until the shearing. George and Josh hold Orr. Cait is weeping and can't wield the imaginary shears. Once again, Lorna plays the villain. The moment she touches Orr's head, the wind whips up in the trees outside, and Orr's body convulses so hard someone screams. Scout barks and barks.

Orr is changing, too rapidly to track.

Deer to brother. Brother to deer.

They are all frozen. Watching.

Deer to brother, brother to deer.

Orr's strobing form flickers with the firelight, transforming faster and faster.

The cycle begins again, so fast Iph worries Orr will fly apart. She throws herself on him and holds with all her might.

He is now the fish from Plum's dream, the embryo in her belly. He is the tiger! The white hound, her arctic minion. A redwood tree. He is teenage Mom on the slide and Dad mourning his brother on the shore.

Iph holds him through every change until finally Orr is still.

The others are holding hands in a circle around them.

Applause sounds from an invisible audience in the house.

A spotlight shines in Iph's eyes.

Orr stands. Holds his hand out to her as if they're preparing to take a bow.

The antlers are gone.

She presses her forehead to his forehead. They stay this way for a long time.

The applause dies. The cottage is silent. The trees are still in the breathless night.

Iph knows before he even moves. Before he says a single word.

"No!" she says.

"I'm sorry," he whispers.

He holds her close again. "I love you," he says.

Then he turns and walks out of the cottage. When Iph reaches the doorstep, there is a pile of clothes on the flagstone path.

Orr is gone.

20

VOICE &
SPEECH

ph makes the call from a laundromat on Northwest Thurman, a few blocks away from the trail leading to the Witch's Castle. Being in the real world is decidedly surreal.

"Hello?"

Mom! Iph can't speak. She can only cry.

"Orr?"

"No—Mom! I'm sorry. I'm so sorry."

"Where are you? We're coming right now. I'm putting my shoes on. Theo!" Mom yells, forgetting to cover the receiver. "It's Iph! Get the keys!"

"How are you home?"

"Later," Mom says. "I have to find my other shoe. Here—tell your dad where to go."

"Macleay Park," she tells him. "Bring Orr's cello."

CAIT'S PURPLE BMW AND the Furies' van are next to each other in the laundromat parking lot. Lorna has to work, and Cait is looking rough. The night has been hard on her.

"I don't even know how to thank you guys," Iph says. She has phone numbers for Cait and Lorna. "Where can I find you?" she asks Josh.

"Around," Josh says, opening his arms for a goodbye hug.

"No bardic comeback?" Iph smiles a little.

"Too tired," Josh says.

"Come stay at my house," Cait says to him. "My parents left for Europe two days ago."

"See you soon, Iph." Mika smiles and shakes Iph's hand. She and Allison are cramming into Cait's car, too. Mika also has to work, and Allison needs her pain meds. Her broken arm has been throbbing all night. "Too much bonus rocking," she says, looking like a debauched empress in her disheveled red toga and raccoon eyeliner.

Iph grabs Lorna and hugs her tight. "Thank you for being so strong," she says.

"What do you mean?"

"You held the shadow for us tonight. We needed that."

Lorna rolls her eyes, but she's smiling a little as she reaches into her ever-present duffle. "Here," she says, taking out the gold shoes. "Give these back to your mom. Or maybe they'll fit you now. They don't feel like mine anymore."

Iph looks down at the boots that have basically become a part of her body. "No." Lorna smiles. "Keep those, too. I've got my own."

Iph waves as Cait's car pulls out of the parking lot and turns left into the ordinary world.

In the van, Jane is smoking. "You all right?"

"Yes, considering."

"I'm gonna go call Plum's dad," she says. Plum and George stayed back at the cottage. "Be right back."

Iph takes one of Jane's cigarettes and lights it. It goes straight to her head. She puts it out, wishing for water.

"We should stop at the store for more of these," she says when Jane starts up the van. "My mom's going to need them."

21

STRUGGLES
WITH OBSTINACY

ph hears the Volvo before it turns into the Macleay Park lot. She runs from the picnic table where she's been waiting—Iph, who doesn't run. Maybe Orr has rubbed off on her.

Mom gets out before the car has fully stopped. Iph is her arms, heartbeat to heartbeat. Mom's patchouli perfume, her essential Momness—ursine, soft, and fierce. Like something that's tamed itself to love her.

Dad gets out and stops, hesitates. "I'm sorry," he says. Iph has never seen him so pale and stricken. He looks thin and hollow—like the ghost in him fled when Orr did.

"It doesn't matter now," she says, trying not to sound cold. The reenactment of Orr's kidnapping was going to be with her for a long time. To her mom she says, "How come you're home?"

"I had a dream," Mom says.

"Me, too." Dad's voice is trembling. "I don't know what it meant, but it was the same dream. We both had it. Your brother—"

"Turned into a deer," Iph says.

They stand in the parking lot at the border between worlds.

"Mom?" Iph says. "It's like your piece—*El Mundo Bueno* and *El Mundo Malo*."

"Yes," Mom says softly, like she already knows where Iph is going with this.

"*El mundo* what?" Dad says, his terrible Spanish accent a little extra terrible. A tiny joke, a tactic that is the start of them making up. But Mom isn't having it.

She strides toward the path.

Iph's stomach flips, full of dream fish. She's never considered her parents breaking up. Not for even a second. But Mom has never, ever been this mad.

"They're the good and bad worlds—but not exactly," Iph says. "It's the multiverse, sort of. Except we keep going back and forth between the two. You have a chance to choose if you pay attention."

"Iph," Dad says like he hasn't heard a word. He's staring at Mom's disappearing back. "Where is your brother?"

"In the forest," Iph says. "Follow me."

22

VALUE OF CHILDISH IMPRESSIONS

Mom has been gone for over an hour looking for Orr. After quickly greeting Jane and Plum and giving a slightly more interested hello to George, Mom asked for a glass of water and headed back out, Scout at her heels. She promised to keep to the trails and not go too far. She didn't speak to or look at Dad, who is now asleep on the sofa. The house took one look at him, produced a turkey sandwich, and lured him to the pillows. George is reading in a chair by the fire. Plum is outside picking flowers and talking to Jane while she smokes.

Iph touches George's sleeve. "I'll be back," she says.

George grabs her hand and pulls her close. Plants a kiss on her forehead. "For luck."

Iph returns the kiss on George's perfect lips. "See you soon." She takes Orr's bundle of clothes and places them in the basket hanging by the front door.

In the woods, Iph wanders. Soon, she hears something—singing. *Mom.* The song Iph hummed to Scout on the bus last night— or no, two nights ago. Or was it three? Iph follows Mom's voice deeper into the woods. So much for staying on the path.

De la Sierra Morena,
cielito lindo, vienen bajando,
Un par de ojitos negros,
cielito lindo, de contrabando.

Iph follows the song to a stream and along the stream past a weeping willow. There, on the mossy creek bank, are Mom and Orr. He is asleep with his head on her lap, and she is stroking his face, now softly furred, and his antlers, which have grown and forked. Sitting there with her long curly hair haloed by a shaft of perfect light, Mom and Orr are a gilded Medieval painting—the Queen and the Stag.

She shifts position and looks around protectively. Now Iph sees Scout, snoring at Mom's side. It's always been one of Mom's gifts, putting babies to sleep. It works as well, Iph supposes, on deer brothers and pocket pits.

"Hey, Mom!" she whispers. "Can we take him back? I have an idea."

23

DON'T SPEAK
OF MY FATHER

Mom. Orr holds her hand as they walk back to the cottage like he is four years old and afraid for his first day of kindergarten. He will stay, he thinks. Of course he will stay. Maybe Iph is right. Maybe Mom's return is the fork in the path they've been searching for. Maybe they will find another cottage with different magic that will help Orr become a human man instead of the thing he is becoming.

He spent the night alone, away from the rest of the herd, although their presence was everywhere in the forest in the scrapes where they'd recently slept and the trees scarred by other new antlers and the rich musk of their hooves and bodies in the wind. He walked at first, his forehead clear of antlers, his legs their normal shape. But then there was a doe. A tilt of her eye, a way she moved. It reminded him of Plum. And he was gone again, farther than ever, as he raced her through the woods. She beat him easily and lost him with as little effort—one moment ahead, melted into the trees the next. Alone again, he'd found a place to rest. He'd slept. Woken up neither boy nor stag. It was then that he heard his mother's singing.

INSIDE THE COTTAGE, ORR stands over his sleeping father. Dad starts and flinches back, bumping his head hard on the window behind him.

"Orestes?" he says.

But Orr is also backing away.

Dad, the brochure, Pinocchio. The hood over his head like he's a hawk bred for hunting. Tamed. Dad trying to talk to him after Mom left. Orr turning his back, damming up, locking down.

"I know what you tried to do," Orr says. "But you shouldn't have trusted those people. I needed you, Dad. Not those strangers."

"They cut your hair," Dad says. Orr sees his reflection in the windows behind Dad and realizes it's a strange thing for him to say, considering the rest of his appearance.

"They hurt you." Dad stands. Takes a step forward. Orr knows this dance—he's learned it from the bucks. Slowly. Head low to show respect.

Orr takes a half step forward and offers Dad his velvet-covered horns, but the moment skin connects with bone, electricity moves through Orr's body.

He is shaking, his abdomen contorting. Something last night—a shifting, rending, dizzy thing too fast for memory to process. It's happening again. Happening now.

Orr's knees buckle, but Dad is here. Holding him.

"Don't let go!" Iph says.

"I won't," Dad says in Orr's ear. "Not until you say so. Never again."

24

OUR HOME THEATER

Orr is improvising on the cello. His notes soar and break into flower petals that float away on a river, gathering mass as they slither to shore.

Jane plays with him, flamenco runs that start soft but gather in speed to pound like a herd of hooved animals. She's changed clothes somewhere along the way, into jeans and a plain white T-shirt. They are both in the zone, loose and aware.

"She never plays the acoustic guitar anymore," Plum says. "I was surprised to see it at the show."

"She's amazing."

"My mom met her when she was my age, living on the street in Old Town. My dad—well, he used to restore and repair old instruments. He redid that guitar for Jane. She was like, practically a professional as a kid."

"Is she Latina?"

"Argentinian." Plum smiles. "She can dance, too, but she never does it. Says she's so sexy when she tangos, people start calling 911."

"Believe it," Jane calls in her alley-cat voice.

"Like me with these," Orr says, cocking his head to show off the antlers. Are they . . . joking about this?

"Iph." Plum pauses to take a sip of water. "Jane had to leave for a while, too, you know."

"When your mom died?"

"Before that. When she was sixteen."

"What did you turn into?" Orr asks.

"A boxcar kid, babe," Jane answers. "For about a year."

"She really was," Plum says. "But she won't tell me how to hop a train."

"I'll tell you how," Jane says over a sassy stumming pattern. "Go to Union Station. Buy a flipping ticket."

Orr laughs at them bickering like sisters.

Iph's plan was exactly this—being together, playing music, reminding Orr of things he loves. But Mom and Dad are outside fighting, and the music has turned sad. This isn't her brother deciding to stay. This is Orr saying goodbye.

"Jane," Orr says when the song is over, "thanks for rescuing me that day."

"Who rescued who, babe? That's what I want to know." Jane reaches out and touches the tip of an antler. "Drugs, man. They wreck your brain. Make you see shit that's not there."

Orr laughs. Jane lets out a shaky breath like she feels the end coming, too.

"Plum?" Orr says. "Can we go for a short walk?"

"Sure." She squares her shoulders like Jane did. They all know it's coming, except maybe Mom. Orr and Plum go out the front door. Jane waits a bit, then heads out after them. For a smoke, Iph guesses.

Mom wanders in through the back.

"Where's your brother?" There's a familiar squirt of panic in her voice. They used to lose Orr sometimes in stores. It would be too loud or smell bad, and he'd go find a place to curl up.

"Just out talking to Plum."

"Sorry." Mom's been crying, but that's a good sign. She cries when the fight is over, after she and Dad make up. She paces the workroom, stops at the little library. Iph knows her moods. It will be hard for her sit still.

"Did you see George out there? And Scout?"

"Yes, they're out there talking to your dad," Mom says. "So freaking cute."

"Which one?" Iph smiles.

"Both," Mom says, then startles. "What was that?"

"Did a book just go *pssst* at you?"

"Is that what's happening?" Mom squints at the shelves. This year, she's started to need reading glasses.

"It's a self-recommending library," Iph says. "The books choose you."

Mom cocks her head to listen, then takes a slim volume and goes back outside. The sun is getting low. All day, the dream of Mom and Rob in the park in New York has been floating through her head. Why didn't Mom ever tell them about her past? She could have at least told Iph. There were moments—when they gave money and food to street kids, when Iph asked Mom if she thought porn was inherently sexist—when she could have said something. Looking back, Iph thinks maybe there were times she almost did.

Through the front window Iph sees her mother settle in an Adirondack chair with the book. *Her mother.* Maybe that's it—it's like that old *Sesame Street* song. *One of these things is not like the other.* Maybe she didn't know how to be both that girl in the park and Dad's wife and Iph and Orr's mom. Iph sees how hard she has to work to get the family to make space for her dancing. They try, but they are selfish. Not so much Dad, but definitely her and Orr.

Iph lies down on the rug. Earlier, they all tried to figure out when it had morphed back from a stage. The house does these things so imperceptibly, it's hard to catch the moment of change.

The sun refracts rainbows on the walls as it hits the beveled glass windows. It's warm, but not too hot. A perfect Portland summer evening—except that something unimaginable is about to happen.

Plum and Orr come back inside. Plum looks happy and flushed, like maybe they've been kissing.

Orr starts to play another song on the cello—the Schubert from the soundtrack of Iph's favorite movie about elegant bisexual vampires Catherine Deneuve and David Bowie. Iph grins. Orr grins. They've seen the movie so many times and always fight over who gets to marry Bowie. Even though he's shriveled and dying by the halfway point, he's still so hot. In the end, Iph always capitulates because Orr gives her both Catherine Deneuve and a very young Susan Sarandon. "Two for one," he says.

She can't hear this song right now. She stands up, not sure where she's going. Orr stops playing.

Plum is the one who's brave enough to say it. "The sun is going down soon," she says. "Orr, I think Jane and I should go. Where is she?"

"Out for a smoke." Iph says.

"Should I maybe go see if George wants a ride?" Plum's voice is steady. Whatever she and Orr discussed, she seems sure about it.

"I think George and Scout are out somewhere with my dad."

"I'll go with you," Orr says to Plum.

With everyone out of the house, Iph is suddenly exhausted. She closes her eyes for one second. She drifts.

"Iph," Mom says, rushing back into the house. She holds out the book she's been reading like it's turned into a snake.

The book is open to the poem: "The Boy Changed Into a Stag Clamors at the Gate of Secrets." The same poem from the match-book.

"It's about a mother crying for her son who's changed into a stag and can't come back to her." She chokes back a sob. "Iph. Is he going?"

Iph can't look at her.

Mom drops the book, covers her mouth like she's going to throw up, and runs out of the house. Iph follows, but stops. Across the creek standing next to the redwood where Iph tried to psychically summon Mom is a leggy woman in faded blue jeans with feathery white hair and dangling silver earrings. Is she the cottage's owner? Something about her is familiar. The young white wolf dog is at her feet. She calls out to Mom, but Iph can't hear what she's saying. Mom reaches her, and the woman holds out her arm. Mom takes it, to Iph's surprise. They walk off together on a path Iph didn't notice before.

Iph goes back inside. Her attention is drawn to the cottage walls—the little sock in its carefully constructed shadowbox, the beautifully framed silver spoon. Baby things, but nothing from a child who's grown. Maybe the woman in the woods owns this place, and maybe she has something to tell Mom about loss.

She picks up the book and opens to a random page. It's near the end. She reads.

> *There he stood on the crest of all time,*
> *there he stood on creation's highest mountain,*
> *there he stood at the gate of secrets—*
> *the points of his antlers plated with the stars*
> *and with a stag's voice he cried,*
> *cried back to his mother who'd borne him—*
> *mother, mother, I can't go back*
> *the hundred wounds in me weep pure gold.*

25

THE BOY CHANGED INTO A STAG CLAMORS AT THE GATE OF SECRETS

Blood pounds through Orr's antlers. The boy in the window, the same one who lives in the mirror, strokes the mossy velvet that covers them. Both he and Orr are beginning to know and love the weight of them. Orr almost laughs. He expected aliens, but never this.

The sun is setting.

George and Scout and Jane and Plum are gone.

"It's time," Orr says.

"Can we go out to the meadow first?" Dad asks. "Just for a minute?"

Orr hesitates, and they all see it: the lack of trust, born way before Meadowbrook.

Dad bows his head, bucklike. Orr relents.

They walk together, arms linked like the heroes of *The Wizard of Oz*. First Mom, then Orr, then Iph, then Dad. They hear what Dad made before they see it—a low hum, like the forest opening its mouth to sing.

The desire to find the source of the sound quickens Orr's deeper desire, itching his ankles toward their new shape. He will control it this time, giving in when he's ready—but then he will do what he's been so afraid of all this time. He will fall into it until he's fully submerged. He will know this other self entirely.

Now he walks with his family, who will always be his family. At the top of a small rise are two trees once scorched in a fire, probably years ago. They look dead, but Orr knows they aren't. Under his bare feet, he feels it. Their children, the tall trees that circle them, will feed them as long as they live.

Between these trees, Dad has strung five thick metal wires. "Piano?" Orr asks.

"I was talking to George. We were letting the dog run around, following her, and I noticed something in the bushes over there. There was an old rotting piano that someone must have left out to pasture. I saw these trees. They're hollow—" Dad stops himself. He loves to explain how things are made but worries other people don't care the way that he does.

Orr runs his hand along one tree, then the other. The wind picks up and runs its invisible mane over the strings. Dad has made him a forest cello.

His antlers are tender, so he uses his hands. Later, he won't need to. Already the bone branches are hardening. He and the wind play a duet that rings from the hollowed trees and vibrates the ground as if the song is rising from some deep cathedral.

"Dad," he says. He can't say more.

"Now you can make music," Dad says, "no matter what."

The family gathers around. They hold each other. Night is falling. The forest calls him. He wants to stay but has to go. He pulls away; they let him.

"Iph," he says. "Come to the forest once in a while. Look for me."

"I'm scared I won't know you from the others," she says, so quietly only he can hear.

"You'll always know me," Orr says. "Just like I'll know you."

"Orr?" Iph isn't crying. She is strong. His strong big sister. "I want you to come back. When you're done. You have to remember. It might be hard when things are so different. When you're done, come back to me."

Iph steps away and lets Dad put his arm around her shoulders. Orr reaches out for Mom. When had her hand gotten so small?

"Look," Mom says, "it's our blue."

Linked, they gaze at the sky. The moon is rising.

Mom turns to him, traces his antlers with the palms of her hands. Licks her left index finger. Reaches down to the dirt. Traces a symbol on the back of each hand and one on his forehead. "Protection," she says.

"I'm going into the trees now," Orr says. "I don't want you guys to watch." Orr knows that seeing will frighten them.

"Te amo," Mom says. Love in Spanish.

"S'agapo," Dad says. Love in Greek.

"Don't forget us," Iph says. Love in Big Sister.

Orr can't say anything. The night is pulsing through his veins. His body yearns to meet itself in fur and hoof and strength and speed. He has to go.

Orr walks away slowly until he hits the trees.

Then he runs.

ACT IV

How fares my child? How fares my roe?

1

THE LINE OF
THE FANTASTIC

"This isn't going to work," Iph says, laughing. She's at the basement sink, washing paint brushes while George kisses the back of her neck. "Stop it or else." Iph brandishes a hot-pink paint-covered roller. It took five coats to cover the dining room, but it's totally worth it. The fuchsia looks so decadent with the dark wood built-ins and bookcases.

"*Give me one kiss, and I'll give it thee again, and one for interest, if thou wilt have twain,*" George says, shoving Iph over to help at the sink. "Is everything out of the old house?"

"Almost," Iph says.

Scout was the one to find the new house—they were walking back from the cello spot when she ran off, barking at them to follow. A few blocks from the Macleay Park entrance was a big yellow Victorian—Dad's nightmare and Mom's dream.

"It's your turn anyway," said Dad, lover of modern architecture, clearly hoping to trade this Victorian monstrosity for the doghouse he was still in.

Iph and Mom laughed. You could see the project wheels turning behind his eyes—how to modernize a hundred-year-old house? What would he need from the hardware store?

"Is your mom at the studio?" George has that *Are we alone in the house?* tone that still makes Iph swoon.

"She is," Iph says. "But don't you have to go?"

George is apprenticing with Shakespeare in the Shelter—a paying job that's brought electricity back to Taurus Trucking.

"There's a little time," George says, pulling Iph closer. As always, Scout weaves around their ankles, worming her way in between them. George scoops her up and laughs.

"Tell my mom to get eggs if you see her," Iph says. "And almond milk. And ice cream."

The biggest changes at the end of summer had been Mom's. Since George introduced her to Glow, there's been no stopping her. She wrote a grant and got donations from all the people she charmed at Dad's work events all these years. She found a space in Old Town and opened a movement studio catering to street folks and sex workers. People said it would be vandalized, but Mom put up with the broken windows and graffiti until people on the street started sticking up for the place. When Shakespeare in the Shelter needed a new home, Mom hooked them up.

Iph never returned to Forest Lake High for her senior year. Thanks to a book she found at Powell's, *The Teenage Liberation Handbook*, Iph is unschooling. Mom was for it from the start, but Dad needed convincing.

"It just means taking charge of your education. And that education doesn't only happen in school," she told him. Then she set it out to prove it.

She's teaching with Mom, taking acting classes at the university, and volunteering for RCT Press.

When Iph finally returned to the cottage, it was with Mom, who wanted to have tea with the lanky woman with white hair and her sweet yellow-eyed white dog. She and Mom became friends, and suddenly Iph found herself with a job.

Sylvie is a tough boss, but kind and incredibly well read. Iph proofreads and does deliveries and post office runs now that she has her license. Once in a while, on her way back down the path from the cottage, she sees Sylvie's white wolf-dog and a tall white hound race into the deepest part of the wood.

On less busy days, Iph stays home and sleeps so she can dream of Orr. Lately, though, she's spent most of her free hours haunting the library, researching theater programs, and slogging through applications.

Now that spring is coming, she sometimes takes a sleeping bag to the cello spot and sleeps under the stars. That's where she's going today—not for an overnight, only a quick visit.

She and George kiss goodbye on the front porch. Iph notices the mail. She unlocks the door, throws it on the hall table. A large envelope catches her eye. *American Conservatory Theater.* Her heart pounds. She shoves the envelope in her backpack and hurries into the bright afternoon.

THE PATH TO THE cottage behind the Witch's Castle is easy to find now. The others make the same pilgrimage. At first, no one heard Orr's music. But in the fall, as the weather got cold, visitors to the cello spot often felt the deep resonance through their boots as they tromped up the trail. By the time they rounded the bend and crested the little hill, Orr was always gone.

At the base of the rise, a short way from the forest cello, someone set up an old table with ornate legs and a splintery top under a thick-branched pine. Under the table, out of the rain, is a child's tape player Allison and Mika found at Goodwill—the kind with large simple buttons that might be worked with the tip of an antler or a talented hoof. It was Jane who first started leaving the mixes. First, random stuff she thought Orr would like. Then a two-song Furies demo tape. Then a four-song EP, recorded at a local studio. Now there's an actual full-length release. The Furies are signed to a Seattle label. Soon, they'll be going on tour, opening for Bikini Kill.

Iph sees evidence of Plum in the artful still-life arrangements of forest ephemera on the table. Stuck to the trunk with tree sap are Polaroid self-portraits of Plum as various classical paintings and kiss-printed Post-it notes.

Mika comes more often than Jane or Allison, sometimes overlapping with Iph. She reads *X-Files* novelizations aloud in case Orr might be listening and leaves fresh-baked pies from the bakery where she works and talks to Iph about how difficult it is dating Lorna.

Mom comes less than she used to, but every full moon she is here, doing rituals of protection. Dad has started running again, visiting the spot daily to pour fresh water from his water bottle into a blue ceramic bowl, even though there is a creek so close you can hear it, and placing mounds of organic oats and corn under trees where there are visible hoofprints.

Today under the blue sky, Iph thinks the cello spot looks a little too much like a shrine or a memorial. The copy of the Furies' tape has been there since last week, unplayed. Iph pulls a blanket out of her backpack along with a bag of caramel popcorn and a book—Jung's *Memories, Dreams, Reflections*. Also, a battered pocket copy of *A Midsummer Night's Dream*. She's auditioning for Shakespeare in the Park next week and needs to practice her monologue. The sun feels so good after last week's rain. Iph lies back. Then she remembers—the letter!

How could she forget? She grounds herself, checks in.

Okay—she's scared.

No, terrified.

She takes a deep breath. Asks herself why.

George, she thinks. But ACT is only in San Francisco. She and George have already driven Mom's Volvo down there twice for the auditions. George is saving for a car, too. Dad is making noise about George getting something classic and them fixing it up together. So, no. Not George.

Is she afraid of the program itself? Maybe a little. But in a good way. The way you're scared because it's something you really, really want.

She sits up. *Ugh.* The answer is obvious. It's what she's been afraid of since fifth grade when she realized she'd graduate two years before Orr. She's afraid to leave her brother.

She takes out the envelope and opens it with a long, black-painted fingernail. She doesn't have to pull out the letter to know what it says. Iph feels her path forking, calling her south. She lies back and lets herself read the nice things they say about her audition. She imagines a studio apartment a little like Lorna's, but in a pink Victorian near Golden Gate Park. She drifts, dreamless at first.

Then comes her favorite dream—a deer approaches, hooves silent on the soft turf. A cold nose presses her cheek. She wakes up. She stands—a tip of antler, a flash of white tail. This is not the first time it's happened. As the weather warms, she imagines Orr's memory rousing from its winter slumber.

"Orr," she calls. "I know it's you." The rustling in the bushes stops. Orr has never quite gotten the stealthy, silent deer thing. "See this?" She raises the letter like a white flag. "It's from ACT. In San Francisco. I go in September." She waits, but all is still. "That gives us the rest of the spring and all summer," she says, even though she's pretty sure he's already gone.

She gathers her things. The bag of caramel corn is empty and hoofprints mark her blanket. As she walks down the hill toward the trail she hears a familiar melody. The words of the lullaby rise into Iph's mouth from the forest floor.

> *Cielito lindo, vienen bajando, un par de ojitos negros*
> *Sweet little heaven is prancing down, a pair of little black eyes*

Iph sings in Spanish and in English. At home she'll ask Dad how to say it in Greek. The chorus comes, her favorite part.

> *Ai, ai, ai, ai*
> *Canta y no llores.*
> *Sing, don't cry.*

The notes follow her through the forest and out to the city street.

A NOTE FROM THE AUTHOR

Dear Readers,

First, I want to acknowledge that the land where this story is set, the place I have called home for the past twenty-six years, is stolen land, once home to traditional village sites of the Multnomah, Wasco, Cowlitz, Kathlamet, Clackamas, Bands of Chinook, Tualatin, the Confederated Tribes of Grand Ronde including Molalla and Kalapuya, and many other tribes who made their homes in this green valley and along the Columbia River. It's also important to note that in 1859, Oregon was founded as a "white utopia" and explicitly forbade Black people from living in its borders—the only state to do so.

When I first moved to Portland in the early '90s, twenty-five and pregnant with my first daughter, I wondered where the people of color were. I had a hard time finding stores that carried traditional Latinx foods and strangers often asked if I was just back from Hawai'i because of my winter "tan."

But Portland also met me with midwives and zine makers, sex work activists and unschoolers, misfits and artists both queer and straight—many of them young parents who, like my partner and I, wanted to transform generations-old patterns of trauma into something kinder, healthier, full of possibility and love. Over time, I even found other people of color, some who were raised here, other who are transplants like me, looking for a quiet place to heal. Our stories have rooted here, adding something fertile to a place that has never wholly welcomed us.

At the time when this story takes place, there was a feeling of reinvention in this small uncool Pacific Northwest city, a sense of DIY pride, a feminist and queer resurgence. Still, the term "genderqueer" would only come into use a few years after this book takes place. When I dug into writing the nonbinary character George, I first thought to use the pronoun "they," but doing so felt like an erasure of the experience of a nonbinary person in that era. I reached for a language-based solution that expressed the character's experienced singularity and decided to write George without pronouns, hoping to convey the isolation of growing up with an identity that is unspoken and largely unnamed.

I also hoped to offer a roadmap to readers who are interested in getting to know their own inner landscape. While magical realism is a literary device that lets authors express deep psychological or spiritual ideas in concrete form, for some of us, like me, it's also a way to see the world—enchanted and full of wisdom if you only take the time to look.

There are endless paths to psyche, but these are some that I've found fruitful: the work of Carl Jung and Joseph Campbell, fairy and folk tales, the tarot, the book *Women Who Run with the Wolves* by Dr. Clarissa Pinkola Estés, listening to stories from my elders, reading poetry, exploring diasporic futurism, becoming aware of the cycles of the moon, paying attention to wild animals wherever I go, and writing down my dreams.

A wise friend of mine believes that time is not linear. That by doing our work in the present, we can heal the past—both our own and our ancestors'. My family's journey is the inspiration for this book and my dearest hope is to send some healing to all past/present/future versions of my beloved daughters, my own mother, my husband and my father, who died at age thirty but would have loved this book most of all. I imagine our family line like a battered spine glowing gold, vertebrae adjusting to stack strong, sending us into the future. I wish the same healing for you and the ones you love.

Michelle Ruiz Keil
December 28, 2020

ACKNOWLEDGMENTS

Thank you to the people who inspired this story and whose love and support inspires me every day—my husband, Carl, my beloved daughters, Luciana and Angelika and Kaylib, my sister and the best of friends. To my own parents, Anita Johansen and Patrick Smith, and, as always, thank you to my nana, Luciana Ruiz Dudley. "Cielito Lindo" was her favorite song.

More and more, I find myself telling young writers how much their work will benefit from theater training. I received mine from the famous, fabulous Donna Russell. I will always be grateful.

Lucky for me, the huge bout of writer's block I encountered halfway through *Summer in the City of Roses* was overcome by the radical hospitality of my time in residence at Hedgebrook. The magic of the forest path and my little cottage infuses this story and so does the kindness of my fellow residents, Heidi Durrow, Roja Heydarpour, Jael Humphrey, Diana Xin, Julie Phillips, Liz de Souza and Wendy Johnson. Thank you for sharing your writing, deer sightings and encouragement. The last moments pre-pandemic were well spent with you brilliant women.

Thank you, too, to the writers and readers who answered my late-night Facebook posts about '90s Portland, especially Rene Denfeld, whose experience as a former punk goddess was put to great use in these pages, and to Portland's own Dead Moon for my writing soundtrack.

A massive fan-girl thank-you goes out to the band Bikini Kill, who generously let me use the lyrics to their song "Resist Psychic Death" and to Natalie Garyet of Tavern Books and translator David Wevill, who allowed me to use lines from *The Boy Changed into a Stag Clamors at the Gate of Secrets* to my heart's content.

I wouldn't have known about Ferenc Juhász's poem at all if it hadn't been for the kindred spirit of poet, screenwriter and bruja Stephanie Adams-Santos. I will always be grateful. Thanks also to fairytale expert and tarot alchemist Coleman Stevenson for reading an early draft of this book and for all her inspiration and support. Poets make the fiercest and best of friends.

Thank you to Satya Doyle Byock and the members of the many seminars I attended at the Salomé Institute of Jungian Studies—our conversations are the sea I swam in as I drafted this book. Love and gratitude are also owed to Connor and Sayre Quevedo and Coda Goodrich, who in some deep but indirect way helped me find the boy in this story. And to their mothers, the writers MK Chavez and Talese Babb, who have loved and supported me for all these years.

It was MK Chavez who introduced me to public health and sex worker activism and who connected me with the force of nature known as Joanna Berton Martinez, aka Teresa Dulce, creator of the nonprofit Danzine. Joanna never met a problem she couldn't solve with limitless energy, a movie-star smile and surreal performance art. Thanks for the inspiration and for those Friday nights in the needle exchange van on SE 82nd!

Finally, thank you to my agent, Hannah Fergesen, and the folks and KT Literary and the lovely people of Soho Press for their support of my work, especially Alexa Wejko and Amara Hoshijo. Working with you has been a privilege and a joy.